ANGEL
FROM THE
RUST

ANGEL
FROM THE
RUST

BOOK ONE of EARTH MEDIEVAL

JASON LINK

Phoenix
Forge
Press, LLC

Cover art by Jason Link
Maps by Jason Link
Author photo by Bethany Bracht

Phoenix Forge Press, LLC
phoenixforgepress.com

ISBN: 979-8-9873198-0-2

To Josie,
who's on her journey
to find her song

RAINIER
KINGDOM

WASHO

COLMANE RIVER

STURGEON
GATE

• RED JACK

TUCK

AGATE RIVER

N

THORN
FO

• KELSICA

HOOD PROVINCE

• TERAMERE

TWO
• STEP

MANIFEST

CONDOR MTS.

MILO

BLUE MTS.

BRUIN

ELKHORN VALLEY

WALLWYN MTS.

SERPENT RIVER

UNION of IDAMON

SHROUD
EST

DAWN'S
LANDING

HARD
SCRABBLE

WADE
CROSS

STAG RIDGE
PROVINCE
OF THE NORWESTOR DOMINION

Landsong Gorge
Ech
High Bridge
Ryperia
Welmet River
Moss K
Mts.
Sky's
The Hooded King
Smo
Holl
Urgonia
Bracken Deep Forest
Cascade Range
Far Green

RAINIER KINGDOM

COLMANE RIVER

• PELAWYLD

BULLRUSH
CROWN

STURGEON
GATE

N

• DRIFTON

CHUTES RIVER

AGATE RIVER

MARKENWELL

FOSSIL •

HOOD
PROVINCE
OF THE
NORWESTOR DOMINION

Prologue

Silas had the view of a god. From a vast window, he observed Earth's roundness, a sphere of color. Arctic white and ocean blue, desert gold and forest green: all of it was his to see. The whorls of a massive storm front were heading south towards the equator. It took the form of an abstract shape. Many centuries ago, he had often laid on the grass to look up at the clouds, watching them drift into the shapes of animals and people. It was somewhat disorienting looking *down* on the clouds instead of up. Silas supposed the imagination could sculpt them just as well from this angle as from down below. He saw the clouds beginning to form into eyes, a nose, and a mouth, the likeness of a human face. It reminded him that somewhere down there, scattered across the continents, were people. If they still lived. He wondered how many fell under his gaze at that moment, how many were being born and how many were dying. He would know nothing of them and their short lives, for they were specks so minuscule as to be unseen from the cold heights of orbit.

The face he saw in the storm front became more defined. It was shifting into a woman's face, one all too familiar. A distant memory came to mind and Silas shuddered, turning away from the view of Earth.

All around him were sterile white walls, white tiers, and white tables and chairs. The air here had been pumped in only minutes before he'd arrived and it smelled new—not fresh, new. The powdery and metallic tang of air canisters. The chamber was called the Forum. It was a place where people could gather in the thousands. At least, that's what Silas had intended it to be. People hadn't been gathering for a long time. Nowadays people preferred to lie in their pods and stay plugged into the Dream. Fantasies made reality on demand. Silas couldn't blame them. Who would want to leave an imagined world tailored to their personal desires? Especially when the view from the Forum brought no comfort. The memories of Earth showed in one window, while the terrible black emptiness of space stretched on in the other.

When Silas had taken over the design of the space station Olympus, he had thought people would take breaks from the Dream and come to the Forum to stargaze. Since hardly anyone left their pods anymore, he could see he had miscalculated. Still, he was proud of his creation. Leaving the Dream helped him remember what he had developed: a construction nearly three miles long. More than six hundred years orbiting Earth. Over three million inhabitants, all hibernating and Dreaming in their pods. All safe and snug.

At least, they *had* been safe.

A sliding door hissed open at one end of the Forum and nine figures entered: the other Founders of Olympus. They looked like hospital patients in their white robes and slippers. They were hairless; even their eyebrows and eyelashes were gone. Their noses had been softened to nubs, their skin was translucent, faces and limbs webbed with veins. Silas looked down at his own hands, his fingers like yellowed glass, his threads of muscle practically visible within. He pulled his hands back into his sleeves, ashamed at his hideousness.

The Founders approached him, the soft whirring of mechanical supports at work under their robes. Silas remembered when he had been able to walk on his own. Now his muscles had nothing to do other than wither away while he hibernated in his pod. There were gyms on Olympus, but Silas suspected they had been left unused far longer than the Forum.

'Where's Dane?' one of the Founders huffed. 'He should have been here by now.'

'You can't expect him to hurry to his own execution.'

The Founders took their seats at the nearest table, Silas sitting at the head. Many of them fidgeted impatiently. Silas understood. Like him, their bodies would long for the comfort of their pods. Even the briefest stint of being ugly and weak was unbearable after spending ages in the Dream being beautiful and strong.

Finally, a pair of doors slid open and in walked another figure robed in sterile white. Silas remembered when Dane had been swarthy and handsome, a stalwart presence demanding respect. Now he was a knobbly, emaciated thing—a fossilized bird-given movement. A pair of red-eyed security droids hovered alongside him like two great insects, their pronged tasers poised in case he should try anything. Silas sniffed at the treatment. What possible threat could this frail man pose to them now? The droids escorted Dane to the table, where he took his seat. The others regarded him with grim looks. He didn't meet their eyes but held up his head with what little of his dignity remained.

One of the Founders said what everyone was thinking: 'Let's get this over with.'

Everyone looked to Silas, waiting for him to begin. He cleared his throat and read from the plex-tablet that lay in front of him on the table. His voice sounded strange to his ears, thick and slimy from long disuse, like an old pipe pumping out sludge. His gums smacked together, his teeth all gone.

'Seventy-two hours ago, Home Tower-257 had a power outage. Of the ten thousand residents occupying the tower, over three thousand were killed when their pods suddenly separated from the system. You have all received and reviewed the files showing what caused the outage. Founder Dane Garrows had been siphoning energy from Olympus's grid in order to power his private projects in Research and Development. As a result of his actions—'

'We all know the story,' grumbled Founder Amir, a withered man who barely filled his seat. 'Let's just do what we came for and be done with it!'

Silas blinked, unused to this treatment. In the Dream he was never interrupted.

'Very well,' he said in a small voice. 'We all know the charges, and each of you has privately reviewed the evidence. Now... I suppose we can come to a verdict. Does anyone think he's innocent?'

No response.

'Does anyone think he's guilty?'

Hands went up, and some Founders even voiced their judgment: *'Guilty!'*

Silas nodded. 'Founder Dane...'

He glanced across the table at the man accused. Dane's eyes had a glaze of rheum (as all the Founders did), but Silas sensed something looking back at him from underneath, a haunting pain that rose from the depths of the man and reached out. In response, there was a stirring in Silas's innards. At first, he couldn't tell what it was. It was nothing he allowed himself to feel in the Dream. The Dream for him was all happiness and pleasure. What he felt now held none of that shine. This was a dimmer, grayer feeling. He remembered its name. Pity. Through the ages of manufactured paradise, he had almost forgotten what it was.

'On with it!' cried Founder Melanie, a woman with papery skin stretched over her skull. 'Has hibernation made you forget your tongue?'

Silas winced at the rebuke. He forced his mind back to the task at hand. All of this would be over soon. He cleared his throat, avoiding Dane's eyes.

'Since you've been found guilty of the deaths of thousands,' Silas said, reading off the plex-tablet, 'you will be taken to an airlock and... ejected into space.'

With a claw-like finger, he numbly scrawled his name on the plex-tablet. Such an easy gesture to send a man to his death. It was best not to think about it too much. He passed the order along for the others to sign.

'Can't believe I woke up for this,' muttered the woman with a pinched face seated next to him; Silas couldn't remember her name. 'Just a stupid formality. Droids could have thrown him out on their own.'

As the others signed, Silas remembered when they had gathered like this before—not to discuss a man's fate but to dream up Olympus. Earth's most brilliant minds brought together to complete the impossible: taking the remnants of their civilization up into orbit. It had been so long ago. The memory rose up through the haze of centuries—how their work sessions had gone on late into the nights, blueprints and holo-files laid out next to pizza boxes and Chinese takeout, their minds growing so fatigued that everything became hilarious. They'd laughed together in those days. Now they barely acknowledged each other, and no one showed an ounce of remorse even now that one of them was about to be cast into the abyss.

This was the Olympus they had dreamed up. Here was its justice at work. Quick. Efficient. Cold.

Once they had all signed, there was no ceremony of closure. They made to get up and leave, to hurry back to their home towers and pods. But then Dane spoke up.

'I don't want to go alone.' His voice, though quiet, was firm. 'If I'm going to walk to my death, I want someone to go with me. Not just these machines.'

The Founders stilled and then looked to one another, not knowing what to do. They may have been an unfeeling lot, but none could bring themselves to deny the man his dying wish. Still, no one volunteered. After a moment, all eyes fell on Silas. He shrank under their stares, feeling as though his robe had dissolved, leaving him naked and exposed. He could feel their impatience growing to heated irritation as his hesitation held up their exit. Nostrils flared. Knuckles rapped the table. Silas wanted nothing more than to flee from that moment and return to the Dream where he could get back to writing his music and forget this whole meeting had ever happened.

'I'll go,' he said at last.

The ride on the monorail was short but miserable. The ovular car that carried Silas and Dane was too cramped. It wasn't that Silas was unused to small spaces—he lived in a pod, after all—but rather that the compartment put him much too close to Dane. Their knees were nearly touching. Silas fidgeted with the hem of his robe and looked at the floor. He looked anywhere but at that haunting expression just across from his seat. The moment demanded something of him and pressed in from all sides, squeezing his throat—he felt he should say something. Parting words, perhaps. But what could he possibly say to the man he had sentenced to death? Goodbye and good luck? The monorail car hummed as it sped down one of Olympus's many tubes, and the security droids buzzed on. The moments stretched out in the awkward lack of words, and the droids' buzzing and buzzing filled Silas's ears until he couldn't take it anymore.

'Did you say goodbye to Helen?' he said at last.

Dane looked up from his thoughts. Unlike Silas, he appeared collected, as though evaluating something other than his impending doom.

6

'Helen? No, I didn't say goodbye.' He shook his head. 'I'd prefer if she never learned of this.'

'But won't she notice her husband gone?'

'I doubt it. We haven't spoken in two hundred years.'

Silas was unfazed at the mention of such a passage of time. He understood. Time was a funny thing in the Dream. One moment, he would be composing music so powerful it could raise islands from the sea, and then in the next, a decade would have passed. The centuries went by too fast.

'That is to say,' Dane went on, 'our *physical* versions haven't spoken. I had her persona, and I'm sure she has a copy of mine. She won't miss this,' he said, pinching at the flesh of his arm.

It was a common practice in the Dream to make mental copies of people known in real life and turn them into virtual versions—perfected versions—of themselves. Pull them up whenever; no need to suffer the inconvenience of setting up a meeting with their real self. Silas had his own library of digital personas filled with all the people he cared about. All but one.

When the monorail car came to a stop, it jolted Silas from a memory. Here they were: end of the line. Silas and Dane got out at a dimly lit platform that reminded Silas of the old subway stations on Earth, only this one was much smaller, cleaner, and devoid of other people. Dane and the security droids moved towards the platform's sliding doors, but Silas hung back towards the monorail car, wondering if he had come far enough. Maybe he could go back to his pod now. But Dane stopped and looked back at him.

'We're not done yet.' He proceeded forward.

Silas cowered and obeyed, following after. Looking down, he remembered the plex-tablet in his hands. Of course, he couldn't leave now. He hadn't given the droids the order of execution yet. One more terrible duty to come.

Doors slid open for them and they entered a square chamber. Unlike the Forum, this room wasn't bathed in sterile white; rather, it was a metallic gray, marking it as an area only authorized personnel could enter. One end had an observation deck with a control panel and a large window looking out at space. Next to it stood a round door of industrial steel with great pistons for opening and closing. The airlock and, beyond it, the infinite nothingness. As Silas and Dane neared the door, Silas's knees began to shake, his mind reeling with the coming judgment. Dane was only a few paces away from passing into eternity.

The two of them came to a stop by the observation deck, the closest Silas was willing to come to that dreaded door. The security droids hovered nearby, awaiting his command. All he had to do was wave the plex-tablet before their red-eyed scanners. They would take care of the rest. Silas nervously fingered the glassy tablet as he looked out the window. An image intruded into his mind: a tiny frozen body spinning away and disappearing into the black. Silas's breathing grew shallow and quick as an old feeling welled up from the pit of his being. He remembered its name immediately. Fear. The cold that crept over his skin even as it made his brow bead with sweat.

A frail hand touched Silas's shoulder. 'What's wrong, my friend?' Dane asked.

Silas recoiled at the touch. 'Don't call me that! I'm not your friend! I can't be.'

He backed away until he leaned against the glass, his breathing heavy. The plex-tablet fell from his grip.

'I can't do this.'

'Of course,' said Dane in a sympathetic tone.

In this dim and ominous place, it was the last response Silas had expected to hear. So empathetic and assuring— and from a man going to his death! It gave Silas pause, and he studied Dane.

'Why are you so calm?'

'Because you know I don't deserve this.' He casually strolled by the airlock and tapped his knuckle against the steel door.

Silas grew still, intrigued. 'What do you mean?'

'I was dealt a losing hand,' Dane continued, pacing across the chamber. 'The Board put me in charge of Research and Development and gave me a job to do: make advancements for Olympus. Why? Because lying around in pods forever and winding up like this—' his hand motioned to his body, his expression betraying his disgust '—was never the plan. The pods were meant to be temporary until my department figured out a way to advance our society. Maybe we could have expanded Olympus, made it a grand city in the stars. Maybe we could have gone out and explored other worlds. But none of that was meant to be.

'We grew too comfortable and the Board's interest in R and D faded to nothing. Every time there was a resource audit, it was my department that got the cuts. Less staff. Tighter rations on energy. One day it was just me, and I had barely enough power to keep the lights on in the workshop. Almost all the power had been allocated to the Dream. And what of the original dream, our advancement?'

He shook his head and turned back to the window, his rheumy eyes seeming to grow foggier still. 'Perhaps I got a little over-ambitious, but only because I had no other choice. I was trying to do my job. With one hand you and the others gave me responsibility, and with the other you cut me off at the knees. So, in truth, you're just as guilty as I am. Of course, I'm the one who's paying the price.'

Dane stopped his pacing and stood before Silas, looking him dead in the eye.

'You can make this right.'

Silas grew rigid. 'How?'

Dane looked from Silas to the large window. 'There's a way.'

Silas followed his gaze to Earth below.

'You can't be serious.'

'I realize I can't stay on Olympus, but that doesn't mean I have to die. There's exile. A fate better than death. Not much better, but we work with what we get.'

'But...'

'The other Founders would never have to know. Besides, I doubt they'd care. They'd get me off Olympus. I'd get to live. Win-win.'

Silas stared at him in disbelief. 'You want to go down *there*?' He pointed a crooked finger at Earth. 'What will you do? Sweat, bleed, work—knowing death is just around the corner after a mere eighty years?' He shook his head. 'What am I saying? Eighty years! Look at you! You wouldn't survive a day among the savages.'

'True,' Dane replied, nodding in agreement. 'I wouldn't make it. Not as I am. But if I brought a few things from my workshop to help me, I might survive. All I need is your permission. Only you can unlock the shuttles.'

'I can't believe you're considering this. Even if you had the tools you need to survive, you're not allowed to go down there.'

'Why not?'

'Because of the Treaty.'

Dane rolled his eyes. 'That antiquated law? You'd bring that up now in a life-or-death situation?' He tapped a finger against the window. 'Do you think there's anyone alive down there who even remembers the Treaty? At best, it's ancient history to them. Most likely it has become a myth.'

'I don't know,' Silas said, his uncertainty growing and compounding his discomfort. They had wandered into forbidden territory. Life off Olympus? An unspeakable heresy. 'I'll need to think about it.'

'What time do we have to think?' Dane snarled, throwing his hands up in the air.

His face was red, and Silas shrank back from the sudden outburst of anger. For a moment it looked as though Dane was about to yell. Then he let out a long breath.

'Here, let me show you something,' he said, forcing calm into his voice. 'I've already done some investigation into where I'd like to go.'

He swiped his hand across the large window and an image appeared on the glass: a wide-angle scene showing a desolate land of gray hills. It was still and quiet until, after a moment, people came into view—dirty, barefoot, pathetic people walking in a line. Coarse ropes tied them together at the wrists. Silas felt his stomach turn at the sight. More horrors appeared. Towering over the line of prisoners appeared grotesque ape-like creatures. They had snouts and tusks like hogs, small eyes hidden beneath thick brows, leathery skin like the dry flinty hills over which they tromped, and long limbs dragging knuckles over the dust. They marched the prisoners up to a cave in a hillside where there emerged another one of the creatures, this one larger than the others. Upon seeing the prisoners, he howled in savage glee and leaped on them.

Silas turned away before he could witness the gore.

'Enough!' he cried. Trembling, he stepped back from the window. 'Why show me this?'

'I thought you would want to know. The land that you saw... it is where your daughter is buried.'

His daughter. Silas thought of the photo he kept clipped to his pod, the only possession he had taken from Earth and the only image he had of her. Memories welled up to the surface, and with them came an emotion he had tried to get rid of. Grief to drown him in bitter waters. He swallowed hard and gripped at his chest, but he couldn't clutch the pain within. He may have forgotten many things, but he hadn't forgotten where his daughter was entombed. A cemetery of green lawns and stately oaks. Not these grey hills.

'It can't be,' Silas murmured.

'Six hundred years have passed. Much has changed on Earth.'

Silas shook his head. He remembered his daughter's funeral. It had been the last time he visited Earth. He had never returned. Good riddance. That planet had taken her away from him. He had begged her to come with him to Olympus. She had refused. She said there was still work to do, that she couldn't abandon her home. Foolish child. Beautiful, wonderful, foolish child.

'Her resting place doesn't have to remain that way,' Dane whispered. 'I could fix it. I'll just need a few of my things to make it happen.'

Silas stood unmoving. After a moment or two, he handed the plex-tablet to one of the security droids. 'Dispose of this and then dock at your posts.' The droids left to carry out his orders.

Silas thought of the creatures desecrating the land where his daughter lay entombed. Something he hadn't felt in a long time welled up within him. Anger. It burned in his stomach and made his frail body tremble. Never had he allowed such an emotion to touch him in the Dream. Now his blood began to boil. He couldn't bear to endure it. As it threatened to erupt from the surface of his being, his gaze fell upon Earth.

'Go,' Silas said, 'but make sure no one finds out.' He headed towards the exit and the monorail platform, longing for his pod where he could extinguish his pain. Then, over his shoulder, he said, 'Murder those beasts while you're at it.'

Chapter 1

It was a well-known truth in all the Elkhorn Valley that Corvala Keen would one day fall into madness. Now at seventeen, her wits were still intact. But give it a year or two and she would go the way of her mother—chasing voices that weren't there and disappearing into the deep dark woods. It was a hereditary madness, going back to her great-grandmother and beyond. All the women of Corvala's line began with right minds, but when they turned eighteen or nineteen, they started to have strange dreams and hear voices calling to them. They disappeared one way or another. Corvala was bound to follow their fate. And though she wasn't crazy yet, people could only see her for what she would be, not what she was. And so they talked, but always behind her back for fear of her father, the local Judge.

Corvala led a life set apart from everyone else in the valley. It was a lonely existence, and she longed to be free from her parents' shadow. Mostly she longed for a cure. Anything to make her normal.

For now, all she had was her fiddle, the last gift from her mother. It was a funny little instrument with a face carved into the scroll on top. The face had a pointy beard, a sharp nose, and little holes bored into the wood to make eyes. Sometimes Corvala would look into those wooden eyes and say, 'Just wait, Sir William. One day we'll get the chance to escape this place.'

And indeed that chance came.

It was late spring in the Elkhorn Valley. The oaks and maples were beginning to take on the deep greens of summer, the early corn shoots were spearing from the soil, and the evenings were growing warmer. The Windborne, a traveling troupe of performers, had come to the valley and set up their colorful tents outside the town of Dawn's Landing. They came only once a year, staying a few days and then continuing on their way. Performers—jugglers, fire breathers, magicians, and others besides—would entertain in the evenings. Their most spectacular show always happened on their last night in town. It was on this night that Corvala came to the Windborne camp with her fiddle, Sir William, sheathed at her back.

The tents and wagons spread out in a wide circle lit with torches and bonfires. All around the circle, merchants' booths displayed goods from faraway lands. Colorful silk scarves and music boxes; vessels of bronze and blown glass inlaid with gold; beads for girls to put in their hair, some made of rare and expensive plasteek—treasures rarely seen in this valley of farmers and ranchers. There were caged exotic beasts: tigers, rhinos, even a chimera. The grounds were packed with people perusing the vendor booths or gathered in groups to socialize. Corvala entered the camp circle and headed towards the far end where the largest tent stood. Inside, the main show was already in full roar with its drums rumbling, horns blaring, and people cheering. Corvala made straight for the entrance, determination in her step.

On her way, she passed the Capel brothers gathered near the caged beasts—*Fitting*, she thought. The thirteen brothers, all rough and surly, passed around a huge jug of mud-wine, filling the air with curses and coarse laughter.

Whenever a woman passed by, they'd whistle and catcall. But not at Corvala. She wasn't wearing anything that called attention to herself—trousers and a tunic with a buckskin vest. Her eyes were dark and quick, and her raven hair was tied in a braid down her back. Her frame was lithe like a willow, and she carried herself with the steadiness of an oak. The Capel brothers watched her and said nothing. Knowing word could get back to the Judge, they wouldn't dare harass her. They weren't that stupid— at least, not this early in the evening, with their drinking just starting. So Corvala passed by, forcing them to lock their vulgar spew behind their teeth. Even Gage Capel, the middle brother and the unruliest of their lot, kept quiet as he stared at her.

Corvala was used to the stares—sometimes accompanied by snickers and snide whispers that followed just out of earshot. Did they bother her? No! Never! Not in the least! That's what she told herself, and she nearly believed it. And why should she let that kind of treatment bother her tonight? Tonight, she was going to break free from this valley and leave her reputation far behind.

Corvala entered the main tent, stepping into a colorful place full of humanity and the smell of popcorn and spicy sausages. Here the wooden bleachers formed a vast semicircle curving around the stage, creaking under the rollicking weight of spectators. The stage now featured the classic Demon and Clumsy Priest act, a standard for any show. A portly, balding man in an oversized robe played the part of the Clumsy Priest. He waddled from one side of the stage to the other, always searching for the Demon while tripping on his robes and falling on his face, his ungainliness tickling the crowd to laughter. Meanwhile, the Demon kept barely hidden behind a large wooden box. He was a character costumed in black and green with horns on his head and machine-like parts attached to the arms and chest. He appeared throughout the show, sneaking on stage while other performers had their backs turned. No matter how loud the audience yelled and pointed, the performers would feign ignorance. All the while, the Demon would creep about and duck behind curtains, stealing props and putting strings out of tune.

As Corvala entered the show and walked the opening between bleachers, she felt a hand pat the top of her head. Looking up, she saw a bright-faced man leaning over the railing and looking down at her from his high seat in the bleachers.

'Hello, Miss Keen,' he said, smiling broadly.

'Hello, Gilly,' Corvala replied, smiling back.

Gilly was perhaps the only person in the valley who sought out Corvala to talk with her. But, then again, he sought everyone out. He was a man with the mind of a child, wandering about town with his shoes untied and handing out dandelions to everyone he met.

'Come and sit with me?' he asked.

'I'm sorry, Gilly. I can't tonight,' she said. 'I'll find you tomorrow and play a song especially for you. Would you like that?'

Gilly lifted his fists to his mouth and nodded vigorously. Then he returned to watching the show, rocking back and forth and laughing with the children.

At any other time, Corvala would have sat with him. Tonight, she wasn't here for entertainment; she had an important matter to take care of, and so she went around the front seats to the far end of the bleachers. A curtain spanned the width of the tent, dividing it in two—the front half for the audience and the stage and the back half as a backstage area. Corvala stood off to the side near the tall curtain. Normally there was a guard keeping watch here, making sure none of the audience would enter. Tonight, though, there was no guard to be seen. Perhaps the Capel brothers were causing a ruckus outside, taking security from their posts. Whatever the reason, Corvala was thankful for her luck.

On stage, the Clumsy Priest accidentally bumped into the Demon, causing the Demon to stumble backwards and fall through a trapdoor on the stage floor. There was a big puff of smoke from the opening, and the Demon was gone. The crowd cheered. Corvala took advantage of the diversion and slipped through the curtain.

Here the sound of the show came as a muffled roar. In this mess of tables and boxes, performers waited for the final act. Corvala stood hidden behind a rack of props and costumes. She scanned the troupe, looking for someone in particular. There were performers tuning instruments and others applying makeup in front of mirrors. Then she saw him—a tall bald man with a tremendous moustache twisted up at the ends. Solomon Swain, the master of the Windborne. He was with the unmasked Demon who had just come off stage. Fixing her eyes on him, Corvala took a deep breath and left the cover of the props and costumes.

'Mister Swain,' she said, walking right up to him. 'I'd like to talk to you about that audition.'

'You again!' he said, both surprised and bothered by the interruption. 'How did you get back here?'

'I just need a minute of your time.'

'I'm too busy. Get back outside where you belong.' The troupe master walked away to tend to other business. Corvala followed.

'You were too busy yesterday and the day before that. You promised me an audition.'

'I did?' Solomon asked skeptically.

'Yes, you did. You said to come by later. And seeing as you're leaving tomorrow, I reckon later is now.'

Before he could refuse her, Corvala took the fiddle from its sheath and brought it to rest on her shoulder. She drew the bow across the strings and sawed out a jig, a popular song in the valley, one the bands always played at the summer parties and harvest festival. Corvala had mastered the tune, her fingers skipping up and down the neck like nimble dancers. The music raced from the strings and even caught the attention of several nearby performers. Some stopped what they were doing and listened, tapping their feet to the music. By the time Corvala drew out her final note, she had a little audience of her own, a dozen or so people who gave her quiet applause. Corvala only cared about Solomon's response. His arms were crossed, and he looked at her with a sideways glance, an amused smile on his face.

'You're good, kid,' he said. 'Real good.'

'Thank you,' Corvala replied, feeling her cheeks flush.

'But,' Solomon added, putting a hand on her shoulder, 'every bumpkin can play that tune. True, you saw it good. But I'm not looking for good. I'm not even looking for great. I'm looking for something special. You're not there yet.'

Corvala stood, stunned.

'What— what do you mean?' she murmured.

'You know how to play the fiddle, that's for sure. But you haven't yet learned how to play the soul.' Solomon looked down at her with an intent stare. 'Every musician has their song. Now I'm not talking about a piece of sheet music or a collection of notes. I'm talking about a sound that comes from deep within your being. *Your* song. When a musician finds their song and taps into it, the earth and sky tremble. You're not just playing your instrument; you're playing the souls of those who hear you. And they think to themselves, "*That's* what I needed to hear." Every musician has their song, but few find it. You haven't. Not yet. Come around again when you have.'

With that, he gave her shoulder a pat and turned away to prepare for the final act. Corvala's cheeks burned with shame, her failure witnessed by the performers around her. One woman gave her a pitying look. A young man shrugged his shoulders and said, 'Tough break.' Not knowing what else to do, Corvala retreated the way she had come, leaving through the curtain. She hurried past the stage, past the audience on the bleachers. All about her were bright lights and cheering, but she was numb to it. Arms wrapped about her chest, she left the main tent and headed home.

That had been her chance to join the Windborne, to escape this valley. Now it was gone. For years she had dreamed of leaving this place behind and making music in faraway lands. True, the madness of her mother would have followed her—but she could have learned how to cope with it and hide it, to ignore the voices if she had to. Dealing with it would have been tough anywhere. As a traveling musician on the road, at least she wouldn't have had her old reputation following her. She could have been anyone. She could have been Corvala the Magnificent.

Not anymore.

She walked around the outskirts of Dawn's Landing until her father's little log house appeared. She entered the house to find it dark. Her father must be out. He was always out working on something. That was fine with her. Right now, she wanted to be alone. She went straight to her room, where she collapsed on her bed. For a long time, her eyes stared up at the ceiling beams. Then the tears rushed in, and she wept.

How long she lay in her misery, she couldn't tell. A few hours, maybe. It didn't matter. She wanted to be holed up in the dark for a hundred years. Her shame was still raw, the wound of rejection wide open. Solomon Swain's words cut into her mind. *You're not there yet... you haven't found your song.* As much as she wanted to, she couldn't get those words out of her head.

After a few hours of drifting in and out of restless sleep, a sudden knock on the front door shot her bolt upright from the bed. She sat there, listening. Who would be knocking at this hour? The house became quiet again and she wondered if she had imagined the knocking. Then it came again.

Rubbing her eyes and wiping her cheeks, she left her room and looked out the front window. A man stood on the front porch. He wore a wide-brimmed hat and carried a short sword sheathed at his side. Corvala opened the door just wide enough to face the visitor.

'Sheriff Kilagrin,' she said, her voice wary. 'What brings you here?'

'I've got some news,' he said, scratching the palm of his hand. 'Your father just killed Gage Capel.'

BUNKER 610 REPORT_____

...

SERAPH CLASS 7

...

RUN DIAGNOSTICS

...

PROCESSING

...

STATUS: HIBERNATING

...

SYSTEM: STABLE

...

BATTERY LIFE: 9.7% - CRITICAL

Chapter 2

Corvala found herself on a long stretch of road in a vast empty field. In the distance, she could see the Windborne caravan of wagons moving towards the horizon, heading to the next town.

'Don't leave me!' Corvala called out.

She ran after the caravan but, no matter how fast she went, their slow wagons somehow kept getting farther and farther away. They disappeared behind one of the rolling hills.

It seemed like forever and a day had passed before Corvala reached the hill. When she rounded the top, the Windborne were nowhere to be seen. Instead, she saw the road ending at a river and, across it, a deep dark wood, its trees tall and ominous. Corvala knew that place and feared it. She knew what she was looking for lay on the other side.

Then, walking into her vision, came a figure on the opposite riverbank—a woman with long black hair and a white dress. When Corvala saw the woman's face, she cried out, 'Mama!'

The woman gave Corvala a sad smile then turned away, walking into the forest and disappearing among the trees.

'Mother!' Corvala cried out again. 'Don't leave me. Don't—'

'Miss Keen?'

Corvala heard a voice calling to her.

'Miss Keen?'

She woke up with her head on her desk. She must have dozed off during class. Looking up, she saw her teacher standing nearby. The old woman's owlish face studied Corvala intently, her expression concerned. The two dozen students in the schoolhouse were looking at her as well. Tessa, the daughter of a wealthy landowner, was in the front row smirking. Sitting up, Corvala ignored her peers and gave her attention solely to her teacher.

'Miss Keen?' the teacher asked. 'Are you all right?'

'Sorry, Mrs. Laskin,' Corvala said in a flat voice. 'Didn't sleep well last night.'

Mrs. Laskin's eyes were soft with understanding. 'Are you feeling well? You look pale.'

'I'm fine,' Corvala lied, sitting up straighter and holding her head up firmly.

'Are you sure?'

'Never better.'

'Hmm.' Mrs. Laskin gave Corvala a doubtful look. 'If you feel the need to go home and rest, I understand.'

She returned to the chalkboard at the front of the classroom and continued with her history lecture. Something about the Ancient people and their demonic machines. Corvala wasn't really paying attention. She just stared at her desk, running a finger over its wooden grain.

When the midday bell tolled, she and the other students went outside for their lunch break. It was a bright sunny day, so some gathered on the lawn for a picnic. Corvala sat alone on a bench and laid her fiddle case and knapsack at her side. She had packed bread, dried meat, and some cheese for lunch. She wasn't hungry. She looked to the schoolyard, where a couple of boys kicked a ball around. More boys joined in and, eventually, a game of rutball started up. They dribbled up and down the small pitch and tried to kick the ball through the standing hoop. Corvala watched the game, her face blank. The wheels of her mind were spinning. She was sorting through what Sheriff Kilagrin had told her the night before.

Her father had put Gage Capel to the sword. She wasn't too shocked about his killing a man. She knew her father killed bad people. Sparingly, sure, but it happened. That's what Judges did. And besides, Gage had it coming.

Rumors floated around Dawn's Landing—some having leaked from the Sheriff's report, some pure speculation. After the Windborne had finished their show, Gage had gone wandering the town, drunk and looking for trouble. What he found was Gilly. The poor simpleton had just come from the show when Gage grabbed him and dragged him into a dark alley. Then the beating began.

It wasn't the first. Gage had a thing for making Gilly feel pain, beating the poor man within an inch of his life and then leaving him bloody and bruised in some out-of-the-way place. After each incident, Gilly would never say who did it; he was too scared of the Capels to talk about it. Everybody knew it was Gage, but there was never sufficient evidence to bring him in. It didn't help that Sheriff Kilagrin was a cousin of Old Roman, the patriarch of the Capel family. So, Gilly kept getting beaten up, too afraid to speak. Justice was barred.

It was in situations like these that a Judge would step in.

According to Kilagrin's report, Gage had started with punches. Something must have angered him because the situation got worse than usual. Maybe Gilly had decided to stick up for himself, throwing a punch of his own. Whatever the reason, Gage got mad and pulled out his knife, stabbing Gilly viciously. Then Corvala's father appeared. The Judge had warned Gage many times to stop the beatings and leave the poor man alone. Gage wouldn't listen. So, the Judge ran him through with a sword.

Gilly had been rushed to Doctor Hearthwood. His wounds were grave, but he arrived in time. The doctor stitched him up and said there was a chance he'd survive. Gage's body, on the other hand, had been sent to the Capels. They already had their own version of the story spreading through the valley. According to them, Gilly had gone into the alley to pick through trash and had fallen in a bin. Broken glass had cut him. Gage had merely been trying to help Gilly out when the Judge came along and murdered him.

Normally such a lie wouldn't have bothered Corvala. There was always some backlash when her father enacted justice. She knew Gage had gone too far by bringing a knife into it. Her father wouldn't have killed anyone for something petty. Still, even though he had done his job, he had kicked the hornets' nest this time. The Capels were a large family and people were afraid of them. They could stir up a lot of trouble.

Corvala thought this all through as she slumped on the schoolyard bench. Out of the corner of her eye, she could see Tessa Jones and the other girls sitting on the lawn, looking at her and holding their hands to their mouths, whispering. They were almost certainly gossiping about her father. Corvala couldn't blame them. She'd probably be talking about him, too—if she had anyone with whom to talk. Her father's annual trial was only a few days away. Since he had killed Gage, he now had the wrath of the Capel family to contend with. Just thinking about it made Corvala's stomach knot.

Her thinking and worrying were suddenly interrupted by a strange noise. A distant roar with music in it—something like a mournful trumpet call. The boys playing rutball stopped their game, and everyone in the schoolyard looked in the direction of the noise. It had come from the forest on the valley's western slopes.

Thorn Shroud Forest. Its ancient needle trees were dark and foreboding, and its shadows held goblins and all manner of fearsome beasts. The call the students had heard was distinctive: long and clear, as richly beautiful as it was deeply disturbing. The call of a manticore.

'I heard they're big enough to take down a horse and rider,' said one of the rutball players.

'Hog slop!' said a boy by the name of Arlo. 'My uncle up in Hard Scrabble killed one. He was going on about how big it was. Only we find out its hide makes a rug you can barely wipe your feet on. I bet I could chase one off with a stick.'

Mrs. Laskin didn't share Arlo's confidence.

'Maybe we should finish lunch inside,' she announced, ushering the students back into the schoolhouse and casting a leery eye towards Thorn Shroud.

Corvala got up from the bench and started to follow the others in. Then she stopped. Why should she go back to class? With everything that was going on, she wondered why she had come to school in the first place. She supposed she had gone out of habit, not knowing what else to do. Now that she was here, she was distracted and had dozed off in class. She thought about Mrs. Laskin's offer to go home and rest. She knew she couldn't. Being stuck in her house would only drive her stir-crazy. Yet there was no point in staying here either. Antsy, she decided she needed to do *something*. Usually, she'd play music when she was down. Since she had failed her audition with Solomon Swain, however, she'd not been in the mood.

You're not ready yet... you haven't found your song.

Even though her father's predicament far eclipsed her own, she couldn't help but think about how the performing troupe had packed up their tents that morning and moved on without her. Now she was stuck in this valley. Where was she to go?

Before she dipped too much into despair, she remembered there was something she could do. She remembered the promise she had made Gilly last night: a song. The poor guy, all stitched up in bed, could probably use some music to cheer him up. Corvala looked out beyond the schoolyard, her fingers tapping pensively against Sir William. Maybe she wasn't in the mood for playing for herself, but she could play for someone else. She left the schoolyard with her fiddle case slung over her shoulder and started on a path towards Gilly's home. It was a beautiful day to be out in the open fields, and being on the move did help her spirits some. It was certainly better than being stuck behind a desk. Corvala felt some apprehension as she walked. Since Gilly's house was on the far western side of the valley, she'd have to pass uncomfortably close to Thorn Shroud. Although the sky was clear and bright, the forest atop the Gloaming Hills on the valley's western border reared up in her view like a wall of darkness, its heights bristling with trees.

Corvala thought of the manticore call they'd heard at school. According to the hunters, manticores were on the move, leaving the forest's interior regions. Something was pushing them outward. A large male expanding his territory perhaps. Or maybe something bigger. Whatever it was, manticores had been spotted at the edges of Thorn Shroud Forest. Grail Stevenson said he had seen one recently, prowling through one of the fields on his farm. Corvala swallowed, trying to keep the neck-prickling apprehension at bay by convincing herself that Grail

27

Stevenson was just telling stories. The geezer was as blind as a bat and couldn't see a lit candle in a pitch-black room.

There was something else besides the beasts that unnerved her as she walked—a fear all her own. The forest was where her mother had disappeared. During one of her episodes, she had heard voices and followed them into those dire trees, never to be seen again. A similar thing had happened to her grandmother, except she had wandered into a marsh, lost forever. Not wanting the same to happen to her, Corvala avoided the western part of the valley when she could. Heading in the direction of the forest's border, her resolve began to waver.

But she had made a promise to Gilly. She couldn't bear to break it, especially since he was fighting between life and death. If there was ever a time he needed a song, it was now. It was worth the risk—if 'risk' it could be called. It wasn't like she was going to climb the hill and venture into Thorn Shroud. That said, she'd get closer to the forest's edge than she'd like—but the path to Gilly's house would keep her in the valley. Assuring herself there was no need to worry, Corvala hurried on.

As if to affirm her choice, her route brought her to a welcome sight—an open meadow of tall grass flecked with yellow wildflowers and bearing the peaceful hum of grasshoppers. Rising from the middle of the meadow was a grove of twelve beech trees, their bark light and smooth. Above them stood a venerable atlas fir, its branches outstretched to shelter the beeches below. With Thorn Shroud looming bluish-gray in the background, this nearby grove came as a patch of verdant green in the foreground—light set against the darkness. Apostle's Grove it was called, a holy place in the eyes of the valley's inhabitants. That's where people prayed, for it was said the presence of God and angels could be felt among those trees. Corvala wouldn't have been surprised if Gilly's parents had already paid a visit that morning. Since she avoided the valley's far western side, Corvala rarely came to Apostle's Grove. With her path taking her so close, she wondered why she shouldn't visit it herself. Just a quick stop and she'd be back on her way to Gilly's house.

She crossed the meadow and entered the grove. The beech trees formed a ring—a natural bowl in the earth, a shady amphitheater layered by small boulders and winding tree roots. Corvala could see how people believed this place to be holy. Hemmed in within the trees, there was an air of protection and tranquility. She descended into the bowl and knelt on the bed of moss at the center of the ring. She closed her eyes to pray.

It was a funny thought to Corvala: her, praying? She was a child the last time she had prayed. She would kneel at her bedside every night and ask for her mother to be healed of her madness. She'd pray to be healed herself, too. After her mother disappeared, she didn't see the point. Her prayers grew infrequent and she held long silences between her and God. Now, however, was perhaps the time to speak up.

'Dear God,' she whispered.

A twig snapped behind her. Corvala yelped, twisting around. Prepared for a beast, she was somewhat relieved to see it was just a boy. Placing a hand on her chest, she caught her breath. The boy stood at the edge of the grove and looked down at her. It was Rhonie Capel, the youngest of the Capel brothers. Even though he was about fifteen, two years her junior, he stood a little taller than her. His limbs were awkward and gangly, but there was a wiry strength in them. He wore clothing common among the men of the valley: buckskin pants and shirt. Hanging from his belt were trophies from the little animals he had tortured and killed— pheasant feet and squirrel tails. Although it was no delight to see him, he was a better sight than a beast of Thorn Shroud. Not by much...

'What are you doing here, Rhonie?' Corvala demanded, rising to face him. 'Shouldn't you be at school?'

'I could ask you the same,' he said as he tromped down into the grove's natural bowl, tearing up the soft moss with his boots.

'What do you want?' she asked sternly, her eyes going to the knife on his belt.

'Don't worry, girl,' Rhonie grunted. 'I'm not here to wolf you. Fah sent me to give you a message.'

'You followed me here?' Corvala said, levelling a cold stare at him. 'You and your father have nothing to say that I want to hear.'

'It's about *your* father,' Rhonie grinned, showing his crooked teeth. 'We've got a proposition for him.'

Chapter 3

'Fah wants to let you know the deal's still on the table,' Rhonie said, picking up a rock and tossing it at one of the sacred beech trees.

Corvala had to think for a moment. There was only one thing he could be talking about.

'Is Old Roman still going on about his stupid plan?'

Rhonie scowled. 'It's not stupid.'

'So that's why you're here,' Corvala sighed, shaking her head. 'Heaven's piss, Rhonie! Your brother's not yet in the ground, and your fah can only think of how he can climb the ladder. Isn't even *he* capable of mourning his son before he hatches his schemes?'

'My fah is a great man!' Rhonie asserted. 'Everybody knows it. He should be in charge. Instead, we got Mayor Green, old and weak. Fah would run things so much better.'

'Yeah, run them into the ground.'

'Don't you dare talk bad about my fah!'

Rhonie moved in towards Corvala, his eyes flashing. She had pushed too far—not a wise thing to do while out here in the fields, alone with a Capel. She took a step back, ready to bolt if she had to. Rhonie restrained himself, clenching his fists at his side. Something was holding him back—the message he had come to deliver. He checked his temper with a huff.

'The deal is pretty much the same as before,' he said. 'We want the Judge to run Mayor Green out of town.'

'My fah already told you no.'

Rhonie's expression turned to a sneer. 'That was when he was offered money. Now my fah has something better to offer. The chance to live.'

Corvala winced. She had been thinking about the coming danger to her father all day. Having one of the Capel boys voice that threat—it was like a hornet's sting to the back of the neck. She tried to keep her composure, not wanting to let this valley scrub know he had got to her.

'Run along then,' he said. 'My fah gets impatient and might change his mind.'

Corvala didn't budge.

'There's still time for my fah to end you,' she shot back. 'Your whole family—gone! You know he could.'

Rhonie grunted with a laugh. But was there a flicker of fear in his eyes?

'He wouldn't. It's not in him.'

'You don't know that. Judges are unpredictable men, full of bloodshed. Remember what happened in Haverston? The Purghett house got bigger and more powerful than what was good for them. Bullied people and took what wasn't theirs. So, their Judge put them to the sword. Every man, woman, and child. My fah could do the same.'

That was the power each Judge possessed. No one was beneath their blade. Not even the Archon himself. Any Judge could run the prime leader through while he sat on his throne in Belcastan, and no one could do anything about it. Not until the day of the Judge's trial. It was how the powers kept each other in check.

Rhonie opened his mouth, ready to spew what Corvala could only assume would be more nonsense, when a loud noise bronzed the air around them. A trumpeting roar—long, clear, and eerily beautiful. Corvala and Rhonie froze.

The manticore was close, the call having come from the meadow. Rhonie dropped and lay on the steep side of the bowl. Not knowing what else to do, Corvala did the same. Belly pressed against the dirt and tree roots, she listened. She could hear paws treading through the tall grass, the *swish-swish* growing more pronounced as the steps drew closer. She dared to peek up from the dirt and saw a four-legged shape obscured by trees and underbrush. Its snaking tail ended in a wicked barb. Arlo from school was wrong. This wasn't a small thing you could chase away with a stick. This was a beast.

It came around the edge of the grove, near where Corvala lay hidden. She gripped clods of moss as her body tensed, the suspense playing her spine like the high strings of her fiddle. She kept as still as she could, her racing heart thumping out the rhythm of the terrified— the primordial beat known to all creatures considered prey. The mouse in the hawk's shadow knew it. The cricket in the mantis's reach knew it. And now Corvala knew it. The rhythm shook her bones and innards and drummed in her ears, and she was sure the beast—and the entire valley—would hear.

The manticore was close now, just on the other side of a nearby tree trunk. Corvala heard its rough breathing—could almost feel the moist heat snorted from its nostrils. Here was the moment the beast would find her. When the terrible music within her would end with a crash—when the teeth and claws would fall upon her.

The moment never came. The beast turned away from the grove and headed back out into the meadow, the sound of its paws fading into the distance.

Corvala released her hold on the roots and moss clumps and let her body collapse in a sprawl on the rocky soil. With the swell of terror gone, something had to fill the void. Her jangled nerves filled it with laughter. She gripped her sides, trying to keep quiet. There was no way to keep it in. Rhonie motioned for her to shut up. He was in mid-crouch, staring at something, his eyes wide with fear. Corvala took enough control of herself to sit up and turn to follow his gaze. Through an opening in the trees, Corvala saw the manticore's face in the tall grass. It had a bright red nose with flared nostrils and blue ridges on the sides of the elongated muzzle. The beast would have had a comical appearance if it weren't for its long, sharp canines and yellow, predatory eyes—eyes that were locked onto Corvala and Rhonie.

The beast lunged.

Corvala and Rhonie bolted, scrambling up the steep sides of the bowl. Rhonie tripped on an exposed root and fell.

'Help!' he cried.

Corvala had a mind to save her skin. But, in that shred of a moment, compassion tugged and got the better of her. No one deserved to be torn apart by a manticore. Not even a Capel. Corvala grabbed him by the hand. In his rush to escape, he pulled too forcefully and brought Corvala down. They stumbled, and both fell in a heap at the bottom of the grove. Corvala twisted and, when she looked up, saw the manticore break through the trees. A flash of reddish fur. Raw wildness and a sprint to the kill. It leaped, claws outstretched. Corvala closed her eyes.

There came a loud thud, heavy bodies colliding with one another. But Corvala felt nothing. She opened her eyes. A new shape had appeared—a form she would recognize anywhere. A large man slammed the manticore to the ground, pinning it with his knees. The creature writhed beneath. Claws raked the man's arms. The barbed tail jabbed at his side. The man ignored his wounds and stabbed a hunting knife into the red fur. Again and again the blade plunged into the ribs. The sheen of bloodied metal then dove into the chest and belly.

The creature snarled and roared, fighting to break free. The man held it down firmly and kept on stabbing. The tail flailed wildly with jerks and spasms. Eventually, the flailing stopped, and the tail fell limp to the ground.

The man rose from his kill. His muscular, stalwart form could have been hewn from the heart of a mountain. His face was bearded and bore sharp features carved by age and tribulation. He turned to Corvala.

She met her father's gaze with a mixed expression of gratitude and fear.

'Are you all right?' he asked in his deep voice.

She nodded timidly.

Her father took his knife from the manticore's body and walked over to Rhonie, who whimpered and held out an arm to ward off the man. Corvala's father did him no harm; he merely took the boy by the hand and helped him to his feet. After he wiped his knife clean and sheathed it, he picked up the manticore in his huge hands and slung the beast over his broad shoulders. When she had been hiding, Corvala's fear had exaggerated its size. She had imagined something that would have met shoulders with a horse. Now she could see it was no bigger than a cougar. Still, a beast that could kill a man. Unless, of course, that man was her father.

Without a word, he left Apostle's Grove and crossed the meadow. Corvala and Rhonie didn't need to be told to follow. They walked in silence. Her nerves still shaking from the attack, Corvala noticed Rhonie casting wary glances at her father. His eyes were drawn especially to the sword sheathed at his side—the weapon that had killed his brother. Like all blades carried by Judges, it had been forged from torcarda, a rare alloy as lightweight as cedar and stronger than steel. It was said angels had come down from heaven to give the first Judges their blades. It had happened hundreds of years ago, the story went, but Corvala suspected the rumor had been somewhat embellished over time. Even so, a torcarda blade in a Judge's hand was seen as a tool of divine retribution. Rhonie feared it. *As he should*, Corvala thought.

Her father led them onto the road but, instead of taking them toward town as Corvala had expected, he turned down a long path through wide acres where cattle grazed. Corvala looked to her father with apprehension. Up ahead, the Capel homestead sat atop a small hill like a lone fortress. A log wall surrounded the compound, within which stood a large wooden house, a barn, and several shacks where the family's servants lived. The homestead may have been grand and impressive a generation or two in the past, but Old Roman had let his family's estate fall into disrepair. Weeds grew everywhere, and the scattered cattle and deer remains made the place a boneyard. The structures were dilapidated, their wooden boards warped and stained with mold. On the rickety front porch, one of the Capels sat back in the shade with a jug of mud-wine. When he saw the three of them coming up the path, he got up and crossed the grounds—giving a swift kick to a dog lying in his way. Corvala could see it was Morgan, the oldest of the Capel brothers. He was weasel-faced and wiry, with brawling scars over his cheeks and knuckles. His eyes were full of suspicion and loathing when he stopped Corvala's father at the gate.

'Judge Exodus Keen,' he snorted. 'You got some gall coming here. What're you doing with my little brother?'

'He ran into trouble.' Exodus dropped the manticore at Morgan's feet. Morgan eyed the creature for a moment before looking at his brother with a flinty stare.

'Get over here, Rhonie,' Morgan hissed, grabbing his brother by the wrist and yanking him to his side. 'Fah told you to keep this quiet. Did he take?'

Exodus spoke before the boy could. 'My answer is no. I won't take your father's offer.'

Morgan clenched his jaw and nodded. 'Very well, Judge. But don't think what you did today changes nothing. You'll get yours soon enough.' He spat on the dead manticore. 'Now get the hell off our property.'

Exodus, unfazed, picked up his kill and left. Corvala followed and took her place at her father's side. Once they were out of earshot of the Capel homestead, she asked, 'Why didn't you take the offer? They aren't talking about money now. They're talking about your trial.'

'I reckoned as much,' Exodus said. 'That doesn't change my answer, though. I'm not going to let the town fall to ruin on account of me.'

'Mayor Green has already let it fall. You wouldn't be doing any harm running him out of town and letting Old Roman take his place. The old dung practically runs things anyway, what with how weak Green is.'

'Green isn't weak,' her father corrected. 'He's grieving. He's been distracted these last few seasons. To lose a daughter to the pale sickness...' Exodus trailed off, shaking his head. Then he added, 'What are you doing out of school?'

Given that he had just killed a beast and confronted his enemies, missing class hardly seemed important. Now, however, wasn't the time to argue the point.

'Mrs. Laskin gave me permission to go. Said I wasn't looking well.'

'So, you went to Apostle's Grove?'

'I was going to Gilly's house to pay him a visit. On the way, I stopped at the Grove.'

'You know better. You got too close to the Shroud.'

Corvala looked up at the beast slung over her father's shoulders. It was staring down at her with dead eyes, its terrible jaws frozen in a snarl, revealing at least three rows of teeth. She shuddered.

'Manticores always stick to the forest. There was no way I could've known one would come out to the Grove.'

'True. But you knew about something else.'

Corvala's expression grew dark. 'I didn't hear any voices, if that's what you're worried about. I'm not my mother yet.'

'Even so, you took an unnecessary risk.'

'I can make my own choices.'

'You better make them wise.'

The two of them turned off the path and took the road towards Dawn's Landing. Slowly, the town appeared in the distance.

'Why don't you just kill the Capels?' Corvala said at length. 'Kill them all.'

Exodus shot her a stern glare. 'Don't talk that way.'

'Why not?' Corvala cried. 'They'll try to kill you at the trial!'

'You don't think I know that?'

'You're doing nothing about it when you have the power—and the right—to end them.'

'Killing people just to stay alive isn't justice. I'm not going to lose my soul to save my skin.'

'What about me?' Corvala asked. She stopped in the middle of the road and grabbed her father's arm. 'What about protecting me? Does that matter to you?'

Exodus gave her a long look, then said, 'Of course it does. But it sounds like you're moving on. Didn't you have plans to leave town with that performance troupe?'

Corvala's gaze dropped and she let her hand fall from his arm. There was nothing she could say to that. Exodus continued down the road, and Corvala trudged after. A long silence settled in between them. It was only when Dawn's Landing drew close that Corvala spoke up.

'I don't want you to go to the trial.'

'Neither do I,' said Exodus. 'You know I have to, though.'

'I don't want you to... die.' The last word came out weak.

'Don't worry,' Exodus assured her. 'God cuts our path.'

'It's a horrible path.'

'Maybe,' said Exodus. 'You tell him what you think, and then you walk it.'

BUNKER 610 REPORT_____

...

SERAPH CLASS 7

...

RUN DIAGNOSTICS

...

PROCESSING

...

STATUS: HIBERNATING

...

SYSTEM: STABLE

...

BATTERY LIFE: 9.69% - CRITICAL

Chapter 4

No laws apply to a Judge except two:

❖ *A Judge must never consort with demons or the powers of Hell.*

❖ *A Judge must report to his people once a year to stand trial so they may decide by stone whether he should live or die.*

—from The Edicts of the Order of Judges

The sun was peeking over the valley's eastern hills. The day of the trial was here, its light shining through Corvala's window. Corvala sat on her bed with her back leaned against the headboard, her fiddle in her lap, and plucked the same note for the millionth time. The daylight crept down her wall and onto her bed. She pulled her feet back so it wouldn't touch her as it moved across the lower half of her sheets. There was nothing she could do to stop the day from coming. It was already here.

In the past, trials had meant a few butterflies in Corvala's stomach but nothing more. Her father would always come out untouched and she'd laugh at herself afterwards for having had any worries at all. Her father was a good man and the people of the valley knew it. His justice was fair. On top of that, he served those in need, whether it was by helping bring in the harvest or repairing a broken roof. And he always did it without being asked. It was this reputation that had kept him safe in past trials.

Today was different. Now he had the wrath of the Capel family to contend with. Now, Corvala didn't have butterflies in her stomach—she had a whole swarm of locusts.

She looked down at the face carved into the scroll of her fiddle.

'He'll be all right, Sir William,' she whispered. 'Don't worry your little wooden head.'

After the sun had risen fully above the eastern hills, there was a knock at her bedroom door.

'Come in,' she muttered.

Her father entered. Corvala could see he was wearing his uniform today. He wore it to every trial and formal ceremony: the dark gray pants and jerkin with a tan long-sleeved shirt underneath. His sword was at his back, the thick strap of its sheath running over his shoulder and across his chest. On the strap was a bronze buckle that bore the image of broken pottery with fire coming out of it—the mark of a Judge. Corvala couldn't help but notice how dignified her father looked.

'Time to go,' he said.

Reluctantly, Corvala got out of bed and made ready to face the day.

In Dawn's Landing, the smoke of breakfast fires wafted from chimneys and hung low over the cedar-shingled roofs of tightly packed shops and houses. Corvala walked at her father's side as they made their way down the dirt lane through town. She fidgeted with the hem of her sleeves and tried not to pay any attention to the people who stared and whispered as they passed. They entered the main square, where everyone from the valley had gathered. The crowds parted before Exodus and the town guards pushed people back, forming a wide circle. Corvala stood at the edge of the circle; Exodus went on to stand in its center.

At one end of the main square there stood the town's great house with its tall A-frame roof. In front of it was a stone platform that held High Mayor Green, the head of Elkhorn County. He was enthroned on a seat of carved wood, a long olive jacket draped over his stooped shoulders. Seated around him were the lesser mayors from the county's smaller villages. Above the platform flew the flag of the Norwestor Dominion: a white field with a bear standing over eight mountain peaks, each representing the eight provinces of the Dominion). Beneath it flew the smaller flag of the Stag Ridge province: a pair of antlers on a blue field. Both flags fluttered weakly in the breeze as Mayor Green stood up to address the crowd. He looked down upon Exodus with eyes creased by long sadness.

'Judge Exodus Keen,' Mayor Green stated, forcing his voice out so that it could be heard by all. 'You stand here before me, a keeper of the Norwestor Dominion and a servant of our Archon. You stand before the people you have promised to serve. And you stand here before God who bestows all judgment and mercy. Have you this year lived up to your calling as a Judge, giving and maintaining justice?'

'I have.'

'Let the people decide.'

Mayor Green nodded to the guards. They went to Exodus and took his sword and his buckle bearing the Judge's mark. They stripped him of his uniform, leaving him with nothing but the cloth over his loins. The guards then blindfolded him before leaving him naked and exposed to the crowd.

Corvala could see the wounds from his fight with the manticore. The claw marks on his arms and chest still appeared raw. She saw he had tried to patch himself up with a needle and catgut. He had done a shoddy job. She suddenly felt angry at him for not asking her to stitch them for him. He probably hadn't wanted her to worry. Although the wounds he bore weren't serious, he was coming to the trial not fresh but already wounded.

One of the guards sprinkled chalk dust on the hard-packed ground, making a circle around Exodus, carefully keeping to the dimensions prescribed by the law. Once the circle was made, Mayor Green addressed the crowd.

'Do any of you wish to stand with Judge Keen to defend him?'

This was the moment Corvala had been waiting for. All the people her father had helped would gather around him, protecting him from the wrath of a bad man and his kin. Their bodies would block the stones. Maybe so many people would stand with her father that those who wished him harm would be discouraged and leave him alone altogether.

But when Corvala looked around the crowd, she saw no one step forward. Those her father had helped in the past did nothing. She could make out Gilly's parents, their faces turned downwards, each quietly ashamed of their own cowardice. And there, at the front of the crowd, was Old Roman, the patriarch of the Capel family. He stood at the edge of the circle opposite her. Unlike most people in the crowd, he looked very pleased, a smug grin on his bulldog face.

His household gathered around him like a small army—his three wives, thirteen sons, eight daughters, and a slew of servants. By his side stood his second wife, Sesha, Gage's mother. She was a thin woman with a wearied frame, but vengeance burned in her eyes—vengeance she and her entire family would mete out.

Despair overcame Corvala. So many of her enemies stood together, yet her father stood alone.

Then a wild thought came to her mind: he didn't have to stand alone—she could stand with him. At first, it seemed crazy. Then again, what did she have to lose? Her father was about to be taken from her, and her mother's madness would overcome her soon. For her, one rejected by the Windborne, wouldn't it be better to die at her father's side than meet an undignified end chasing voices into the deep dark woods?

Corvala took a step out from the edge of the crowd. Then another. She wondered if she was acting rashly. There was no time for second thoughts. All she knew was that her place was by her father. For as long as her body would hold out, she would block the hurled stones. When she came to stand by him in the center of the circle, he turned his blindfolded face towards her.

'Corvala?' he whispered.

'Yes. It's me.'

'You don't belong here. Get back!'

'I won't let you go through this alone.'

'It's my trial to bear. Now get back!'

'No!'

Exodus snorted at her stubbornness. He then raised his voice just enough for the old man on the platform to hear him.

'Mayor Green… remove my daughter.'

There was nothing that bound Mayor Green to honor Exodus's wish. But under the calm tone of the Judge there was a deep thunder, the distant rumbling of a storm beyond the horizon. It promised terrible things for the mayor if any stone should strike Corvala—if, of course, Exodus survived.

Mayor Green nervously licked his lips and, after a moment's deliberation, he motioned for the guards to drag Corvala from the ring. A pair moved in and grabbed her by the arms.

'No!' she cried, clinging to her father. 'I won't go.'

'You're brave,' Exodus said in soft tones, 'but this is mine to bear.'

The guards tore her from him and brought her to the edge of the crowd where one of them held her firmly by the wrist.

'No!' she screamed. 'Will no one stand with him?'

She looked wildly about and spotted a weathered man with thick eyebrows.

'Mister Delhan!' she cried. 'Who dug irrigation ditches with you during the drought? My fah! You stand with him! You stand with him *now*!' She looked at an older woman, who avoided her eyes. 'Widow Oppet! Who repaired your shed after it fell in the storm? My fah! Stand with him!'

There were more, too—Corvala called them out one by one, reminding them of what her father had done for them. Still, no one stepped forward. She screamed her desperation until a guard tied a thick cloth around her mouth. Gagged and restrained, she sank to her knees in defeat, her arm lifted above in the guard's firm grip.

Mayor Green proceeded with the trial.

'Anyone who has a grievance with Judge Keen may step forward.'

A pair of guards rolled in a cart laden with stones. In the grim ambience that hung over the square, Sesha left Old Roman's side and picked a fist-sized stone from the cart. She marched up to the chalk line and set her fiery glare upon her target. Exodus stood still—a pillar of strength. Sesha took aim and threw the stone. Despite her skinny arm, her throw was powered by all the rage of a bereaved mother. The stone hit Exodus square in the chest. He made no sound, but the stone left the skin red. It was nothing fatal, but this was just the beginning.

The next up was Trajan Capel, Gage's closest brother. He was a savage brawler, known for laughing wildly during fights. He picked out a stone and came around to the other side of the circle to face Exodus's back. With a powerful yell, he hurled the stone, sending it crashing into Exodus's spine. Corvala bit into her gag and gripped her arm, digging her fingernails into her skin. Exodus shuddered before regaining his firm stance. Trajan crowed like a victorious rooster and strutted back to his approving father.

One by one, all of Roman's sons, daughters, wives, and servants came to the chalk line to enact the patriarch's revenge. The stones rained down on Exodus, smashing into his flesh and bone. The stitches on his arms and chest were broken open. His head became so bloodied his blindfold turned red. His stance weakened, and he teetered like a wobbling drunk. Corvala couldn't bear to see her father this way, but neither could she let her eyes abandon him. So, she wept and watched his strength slowly crumble as the stones flew.

Rhonie was one of the last to throw. He plodded over to the cart, where he half-heartedly picked up a smaller stone. When he threw it, it barely grazed Exodus's leg. Slinking back to where the other Capels stood, Roman gave his youngest son a look that promised punishment later.

There were only two Capels left: Morgan and Old Roman himself. Corvala knew Morgan was a powerful thrower. In passing, she had seen him play his drinking game out in a field—knocking deer skulls from the top of a pasture fence. Even when he was drunk, he was a good shot, hardly ever missing his mark and shattering each bone he targeted. Today, he came to the trial sober, his arm twitching to throw. And when he threw his stone, it hit Exodus hard on the side of the head, making a sickening crack for all to hear.

Corvala screamed into her gag. She tried to run to her father but the guard held her back. She pulled against his hold like a mad dog tied to a stake, unable to break free. She shook her head wildly until the gag dropped from her mouth, and cried out, 'No! Leave him alone. Isn't this enough for you?'

Exodus swayed and, finally, fell. For a moment he lay still, his face pressed into the blood and dust, his breath heavy and labored. Then, with trembling limbs, he pushed himself up. He tried to stand, but could only manage to kneel.

Old Roman could grin no wider. The patriarch sauntered over to the cart, savoring Exodus's fallen state. His family must have left the largest stone for him, for he came up to the chalk line with a rock that took two hands to carry.

This was it. The killing blow. Corvala looked away.

A bright light flashed above. A thunderous roar shook the timbers of the town's structures. The people looked up in wide-eyed astonishment and fear. A shooting star in a clear sky. Not one of the streaks of glittering light seen in the evening, but a great fiery ball. It blazed a straight line across the sky, roaring its fury and leaving a trail of reddish smoke behind. As quickly as it came, it was gone, disappearing behind the north-western hills.

For many moments, the crowd stood still. Then, at once, they stirred, murmuring and shuffling about like a herd of spooked sheep.

'God is angry with us!' a voice cried out. 'Angry that we would condemn a just man!'

Many other voices agreed. They shouted out at Mayor Green, demanding that he do something. Green held up his hands to calm them, though he looked just as frightened as they did.

'I pronounce the trial over. Everyone to your homes. Kneel and pray.'

The crowd rushed away. Even Old Roman dropped his stone and left in a hurry. Corvala thought little of what the others were doing or what had streaked across the sky. She thought only of her father. Coming over to him and kneeling by his side, she found that he was breathing. Just barely. She dumped the remaining stones from the cart and, with a grunting effort, heaved Exodus's body into it. No one in the crowd paid her any heed. They were too busy getting to their homes and looking up at the sky with trepidation. Corvala gritted her teeth and began pulling the cart and her father out of the town square, winding towards their home.

'I'm going to fix you,' she said, not knowing how on earth she was going to do that.

Chapter 5

Far away in the flinty hills of the wild north, a troll woke from his slumber. Urgath was his name. He rose from the raw stone ground of his cave and, as he did every morning, rubbed his back against the rock wall, giving his thick gray skin a long scratch. He did the same with his boar-like tusks, honing them to a fine point. At the mouth of his cave, he found a puddle where rainwater had pooled. Urgath cupped his hands in the water and brought them to his mouth. Taking a long drink, he looked outside and surveyed his territory. Below him, a ravine cut through the gray hills, and caves pocked the steep cliffsides where other trolls lived. This was the home of his *hrak*.

Before him, Bulnatog the Mountain had been chief. For twenty years, Bulnatog had ruled the *hrak*, earning the title 'Mountain' because no challenger could bring him down. When Bulnatog grew old, Urgath contested his rule. It was a brutal fight, a wrestling match over the rocky earth. All the members of the *hrak* watched in hungry anticipation as the two combatants locked arms and slammed each other against the ground. They roared and drove tusks into each other's hides. In the end, Urgath crushed Bulnatog's throat with a heavy stone. Victorious, he carried the dead troll up the highest hill in the *brak's* territory. At the top stood a pile of skulls—those of the chiefs who had come before. Urgath took Bulnatog's head and placed it on the top of the pile. He stayed on the hilltop in solitude for many days, eating Bulnatog's remains and consuming the former chief's power. When he descended the hill, the *brak* recognized him as chief.

That was over fifteen years ago. Now Urgath was getting old. Despite his size and strength, his joints ached, and he wasn't as quick as he used to be. He knew the younger males were studying him, sizing him up and looking for anything that hinted at weakness. The challenges would come soon. He would fight them back for a while but, eventually, his head would be added to the pile of skulls on the high hilltop.

Along with his age, another circumstance weakened his authority: the year had been a poor one. The deer and brush-hogs seemed to shun his territory, leaving many in his *brak* hungry. And trolls always blamed their chiefs for their hunger. Sensing resentment, Urgath had sent his best hunters south of the great river to raid the human kingdom. It was a bold move. Although humans were weak, they were clever and had numbers. They could amass huge armies to march into the northern troll lands. The chiefs of other *braks* would have called Urgath's move foolish, one that could bring the wrath of the human kingdom down upon them all. Urgath, however, believed he had killed two birds with one stone. Many in his *brak* took his boldness as a sign of strength, keeping his challengers at bay, and his hunters had brought back venison and human prisoners to feed the *brak*.

The thought of food made Urgath's belly rumble. It was time for his morning meal. Like a massive ape, he knuckled his way down the hillside, finding several other trolls stirring in their caves. When he passed, they lowered their heads and laid open their palms before him.

Sometimes he'd stop to sniff them as they bowed, growling to remind them of their place. Entering the ravine, he came to a hollow carved into the steep side of a hill. At the back of the hollow there stood a door made of smooth stone.

How the door had come to be, no one knew, not even the elders of the *hrak*. It had been there long before trolls had moved into these flinty gray hills. Still, since its opening was too small for a troll to enter, the *hrak* didn't see the mysterious door as anything worth worrying about. Now that Urgath had human prisoners, the chamber at last had a use. He pushed the heavy door inward and bent down to look inside. At the center of the small room lay a stone box—likely one of the cages humans locked their dead in. At the back of the room huddled over a dozen men, women, and children, each of them shuddering at the sight of the troll. Urgath reached in to pluck up one of the children. The little girl screamed and a man tried to pull the child back. Urgath grunted, reaching in further to get a better grip, when a thunderous roar shook the hills.

Urgath pulled back and looked out at the hillside beyond the cave mouth. A great fiery ball tore through the ashen sky. It grew larger and louder by the moment, hurtling straight down towards the hills where Urgath and his *hrak* stood. Trolls were bellowing and running, many going so far as to flee to their caves. With no other cover nearby, Urgath crouched in the hollow, clapping his hands over his ears to block out the terrible noise. As the bright light sped closer, it shed its fiery covering and revealed a massive object shaped like a spearhead. To Urgath's surprise, it didn't crash into the hills but gradually slowed, hovering like a great metal bird. As it came down below the hilltops and neared the land, it blew out wind and flame from its underside before disappearing in a cloud of dust.

When the roaring stopped and the dust cloud settled, the trolls looked out from their hiding places. Even some of the human prisoners dared to peek out from behind the stone door. The great metal bird had landed outside the mouth of the ravine. Now that it was close, the trolls could see its immensity, its wings and body nearly filling up the flat space between the hills. The trolls waited for the creature to move. It remained still. The younger males of the *brak* watched Urgath keenly.

Not wanting to be seen as weak and afraid, Urgath approached the metal bird. His ears twitched and nose sniffed as he readied himself for it to rise and attack him. It remained still. Coming in close, he prodded the nose with his finger. Nothing happened. He then struck the nose with his fist. There was a loud clang. Still, nothing happened. Urgath started walking around the metal bird, continuing to prod at it. Suddenly, the thing's insides began to hum and whir. The underbelly hissed open, disgorging a cloud of cold vapor. Urgath snarled and leaped back. Out of the cloud walked a figure clad from head to toe in golden armor.

What lay under the metal coverings must be a man, for he walked upright on two legs and stood at a man's height. Urgath sniffed the air and smelled human within the metal suit. There was also the smell of acrid fluids that the troll couldn't place. Since the man wore armor, he must be a warrior—but he didn't look like any of the human warriors Urgath had encountered before. In the kingdom to the south, soldiers wore assortments of scale and chain mail. Some had pieces of plate. This golden armor, however, radiated with greater strength. It reflected the dawn and appeared to shine with a light all its own. The man's head was covered in a crested helmet with a metal visage, and all about the man's body, golden pieces were fitted together with the intricacy of a beetle's carapace. Not an inch of skin lay exposed. Urgath noticed the warrior carried no weapon—neither spear nor sword.

This oddity was unimportant. What mattered was the man was intruding on Urgath's territory. For all the fire and thunder he had brought by falling from the sky, he was a fool to have come unprepared for a fight.

Urgath picked up a boulder and hurled it at the golden man. The man raised his forearms in a block and the stone crashed against them. By the force of the throw, the man should have been struck down. Instead, he slid back a short distance, his metal boots skidding against the earth, his stance holding.

Impossible. How could a human possess such strength? Urgath stared, toothy mouth agape, dumbfounded a moment too long. The man moved, but Urgath saw only a flash of gold. An armored fist struck him under the jaw. A tusk broke. His head went back in a wicked snap. The world spun in circles around him, and he collapsed to the ground in a crumpled heap.

Through the ringing in his ears, Urgath heard roars and bellows. He opened his eyes to see his *hrak* rushing to battle. They leaped down from their caves and charged the golden man. The younger males, hungry to prove their mettle, led the charge. It looked as though the mass of hulking bodies and thick limbs would crush the man by sheer force. But before the trolls could get their hands on him, blasts of bright light shot from the man's forearms. The younger males flew back, holes torn through their chests, their flesh charred and smoking. More pressed the attack, and they, too, were blasted apart. The terrain worked against them. Confined to the ravine, they couldn't swarm the man, so they funneled towards him in threes and fours. The blasts of searing light cut down row after row.

Desperate to aid his *hrak*, Urgath tried to get up. He couldn't move. There was no feeling below his neck. Able to do nothing but froth and snarl, Urgath watched the massacre. By the time his trolls realized they were charging towards their deaths, it was too late. The few that remained turned and ran, tripping over the dead as they went. The searing rays of lights chased them and struck them down from behind.

Finally, the sound of blasting ceased. Through the smoke rising from the bodies, Urgath saw that none of his *hrak* stood. In one terrible minute, he had become the chief of nothing.

Dane looked at the piles of dead trolls that lay before him. Earth had certainly changed since he had last visited. When he had lived here, biological experiments and genetic engineering had created the creatures of myth all for the sake of amusement—as novelties at zoos and theme parks. Now, six hundred years later, these creatures were out in the wild, long adapted to their environment. Earth had become a strange place indeed.

He was impressed with his mechanical suit. Killing over thirty beasts, it had proven itself. It was his creation, a product of his workshop on Olympus and designed specifically for himself. Though his body was frail and his muscles atrophied, the suit gave him power. Though his face and skin were hideous, the suit gave him a magnificent and intimidating appearance. It was a sleek piece of technology but in its design were nods to the classical armors of the Greco-Roman empires.

Running a quick diagnostic of the suit, Dane found there was no damage and no overheating. The system was intact. Satisfied, he checked his shuttle's systems. The exterior was whole, having sustained minimal damage when entering the atmosphere. There was just a little dent on the shuttle's nose where the troll had struck it. The engine and computer systems were in optimal shape. Everything was in perfect order. Dane was amazed these shuttles could run so well after six hundred years of sitting in Olympus's port.

As he checked the vessel over, he heard a weak growling noise from nearby. There, on the ground, a troll was still breathing. It was the largest and strongest, the one who had approached him first and thrown the boulder. The troll's yellow eyes were full of malice, but he was impotent in his rage, his neck broken.

Dane knelt beside the troll.

'I was hoping you and your lot would've put up more of a fight.'

'*Furtok*,' the troll cursed, barely able to open his mouth. '*Furtok ganash*.'

'Is that so?' Dane replied. He then fired a shot, putting a smoldering hole through the troll's head.

Killing the trolls hadn't been as exciting as he thought it would be. Although they were large and strong, they were clumsy and stupid. Fighting them was nothing like the battles he had experienced before. Hooked up to the Dream in Olympus, he had often relived the exploits of history's greatest conquerors—Alexander the Great, Genghis Khan, Napoleon Bonaparte. Dane had experienced the thrill and glory these figures had felt while on the battlefield. Like them, he had needed strategy and cunning to win. With these trolls, it was like shooting fish in a barrel, their lumbering bodies falling one after the other.

Human voices sounded nearby. Dane looked into the ravine and saw people emerging from a stone door built into a steep hillside. They were filthy, their clothing ragged. As they stepped outside, they stared at the aftermath of the massacre. After a long moment, they began to weep and cheer, clutching at one another. One woman picked up a rock and wildly struck a dead troll, screaming at her former captors. Many mumbled to themselves—no longer stuck in the dark, wondering if they'd be the next meal. Now they stood bewildered, blinking in the daylight.

When Dane approached, the freed captives hushed. Even the woman working out her rage with a bloody stone became quiet. Stepping over the slumped bodies of several trolls, Dane came to a stop. Several of those gathered stepped back in apprehension. A bent old man at the head of the group came forwards to meet him.

'You did this,' the old man said, gesturing at the dead trolls about them. 'I saw you do it… with a strange power.' Then, squinting his eyes, he asked, 'Who are you?'

'I am Dane.'

'Dane,' the man repeated. He looked to the shuttle that stood outside the mouth of the ravine. 'You came down from the heavens. Are you an angel sent by God?'

'No,' Dane said. 'No god sent me. I am God.'

The eyes of his faceplate flashed with electricity and the metal of his suit began to glow. The old man gasped and fell to his knees, bowing to the majestic presence before him. The others did likewise and murmured among themselves, astonishment in their voices. Some reached their arms out to him and wept in gratitude for the salvation he had brought.

As they worshipped him, Dane produced a glowing metal orb—another invention of his, a device he called a patheograph. It focused on the freed prisoners and gathered up their emotions—their wonder, awe, and fear. The more it gathered, the stronger it glowed.

'Rise and go free,' Dane commanded. 'Tell everyone to prepare for my coming.'

Moving in quiet reverence, the people did as they were told. They gathered up the children and left that place, leaving the ravine and heading south towards their homes.

Dane returned the patheograph to a compartment on his belt, satisfied with what he had collected. These people had been ripe with adoration. They would tell everyone they met what they had seen him do here. His legend would spread like wildfire. Soon he would go south himself, but there was one more thing he had to do before he left these flinty hills.

Inside the cave, he crouched through the stone door and entered the small room where the prisoners had been held. In the middle of the room stood a sarcophagus made of plain stone. Long ago, this land had been a cemetery. This was the tomb of Silas's daughter.

Although she had wanted a simple burial, Silas had refused her wishes. As he saw it, if he was going to live through the ages on Olympus, he would make sure her place of rest would endure the test of time as well. What Silas had envisioned came to pass. While the other gravestones had crumbled away, the tomb of his daughter remained, tucked safely in the earth.

On the top of the sarcophagus was a metal crest bearing the image of a tree. Below it were words engraved in stone:

HERE LIES FELICITY FERRER
BELOVED DAUGHTER & FIERCE FRIEND

Dane pressed the crest and a hologram appeared before him, an image of a young woman with short auburn hair and a tattoo of a tree on the right side of her neck. Silas's daughter. She wore a loose-fit shirt and pants of natural fiber weave—the style popular among the natreos during the Divide and the days before the Treaty. Her image started to speak.

'Many people ask me why I have chosen to stay on Earth. The answer's simple: this is home. Here I have the ground beneath my feet, sunlight to keep me warm, and fresh air to breathe. Yes, living here is hard. But it's real. And it's worth—'

Dane switched the hologram off. 'That's enough of that.'

He took a photo out of one of his suit's compartments. It was a picture of Silas and his daughter. The two of them were up on a mountain, their arms around each other's shoulders, their smiles broad and genuine, as if they had been caught in the middle of a joke. Behind them stretched mist-shrouded lowlands and, beyond those, the red sun smoldered low in the sky. Their relationship looked healthy. The picture must have been taken when they were still speaking to one another, before humanity's Divide and the Treaty.

Dane tucked the edge of the photo under the emblem upon the sarcophagus.

'A gift from your father,' he said.

With that, he left the tomb. He had done what Silas had asked of him. Now it was time to make a new home for himself. One suitable for a god.

Chapter 6

Corvala sat at her father's bedside, keeping watch over him. She had done what she could—had stitched his open wounds, cleaned him up, and dressed him in new clothes. Now the only thing to do was wait—wait for some sign that might give her hope. A blinking eye, a muttered word. Something. All she got was silence.

She stared across her father's bedroom at the window and the afternoon light that shone through. The house was filled with an empty stillness that left Corvala alone with her thoughts. Images of the trial that morning came to her unbidden, and she recalled the stones thrown. She wondered what she could have done differently, what she could have said instead of scream like a crazy woman.

There came a knock at the door. Corvala didn't get up. It was probably just another person stopping by with a pot of soup or a sack of potatoes. With the danger over, the people were coming to her aid—a safe act of kindness to help her out with meals as she cared for her father. They had seen the fire fall from heaven and now they brought their meagre offerings, trying to atone for their sin of cowardice. Corvala scorned their food. She didn't need their sympathy; she needed a cure for her father. Chicken soup wasn't going to cut it.

Perhaps something else would. The thought of a cure put an idea in her head, and she wondered why she hadn't thought of it before. Going to her room and kneeling beside her bed, she lifted up a loose floorboard and revealed a hidden compartment below. There, she found a thick book with a ratty leather cover and pages as brittle as autumn leaves. There was no name attributed to the author except for the title 'Reputable Scholar'. The anonymity made sense, for who would openly confess to researching and writing about the forbidden knowledge of the Ancients? Such a crime would get you apprehended by the Rooks.

Corvala had found the book many years ago. It had come in a box of contraband her father had confiscated from a traveling merchant—a man who dealt in illegal goods on the sly. Curious, Corvala had opened the box while her father was out. She found a collection of artifacts that had once belonged to the Ancients—rusty parts of their machines unearthed from ruins. The box also had a dozen or so books, their pages bearing the rough sketches of tall towers, flying machines, and devices that shot fire and metal. Wonders that didn't seem possible. When she came to a book bearing images of the human body, her heart skipped a beat. The book showed the Ancients' methods of healing. If the Ancients had come up with impossible machines, maybe they had come up with impossible cures. Maybe they had come up with ways for healing madness—the kind of madness that would one day consume Corvala, just as it had her mother and grandmother. So Corvala took the book of healing methods and hid it in her room. Later, her father delivered the box of contraband to the Rooks, and nothing was said of its contents ever again. The book was never missed.

Once in her possession, she pored over it in secret, reading and rereading the sections that covered the brain. Unfortunately, nothing mentioned generational madness giving one visions. Disappointed, she thought about burning the book or throwing it in the river. Better her disposing of it than getting caught. But what if she found need of it in the future? What if something terrible happened?

Now, with her father at death's door, Corvala was grateful she had decided to keep it. She began searching the book for something she could do for him. Although the condition of her mind was unheard of, her father's wounds were common. Surely a method on how to treat a head injury would be found within the pages. The book, however, was hardly an easy read. It hadn't been written by an expert in the healing arts but by a scribe copying from the sources he had found—probably torn-out pages and bits of paper preserved in ruins. The result of the author's work was a disjointed and fragmented collection of notes. On one page, Corvala found him changing topics at least three times, first writing about the spinal cord, next the lungs, and then the bones of the foot. Sometimes notes ended mid-sentence, leaving concepts unexplained. Still, what little it offered went far beyond what Corvala knew about medicine, and so she continued to navigate the disjointed text, seeking out anything that might pertain to her father's condition. Her mind quickly grew fatigued.

Her eyes grew heavy. She tried shaking herself awake. It was no use. The dry voice of the text lulled her gently away. Her chin sank to her chest and, in a matter of minutes, she was snoring softly.

Corvala found herself standing in the middle of the town square. It was a quiet morning and the streets were empty of people. A bright light flashed above and a great fiery ball tore across the clear sky, arcing brilliantly downwards. When the falling star disappeared behind the hills to the north, the sky grew dark. Corvala now stood on the banks of a river. It was night and the moon was out, larger than she had ever seen it before. It colored everything with a soft cool glow. On the other side of the river was a deep dark wood and, at the forest's edge, a woman stood. She wore a long flowing robe of white and had the same straight raven hair as Corvala.

'Mother!' Corvala cried.

She waded across the river. When she made it to the other side, she saw her mother following the river downstream.

'Wait for me!' Corvala cried. 'Don't leave me.'

Corvala ran after her along the banks. Her mother strolled with no hurry but, no matter how fast Corvala ran, the distance between them remained the same.

'Mother, wait!'

The woman in white gave no reply as she rounded a river bend and went out of sight. When Corvala swept round the corner, she came upon a small creek feeding into the river. At the place where these two waters met stood her mother. No, not her mother—her grandmother. She didn't look old and wrinkled the way Corvala had last seen her—now she was young, still in her prime—but Corvala knew it was her. She had that same smell of cinnamon that Corvala remembered so well. Like her mother, she, too, was wearing a white robe.

'It's you. Mother needs to see you. It has been so long.'

Grandmother only smiled at this. Then she lifted her arm to point up the creek.

'You want me to go?' Corvala asked.

Her grandmother nodded slowly. Corvala turned in the direction her grandmother had pointed. The water flowed deeper into the forest, coming out onto a ravine filled with ferns.

'Where will that take me?' Corvala asked, turning back. Her grandmother was gone. Corvala looked all around, but there was no sign of anyone. Not knowing what else to do, she followed her grandmother's instructions and began walking up the creek.

It wasn't long before Corvala encountered another woman in a white robe. Even though Corvala had never seen her before, she knew there was a connection between them. She had her mother's eyes.

'You must be my great-grandmother.'

The woman gave a slight smile and pointed into the ravine. Corvala continued along the creek, finding as she went more women in white robes, each standing at a different bend. Not only was she going upstream, but she was also going further back in her bloodline. Generations and generations back.

At last, she came to a woman who stood in the middle of the creek. She had short auburn hair and a tattoo of a tree on the right side of her neck. Her arms were held slightly out to her sides, instructing Corvala to come to a halt. Corvala paused in the ankle-deep water. The woman pointed to a crevice in the ravine's wall.

'You must go in there,' the woman said.

'What's inside?' Corvala asked.

'You must see it for yourself.' She smiled, eyes twinkling. 'Come and find it.'

Chapter 7

It was a quiet night in the town of Dawn's Landing. Corvala stopped running only when she came to a house with a wreath of herbs hanging on its door. She knocked, trying to catch her breath, and when the door opened the overpowering smell of garlic and rosemary spilled from inside. There appeared a man, tall and thin like an egret, his hair stuck out at the sides like wild feathers. He opened the door with a casual air—a man used to callers at odd hours. Upon seeing Corvala there, a look of surprise sprang to his face.

'Miss Keen!' he gasped. 'What are you doing—I mean, what can I do for you?'

'I need to come inside, Dr. Hearthwood,' she implored. 'I have something very important to ask you.'

'It's about your father, isn't it?'

Corvala nodded. She was putting him in a difficult spot. She could tell he wanted to help, but the rules forbade it. Doctors weren't allowed to help Judges after trials, since any aid given to a Judge was seen as undoing the justice enacted by the people.

'Please,' Corvala said, 'all I have are a few questions.'

Dr. Hearthwood pursed his lips and scrunched his brow. Then he looked both ways to make sure no one was watching. The street was empty.

'Come in, come in,' he whispered, motioning Corvala inside.

She came to a lantern-lit room where bundles of herbs hung from the rafters. Countless glass bottles of different shapes and colors lined the shelves.

'Can I interest you in some biscuits with honey?' Dr. Hearthwood asked, going into the kitchen to put a kettle over the fire in the fireplace. 'Perhaps some tea?'

Corvala agreed to both, taking a seat at the room's small round table. She hadn't realized how hungry she was until he had made the offer of food. She couldn't remember when her last meal had been—indeed, a part of her regretted ignoring all those people who had come with offerings of meals. When Dr. Hearthwood laid a basket of biscuits before her, it took her a good amount of effort to refrain from wolfing them down two at a time. After she had eaten a little, she took out her papers and laid them on the table.

'What's this?' Dr. Hearthwood asked.

'A cure, I think. Can you tell me what it means?'

'A cure, eh?' he said, giving her a sympathetic yet dubious look. 'Let's see here.'

Dr. Hearthwood put on his glasses and began to read over Corvala's notes. It didn't take him long, however, to realize what he was reading. He put down the first page and pushed it back to Corvala. His face was set and grim.

'*Contusion. Cranial bleeding.* These aren't common terms used by girls in a backwater valley. Not even doctors speak this way. This is old language. Where did you find this information?'

'Where I found it doesn't matter.'

Dr. Hearthwood bowed his head and rubbed his temples. 'Were you reading forbidden knowledge?'

'I wasn't reading about anything demonic if that's what you're asking. No unholy machines or weapons. No potions for unnatural abilities.'

'It doesn't matter. You can't go rooting around in the world of the Ancients. It's against the law.' Dr. Hearthwood looked over his glasses at Corvala. 'Even for the daughter of a Judge.'

Frustrated, Corvala steepled her fingers and pressed them to her chin. 'I'm just trying to learn how to save my fah. Is that wrong?'

'Whatever your motives, you need to be careful, Corvala. The knowledge of the past is forbidden for a reason. The demons promised the Ancients many good things. And those good things came at a heavy price.'

'If you want to talk about a heavy price,' Corvala said, putting flint in her voice, 'let's talk about my fah. Look at the price he paid. He's battered and near dead because no one in this town had backbone enough to stand with him at his trial.'

Corvala drove a glare into Dr. Hearthwood. The old man looked away, his expression sunk in guilt. He tapped his fingers on the table and then let out a deep breath. With a resigned hand, he reached across the table and pulled the papers back.

'God forgive me,' he muttered.

While he read over her notes, Corvala took the kettle from the fireplace and poured them both a cup of tea. The doctor left his tea untouched, too deep in his study. He was good at what he did, having proven himself a true healer time and time again, just as he had with Gilly. Corvala trusted he would see logical patterns and answers where she had been confounded, and so she drank her tea quietly so as not to distract him from his work. He pored over the pages, so enraptured with the material before him that he appeared to have forgotten all about the laws regarding forbidden knowledge.

Right about when Corvala was finishing her second cup, Dr. Hearthwood slapped his hand on the table and looked up at her victoriously.

'Got it! It's all in here,' he said, gesturing towards the notes. 'How to reduce the swelling around the brain without opening the skull or thinning the blood. I didn't think such a thing was possible, but those Ancient buggers found a way.'

'So, you can cure my fah?' Corvala asked expectantly.

'Well...' The doctor tapped his fingers together. 'I'm not sure I can.'

'What do you mean?'

'According to your notes, there exists an anti-inflammatory agent that could help your father's head injuries heal. I have *most* of the elements needed to make that kind of agent. But not all.'

'Are you sure? Can't you check?' Corvala asked, sweeping an arm to the shelves on the walls.

'I know my collection of vials and herbs better than the end of my nose. Most of what I have helps with fevers and sour stomachs. Not what your father needs. The missing ingredients are too rare.'

Corvala set her jaw. 'So, there's nothing you can do for him.' Her voice demanded the doctor say otherwise. The cure was right there on paper, and he had the mind capable of making it. Too close to give up now.

Dr. Hearthwood scratched his head and rubbed his chin. 'There is... ember-tail,' he said at length. 'It's a medicinal fungus. It could perhaps—*perhaps*—make up for what I lack here. Sort of like swapping wheat flour for cornmeal. It wouldn't produce the same thing the Ancients made, but it would be something.'

'Something is all I need.'

'Don't get too hopeful. Even though ember-tail might not be as rare as the compounds I'd rather use, it's still hard to find. I've only seen it a few times while foraging deep in Thorn Shroud.'

'Then what can we do?'

'It will take a few days. I can send word to the herbalists in the villages and see if they have any.'

'Fah doesn't have that kind of time. And what if they refuse to give up their supply? Or, worse—what if none of them have any?'

'It's the best option we have,' the doctor said, patting her on the hand. 'Let me do what I can, and I'll see if I can't get ember-tail for your father.'

Discouraged, Corvala looked down into her empty cup. 'Could you fill me up?'

Dr. Hearthwood took her cup into the kitchen and began pouring her some more tea.

'Don't worry,' he called back over his shoulder. 'I'll send messengers first thing in the morning. It's better than traipsing about in the Shroud. The forest is even more dangerous now than it was before. You of all people should know that. Better if we stick to my—'

But when Dr. Hearthwood returned to the main room, he cut himself short. Corvala's chair was empty, and her stack of papers was gone.

Once, when Corvala was a young child, she had been walking with her father near a marsh. It had been just after sunset and, through the rushes, they spotted a faint glow. Her father pushed the rushes aside and revealed a mushroom that shone with a calm bluish-green light. It was slender, with spiraling tendrils hanging from its cap.

'Ember-tail,' her father whispered.

'Can we take it?' Corvala asked.

'Let it be. If we remove it, its light will go out.'

Corvala remembered watching the ember-tail in silence for several minutes, enthralled by the mushroom's glow the same way weary travelers watch a campfire at the end of a long day's walk. It wasn't a memory Corvala recalled often. Still, she was grateful for that moment with her father—now she knew what she was looking for.

Guided by a lantern, Corvala followed a meandering path towards the western side of the valley. Beyond the circle of the lantern's glow, the world was a charcoal smudge where amorphous shapes like silent men roved just beyond the rim of sight. Corvala felt the temptation to fear the dark. She distracted herself by looking to the ground and watching her feet move in rhythm. Her path took her to a small river known as Gray Run. Lifting her lantern high, Corvala peered through the dark. On the opposite shore, there rose an ominous wall of pines and firs. Here stood the border of Thorn Shroud.

The last time Corvala had come this close she'd been a child, before her mother's disappearance. She couldn't remember what had brought her there. Curiosity, perhaps. As did all parents of the valley, her mother and father had warned her not to go near that forest, which of course made her want to go all the more. When she came to the banks of Gray Run, she'd seen the tall forms of trees as cold and dark as slate. Between the trunks and branches sank the oily gloom of the depths beyond, promising lostness and despair. After one look, she had fled in terror.

Now, as a young woman, she stood transfixed, feeling just as she had back then. A shudder ran through her bones. Her skin prickled with gooseflesh as cold spread across her back. There she was, so small against the heights of forest murk. With no wind that night, the trees kept still. Not the stillness of peace, but of a predator in wait. The memory of the manticore appeared unbidden in her mind. She envisioned the creature waiting in the depths, then growing and melding into the forest itself. The reddish dappled coat changed to deep greens and grays and blended into the bristling branches. She could *feel* the forest, a giant living thing, sensing her, watching her. It became a beast in her mind—every beast that had ever walked the earth. Every creature with claw and fang and taste for blood. And she was every prey, small and shivering under the gaze of hunger and madness. Now the forest towered over her, ready to fall upon her and swallow her up. Just as it had done to her mother.

Corvala's hand went involuntarily to her father's hunting knife, which was sheathed at her side. The touch of its handle offered little comfort. A part of her mind told her to turn back, to flee, just as she had done as a child. It had been one thing to walk up to the forest. But to go inside...

She backed away from the river, the thin watery band that kept the wilds at bay. How could she possibly cross over into those woods? She would return home and think of another way to save her father.

Her father.

The thought of him lying in bed near death made her stop. Deep down, she knew there was nothing else she could do for him except find ember-tail, and ember-tail grew in Thorn Shroud. Because of its glow, it was best found at night. True, the forest held doom. But hadn't she been willing to walk to her doom earlier that day, to stand with her father as he faced the stoning? Now her father's life was quickly ebbing. Besides, it was surely only a matter of months before her mother's madness would overcome her. There was nothing to lose and her father to gain.

She looked back at the forest. This time, amid the terror, there was a flicker of defiance within her. Across the Gray Run lay a fallen tree leading from one bank to the other, its trunk wide enough to serve as a bridge.

This isn't a good idea, she thought to herself.

And she crossed into Thorn Shroud.

Chapter 8

The forest air, heavy with the scent of resin and moist decay, closed in around Corvala. She walked the narrow tunnel-like spaces between tree trunks and under branches, her steps muted by the bed of fallen needles. Multiple ways lay before her, each one disappearing into the inky dark beyond the reach of her lantern light. The plan was to stay as close to the Gray Run as possible so as not to wander into the forest's depths and get lost. Although Corvala couldn't see the river in the dark—she doubted she'd have been able to see it through the thick trees even during the day—she made sure she could hear its babble at all times. It would be her lifeline during her search. If her memory served her right, ember-tail grew near water, which was another reason to stick close to the river. Intermittently she'd close the shutter of her lantern and peer out into the forest, looking for any sign of the glowing mushroom. All she found was darkness.

The minutes passed. Each time she opened the lantern shutter, the world would split into long shadows. They shifted and contorted as she moved, warping and breaking into the semblances of human figures. A woman with several arms. A man with his head twisted on backward. Despite her better sense, Corvala couldn't help but envision something reaching out for her.

When she'd been a little girl afraid of the dark, her mother had sung her a lullaby at bedtime. It was unknown to the people of the valley, and her mother said it was very old, perhaps going back to the time of the Ancients. It had soothed Corvala then—maybe it would work for her now. So, quietly, she began to sing.

> *When peace like a river, attendeth my way,*
> *When sorrows like sea billows roll...*

It came out weak and quivering, her voice hesitant to venture out into the silent forest. She urged herself to sing louder.

> *Whatever my lot, thou hast taught me to say*
> *It is well, it is well, with my soul.*

Now she sang in full voice, defying the dark.

> *It is well,*
> > *it is well,*
> > > *with my soul.*

Corvala halted. There stood a woman in her path.
Her mother. White gown and all.
Corvala gasped and staggered back a step. 'Moth—'
But the woman had vanished. In her place stood a tree. By the lantern light and shadows, the smoothed burl had given the appearance of a head, and she'd mistaken the moss hanging from it for hair. Just her imagination playing tricks. Or was it? The image of her mother—even if it had only been there for a fraction of a moment—had seemed too real. Corvala scolded herself for singing that lullaby. This forest could trigger madness, and a memory

of her mother here and now could be enough to tip her over the edge. She couldn't let it take her. Not now.

She placed a hand on her chest and took several shaky breaths. She assured herself that nothing had shifted in the dark. The shadows weren't after her. And she certainly wasn't going mad like her mother. If she closed her eyes and forgot about the forest, she could imagine herself in a peaceful, quiet place. All was silent out here in the woods.

Silent.

No sound of the river.

Sudden dread fell over her. When had she wandered from the river? Where was she? All around: darkness. Something hissed nearby; an owl hooted. Corvala fought down her rising panic. The Gray Run had to be close— she couldn't have wandered that far. She'd just have to find her way back. And which way was that? It all looked the same. There, to her right—yes, that seemed correct. Follow the downward slope in the land, the way water flows. Out in the valley, the Gloaming Hills looked like smooth slopes sweeping from the hilltops down to the banks of the sunken Gray Run. As Corvala walked, she learned that the hills were deceptive; they were anything but smooth. Thorn Shroud covered land deeply pocked and wrinkled with contours. Here, Corvala plunged into a gully. There, she rounded the top of a wide mound. The shape of the terrain was a false guide. Did that mean she was...

...lost?

The thought quickened her pace and sent her pushing through the branches. Her breaths became shallow, hurried rasps. She should have found the river by now. Where was it? *Where where where?* Frightened tears welled up in her eyes.

Then she heard it: the babble of running water. Corvala's face lit up and her heart leaped inside her chest. Only men dying from days of desert thirst would have loved that sweet trickle more. Corvala ran through the forest, chasing the sound. She hopped down an eroded lip of earth and landed on a gravelly bank. Here ran water. On the other side, there weren't open fields or farmland, but more forest thick with trees. This wasn't Gray Run. It was smaller, a creek running out from the depths of Thorn Shroud. Even so, it was something. It would certainly flow into the river. Getting back to the forest's edge would just be a matter of following the creek downstream.

Corvala found herself lingering. She studied her surroundings like someone who had walked into a place of distant memory. It was all vaguely familiar. How could that be? Before tonight, she had never ventured into this forest or come upon this creek. Maybe she had seen it in a dream. She noticed her body was relaxed here, her muscles losing their tension and her breaths growing easy. Her fears were muted and she forgot about the shifting shadows. She felt at peace—the same kind of peace when safe at home. It was as though she were meant to be here, as though something subtle in her mind had been guiding her steps towards this creek all along. Curious, she wondered what might be upstream. From her lantern light, she saw the land rising steeply on either side of the creek, the water flowing out from a fern-clad ravine. And up in the ravine, she saw the faint glow of bluish-green light. She shook herself from her stupor.

'Ember-tail!' she cried.

She hurried up the gravelly banks into the ravine and towards the twinkling light. The smile that had sprung to life on her face was quickly snuffed out. Fireflies. They danced and shimmered about the ferns like low-hanging stars. On any other night, they would have been beautiful. Now, they brought only disappointment. Still, they did at least remind her of her task. She had been so preoccupied with the shadows and trying to find a way out that she'd nearly forgotten why she had come here in the first place. She thought of her father lying in bed, close to death. And here she was, stumbling through the trees, spooked by childish fears. Some help she was turning out to be! A tinge of hot shame touched her cheeks. Cutting straight through the insect galaxy, she continued in her search.

The creek provided a way for her to go deeper into Thorn Shroud without getting lost. It was the kind of damp place where ember-tail might grow. She tried to stay focused on her search, but she couldn't shake the feeling that she had been here before, walking down this same gravelly bank. Bend after bend in the creek, she kept on the lookout for glowing lights. She would wonder to herself, *Hadn't there been women here before? Women in white gowns?* Maybe this was the first sign of madness. Such a thought should have worried her. Strangely enough, it didn't. She felt calm and relaxed. A walk through a waking dream.

Distracted, she slipped on a slick rock and fell to her hands and knees in the shallows. Her lantern was nearly put out, and the fireflies blinked above in mocking light. Wet and cold, Corvala crawled to the bank. As she shook out her sleeves, she noticed a cleft low in the ravine wall, down beside where she sat. If she had been walking, she would have gone right by it. Here was something odd— she had seen this opening before. She was certain of it. With her certainty came an impulse telling her to go inside. The higher levels of her mind questioned such thinking. But the deeper, more primordial parts bid her forwards.

You must see it yourself, a voice in her mind seemed to say. *Come and find it.*

She ducked her head inside the cleft. A tunnel went deeper down than her lantern could shine. There was something down there, something for her. She was about to crawl inside but then stopped herself. What was she doing? She was out here to save her father, not to go exploring. But what if there was ember-tail down in the tunnel? Mushrooms did, after all, grow underground. It was worth a look, she decided. It would only take a minute or two.

The tunnel went down into the earth. There was something more than concern for her father that pushed her onwards; something stronger than curiosity that had her squeeze through that cleft in the ravine wall. There was a primal force that led her: the force that guided geese south for the winter, that pushed salmon against the river currents. She couldn't explain it, but it felt old and familiar.

Down she went, twisting and turning in the dark. She went first on hands and knees, then stood to full height when at last the tunnel widened. Then, suddenly, her way came to a stop, ending at a rectangular metal slab in the raw stone ground. It looked like a door. What was a metal door doing out here in the Shroud? Was this an old mine? She pressed her hand to the door to see if it had any give. As soon as she made contact with its surface, lights suddenly came to life around her—she jumped back, eyes darting left and right. Then she saw the source of the light: a pair of lanterns the likes of which she had never seen before, one on either side of the door. They didn't burn with flame but glowed, fed by an unidentifiable fuel. Was this demon magic? She wondered at this for only a moment, for the door hissed open in front of her. And although it was strange that such a thing should happen on its own, Corvala wasn't afraid. Her instinct invited her in. So, with a deep breath, she passed through the threshold.

BUNKER 610 REPORT_____

...

SERAPH CLASS 7

...

RUN DIAGNOSTICS

...

PROCESSING

...

STATUS: HIBERNATING

...

SYSTEM: STABLE

...

STATUS: BUNKER BREACH

...

PROCESSING

Chapter 9

Corvala entered a small round chamber. Lights, identical to the pair by the door, flickered to life about the room. The low light revealed not a cave formed of raw stone but metal walls and metal beams—all flat surfaces and hard angles. It reminded Corvala of the structures she had seen in the forbidden books. At the center of the chamber stood what looked to be a large machine—a bronze egg with a thick tangle of silvery cords leading from its base. A walkway went from the door where she stood towards the machine and ended up on a pedestal of some kind. On the glassy surface on top of the pedestal, the shape of a handprint began to glow. Drawn towards the light, Corvala instinctively pressed her hand against the glowing print. When she did, the pedestal began to vibrate and the light shone brighter under her palm. Then a voice sounded throughout the chamber, disembodied and unnatural:

'Bunker Six Hundred and Ten. System initializing. Please standby.'

'Who's there?' Corvala called.

The strange voice didn't answer. Instead, there came another noise—one from behind her. It started low and then grew to shouts clanging through the tunnel. A gang of rowdy men. Had the shadow-figures of the forest taken on substance with throats and mouths? No, that was a foolish thought. It didn't take Corvala long to figure out who was coming.

'Capels,' she hissed.

Trajan's feral laughter echoed before them. And there, Deker Capel complaining again. It was said throughout the town that you could spend an hour with Deker and learn a million things he hated.

'I hate cramped spaces,' he said. 'Especially when they're wet and cold. I bet there're lots of rats down here. I hate rats.'

Corvala stared at the chamber door, frozen. How had the Capels followed her here? Such a question was enough to puzzle over, but it was swallowed up by a thought far more terrifying. *Why* had they come for her?

She barked out a laugh. A single, harsh syllable void of any mirth. Of course they'd come! With everything that had happened that day—her father's trial and her wandering lost through Thorn Shroud—of course the Capels would then show up. Corvala still possessed enough wit to look for somewhere to hide. There wasn't much in the small chamber—just a mess of metal cords behind the room's central device. She crouched beneath the thick tangle, hoping to go unnoticed in the low light. She held her father's knife in a shaking hand. Maybe she could take one of them by surprise. But the whole gang of brothers? This sent her into a fit of nervous giggling, one she was barely able to stifle as the Capels entered the chamber. Their footfalls came to a halt and their voices grew quiet.

'What is this place?' one of them said, apprehension coloring his voice.

'I don't know,' another replied. Corvala recognized the voice as Morgan's. 'All I know is that she's down here somewhere.'

Corvala heard the men spreading out around the chamber. They stepped quietly as if trying not to wake something.

'I don't like it here. This place gives me the creeps.'

'By the wreck, Deker!' Morgan huffed. 'Don't be such a coward. If a little girl can hide here then you'd better have the stones to walk where she treads.'

'Here kitten, kitten, kitten,' Trajan purred.

Corvala could hear their feet shuffling over the metal floor. They were everywhere. Ducked in hiding as she was, she didn't dare risk lifting her head to look.

'I don't know, Morgan. You hear stories about these kinds of places out here in the Shroud—the kinds of places people wander into and never escape from.'

'Shut up, Deker!'

'What if there's something here that got the girl?'

'I wouldn't worry about that,' said a voice much too close, 'because *I* got her.'

A hand grabbed Corvala by the ankle and pulled her out from behind the metal cords. Corvala yelped and came face to face with Trajan Capel. He took her by the arm and looked at her with that manic grin of his. Corvala lashed out with the knife in an awkward slash, cutting the sleeve of his shirt but nothing more. Trajan cackled. He knocked the knife from her hand and sent it clattering to the floor. Then he grabbed her around the waist and pulled her towards him.

'You've got some teeth, little kitten. Got any bite for me?'

No matter how much Corvala kicked and squirmed, she couldn't break from his wiry arms. Trajan licked his lips and pushed in for a kiss.

'Enough!' Morgan shouted.

Trajan paused. He and his older brother met eyes and stared—two wild dogs sizing each other up. Morgan puffed up his chest and cracked the knuckles of one of his fists. Trajan grunted and relented, dropping Corvala to the floor. On her hands and knees, she saw her knife by Morgan's foot, just out of reach. The Capel brothers stood over her—a hungry pack circling their prey. She noticed Rhonie at Morgan's side. He had a swollen lip split down the middle and a black eye. With his good eye, he looked at Corvala almost apologetically.

'Looks like my brother's good at something after all,' Morgan said, grabbing Rhonie by the back of the neck. 'Has a knack for tracking you down.'

Corvala didn't say anything but stood up with as much dignity as her trembling legs would allow. That's what her father had taught her: never to let the bad guys see you unsettled. It was hard advice to follow in the thick of things.

'What are you doing here?' she managed to get out.

'Can't you see?' Morgan replied. 'We're here to skin ourselves a pretty pelt.' Morgan grabbed Corvala's raven-colored braid and stroked it with his fingers.

Corvala pulled back. 'Don't you dare touch me,' she hissed. 'My fah's on the mend. If he learns anything happened to me, he'll use your skins to make his boots.'

Morgan grinned, picking up the knife from the floor and passing it from hand to hand as he stepped towards her.

'Your fah took a brother from us. It's only fitting we take something from him. We tried for his life. But his daughter will do.'

He pressed the knife against Corvala's throat. This was it. Just a flick of Morgan's wrist and death would have her. Her body tensed, the cold winds of the underworld howling up and down her nerves. Her mind, however, felt detached, not sure what to think. If anything, it was annoyed. This wasn't how things were supposed to happen! That morning, she had been ready to meet a noble end beside her father. Now she'd die surrounded by these gloating lowlifes. A humiliating death lost somewhere underground, out in the Shroud where no one would know. Was this the way of fate?

As Morgan leered over her, the disembodied voice filled the chamber once more.

'Initialization complete. System diagnostics complete. Eighty-six percent intact. Functional.' A pause. 'Warning. Intruders.'

Morgan's eyes grew wide as he cursed and shot frantic glances about the chamber.

'We shouldn't've come here,' Deker quavered.

The chamber began to hum and steam hissed as if from metal throats. The large device at the center of the chamber began to move. Great metal arms pulling, hinges groaning... and then the lights flickered and went out. For many moments, the noises continued as parts moved. There came a loud bang, the sound of great metal slabs settling into place—heavy and final. After this, silence.

The lights flickered back on, revealing the central device, which now lay open. The interior cavity looked like it should have held something—something as large as a person. Now, though, the space was empty. The Capels looked warily about the chamber. A moment or two passed but nothing else happened.

'We've got to get out of here,' Deker whimpered, unplacated by the quiet in the chamber.

'Just a moment,' Morgan hissed, but Corvala could see the sweat beading on his brow. 'I got to finish what I came here to do.'

He pulled on Corvala's hair so that her neck bent back. Leaning in close, he hissed, 'This one's for Gage.'

Then many things happened at once.

A figure dropped from the beams above—a dark-skinned woman clad in gray. She grabbed Morgan's arm and used her fall to slam him to the ground. Then a fluid leap upwards as she smashed her fist into Deker's nose. Coming back down, she landed a hard kick to Trajan's shin—a sickening snap of bone. The woman moved so quickly—several of the brothers were down before any of them had moved. Heyworth Capel was the first to snap out of his surprise and made to tackle the woman.

She ducked beneath him and flipped him over her back. He flew into two of his brothers, knocking them to the ground.

Amid the sudden chaos, Corvala backed into a corner and took cover behind a metal column. It was all she could think to do. She watched for an opening in the fight, but there was too much movement. Whoever this dark woman in gray was, Corvala didn't care. Her attack on the Capels was just the diversion Corvala needed to get out of there. She would have to move fast. How long could one woman fight a slew of brothers? But—surely not, Corvala thought—the woman was holding her own. No, more than that—she was *winning*. Wherever she threw a fist or sent a kick, it met flesh and bone with precision and power. And whenever the Capels tried to strike her, they met only air. This gang of men who had once been so terrifying changed suddenly into a pitiful band of the lame toppling before the grace of a dancer.

Morgan rose from the ground and took the woman from behind. Corvala felt a warning cry rise in her chest. Before she could get the words out, Morgan drove the knife into the woman's back. The woman stopped punching Heyworth and let him fall to the floor. There was no surprise in her face. No anger or pain. No emotion at all. She merely pulled the knife from her back, the blade clean, and tossed it away. Corvala watched in disbelief.

'That ain't possible,' Morgan gasped, voicing Corvala's thoughts.

The woman kicked Morgan in the chest, sending him flying down the chamber's walkway.

'Demon!' he cried, scrambling to his feet. 'Run!'

He fled through the chamber door and into the tunnel. His brothers picked themselves up and followed, whining like whipped dogs. Corvala hesitated, questioning whether or not she should leave now and run with the men who had tried to kill her. She deliberated a moment too long, for the woman in gray came to stand on the walkway between her and her way out. The woman looked down on a figure clutching at a broken leg. It was Trajan, the cocky fighter in him gone. No laughing now—just whimpering and moaning. His break was in the middle of the shin, and Corvala saw that his lower leg bent oddly to the right, the bone bulging under the skin. In the presence of the woman, he lifted his hands to shield his face. She grabbed his arm.

'Leave me alone,' Trajan cried. 'I don't want no trouble.'

The woman took him to the pedestal near the chamber's center and placed his palm on its glassy surface.

'Computer,' she said in a flat tone. 'Identify.'

The surface of the pedestal glowed as it had when Corvala had placed her hand upon it. There came a sound like an angry horn blast.

'Identity does not match,' the disembodied voice of the chamber announced.

Corvala peered, wide-eyed, from behind her pillar. Trajan was wincing, his eyes squinting open and closed—but the woman merely took his leg and bent it back to how it had been before, setting the bone. Trajan gnashed his teeth, a howl lingering on his lips. The woman then produced what looked to be a spur from the lower part of her palm. She inserted the point into his leg and placed her hands over the break. Corvala thought she could see a warm glow coming from the woman's palms. Trajan was breathing heavily but then calmed, some color returning to his pale face. The woman helped him to his feet. He tapped his foot against the floor to test his leg. His break was healed.

'Leave this place,' the woman commanded, her voice just as emotionless as before.

Trajan backed away from her, confused. Then he loped away, out the doorway and up the tunnel.

The woman gave no pause, instead walking over to where Corvala was hiding behind the pillar. Before Corvala could figure out what was happening, the woman had her by the wrist and was dragging her out from hiding. The woman took her to the pedestal and pressed her hand on the glassy surface.

'Computer, identify.'

The surface of the pedestal glowed and hummed.

'Identity matches,' said the disembodied voice of the chamber.

The woman let go of Corvala's wrist. Corvala could now get a good look at this woman. She was like no one Corvala had ever seen in the valley—or in the Norwestor Dominion for that matter. Here was a woman whose eyes flashed with deep amber. Her dark hair was short and swept back as if blown by the wind. The clothing she wore fit tight against her agile frame, was cut from a sleek material Corvala didn't recognize. She wasn't haggard or worn like the women who slaved away on their farms; instead, she was clean and fresh. There wasn't a speck of grit under her nails, nor the slightest wrinkle cornering her eyes. It was as though she possessed the unblemished freshness of eternal youth. How could that be? Had she not just emerged from a tomb?

Morgan had called her a demon. She didn't look like one. When Corvala thought of demons, her mind immediately went to the Dominion-issued history books she read in school—books that warned against the evils of the Ancients. The drawings in those books depicted demons with horns, hooves, and fire. They usually stood behind the Ancient people, whispering in their ears and tempting them to build weapons, towers, and flying machines. Sometimes the demons inhabited metal shells and walked around like mechanical people and mechanical beasts. No hooves. No horns. But looks could be deceiving.

'Do not be afraid,' the woman said in a flat voice, responding to Corvala's shrinking posture.

Corvala looked into the woman's eyes and couldn't sense any spark of emotion. There was only the coolness of metal.

'I saw them stab you,' she said. 'You should be dead.'

'I am not a living organism. So, technically, I cannot die.'

'Then what are you? A demon?' Corvala took a step back towards the exit.

'No, I am not. I am an instrument. I am Seraph Raphaela. My creators called me Serapha. You may choose to call me that as well if it suits you.'

She spoke strangely, too, Corvala thought. Too rehearsed.

Corvala shook her head. 'I shouldn't be here.'

'I am not going to harm you.'

'You thrashed those guys.'

'They were intruders. You are not. You have no reason to fear me.'

'I have to go.'

Serapha took hold of her arm. 'We have matters to discuss.'

'Let me go!' She tried to pull away, but there was no breaking from that iron grip.

Serapha, undisturbed by the struggle, addressed her frankly. 'You were told to come down here, to find what is inside. "You must see it yourself. Come and find it."'

At this, Corvala stopped struggling. She recalled her dream and her walk along the creek. The memories that had come all on their own.

'What did you say?'

'You were led here by something you do not understand. Your ancestors pointed the way.'

'Yes... but how did you know that?'

'It was a message, a signpost to guide you to me. You woke me from my casing.' Serapha motioned to the device in the middle of the chamber and the person-sized cavity at its center. 'Something you saw or experienced triggered the dream. I need to learn what that trigger was.'

Serapha then reached out her fingers towards Corvala's head.

Corvala squirmed back. 'What are you doing?'

'I am trying to connect with your mind to find out what triggered your dream.'

'No,' Corvala said, covering the top of her head with her free hand.

'I told you that you have no reason to fear me,' Serapha assured.

'You want my mind! Why shouldn't I fear you?'

'I cannot force you to open your mind to me. The connection is only possible if you permit it willingly.'

Corvala took her hand from her head and stood up a little straighter now that she knew she had some control over the situation. 'I'm not willing.'

'If you do not allow me to connect then we will not be able to learn why you have come here.'

'I have enough madness when it comes to the minds of my family. I don't need any more.'

'If you refuse,' Serapha continued, 'then I must hold you here until you reconsider. I must know what triggered the vision that brought you here.'

What little confidence Corvala had gained a moment ago quickly withered away. Although Serapha may not have been able to force herself into Corvala's mind, Corvala was certain she could force her to remain in that underground chamber for as long as it took her to give in. As she thought her situation over, her eyes fell upon the spot where Trajan had been nursing his broken leg.

'You can fight,' she said, an idea coming to mind, 'and you can also heal. So let me make you an offer.'

Corvala had heard the fairy tales where people made deals with imps and malicious elves of the forest, bartering their names or their souls so they could save the people they loved. In the end, they were somehow able to use their wits to get out of such contracts, saving both themselves and their loved ones. Maybe Corvala could pull off the same thing.

'You heal my fah. Then—and only then—will I let you connect with my mind. Save us both time. And we both get what we need.'

She tried to keep a straight face, acting as if she were holding her own in this situation. Serapha's expression, however, was steel, revealing nothing.

'Your request is reasonable,' she replied. 'We have an agreement then: I do the healing you desire, then you give me access to your mind.'

Chapter 10

It was still dark out when Corvala arrived home. The guard assigned to watch over the house was half-dozing on the porch. He was a thick-necked man with a nose flattened from a badly healed break; not a deputy on Sheriff Kilagrin's payroll but a member of Mayor Green's personal security team. Corvala wouldn't have left her father alone with one of Kilagrin's men; the sheriff was too close in blood to Old Roman. Green had posted the guard there after the trial so that no one would try to finish off the Judge while he recovered. The guard tipped up his chair and shook off his sleep at the sound of Corvala's approach. His eyes looked out from beneath pudgy brows and regarded her with a look of suspicion. She had been in and out a lot that night, and now she was coming back near dawn. Corvala gave him a nod, not meeting his eyes, and entered the house, locking the door behind her.

She went straight to her father's room and found him just as she had left him: barely breathing, making no other sound or movement. Yet he was still alive—thank heaven! She took away the night's soiled sheets and clothing and then dressed him in clean garments, allowing him as much dignity as she could. A guest was coming, after all.

Corvala went to the back room and opened the window. The sky was mostly black, fringed with indigo at its eastern edge. Corvala peered out into the darkness. The meadow behind her house lay still—but then a silent shadow ran across the grass, coming to the house and up to the window.

'Did anyone see you?' Corvala asked.

'No,' Serapha replied. Without waiting for permission, she slipped into the house. 'My energy is limited, so we must be efficient. Show me to your father.'

Corvala led Serapha to her father's bedside. Seeing him so weak and vulnerable, she immediately had second thoughts about letting this strange woman—whatever she was—anywhere near him. Serapha produced a spur from a hollow between her palm and wrist but, when she went to insert it into Exodus's neck, Corvala reached out to stop her. Serapha caught Corvala's hand and met her eyes.

'Do not be afraid. I will heal him.'

Corvala bit her lip and reluctantly pulled back her hand. She reminded herself that if this woman could heal Trajan, she could heal her father. Serapha inserted the spur and then began moving her hands over Exodus's head, her palms glowing. Corvala watched intently as Serapha worked. The hands glided over Exodus's face and before Corvala's eyes the bruises there began to fade, the angry black and purple splotches turning a healthy ruddy color. Serapha moved from the head down to the chest and stomach. Everywhere her hands went, the bruises disappeared. Even Exodus's manticore wounds sealed up, pushing out the stitches and leaving a scar. Serapha went from head to toe, front and back, addressing every wound. When she finished, Exodus was taking full and easy breaths at a comfortable rhythm. No longer a man on his deathbed but a man in pleasant rest.

'You fixed him,' Corvala breathed.

'Yes. I took care of the pressure on his brain along with the other contusions in his body. He will need to rest before he can move around with comfort.'

Serapha turned from her patient and met Corvala's eyes. 'Now for what you promised.'

Corvala looked from her father to Serapha, her smile falling.

'And if I still refuse?'

'If you do not comply then I will inject a toxin into your father. It will not kill him but will render him immobile and unconscious for the rest of his life—a state similar to how he was before I healed him. It would be as though I never came here.' Serapha held up her palm and the spur reappeared. 'We do not need to go with that course of action. Instead, you could comply and let me into your mind. I sense that you are afraid of this. As I told you before, you have no reason to fear me. The process may give you some discomfort, but there should be no pain. Your mind will not be altered. Now that I have addressed your concerns, do you wish to comply?'

Corvala held still. She could see no way out of this one, no fairy-tale ending where she outwitted the mysterious creature. All she could do was trust this strange woman. Corvala gritted her teeth and nodded. Seemingly satisfied, Serapha put her fingers on Corvala's temples and looked into her eyes. Corvala felt uncomfortable looking into that empty gaze, but it was impossible to look away—Serapha's eyes seemed to draw her in. Then, Corvala's brain began to tingle. It was as if a million intruding fingers were sifting through the pieces of her mind. After a few moments, the fingers took hold of one thought in particular. Corvala saw again the morning of her father's trial: Roman Capel carrying the large stone, getting ready to bring it down on her father's head; the bright light above, the fiery ball flying across the sky. The image in her mind froze there. Corvala had the strange sensation that a second pair of eyes was looking at the image, too. The eyes studied it for several moments and then seemed to vanish.

Corvala was released and her consciousness returned to the room. She gasped as though she had just come up from deep water, then sat in a nearby chair to steady herself. Besides being a little dizzy, there seemed to be nothing wrong with her. Her vision was clear, her thoughts unclouded.

'You saw it,' she said, turning to Serapha. 'The falling star. You were really in my head.'

Serapha gave no reply to this. She had gone out into the common room and was looking towards the front door.

'Is something wrong?' Corvala asked.

'We must leave,' Serapha said. 'Now.'

'Why?'

'Something interrupted my scan of your memories. I hear people coming. And I sense they are hostile.'

Corvala went to the front window and looked outside. The sky was a dark blue, a white glow in the east foretelling the coming sun. But there came other lights as well, those of blazing torches. A mob—and, at its head, Sheriff Kilagrin. A company of guards rode with him, all of them armed with stout cudgels. Riding beside the sheriff was Roman Capel. His sons followed in tow.

'What's this?' Corvala hissed. 'A mob comes for my fah? They can't do that.'

'We must leave,' Serapha commanded. 'Follow me.' She made for the back window she'd entered through.

'Wait!' Corvala cried. 'I'm not going anywhere without fah.' She rushed over to Exodus and shook his shoulders; he didn't stir.

The voices of the crowd grew louder. The torchlight began to shine through the windows.

'Leave him,' Serapha commanded.

'You can go if you want!' Corvala snapped. 'You got what you came for, so just go. I'm not leaving without him.'

Serapha stared at her for a moment, evaluating. Then, without a word, she slipped out the window.

Corvala returned to her father. 'Wake up! Please! Wake up!'

She needed him to rise on his own. She couldn't possibly carry him. She shook him harder. Still nothing.

'Get up!' Corvala begged.

Bang, bang, bang! A heavy fist pounded on the front door.

Corvala froze.

Bang, bang, bang!

'Open up!' commanded a gruff voice from outside.

Corvala stood there paralyzed, wracking her mind for some sort of plan.

Bang, bang, bang!

It was too late. Perhaps, if he woke, her father could speak to the men outside. Perhaps he could make this all better. She slapped his cheeks. His eyelids trembled but didn't open.

'Open it up,' came the muffled command of Sheriff Kilagrin.

The doorknob shook. She was stuck—a ground squirrel trapped in its burrow, the hunting hounds digging their way in. Her father couldn't help her. She'd have to take care of this herself. Yes, this was hers to face. Was she a Judge's daughter, or wasn't she? She balled her fists and marched to the door. This was a Judge's house! How dare they come here with fire and harass her! The Order would be furious when they heard of this. With the desperate ferocity of a cornered animal, she threw the door open and faced the mob. The guards who had been fiddling with the knob and lock dropped their tools in surprise.

'What are you doing here?' she demanded, passing severe eyes over the crowd. All were men—Roman's sons, servants, and the bad ilk that ran with them.

Sheriff Kilagrin casually dismounted his horse and approached Corvala. Despite his hardy bulk, his voice was feathery and light.

'We've come to ask you questions,' he said calmly.

'At this hour? Go away. This isn't a time for questions.'

Corvala made to go back inside, but Kilagrin leaned in and stopped the door with his boot.

'I'm afraid it's important.'

'Sheriff, you know you have no business coming here.'

'There has been a report of lawbreaking,' he said.

'And what does that matter to me? Take your investigation elsewhere.'

At this, Roman Capel spoke up, gravel and spite in his voice. 'You're the accused, Miss Keen.' He took a pull on the corn-husk cigarette he was smoking. 'Time to come outside and cut a switch.'

Corvala swallowed hard. Whatever courage she'd had when she'd first emerged began to falter. 'I didn't break any laws. And even if I did, you have no jurisdiction here. Now get out of here before I tell the Order about this.'

Roman gave the kind of smile a gambler gives when he's about to show his winning hand. 'Witnesses say you called up a demon. Witchcraft. That's a mighty hellish crime, Miss Keen. Daughter of a Judge or not, that puts you in Sheriff Kilagrin's reach.' He took another pull on his cigarette and puffed the smoke out his nostrils.

Corvala's brow began to sweat.

'Who are these witnesses?' she asked, but she already knew who.

'My boys told me you went to an unholy place deep within the earth. Called forth a demon in Hell's language.'

'I was out in the forest looking for medicine for fah,' Corvala shot back. 'Ask your *boys* what they were doing following me.'

'She put a spell on us,' said Morgan, taking a step forward and pointing an accusing finger. 'Made us walk where we didn't want to go. Drew us into the forest so that demon could torture and kill us. Luckily, we came to our senses and escaped with our lives.'

Corvala laughed at their outlandish tale. Her laugh was cut short, however, when she saw Kilagrin nodding.

'You can't possibly believe him!' she cried.

Kilagrin absently ran his fingers through his thick red moustache. 'I thought it was an odd accusation at first. But the guard posted here tells me you were out all night. That's suspicious.'

'As I said before, I was out looking for medicine for fah.'

'Perhaps, but I'm going to need to take the necessary precautions to find out what's true.' Kilagrin turned to his men. 'Search the house. See if you find anything.'

'No,' Corvala protested. She knew this was not a neutral group who would merely walk around the rooms. These men would search until they found something incriminating. They would toss every piece of furniture and pull up every floorboard if they had to.

Corvala's face paled. What if they discovered the forbidden book under her bed? Their suspicions would be confirmed. They would call her a witch, and she would be taken away by the Rooks. And when the Rooks had her...

'No,' she cried, putting herself between the guards and the door. 'You'll disturb fah. He needs his rest. Pity a wounded man!'

'Move aside, Miss Keen,' Kilagrin commanded. 'Let us do our work.'

'You don't have any *honest* work to do here,' Corvala shouted in Kilagrin's face. 'You're just here to play along with your cousin's revenge.'

Kilagrin made to push past her, but Corvala grabbed the doorposts and planted her feet firmly to the floor.

'If you're not going to cooperate,' Kilagrin sighed, 'then you'll have to be removed.' He nodded to his guards. 'Take her away.'

The guards grabbed her by the wrists and began pulling her from the house. She writhed and kicked, but it was useless.

Then there came a loud voice from above.

'Stop!' it commanded.

The men froze. All eyes turned upwards. Atop the roof, Corvala saw, was Serapha. The Capel brothers shrank back in fear, and others drew circles in the air to ward off evil.

'That's the one!' Morgan cried. 'That's the demon!'

The guards readied their clubs and pulled knives. Kilagrin put a hand on his sword hilt.

'You will let her go,' Serapha ordered, 'and you will leave.'

'You and this young lady broke the sacred laws,' he managed after a moment, his voice wavering. 'There ain't no witchcraft allowed in the Dominion. She will come with us. And you will burn.'

'You are not in a position to give commands,' Serapha warned.

Then something bizarre happened, like the wonders told in old stories. Serapha began to glow. At first, Corvala thought the sun must have come up over the horizon but, as she watched, she realized the light was coming from *within* Serapha. It grew in strength, pulsing beneath her skin the way distant thunderheads rumble with threatening light. Her eyes flashed white and the air hummed with intensity as though the earth and sky were readying themselves to crack with lightning. Up from this rumbling erupted Serapha's voice, a peal of thunder that shook the bones:

'Do as I command! Leave now!'

The light within her no longer contained itself—she was blazing now, a beacon of terrible omens. The mob reeled and shook, the men aghast, the color draining from their faces. Many dropped their torches and clubs and ran for town. The last to go was Old Roman and a few of his boys, who cast fearful and bewildered glances back at the frightening sight on the roof—and also at Corvala. For a moment, she was confused as to why they would fear her, but she was too shocked by Serapha's display to pay these thoughts much heed. She might have run herself had the mob been safer company. After the last man stumbled away into the dark, only she remained in Serapha's presence. She turned to look up at the roof.

Who *was* this woman?

Chapter 11

Once all was clear, Serapha jumped down from the roof, the light in her gone. When she spoke, it was in her normal voice. Corvala blinked. It was as if nothing had happened.

'We need to go. They will return.'

'What are you?' Corvala mumbled, still stunned.

'What I am is not important now. The focus is on our leaving. This place is not safe anymore.'

She put a hand on Corvala's shoulder. This was no time to be stupefied. What Serapha had just done would confirm Roman's accusation, even though he had been lying. The mob's story would spread like wildfire through the town and then the rest of the valley—Corvala Keen had summoned a demon to attack the Capels. An unforgivable crime. She remembered how the Capels had looked at her as they fled, how they feared her now. The Rooks would be called in to take her away. Not only her, but her father as well. Roman and Kilagrin would find a way to paint him guilty, and his rank wouldn't save them. Indeed, a Judge and his household would be held to a higher standard. The law was the law. *No consorting with demons.*

But Serapha was an instrument, whatever that meant. Corvala was still working that out.

'We need to go,' Serapha repeated.

'Fah…'

'I will get him if it means your cooperation. Take what you need for the journey. We do not have much time. And my energy levels are limited.'

The sky was now a reddish orange in the east. The sun would rise soon, and Corvala was sure that the Capels and the sheriff's men would grow bolder in the daylight. They would come back with a mob even larger than the one before, each man armed to the teeth. Serapha was powerful, but could she hold off an entire town breathing fear and righteous judgment? There was no time to think it over. Preparations needed to be made for their departure.

Going into the house, Corvala took her book of Ancient medicine from under her bed and set it alight in the fireplace. She watched forlornly as the knowledge of healing burned. It was better this way—when the sheriff and his men searched the house, they'd find nothing more to incriminate her and her father. As the book smoldered, she gathered a few things: waterskins and a sack filled with bread and dried meat. She took her father's sword down from where it hung over the fireplace. There was a strict rule in the house that she was never to touch the sword, so now that it was in her hands, she felt a strange burst of forbidden pleasure. She looked down the sword's length—an edge keen enough to cut the east from west, as her father sometimes said. The metal was dark as obsidian with an iridescent sheen, and above the hilt was stamped the pottery and fire symbol of the Judges. If the angels had indeed descended from heaven to give the first Judges their swords, could this have been one of the originals? Or had it merely been hammered out in the same style as those first awarded? Either way, it was too valuable to be left behind. Corvala added it to her supplies.

Just one more thing. Going into her room, she picked up Sir William in its sheath. Only a handful of days ago she had been ready to leave her home and head out on the road with the Windborne. Now, with these circumstances thrust upon her, the thought of leaving was no longer enticing. Not an invitation to song and adventure, but a harsh crack of the whip driving her from what she knew. She gave her room and house one more look over, not knowing when she'd return—or whether she'd return at all.

'Don't worry,' she said to the little wooden face on her fiddle. 'We'll be all right.'

Picking up the rest of the supplies, she slung Sir William over her shoulder and walked out the door. In front of the house stood Serapha holding a horse by the reins. It was Kilagrin's. During all the commotion, the sheriff must have fled on foot—too scared even to mount his horse, Corvala thought with a snort. Whatever the case, Serapha had decided it was now theirs to use. Corvala knew this kind of theft was a noose-worthy crime. Given the heavy accusation of witchcraft on her head, however, she hardly cared. She might as well take part in stealing, as deep in as she was. Besides, she felt some dark satisfaction knowing Kilagrin would be short his mare. The horse would carry her father, who Serapha had laid over the saddle. This show of strength would have been impressive if Corvala hadn't just seen Serapha make a storm of herself. Of course she could lift a large man.

Once the supplies were attached to the saddle, it was time to go. Serapha led the horse by the reins and took a path heading away from town. Corvala walked beside her, casting one more glance back at her house. Who knew where they would go from here? For now, all she knew was that they needed to get far from this valley. Perhaps beyond the borders of the Stag Ridge province and maybe even the Norwestor Dominion entirely—they could flee to the kingdoms of the north. Corvala shivered at the thought. Not only were they foreign and far away; on top of that, Rainier and Washona had just as strong a presence of Rooks as the Dominion. Corvala hoped their flight wouldn't take them that far from home.

She noticed Seraphia was leading them west towards the Gloaming Hills. The heights bristled with pointy trees, the coming day turning their tops to red—a million bloody spearheads.

'We should go north,' Corvala said warily. 'That will take us out of the valley and up to the main road.'

'This is the most direct route to where we are going,' Seraphia replied.

'And where are we going?' Corvala asked, suddenly suspicious of Seraphia's purposeful direction.

'To the Elijah Tree.'

'Never heard of it. Is it some sort of hideout?'

'No.'

'Then why are we going there?'

'It is there that you will complete your mission.'

'Mission?' Corvala snorted, turning a quizzical look on Seraphia. The idea took her off guard. She'd thought they were just trying to put distance between themselves and the law. 'I'm not a part of any mission.'

'But you are,' Seraphia replied. 'You are a Sentry. That is why you must journey to the Elijah Tree.'

'Is this about reading me?' Corvala put a finger to her head. 'Because I already let you in. Done deal.'

'My reading your mind was only part of what was needed. There is more to do.'

'Listen,' Corvala said, putting up her palms. 'I don't know anything about this Sentry business. Once we get well enough away from this valley, my fah and I will take our *own* road. As soon as I can figure out which way, that is. I didn't sign up for any mission.'

'It is not something you elected. It comes from something you were born with—a trait you inherited from your mother.'

'I don't know what you're talking about.'

'It should be familiar to you. It guided you to me.'

Corvala thought for a moment and remembered her dream—her female ancestors standing along the creek, leading Corvala to the tunnel. It had guided her to the underground chamber. Something was in her that linked her to those women, something more than blood alone. She wanted to baulk at the idea and dismiss it as foolishness. But she couldn't; she knew it was true. Her mother had given her something.

'The madness,' she whispered.

'It is called Sky Mantle,' Serapha explained. 'It is a code found in your DNA.'

Corvala shook her head blankly.

'If I were to describe it as patterns of information written into the fiber of your body, would that make it clearer?' Serapha said.

Corvala looked down at her arms, picturing strings of letters and numbers running through her veins. She realized she had stopped walking, the urgency to escape the valley momentarily forgotten.

'Sky Mantle,' she said, testing the term, weighing it. The pain of women in her line—now it had a proper name. 'It's brought nothing but misery. What's it good for?'

'It appears the code produces side effects in your bloodline.'

'Madness,' Corvala snorted. 'Like a wound in my head.'

Her gaze drifted to her father's once-beaten brow. Then, as the sun rose over the hills and lit the valley, an idea came to her.

'If you healed him then you can heal me.'

'What kind of healing are you referring to?' Serapha asked.

'I want you to get rid of that code,' said Corvala. Expectancy lit her eyes. 'You can do that, can't you?'

'You ask if I can remove the Sky Mantle code. It is possible. However, you need the code to complete your mission. Only when it is complete will I be able to dismantle the code.'

'So I can be cured!'

'Technically you are not diseased. But by your understanding, yes, you can be cured.'

Corvala felt the pleasant burn of happy tears and the sudden thrill of hope catch in her chest. She looked to Gloaming Hills and the trees of Thorn Shroud—the wilderness where the mission would take her. She'd cross that forest and the rest of the world a dozen times over if it meant she could be cured.

'I'm in,' she said with an eager nod. 'What am I supposed to do?'

'Follow me,' Serapha replied, 'and I will show you.'

Chapter 12

Rising above the Moss Kettle Mountains, the sun cast its light into the wide Landsong Gorge, where the Colmane River flowed. On the southern shore of the river and at the foot of the mountains stood the city of Ryperia, the capital of the Hood province of the Norwestor Dominion. The rising sun chased back the gorge's shadows and colored the city's basalt structures a warm orange. Light streamed into the tall windows of the highest building in the city, the governor's palace.

As the light inched its way across the stone floor, Governor Grimshaw, an ageing man with a heavy brow and beady eyes, winced. 'Careful,' he tutted, and the servant shaving his face—a young man, not his usual barber—bowed apologetically.

After breakfast, he was scheduled to meet with the captains in charge of defense along the river. The trolls to the north had raided one of the villages and carried off several prisoners. Strange—the brutes usually kept to themselves and rarely crossed the river. Grimshaw wondered why they were giving him trouble now. Maybe it had something to do with the falling star that had flown over the city the other day. The priests had tried to read it as a sign of what was to come. Their interpretations were mixed, some looking to the light and calling it a blessing while others saw the fire from heaven and named it judgment. Grimshaw didn't place much stock in vague signs. All he knew was that he had fallen upon strange times.

The servant was finishing up the left half of his face when the captain of the city guard burst through the bed-chamber door. Startled, the servant nicked the governor's cheek again, but Grimshaw was too surprised to scold the boy.

'By the wreckage! What on earth are you doing, Robert?'

'Forgive me, governor,' said the head guard, coming to kneel at his master's feet. 'It's urgent.'

'It'd better be,' Grimshaw warned, perturbed that business had broken into his day before he had had the chance to eat.

'A mob is coming down the gorge from the east, heading towards the city.'

Grimshaw stared at the captain. It was too early for this kind of news. 'What? An army?'

'We're not sure. I sent scouts to find out, but none of them have returned. I rode out to see the mob from a distance. They're less than two miles away and will soon be at our gates.'

Grimshaw kneaded his thick brows. 'How many?'

'It's hard to say. With each report I get, their numbers grow. Last I heard, they were well over seven thousand.'

'Seven thousand,' Grimshaw repeated to himself. 'You didn't see this coming?'

'No, sir,' the captain said, looking to the ground. 'They came out of nowhere.'

Grimshaw stood up from his bed and went to the window, staring out at nothing. Lathered soap still covered half his face, but he didn't think of it.

'Bar the gates,' he said. 'Put all your men on the walls. And get my escort ready. I need to see this for myself.'

In less than a quarter of an hour, Governor Grimshaw came to stand on the parapets of the city walls, the banner of the Norwestor Dominion snapping in the breeze. Gathered around him were his company of personal guards, each wearing a helmet plumed with pheasant feathers and a full chest plate that glinted in the sun. Grimshaw had prepared and dressed as smartly as the short time had allowed—a ceremonial breastplate and scarlet cape with a collar made from a fox tail. He rubbed his chin, irked that half his face was cleanshaven while the other half bore stubble. It shouldn't have bothered him; there was a far more important issue at hand.

He looked out to the east, to the gorge where the river ran. Along the banks of the Colmane flowed a river of people from around the nearest bend, a multitude ten thousand strong.

'Salt and fire!' he murmured to himself.

He called for his spyglass and put it to his eye. He was expecting to see warriors armed with spears. What he saw instead were men, women, and children. Not a single weapon among them—not even a shovel or a simple club. This was no army but a crowd of common peasants from the surrounding villages, some of them singing and dancing as they went.

'Captain, is there a holiday or festival I'm forgetting?'

'No, sir. Not that I know of.'

Perhaps the death of a great person could call forth a wake of thousands. Strange—Grimshaw hadn't heard the news of anyone of consequence dying. And besides, the people looked happy, not mournful.

'What in the name of heaven is this?' he said, turning his spyglass to the head of the crowd.

There walked a man adorned in gold armor from head to toe, a great white light held in his hand. He held the attention of the entire crowd. All vied to be near him.

'This isn't right,' Grimshaw said, lowering the spyglass. 'I sense a trick. When they come in range, have the archers fire.'

'But sir,' the captain objected, 'there are women and children among them. Can't we at least send out a runner to give them warning to back down?'

'You yourself said our scouts haven't come back. Why do you think sending a runner now would be any different? Besides, I sense something wrong here. Those people out there… some devilry is driving them.'

The multitude came ever closer, the golden man leading them straight to the main gate.

'Archers, Robert,' Grimshaw said, his words a command.

The captain met his eyes, his expression dark and near-defiant. 'There aren't enough arrows here for a crowd like that. With what we have, we could barely take down a quarter of them.'

'We don't have to.' Grimshaw was growing irritated. 'Once a few fall, the rest will scatter. Now do as I say!'

The captain looked to the men around them and saw their growing fear of what was to come. Bowing his head, he shouted, 'Fire on my word.'

The archers at the walls nocked their arrows and drew back their strings. The multitude was nearly in range. The captain raised his hand, ready to send the arrows loose.

As Grimshaw waited for the volley to fly, he looked at the golden man coming down the road, the bright light held aloft in his right hand. It wasn't a torch, for the light didn't flicker; instead, it held a glow that pulsed in a steady rhythm. It was like nothing he had seen before. Beautiful, Grimshaw thought. Whatever it was, it emanated more than just light. He could feel it. New moods began to wash over him.

It started as a mild curiosity. As the light drew nearer, the feeling grew into glassy-eyed wonder. He forgot all about the archers and the order to fire. It didn't matter. They had already laid down their weapons of their own accord. They, too, stared at the light, transfixed by it.

'Open the gates,' Grimshaw said. 'I would like to speak to the man who leads them.'

The governor came down from the parapets and stood at the city's threshold as the gates opened before him. The multitude came down the road, shouting praise. As they drew nearer to the city, Grimshaw could see the golden man more clearly. Heaven above—wasn't he magnificent! His armor was unlike anything Grimshaw had ever seen. It was nothing like the heavy plate of the Dominion's elite warriors. It looked light but stalwart, a million pieces of finely crafted metal intricately and firmly sewn together. A slight glow radiated from the nearly seamless joints. How could the clumsy hands of men put such a thing together? It was flawless work, not of earthly making. This man in the golden armor was no mere mortal.

Grimshaw suddenly felt inadequate in his ceremonial breastplate and scarlet robe. He might as well have been wearing a tarnished piece of tin and a rag draped over his shoulders. And how could he forget the shameful state of his half-shaven face? It had been foolish to think a man of his meagre station could walk up to such a being and demand an audience. When at last the golden man came to the city gates, Grimshaw was kneeling in the dust, his eyes looking up in amazement as the light reflected off the golden man in a heavenly sunburst.

'Who are you, visitor,' Grimshaw said, 'that you would come to our humble city?'

'I am Dane, God of Olympus,' the golden man stated, his voice seeming to reverberate throughout the gorge.

'Welcome to Ryperia, God Dane. May we serve you as best we can.'

'I am pleased by your welcome and promise of hospitality.'

'And I am pleased as well,' Grimshaw sang with glee, meaning every word he said wholeheartedly. 'Let me show you to the palace.'

Grimshaw led Dane through the gates and up the main road the way an innkeeper would lead an esteemed guest to his room. The governor began to scrutinize his city, hoping it was good enough. The stone structures and paved streets that he had once taken so much pride in were suddenly filled with imperfections. All Grimshaw could see were the cracks in the stonework and the weeds infesting the shingled roofs. He cringed when he saw small piles of rubbish in the alleys. It was a miracle that the god following didn't turn away in disgust. No, he remained despite the city's shortcomings—such was his graciousness.

The multitude followed them as they went. Grimshaw occasionally looked back, finding his citizens and soldiers now among those singing.

'He killed a hundred trolls!' some cried.

'He'll kill a thousand more!' others responded.

The people were right to praise him, Grimshaw thought.

They reached the palace, a grand three-story structure of columns and arches. It sat upon a large rocky prominence surrounded by tiered gardens and a tall iron fence. It was the pride of Ryperia, and Grimshaw hoped the god would find it pleasing. Once they reached the iron gate to the palace grounds, Dane stopped and turned to face the crowds.

'My followers, here is where we must part. Many of you have traveled far, leaving your homes to follow me. Please find rest in this city and make new homes here.' He then spoke a word with Grimshaw. 'Would you show me in?'

Grimshaw was overjoyed. How privileged he was to escort a god! He took Dane directly to the throne room, where ornate wooden pillars held up the vaulted ceiling. At the end of the room and elevated on a dais sat the governor's throne, a chair of cedar ornately carved to resemble lions and eagles. Still, it didn't seem so impressive next to Dane.

'This can be yours if you like,' Grimshaw said meekly, a silly child offering a piece of wood to a venerable and kindly grownup. It was the best he could offer a god.

'I'm pleased by your gift,' Dane stated. 'I will take this place as my sanctuary.'

'Of course, my master.' Grimshaw bowed and left the throne room, delighted that a god was now residing in the palace and that he himself would get to be the god's servant.

Dane watched as a group of men dragged several metal cases into the throne room. The cases were large, each hauled by a pair of men. They held power cells to charge his suit, tools for maintenance, and various other bits of equipment he might need. The shuttle that had brought him to Earth could have carried him to this part of the gorge—indeed, its flight over the city would have been a marvel to the people, solidifying his reputation as a god even further—but it could be tracked from Olympus, and Dane didn't want anyone to know where he was. He doubted Silas would care or that the other Founders would learn of his exile, but he thought it best to take the extra precaution. So, he had come to the city on foot, amassing worshippers as he went.

He grinned to himself within his helmet. He was reminded of the conquistador Francisco Pizarro who had used 186 Spanish soldiers with steel weapons and armor to defeat eighty thousand Incan warriors armed with clubs. Dane had done better. He had taken a city of nearly a hundred thousand all by himself. He passed the glowing patheograph from one hand to the other. The little device had worked like a charm. A new page in the history books where technology had won the day. Waging a battle would have been more fun, but it didn't fit into Dane's plans. He needed people alive and willing to serve him.

There was one more thing left to do to make sure the city would remain his. He climbed out of one of the throne room windows, leaving the men to their work, and scaled the palace walls, coming up to the large domed roof rising up out of the palace's center. The palace was the tallest structure in the city and its central location gave it a commanding view of most of the other buildings. Dane took the patheograph and attached it to the palace's iron spire with some fusing wire. Now the patheograph would reach out to the entire city, simultaneously broadcasting and collecting feelings of wonder and awe. It was a system that perpetually fueled itself, working *ad infinitum*. Anyone who entered the city would be touched by the patheograph's power. All would be pulled in, unable to resist the urge to worship.

His sense of accomplishment was interrupted by the pitiful growling of his stomach. He bent over and folded his arms across his belly. The hunger pangs were growing more frequent. Since leaving Olympus, he hadn't had any sustenance. His worshippers had been more than willing to give him bread and meat, but he couldn't take their solid foods. He had lost all his teeth centuries ago. When he had managed a moment away from the crowds, he had tried some boiled water with sugar mixed in, but even that upset his stomach and left him vomiting. His body wasn't accustomed to eating and drinking the way it once had—on Olympus, machines had fed him while he hibernated in his pod. Tiny needles dripped sustenance into his veins, and those fluids came from machines that converted solar energy. A kind of artificial photosynthesis. When it came to 'eating', Dane was now not so different to a plant, and his innards had atrophied from disuse. All they were good for now was letting him know he was hungry.

Another growl from his shriveled stomach. Dane had never known hunger while in the Dream and had all but forgotten the bitter emptiness that gnawed from the inside. Now it doubled him over. He had to find sustenance soon or he would starve. Artificial photosynthesis wouldn't work—the process provided just enough energy for a body in hibernation, and he had no pod to sleep in. Even if he had brought a pod down to hibernate in, where could he get the power to run it? On this primitive world, he would need a different source of sustenance.

Dane looked down at the city below, at the humanity flowing through the streets. Many of the worshippers still gathered outside the palace. Dane thought of how the gods of Greek mythology had required burnt offerings from their worshippers, of how the smoke from the altars had risen into the heavens and brought sustenance to the gods. He, too, would require sacrifice.

His stomach complained again. 'Soon,' he said, wincing and pressing a hand to his belly. 'Soon.'

Chapter 13

The sun had vanished. Serapha bobbed in and out of view ahead and Corvala hurried after her, heading deeper into Thorn Shroud. A labyrinth of trees grew up about them. The monotonous columns of pines, firs, and spruces in the highlands; the gnarled trunks of oaks and maples in the lowlands. Despite every direction appearing to twist into lostness, Serapha moved with purposeful steps as if she knew where she was going. She walked at an unflagging rhythm, leading the horse with Exodus laid over its back. A dull pain burned in Corvala's legs, and weariness weighed her feet down. The sleepless night was catching up with her, and her thoughts and senses had become warm and sticky, like molasses being stirred into porridge. Her body moved to the monotonous rhythm of her steps, but her mind did no navigating. All she could do was keep Serapha in front. Even though she longed for rest, there were powerful forces that kept her going. The thought of Rooks coming after her whipped her from behind. What was more compelling, however, was the hope that pulled from ahead. As soon as this mission was over, she would be cured of the coming madness.

During their travels, Serapha had explained a little more about the mission. According to her, the Sky Mantle code was supposed to have remained dormant in Corvala's bloodline until it was triggered by certain sights or sounds 'deemed possible threats to global safety'. Unfortunately, the code prompted side effects: it created visions that called women to missions that didn't yet exist. An error. A fatal one. Unlike the women before her, however, Corvala had a different reaction: the code had done what it was supposed to do. The sight of the falling star at her father's trial had triggered the code, which had then given her a dream, and the dream had, in turn, led her to Serapha. It was all very complicated, and Corvala was sure she didn't understand everything Serapha had said. Her sluggish mind wasn't helping. It didn't matter though. Soon, all of this would be over. They would reach their destination—something Serapha had called the Elijah Tree—and Corvala would get her cure.

'So we go to the tree,' Corvala huffed as she marched herself up a hill, 'and then what?'

When Serapha replied, she sounded not in the least bit winded. 'You will make physical contact with it, thereby establishing a connection between the code within you and the Elijah Tree's programming.'

Corvala nodded slowly. This woman spoke so strangely. Many of her words were unfamiliar, and her voice was too... precise.

'I don't understand.'

Serapha didn't respond right away—instead she paused, trying, it seemed, to put her thoughts into simpler words. 'You will place your hand against the tree. The tree will do the rest of the work.'

'But why? Why go through all this work just to shake hands with a tree?' Corvala looked up to where they were going, but too many trunks and branches hid the hilltop ahead from view.

'The Elijah Tree is part of a defense system,' Serapha replied. 'You need to activate it because a possible threat has been detected.'

Corvala *hmph*ed. How a tree in the middle of the forest could be some sort of defense for anything was beyond her.

'And what is this threat?'

'The shuttle.'

'Shuttle?'

Corvala felt like a child asking too many questions, but she was too weary to care. If she was going to tromp miles and miles through this wretched forest, she had the right to know why. Besides, Serapha didn't seem bothered by her querying.

Again, the strange woman paused before giving a reply. 'What you call a falling star is not a falling star. It is a vehicle—a vessel.'

'You mean... a flying machine?'

Images came to mind, drawings she had once glimpsed in the forbidden books—drawings of flying machines with great tails of fire streaming behind them. Those were Ancient things. Could one of them have flown over her father's trial?

'Where did it come from?' she asked, her voice equal parts wonder and doubt.

'It came from the space station, Olympus, which orbits Earth...' Serapha stopped herself as though she knew already that Corvala would not understand. 'It is a structure, similar to a city, that floats high above the Earth.'

'A city? In the sky?'

Corvala's eyes instinctively looked up to the patches of blue between the treetops. She suddenly felt very small, although she couldn't explain why.

'The shuttle,' Serapha continued, 'comes from Olympus. This is a breach of the Earth and Sky Treaty. Therefore, it must be treated as a possible threat.'

What Serapha had said was too hard to believe—the return of Ancient things—and yet Corvala found herself believing it. Oddly, part of her *wanted* to believe. It was the same part that had driven her to look through the forbidden books years ago, hoping the Ancients had the secret to cure her. It was the same part of her that hoped Serapha could take away the madness. Maybe her mind was so sluggish she could be convinced of anything right now, but ever since she had joined with this woman who could perform miraculous healings and glow with lightning, she had felt the foundations of her reality shift. Things that had been certain before weren't quite certain anymore. Unformed questions stirred in her head. Maybe there *were* flying machines, or a city in the sky.

At last, they crested the hill. Corvala followed the horse down to what looked to be a wide ravine between the hills. She was just about to put another question into words when Serapha came to a halt. A wide creek lay before them, running along the bottom of the ravine where cedars grew. At the sight of the cool refreshment, Corvala stumbled to the bank and lapped up water, the horse following suit beside her. After she'd had her fill, she checked on her father and made sure he was still breathing. He couldn't be comfortable lying over the saddle like he was, but still he slept.

Corvala turned from him and noticed Serapha was standing as rigid as a plank, her eyes rolled back into her head.

'Serapha?' Corvala said cautiously. 'Serapha?'

She tapped her shoulder. Serapha's eyes shot back to normal.

'You are causing interference.'

'Interference with what? You were just standing there like a snake worshipper.'

'I was doing analysis and found my map is out of date. It does not record this stream being here.'

Corvala looked at Serapha's empty hands. 'What map?'

'The one in my memory. It is no longer accurate. The land has changed since I was put into hibernation. I will need to scan the surrounding area, rebuild my map, and reboot my system.'

'Sounds like a lot of work,' Corvala yawned.

'It is a necessary use of time, for my energy is limited. I did not wake from hibernation at full capacity. There is only enough for this mission. Therefore, we must take the most efficient route to your destination. The rerouting process will take approximately thirty-five minutes. You may use the time to rest.'

Serapha left and went back up the hill, presumably to get a higher vantage point. As much as Corvala wanted to press on and be cured, her weary body welcomed the break. After she tied the horse's reins to a tree, she found a soft bed of fallen needles near the bank. As soon as her head hit the ground, she was asleep.

Corvala opened her eyes. She was in her room, lying in bed. Her mother sat beside her. She was singing that old lullaby she had always sung. It was solemn and haunting, but underneath there sounded a trembling joy. Corvala had never heard anyone else in the valley sing it. It was their secret song, passed down from generation to generation.

> *When peace like a river, attendeth my way,*
> *When sorrows like sea billows roll*
> *Whatever my lot, thou hast taught me to say*
> *It is well,*
> > *it is well,*
> > > *with my soul.*

Her mother sang all the verses and, when she finished, she sat up from the foot of the bed.

'Time to go, little sparrow.'

She walked out of the bedroom and Corvala heard the front door close.

'Mother!' Corvala cried. 'Don't leave me!'

Corvala tried to get out of bed, but something was pulling at her from behind. There was a thread coming out of her back, only... it wasn't a thread. It was *glowing*. Corvala looked closely and saw little numbers and letters running along its length. She turned, finding a massive spool she'd somehow not noticed before filling half her room. She had to give a good pull in order to get the spool turning. Once she released more thread, she followed her mother out the front door and into open fields under gray skies. She noticed the thread ran through her chest and connected to her mother far ahead. Beyond her were other women in white. The thread ran through all of them, forming a great line from Corvala towards the horizon. Corvala tried to catch up to the women in white, but she was slowed by the pull of the thread. She often had to yank it as she trudged forward. The others moved farther and farther ahead until they disappeared over the horizon line. Don't leave me, Mother!' she cried.

Corvala woke with a jolt. She found herself on her feet. Odd. Hadn't she been lying down? Now she was standing in the shallows of a creek. The horse was behind her, her father hanging over the saddle. It was no thread she had been pulling from behind; it was the horse's reins. She had been sleepwalking.

Corvala started to giggle. Then she was laughing. Full belly, hard-to-breathe, tear-streaming laughter. She had to sit on the bank and clap her hand over her mouth even as she kept on laughing. There was no joy in it. Her mind didn't know how to handle—or didn't want to handle—the cold dread that sat in the pit of her stomach.

She had just gone the way of her mother: following visions through the forest.

It took her a minute or two to calm down. She fought off the giggles and tears and reminded herself that Thorn Shroud was no place to lose her head. She needed to get a hold of herself and get her bearings. How far had she gone? A few yards? A mile? She looked around but couldn't see the stream or her bed of pine needles. There were only trees and more trees—it all looked the same.

'Serapha!'

She called again and again, but there came no voice in reply. Instead, she heard another sound: sticks snapping in the distance.

'Serapha?'

The noise stopped. An unsettling feeling crawled prickles over her back. She climbed up onto the saddle. It felt better to be off the ground, and having her father at her back—even though he was unconscious—gave her some comfort. She turned the horse around and rode it down the creek in the direction she had come. She told herself she'd eventually find Serapha or that Serapha would find her. She couldn't have wandered that far.

There was another noise, this one closer than before. She stopped the horse and listened. There was a cackle in the distance, but it could have been a startled bird. Corvala felt her skin tingle with goosebumps. The horse grew nervous. Its ears were back as it snorted and stomped its hooves.

'Let's go,' Corvala whispered, spurring the horse onward.

At that moment, a shadow leaped out from the trees—a squat figure half Corvala's height. It was bent, its skin brown and warty like a toad's.

Goblin!

It landed in front of them with a hiss and thrust a sharp stick at the horse's chest. Spooked, the horse turned and bolted away, charging into a full gallop down the creek. It was all Corvala could do to grab hold of its neck and hang on for her life. As the trees rushed by, she could make out the shapes of other goblins moving after her through the branches. Their cackling laughter grew louder. It came from above and behind—all around her, filling the forest. The horse bucked and whinnied, froth whipping from its mouth. Corvala could feel her father's body jostling against her back. She turned to grab the collar of his shirt—but she wasn't strong enough. He slid off the horse and tumbled to the bank.

'No!' Corvala cried, the horse leaving him behind.

She managed to get hold of the reins and tried to get the horse to stop, but it ignored her. On and on it ran, trying desperately to escape the relentless pursuers.

'Easy! Easy!' Corvala screamed, failing to calm the horse with her frantic voice.

One of the goblins nimbly climbed out to a low branch hanging over the bank. Corvala ducked the branch. But she wasn't quick enough to dodge the goblin's club. A riot of pain burst across the side of her head. Sparks and wild colors spun in her vision. Then all the lights went out, and she fell into darkness.

Chapter 14

Hobb spurred his horse on through the rocky heath, clouds of sulphureous steam coughing up from the thermal springs pockmarking the earth and soaking everything with the smell of rotten eggs. Here the landscape hissed with desolation: craggy outcroppings jutted up from the earth and there was nothing but thistles and scrub to call life. Hobb took out a handkerchief and wiped the sweat from his balding head. It could have been from the heat rising from below the ground. Or he could have been nervous.

A man like him with a hefty paunch and soft hands wasn't used to being on his own in a place like this. He was much more comfortable behind his desk, counting coins and checking the budget. If he did go out, it was usually with the company of bodyguards. But he didn't trust hired muscle anymore—not since his last pair of men sold him out and left him to the thieves. Trust? Bah! What had that got him? A beating and a night spent in a ditch. All the fine cloth from his wagon stolen. No, the only person he could trust was himself. Next time he was out on the road to deliver a trade, he'd have more reliable protection. Which was why he had come out to this infernal land.

As he directed his horse around a bubbling pool of mud, he thought he saw something move in the corner of his eye. A fleeting shadow. He stopped his horse and looked around. There was nothing. Just steam wafting across the wild heath. It was probably the clouds playing a trick on him. Of course—nothing. He had made sure he was out here alone, taking empty roads at unsightly hours. He got his horse going again. Soon he'd be done with this secretive business. He'd get what he had come for and get out. Then he wouldn't have to worry anymore.

Through the steam, he saw a lone shack and, beside it, a barn. It was still and quiet. If it weren't for the goats in the pen, the place would have looked abandoned. Hobb dismounted and cautiously came up to the shack to knock. The door opened a crack to reveal a woman. She was broad-faced and plain, her features weathered from living on this harsh land. Not what Hobb had expected a witch to look like. In the tales he'd grown up hearing, witches had warts at the end of long noses and they wore black cloaks. This woman looked like the average goatherd in brown buckskins.

'Who are you?' she growled. 'What are you doing on my property?'

Hobb understood her suspicion. Wasn't he himself out here because of distrust?

'I'm here to make a deal,' he said. 'I understand you have… *interesting* goods for sale.'

'Don't know what you're talking about,' the woman spat. 'Now get out of here. Get off my land.'

She went to shut the door, but Hobb stopped it with his foot.

'Wait! Kendon told me to tell you: the ghost of Samuel is at rest.'

This gave the woman pause and she stared at him, scrutinizing. One of the goats bleated in the yard. Hobb began to wonder if he had been given the right code phrase or if he had just uttered nonsense.

'You bring money?' she said at last.

Hobb held up a sack that jingled with coins. The woman snatched it and looked inside. Satisfied, she pocketed the sack.

'Give me a moment,' she said, and crossed the yard to the barn.

Hobb noticed she carried a broom. For some reason that seemed appropriate for a witch. Weren't there old stories about witches using brooms to fly and cast spells? What she'd use it for he couldn't tell. Probably just sweeping floors.

She came out of the barn leading a mule by a rope. She handed Hobb the rope and then went back into the barn to retrieve her broom and a long metal pole ending in a hook.

'Follow me,' she said.

The woman took Hobb out to one of the hot springs, its bubbling water warning of scalding heat. She dipped the pole with the hook into the water and, after fishing around for a while, pulled up the end of a chain. She hooked the chain to the mule's harness, working with gloves so as not to get burned. She gave the mule a hard smack to the hindquarters and it lurched forwards, dragging up something large from the depths. A metal container shaped like a coffin emerged from the boiling water. Once it was on solid ground, the woman flipped the latches and lifted the heavy lid. Curious, Hobb came in close, surprised to feel cool air coming out of the container. He looked inside and saw half a dozen long metal objects with a variety of oddments attached.

'Are those—?'

'Guns,' the woman said flatly, finishing his guess.

'Guns,' Hobb repeated. These were tools of the Ancients, enchanted devices imbued with strange magic. What lay before him was a dangerous and forbidden power. It took a great effort for Hobb to stifle his wonder and desire. Being an experienced businessman, he knew it was an amateur move to show he wanted something during a buy. Revealing his interest would mean higher prices.

The woman took one of the objects from the container. It opened up wide at one end like a funnel.

'This is what they called a *shotgun*. It'll make you stronger than twenty men.'

Hobb felt the lust for power bubbling up inside him. His fingers itched to reach out and grab the thing. Instead, he kept a hold of himself and put on an air of mild amusement.

'Kendon said you had a weapon that would make me stronger than a *hundred* men.'

The woman eyed him dubiously. 'You sure you need that?'

'I'll be the judge on what I need. Now show me the gun I came to see.'

The woman reluctantly put the shotgun back and pulled out a gun that looked to be made of many different pieces of metal fused together. She pressed a small circle on the side of this new object and Hobb heard it start to hum with energy.

'This is a *laza ryeful*. It fires the devil's flaming arrows. More shots than I can count. It'll kill you a hundred men and then some.'

'How does it work?'

The woman held out the laza ryeful before her and explained how to make its magic. She dragged her finger across the device and pointed out its various parts. This end was the *barrel*. This end was the *stock*. This is where you put the *power cell*. And on and on.

When she finished her droning monologue, Hobb gave a sickly-sweet smile. 'Of course,' he said, 'I'll need to see what it can do before I put any more money down.'

The woman rolled her eyes but tromped over to a large boulder and started to set up little rocks as targets. Then, suddenly, she stopped, perking up and looking all around like a dog catching a new scent on the wind. She clutched the laza ryeful and crouched down, keeping close beside the boulder, the broom still at her side.

'What are you doing?' Hobb called across the short distance between them.

The woman ignored his question and kept low. From where Hobb stood, he could see her take on a strange new position: her elbows propped on the outcropping and her cheek against the gun, one eye squinting down its length. If he had his terms right then her finger was on the *trigger*. Whatever she was doing, it made Hobb suddenly feel exposed—why was he just standing there like an idiot? He crouched down beside the metal container. What they were hiding from, he couldn't tell. Then a worrisome thought crept into his mind. Had he been followed? No, that couldn't be. The roads were empty. He had been all alone; he had made sure of it. But still…

He peered out from behind the metal container and looked out onto the barren landscape hissing with steam. Then, he caught a glimpse of something—a figure like a fleeting shadow. It moved silently from one column of vapor and disappeared into another. The woman must have seen it, too, because she let loose her weapon. The laza ryeful fired several streaks of red light. Some disappeared into the steam. Others crashed into the outcroppings, cracking rock and blasting stones into dust. Hobb watched from behind the container, an expression of fascination and bewilderment slapped on his face. Here was the magic of the Ancients playing out before his eyes. The devil's flaming arrows indeed!

The figure was nowhere to be seen among the boulders and steam. Who knew if the shots hit their mark? The woman repositioned so she could track where she thought the figure had gone. Then—to the left of her! A ball of light swiftly flying, wisps of green trailing behind. It screamed through the air and struck the woman, disappearing with a pop. To Hobb's surprise, the woman was unhurt. Only her short hair tousled as if caught by a breeze. The laza ryeful, however, had absorbed the green ball of light. Now it sizzled and sparked. When the woman pulled the trigger, the gun did nothing but puff with smoke. She cursed and threw it aside. Whoever was out there in the haze had power of their own.

Hobb didn't know much about the secret world of forbidden knowledge and the things of the past. But he did know about the kind of person who could destroy magic.

A Rook.

The woman looked back towards him, evaluating whether she should break cover and make the short run for the metal container. Thinking better of it, she instead did something odd. She lifted her broom and spoke to it.

'Enemy detected!'

The words must have been a spell because out of the bristles burst a spider. It was larger than a person's hand and unlike any spider Hobb had ever seen, its body made of metal and its head bearing a single red eye. It landed before the woman and awaited her command.

'Over there,' she said. 'Behind those rocks.'

The spider chirped in response. On legs like long sewing needles, it skittered across the ground and disappeared into the patch of mist where the woman had pointed.

Hobb wondered what he had got himself into. Witches and spiders! And a Rook on the prowl. This was too deep for him. His legs trembled and he wondered dimly whether he should flee or stay put. Before he could decide, the air erupted with a terrible boom that knocked him off his feet.

Out behind the rocks blossomed a fireball—a blast with the force to destroy a house. Coughing from the cloud of dust, Hobb picked himself up. His ears rang and he gripped the metal container to keep steady. The explosion had come from where the spider had been heading. Had that creature done that? Such a small thing with such great power of destruction? Hobb had seen enough that day to believe it could be so.

The woman cautiously rose from behind the boulder and hurried over to the metal container.

'Did you get him?' Hobb quivered.

'Not sure,' the woman said, grabbing another gun out from the container; this one looked more like the shotgun than the laza ryeful. With a careful tread and the weapon held out before her, she disappeared into the clouds of steam.

It was quiet. Hobb could hear his nervous heart pounding in his ears. He sat in the dirt. What was he waiting for? He got the sudden urge to take what he had come for and run. The Rook could still be out there. Maybe the explosion had killed him; maybe it hadn't. No point in sticking around to find out. Hobb crept up and looked inside the container. There lay all those guns, all that power.

He knew the deal wasn't fully complete. There was more money to pay, and Kendon had told him the trade would probably end with him drinking a potion of some kind—one that would clear his memory a bit and give him no recollection of the witch or where she lived. That way, if he was ever captured or questioned, he couldn't rat her out. Witches were strict about that part of the deal, and it was unwise to cross them. But she was gone, and jittering instincts told him to get out of there. If broken rules meant Hobb would be on her bad side, so be it. Surviving this thing was worth risking her anger.

Hobb reached into the container and took out a gun: the only other laza ryeful in the batch. He then hurried across the heath, going in the direction he thought would take him back to the shack and barn. It was hard to tell in all the haze. He'd get back to his horse and ride far away from this place.

Then a violent string of cracks and bangs rang out through the air. Hobb stopped in his tracks. It was hard to place where the noises had come from. He couldn't tell if he was heading away from the danger or towards it. Before he could figure it out, he saw the woman appear from the haze. She didn't look at him—instead, she kept glancing over her shoulder. Something was after her. She held her arm, a fletched bolt sticking out of it. Blood colored her sleeve. Hobb debated for a moment whether or not he should call out to her. Before he could speak, another bolt flew through the air and struck her in the back of the thigh. She screamed and fell to the ground, the gun tumbling from her grasp. A jolt of fright dropped Hobb behind a clump of sagebrush. No courage now. Just instinct to save his skin.

Lying on his belly with his face in the dust, he heard something coming. Footsteps crunching on gravel. Hobb looked through the twigs of sagebrush. Out of the steam materialized a man cloaked in dark gray. In one hand he carried a crossbow and, in the other, a metal staff topped with a jade cylinder. His face was covered by a dark metal helmet that gave him a fearsome appearance. Jade glass filled the eyeholes. Even though Hobb lay behind a thick growth of scrub, he had the sinking feeling no cover could hide him from the gaze of those green eyes. He tried to make himself as small as possible, pulling his arms and legs into his chest. The terror within him begged his body to keep still even as it twisted his innards and made his limbs tremble.

The Rook approached the woman, his bow trained on her. He kicked aside her discarded gun.

'Where did you get these, witch?' he said, his voice cold steel.

The woman gave him no reply but glared at him with the fierce eyes of a wounded animal. The Rook studied her for a moment, evaluating.

'Your sister didn't speak at first either,' he said.

This made the woman flinch. Hobb saw the hate in her eyes flare.

'You don't have her.'

'She says she picked up the unholy trade from you.'

'You lie!'

'We went to work on her hands. She held out for a little while. Now she has only one finger left. Would you like to know which one it is?'

'Go rot!' the woman growled.

Hobb swallowed. The thought of being captured and tortured made him break out in a cold sweat. He held the ryeful the way a frightened child would clutch a stuffed animal. Then it dawned on him—he had a weapon that made him stronger than a hundred men. Why was he afraid of one Rook? He focused on the feel of metal in his hands, and a fire began to stir in his belly. He lifted himself off the ground and carefully moved into a crouch. Looking through the sagebrush, he saw the Rook standing over the woman, his back to Hobb. Hobb trembled, the thrill of power now mingling with his fear. He looked the gun over and remembered there was something he needed to do to wake its magic. His finger found the circle at its side and he pressed it just as he had seen the woman do. The weapon hummed to life.

It wasn't a loud noise, but it was enough to catch the Rook's attention. He shot a glance towards Hobb's position. Taking advantage of the distraction, the woman yanked a small device from her boot. As she aimed, the Rook moved with a viper's speed. He leaped to the side, dropping his staff. A shot from his crossbow and the woman threw her arm back, the device in her hand firing with a bang.

The woman gripped her neck where the bolt had pierced her. The sound of despair gurgled in her throat, and she slumped back, dead.

Hobb stared, stupefied. He saw the witch's body lying on the ground, her blood mixing with the dust. The Rook stood still, his arm halted mid-reach. It was then that Hobb realized he had the gun pointing at the Rook—a move done in mere reflex. Trembling as he was, Hobb didn't wield the gun so much as hide behind it.

'Well played,' the Rook said, his voice unwavering.

He had no bolt in his crossbow and Hobb had the gun trained on him. As the saying went, the boot had pinned the snake to the ground. But that didn't mean the snake was any less venomous. And it didn't make Hobb any braver.

'I'll admit,' the Rook continued, sounding as though he had lost nothing more than a hand of cards, 'I didn't take you as a threat. Do you know how to use that thing?'

'I know enough,' Hobb sniffed, adjusting his grip on the gun.

'Just be careful. That looks to be the patched-up remnants of an old KX-370. Who knows how corroded its wires are? Pull the trigger now and it could explode. A good way to lose an arm. Or a face.'

'You're just trying to scare me.'

'You're scared already.' The Rook made a long low whistle that rose to a high note.

'Stop that! What are you doing?'

'Calling for help.'

'You're not alone?' Hobb's eyes darted right and left, searching for anyone else who might be lurking in the columns of thermal steam. 'Who's with you?'

'A friend. You still have time to give up.'

'You're bluffing,' Hobb managed to get out, his voice shaky. 'You lied to the witch about her sister, and you're lying to me.'

'Are you sure about that?' the Rook said, following this with another whistle.

'You're in no place to make demands!' Hobb cried, brandishing the gun. 'I've got the upper hand!'

The Rook stared at Hobb for a moment. 'Last chance,' he said at length. 'Put down your weapon, and you'll live.'

'Enough of this!' Hobb barked.

He put his finger on the trigger just as he had seen the witch do. But he didn't fire. A gruesome image came to mind—his pulling the trigger only to be torn apart by wild magic. He shook his head. He couldn't just stand there in fear and doubt. A move had to be made. This was just like dealing with traders in the market, only the stakes were higher. And Hobb was going to get the bad end of the deal if he didn't keep his head on straight.

'I'll tell you what we're going to do...'

He didn't get to finish his proposition.

There was movement in the corner of his vision. With it came the sound of feet padding across the gravel. When he turned to see what it was, it was too late. A large silver shape leaped at him. At its front, a large maw filled with teeth. Its sudden dark clamped down hard upon Hobb's head and shoulder. He felt his nose crunch and face smash in with the pressure. Pain and terror rose in shrill volume, viciously muted in his squashed mouth. He felt himself lifted from the ground and shaken. His arms and legs swung one way, his body another. If his finger pulled the trigger, it wasn't to put up a fight; it was to grab hold of something—anything—that might save him. The screaming. The aimless blasting. Then a snap of his neck. And it was quiet.

Rook Vlaren watched his wulgyre make the kill, shaking the man like a rag doll.

'Lobeka! Enough!' Vlaren commanded.

Lobeka obediently dropped the man's body.

The wulgyre was a powerful predator, something between a wolf and a tiger, as if the two creatures had been perfectly melded together. Her fur was light silver, except for her paws and the tips of her ears and tail, which darkened to an almost indigo color. Although she was large—just a few hands shy of meeting shoulders with a horse—she had moved silently upon the hapless merchant. He had been warned. Fool.

Here marked the end of this Hunt. Two dead. Sloppy work considering he had wanted prisoners for interrogation. There were always questions, always more to find out. More mysteries of the Ancient world to seek out and destroy. So, in a way, the Hunt was never really finished.

Vlaren took off his metal helmet, revealing a lean tawny face and eyes so dark they were nearly black. He looked over the dead witch. In her lifeless hand was the small device she had tried to kill him with—a gun the Ancients called a *9mm pistol*. From his studies at Pillar Dark, Vlaren knew its magic was older than that of laser rifles. Instead of the devil's flaming arrows, the pistol held metal capsules filled with black powder—a powder that ignited into small bursts of hellfire. He had expected the witch to have some tricks up her sleeve, but the merchant shouldn't have been a factor. Vlaren had pegged him as a coward who would run at the first sign of danger. Still, Vlaren supposed, he couldn't predict everything.

He took the pistol and gathered up the guns from the container—amalgamations of an AR70/90, an AK-47, a DRT-570, and other enchanted weapons with strange names given by the Ancients. They were crudely put together, and he hadn't been lying when he had warned the merchant; shoddy examples like these could easily explode when their triggers were pulled. All of them he threw into the middle of the boiling spring, putting them out of reach of anyone who might want to use their demonic magic.

There were dozens of thermal pools on this vast rocky heath, and Vlaren suspected the witch had other containers hidden in the depths of their scalding waters. Taking up the pole with the hook, Vlaren began checking them, fishing around for any chains. When he reached the fourth pool, Lobeka raised her head in alert.

Out from the steam came a figure. Like Vlaren, he was cloaked in gray and wearing a jade-eyed helmet. He rode on a reddish wulgyre, the beast padding across the heath in an unhurried yet purposeful approach. Upon reaching Vlaren, the old Rook took off his hood and helmet. He had sharp angular features, and his shock of white hair stood out against his brown skin.

'Rook Eramez,' Vlaren said, uncertainty in his voice. It was unusual for his former master to follow him out to a mission like this.

'Two dead,' said Eramez, his voice as subtle as a breeze through sagebrush. 'Not your best. They should've been brought in for questioning.'

'Things can get messy when you bring a crossbow to a gunfight.'

'Excuses,' Eramez sniffed. 'And what about that empty container? I should have seen guns inside.'

'I threw them in the pool,' Vlaren said, waving a dismissive hand. 'Anyone who wants them is welcome to burn their hands off.'

'You know that goes against policy,' Eramez said, poking the tip of his staff into Vlaren's chest. 'They are to be collected for study and proper disposal.'

'Pillar Dark has enough of these things. And I don't have time to do the paperwork or to wait around for a collection crew. I've got another lead on who supplied this witch.'

'That can wait.'

Vlaren grimaced. He knew the old man hadn't just come to criticize his work.

'I have another mission for you,' Eramez said. 'There's been a demon sighting near here.'

'Another superstitious old lady afraid of the shadow under her bed?'

Eramez shot him a stern look. 'Do you think I would come with trivial matters? They say a girl summoned the demon to save her father. Her father is a Judge.'

There was a hint of bitterness in the last word, the longstanding rivalry showing itself. So that was why Eramez was here in person.

'Two Rooks to take a Judge,' said Vlaren. 'That's certainly thorough.'

'No. You're on this one alone.' Eramez looked out across the thermal pool, stroking the tuft of beard on his chin. 'I'm going to the Landsong Gorge. Reports have been coming from there, claims of villages emptied of people. It's said they were led away by a man in gold, like in the tale of the Pied Piper. Whether these reports are exaggerated or not, they're worth investigating.'

'The two cases could be related.'

'We'll find out,' Eramez said, prodding his wulgyre's sides with his heels and getting his beast on the move again. 'Go to the town of Dawn's Landing. And go quickly. The Judge is on the run.'

Vlaren watched as Eramez rode away. The older Rook had taken the bigger job for himself, sending his former pupil out to poke a scandalous hole in the reputation of the Judges. No matter. Vlaren cared little for reasons behind his assignments. The only thing he cared for was the Hunt. And a Judge was formidable prey—one he had never pursued. The thought of it sent a familiar thrill through his limbs. He jumped onto his saddle and directed Lobeka west towards the town of Dawn's Landing. Unlike his last job, he'd complete this next mission right. Two prisoners—the Judge and his daughter. They would run and probably put up a fight. But like all the others he had Hunted, they would be his in the end.

Chapter 15

It was more of a memory than a dream. Corvala was six or seven years old. She ran home crying. Bursting through the front door, she found her mother in the kitchen and buried her face in her mother's apron.

'What's wrong, little sparrow?' her mother asked.

'I was playing on the hill,' Corvala wailed, 'and I fell down and bumped my head.'

She cried, and her mother stroked her hair and spoke soothing words. After a while, Corvala caught her breath and wiped the tears from her cheek.

'Are you crazy, Mom?'

Her mother stopped stroking her hair.

Most of the time she was what Corvala would call normal, going about her days like any other woman of the town. But there were occasions when she changed, when voices and visions would fill her head and she'd seem to shut out the real world. She always told Corvala those were her 'dizzy spells.'

'Why do you ask?' she said with a sad smile.

'Tessa Jones said so. She and the other girls laughed at me when I fell. Tessa said the bump I got would knock the crazy loose in my head. Crazy I got from you. The girls laughed.'

Corvala felt like crying again, the humiliation still raw. Her mother stroked her cheek and made the two of them meet eyes.

'You listen to me, little sparrow. Those girls don't get to say what is and what isn't. They're caught up in their little flock, following each other like sheep. When one laughs, the others laugh. Don't do the same. Don't toe the line just because. "If you can keep your head when all about you are losing theirs..."'

Her mother would often quote that line of old poetry, leaving it unfinished. Corvala could never figure out whether her mother had forgotten the rest or was intentionally leaving it open for Corvala to fill with her own ideas.

'Let me have a look at you,' her mother said, kneeling to her level. She pushed some hair from Corvala's forehead. 'Oh, there it is.' She kissed the tender bump above Corvala's brow. Corvala sniffed and wiped her nose.

'Will I go crazy, too?'

Her mother's expression remained kind even as her eyes narrowed, betraying an internal wince.

'Let's get a cold wet rag on that bump and see if we can get you feeling better.'

The pain in Corvala's head lingered. She felt it in her temple, a dull throbbing that sent tremors through the fault lines of her skull. A newer memory came to mind—one with blood only recently dried. She made to touch the spot the club had hit her, but her hand wouldn't come forwards. She was seated on the ground, her arms pulled back around a tree trunk, the muscles in her chest and shoulders so taut it was hard to breathe. The knobs of the bark dug into her back and rough cords bound her wrists and ankles. Another cord squeezed around her waist and lashed her to the trunk. She convulsed with a jolt, her stupor vanishing, cold shock filling its place. Her body writhed against her constraints but, in her panic, her bonds only seemed to grow tighter, slithering around her body and twisting into her skin.

Her eyes darted about her surroundings as she tried to figure out where she was. Far from the house where her mother had once comforted her. Here stood the tamaracks and pines of Thorn Shroud, now gray and blue in the low light of ending day. There were other forms among the trees, forms that didn't appear to belong in a forest. Nearby there loomed a great metal beam, twisted and rusted, supported by a broken section of crumbled wall at its base. Around the edge of a clearing stood more fragments of ruins. They rose from the ground like the broken ribs of the earth. Whatever the whole structure had been before, it hadn't been built by the people of the Norwestor Dominion. It was much older. Something Ancient.

Strung about the beams and nearby trees was a vast collection of forbidden objects—tarnished bits of metal and pieces of machines tied to cords—thousands of metal insects caught in a messy web of twine. Closest to Corvala were the newest objects in this odd collection: the saddle with the bags she had packed for the journey. To one side hung her fiddle; to the other, her father's sword in its sheath.

Her father. Maybe he'd been caught like her. Searching, she craned her neck this way and that. He was nowhere to be seen, no shape of him. Instead, she saw animal skin tents forming a camp at the center of the clearing. A goblin nest. The creatures were drawn to the remains of the Ancient world the way flies were drawn to dead animals. Dozens of them were gathered around a fire at the center of the camp. By the firelight, Corvala could see their apelike forms. Their snouts were bloody as they feasted on a large body.

Corvala's face paled at the sight of it—but, after a moment of wordless mortification, she realized it wasn't her father. The body was too big and, by the firelight, she could make out the four legs and the long head of the horse. Despite the momentary relief, the scene was far from comforting. A gruesome split had opened the horse's underside, and a slew of goblins crammed in all at once. They shoved their faces into the guts and tore out whatever they could gobble down, ramming heads and shoulders, biting and snarling in a ravenous frenzy. It was a wonder they didn't eat each other. The largest of them held the prime spots, kicking away the smaller goblins who tried to wriggle into the mess. The subordinates circled the carcass and sniffed the air with longing. Near the fire sat an especially large and grotesque goblin, her skin layered with folds of fat. A brood of squirming young suckled on her rows of teats. She would often bark at the others feasting on the horse, who would then hurry to the matriarch, cowering and with ears back, before dropping strips of flesh and viscera into her greedy maw.

The feast continued to rage, and Corvala was grateful that the nearby portion of wall blocked most of it from her sight. Even so, she couldn't push away the horrifying thought of *her* blood staining the goblins' snouts. Maybe that was why they had her tied up—to keep her alive and fresh for a later meal. The thought drove her to another panicked attempt to break her bonds. She used what limited range of motion she had to rub her wrists against the tree, hoping the rough bark would eventually wear through the cord.

The goblins were too occupied with the meat to pay her any heed. After the larger ones had stuffed themselves, they turned away from the carcass and retired to their tents, filling the camp with wheezy snores. Even the fat matriarch who had eaten so greedily appeared appeased, and her wide head lolled to the side in a doze. Her young nestled themselves in the folds of her skin like rodents squeezing into burrows. With the feast winding down and sleep falling over the camp, Corvala felt a faint hope return. She would break her bonds before they woke and escape without notice. Rubbing the cords against the tree trunk, she felt some of the fibers snap. She worked vigorously yet carefully, keeping an eye on those among the goblins who were still awake.

A few smaller ones fought over what remained of the carcass. Two of them were locked in a pulling match over a foreleg. The smallest of their lot took advantage of the diversion and broke off a rib bone with some skin still attached. The others snarled and chased him away, sending him scrambling up a tree near Corvala. She stopped her work on the cords and pretended to be asleep. She watched the goblin with one eye half-open. At first, he took no notice of her as he huddled over his prize, eating what little meat and marrow he could find. As he chewed and sucked on the bone, however, his watchful gaze happened to fall upon her. He stopped chewing and stared at her for a long time. Then a mischievous grin of sharp yellow teeth spread across his beastly jaws. Dropping the bone, he crept down the tree and limped over to where she was tied. He cast a wary glance at the others. They were still fighting over the scraps. Corvala could see the goblin's little mind at work. He was wondering if he could get away with taking this prize for himself. He was behind the section of ruined wall, after all—no one would notice him steal a few bites in secret. He turned his yellow eyes back to Corvala and licked his lips.

Too frightened to feign sleep any longer, Corvala began to tremble. The goblin came in close and clamped a warty hand over her mouth, cutting off her scream. With his fingers pressed under her nose, the stench of rotten frog burned in her nostrils. The goblin looked her body over, deciding where to begin. His eyes locked onto her throat. Before he made his bite, he turned one more glance at the camp to make sure the others weren't looking.

Crack!

A large stone smashed into his head. The goblin fell to the ground in a lifeless heap, half his skull caved in. Corvala looked up. There in the darkness holding a bloody stone stood a figure—a bearded man, tall and broad-shouldered.

Fah!

Corvala gasped. Life and death roiled inside her, and a wet cry welled up in her throat. Her father knelt beside her and put a finger to his lips. Time to focus; time to stay quiet. Exodus put a hand on her bonds and pointed to the nearby branch where his sheathed sword hung. Corvala choked back her sobs of sudden relief and nodded.

Crouching low among the stunted trees, Exodus crept over to his sword. He didn't grab it right away. Corvala understood why: it seemed too easy, the belt and sheath just left out for the taking. Although goblins acted like wild beasts, they were sly and sometimes known to outwit humans with clever tricks. Sure enough, Exodus pinched something that took Corvala a long moment to make out—a black thread, practically invisible in the dark, tied to the pommel. The string went up into the trees and connected to a dozen tiny bells hidden in the branches. Carefully, Exodus gently held the thread and gnawed through its fibers. Once the sword was freed from its alarm, he cut his daughter's bonds. Her arms and legs felt sweet release, and relief flooded her. Freedom from this horrible place was at hand. Exodus came back around the tree to face her, making gestures and trying to communicate something. Through her teary eyes, she couldn't perceive his meaning. She cared only that he was with her and swung her arms around his neck in a tight embrace.

As she leaned into her father, Corvala felt a pull on her tunic. There, on her sleeve, the end of a black thread had been sewed into the hem. The other end of the string ran up into the trees. It pulled on an assortment of tiny bells that, at once, chimed in alarm. The few goblins gathered around the carcass looked up from their feeding. Upon seeing Corvala free and a man with her, they let up shrill cries for all of the camp to hear. Corvala froze, but her father left no room for panic. He took her by the hand and pressed her into the corner of the ruined wall. Pushing her behind him, he took up a fighting stance with his sword.

'Get ready,' he said.

She wanted to run and get out of there. Foolish maybe—to stumble through a darkening forest at the end of the day. The goblins would come after her and overwhelm her as they had before. At least with their backs against the wall, they wouldn't get taken from behind. It was a small assurance, however, in the face of so many goblins springing from their tents with clubs and spears in hand. Too many for her father to face, even with his size and steel. He stood as a deep-rooted oak in the face of a torrent. How long would he hold before they brought him down? The goblins howled and charged, gibbering and bristling with spears.

Then, from beyond the clearing, a new figure arrived: a dark-skinned woman clad in gray, her short hair swept back and her eyes bright with lightning. Serapha leaped from the tree line and ploughed into the charging goblins' flank. She took two by the throat and slammed them to the ground.

What happened to Serapha after, Corvala couldn't tell. A bloodthirsty mass of chaos engulfed her view. Whatever Serapha had done, it was enough to throw off the goblins' charge and keep the full brunt of the attack from coming down on Exodus. The first wave of the creatures crashed against the edge of his torcarda blade. A deep gash blossomed across the lead goblin's chest.

Before this, Corvala had never seen her father deal out death with his sword. She knew he used it to kill men, but he never talked about it. She had only seen his sword clean and sheathed, hanging above the fireplace as if it were nothing more than a relic in long slumber. Now it had awoken—wild and naked, flecked with gore and red with firelight. It was a flashing terror in her father's hands. Grim-faced, he lunged at the goblins, cutting them down one after the other.

A dead goblin fell at Corvala's feet. She stared for a moment. To her surprise, she snatched up the dead goblin's spear, her hands acting of their own instinct to survive, to grasp onto something in the heat of battle. She'd never held a spear before, let alone used one, and this one was tiny in her hands. In her desperation, she stabbed at anything that drew near, her thrusts aimless amid too many moving bodies. She did manage to poke a goblin in the shoulder. It turned its attention to her—a fatal distraction as her father cleaved into its skull. The sweeps of his sword cut a wide semi-circle around the beleaguered pair, but the goblins had numbers, and step by encroaching step, they pressed their attack. The semi-circle grew smaller and smaller.

The heat of survival kept Corvala stabbing into the bristling mob. An enraged cry rose around her and dimly she realized it was her own. Then a tooth-studded club struck her in the leg, her battle cry turning to a yelp as she stumbled. The club-wielder raised his weapon but, as he did so, Exodus drove his sword through the goblin's chest. The move exposed his side and Corvala saw it and shouted a warning—all too late. Two goblins speared her father in the calf and thigh. Exodus pivoted and came down on his attackers, hacking away an arm, severing a throat. Spears stuck out of him and his wounds bled freely. While he made no wince or grimace, his wounded leg shuddered beneath him. Sweat dripped from his brow. The goblins must have sensed his weariness, and their snouts twitched at the scent of his blood. With savage cries, they surged forward. Too many spears and clubs. Too many toothy mouths hungry for human flesh. Corvala felt the building despair within her break and spill its icy flow through her veins. She knelt, frozen before the coming onslaught.

Then a sleek form broke through the goblin wall, knocking several down. *Serapha*. Corvala half-rose as the woman strode towards Exodus, snapping limbs and necks with brutal efficiency. Exodus lunged to meet her.

As Corvala watched, her fear gave way to awe. Serapha's inhuman speed and precision; Exodus's sword ringing a song of scarlet violence. The goblins crashed upon fist and sword, the dead and wounded strewn around Exodus's and Serapha's feet. A collective shudder went through the mob and, at once, its ferocity burst. Those goblins who could still run fled into the woods, while the wounded limped and crawled away. The camp emptied, leaving only the matriarch, who was too slow to keep up with her brood. She squawked in fright, and her terrified young sought refuge deep within the folds of her fat as she waddled into the depths of the forest. Goblins were creatures of ambush and quick swarming, and the fight had been taken from them—a battle drawn out too long. The smell of their blood hung thick in the air.

Exodus, his daughter now safe, knelt beside Corvala to check her over. She was more worried about him.

'You're bleeding,' she said, looking to the ragged holes in his leg. 'We need to see to that.'

'Later,' he said. 'We need to get moving. The goblins could regroup and return.' He wiped the blood from his sword and sheathed it. Corvala stilled his urgency by taking his hand.

'You're alive,' she said.

She pressed her forehead into her father's chest and hugged him. His body was tense for a moment, the vestiges of violence still thrumming through his sinews. Then he loosened and put a hesitant hand on Corvala's head.

'But how did you find me?' she asked.

'I came with her,' he said, nodding to Serapha. Corvala looked over to see Serapha standing just a few paces away, unobtrusive and silent, waiting for the two of them to finish their reunion.

'She found me belly-up in a creek,' Exodus continued. 'Told me she'd been tracking you after you ran away.'

Corvala looked to the ground to hide the hot flush of embarrassment in her cheeks.

'I went looking for tubers to add to our food bag,' she lied. 'Then the goblins found me.' She couldn't bring herself to tell him the real reason—that she had gone the way of her mother, chasing dreams and visions into the woods. She added, 'You must be wondering why we're out here in the first place.'

'She told me the story,' Exodus said, waving a hand at Serapha. 'At least, what could be said while on a goblin hunt.'

'So… you know what happened after the trial?'

'I learned enough.' He turned away from Corvala and faced Serapha. 'I know we're in something deep.'

Corvala nervously looked back and forth between her father and Serapha. Whatever cohesion these two had shared in the battle gave way to something else. Exodus now filled the space between them with a hard look. Serapha, of course, revealed nothing of what she thought or felt.

'Why do you want my daughter?' Exodus asked.

'I am to escort her to the Elijah Tree so that she may use the code within her to activate the defense system.'

Exodus took several pained steps forwards, putting himself between Serapha and Corvala. Corvala instinctively moved in to help him, but Exodus shot her a stern look.

'I agreed in desperation,' he said to Serapha. 'You would help me find her. In exchange, I would aid in whatever you planned on doing. Now you've told me what that is, and it sounds like witchcraft. And that's something we can't join.' Exodus reached for Corvala's hand and began backing away. 'You helped me save her, and for that I'm grateful. But we'll be going our separate ways.'

'We made an agreement. There is no time to re-establish the terms. We need efficiency; my energy levels are limited.'

'I have always been a man of my word... until now. I can't keep my word when it's given to a demon.'

A swift punch struck Exodus in the chest, knocking him back several feet. He swiftly recovered his balance and readied his sword before him. Serapha stood in a fighter's stance, her fist held out.

'What are you doing?' Corvala cried.

'This is not a negotiation,' Serapha said flatly, her words directed at Exodus. 'I am taking your daughter to the Elijah Tree with or without your approval. You can comply, or I will incapacitate you.'

Exodus stood ready, expression dark, set to fight to whatever end.

'Stop!' Corvala jumped between them and turned to her father. 'Don't do this. You can't beat her. She's too powerful. Just look at what she did here—without weapons, even. You can't beat that.'

Exodus didn't back down.

'Come on, fah,' said Corvala. 'It's just a walk to a tree. It can't be that bad. We'll go and be done with it. Please, I can't lose you again.'

Exodus eyed his opponent.

'I'm sorry, Corvala,' he said at length, 'but I can't lose you either.'

He sprang forwards in a charge, making to drive the sword into Serapha's chest. Serapha was too quick. She blocked the strike with her arm, and the impact sounded with a metal clang—as though her bones were made of iron. A brief moment of faint astonishment passed over Exodus's face. However small, it was all the distraction Serapha needed. She delivered a strike to his arm, knocking the sword from his hand and sending it spinning through the air. It landed with a thud in the middle of the goblin camp. Then, in one swift move, Serapha twisted his arm and slammed him belly-first into the dirt. She drove her knees into his back and pinned him to the ground.

'Do you yield?' Serapha said.

He pulled against her hold. She wrenched his arm higher, up between the shoulder blades, driving the side of his face deeper into the dirt.

Corvala cried out and rushed to her father's side. She tried to drive a wedge between the two. Serapha wouldn't budge.

'Do you yield?' she repeated.

Exodus didn't. Still, he pulled against her and pressed his free hand to the ground in an attempt to rise. Serapha's hold over him, however, was just as strong as his will to resist it.

Serapha's free hand grabbed hold of Corvala's wrist, and Corvala felt her arm light up with pain. The shock swept a sharp edge through her body. She screamed: a cry to strike against her father's ears.

Exodus groaned, his muscles swelling, veins popping beneath his skin. Steadily, his wrists shifted in Serapha's hold, and she had to reposition her grip. It was all Exodus could do. Corvala saw her father's body trembling, straining against his limits, sinews thickening horribly. Then she felt another shock and screamed again.

'Stop!' she cried, but not to Serapha. She leaned into her father's ear. 'Stop fighting,' she trembled through gritted teeth.

'Yield,' Serapha commanded.

Exodus stopped pulling, but his body was still tense. Corvala could see the fire remained in his eyes.

'I'll make no pact with a demon,' he said in a low growl.

'I am not a demon,' Serapha replied.

'Then what are you?'

'I am an instrument.'

Corvala could tell the answer didn't satisfy him. She bit her lip, hoping he wouldn't start another fruitless match of strength—and that she wouldn't get shocked again.

'I can see that there is a moral code you follow,' Serapha said. 'I do not know all that your code entails, but I would conjecture that my mission would align with it. The object that fell from the sky during your trial was not a falling star. It was the transport of an intruder who is not permitted on this world. The intruder may be a threat. My mission is to address this possible threat, and your daughter is a critical part of this mission.'

Exodus grunted in frustration. 'What are you asking her to do?'

'She will need to make contact with the tree in order to connect with it. Once she does, the Elijah Tree will activate its defense system.'

'What would the tree do to her?'

'It will receive the code within her. She will not be harmed.'

'And what would you do with us after that?'

'Nothing. I will be done with her. So, both of you would be free to plot a course of your choosing.'

Corvala watched her father. For a long while, he said nothing, his mind weighing heavy on the options. There was still resistance in him.

'I have to complete this mission,' Corvala said, coming in close to him. 'It's the only way I can get this code out of me. Mom had it, too. And grandma. It runs in the blood. That's where the madness comes from. Now I have a chance to get rid of it. But only if I complete the mission first.'

Exodus met her eyes. He stared deeply for many moments, reading what all of this meant to her. Then his body fell slack.

'I yield,' he breathed.

Serapha released Corvala but kept Exodus pinned down. She produced the spur at the base of her palm and jabbed it into his leg. Exodus shook some as Corvala took his hand.

'Don't worry. I know what she's doing.'

Serapha reached back and placed her hand on where he had been speared. A warm light emanated under her palm. When she lifted her hand, scars lay where there had been jagged wounds. Serapha released her hold and helped him to his feet.

It appeared the fight in Exodus had been gently pushed aside, for he didn't look to strike out at Serapha or make for his sword. Instead, he ran a finger over the new scars on his thigh and calf.

'What are you?' he asked again, his voice hushed. Corvala could swear there was a hint of wonder in his tone.

'As I said,' replied Serapha, 'I am an instrument.'

Exodus scratched his head and looked into the woods, his brow heavy. At last, he walked over to where his sword lay and picked it up. Corvala stiffened, wondering if he'd try something, but he merely slid it back into its sheath and affixed it to his belt.

'God cuts our path,' he said solemnly. 'We'd better walk it.'

Chapter 16

The old beggar Jerum held out his empty wooden bowl. He sat with legs crossed, leaning back against the cracked wall of the pottery shop. It was his usual spot in Ryperia's market—the street corner where Trout Way and Stag Way met. In this part of the market stood the booths of furriers with strings of animal pelts and linen merchants hawking colorfully dyed fabrics. The scent of spices and roasting meat wafted in the breeze from the food vendors down Stag Way. The crowds were packed so tightly that a horse would have had trouble walking through. Over it all was the din of commerce—the sellers calling out, 'What can I get you, my dear?' and the customers haggling, 'Too much, too much.' In the shadows of the background, mongrels and street urchins watched and waited for the scraps of tossed-aside food.

Amid the bustling currents of people, Jerum was a fixed point. Crowds moved here and there, but Jerum remained in his spot, as permanent as the wall against which he leaned. Always there but hardly noticed. He'd picked out that spot many years ago, and it had been his ever since. It was a strategic place for a beggar, one that put him near the flow of foot traffic. The corner also gave him a view of Ryperia's palace rising over the roof-tops. *One day I'll get the honor of walking beneath its high roof.* That's what he used to tell himself when he was younger and full of ambition, but now he knew better.

With the intersection being as busy as it was, Jerum was of course not the only panhandler there. Others had their places, and each tried to catch the windfall of the crowd's charity in different ways. Some juggled, some dressed as clowns. The orphans with soot-stained faces wandered the intersection, using their heartbroken eyes to garner pity and coins. The most successful of all the beggars was Haldo. The bright-faced young man enter-tained the crowds by playing his trilling flute and snapping witty remarks between songs. Everyone knew that once his hat was filled with money he would slip into the tavern down the street.

Jerum was too old for tricks. All he had was his spot and his constancy in sitting there. Every day his arm held out a bowl, a gnarled tree limb holding out a bird nest. And every day he managed to collect a few pieces of copper—just enough for a hunk of bread for an evening meal.

Lately, things had been different. The coins had stopped dropping so regularly. Even Haldo was having trouble calling the crowd's attention. Ever since the gold-en man Dane had arrived in the city, people had been… different. It had not been an obvious shift; rather, it was something only a beggar who spent his day watching the world go by would notice. People moved more slowly and talked more quietly. Even the market seemed to have lost some of its vigor, as if an unseen fog was muting the noise. Whispers about the golden man's wonders passed like blown leaves through the streets.

'And she said when his eyes fell upon her, her ulcers were healed! Right then and there!'

'I heard he came from the heavens and can call upon an entire legion of…'

Jerum was accustomed to people ignoring him, but now they had a slight dreamy glaze over their eyes, like a cloudy film. Strangely enough, he understood. Although his bowl and stomach weren't as full as before, he didn't feel their lack. He felt safe and content knowing that the all-powerful Dane dwelled in the city. Jerum looked to the bright light emanating from the palace's spire. Nothing could go wrong with a god watching over your home.

It was about midday when a pair of city guards came strolling through the market. Nothing unusual—guards regularly passed through this intersection on their daily patrols. At first, Jerum didn't notice them. They stopped and pointed at him from across the way.

'What about that one?' said one of the guards.

The other rubbed his chin and nodded. 'He'll do.'

The two of them walked over to Jerum and looked down to where he sat.

'You there!' said the first guard. 'Come with us. Our master wishes to see you.'

Jerum gave them a leery eye. 'I didn't do nothing.'

'It's not like that,' said the second guard. 'The golden man—he has something for you.'

'The man in gold! Bah!' Jerum grunted, shying back into the wall. 'You think I'm stupid.'

'It's no trick,' said the first guard, his voice growing sharper. 'Now get up!'

'He picked you,' the second guard added. 'It's a high honor.'

'He wouldn't want that,' Jerum huffed. 'You're just bothering an old beggar.'

Then he looked up at the palace with its bright light shining from the spire. As he took in the raw and enchanting light, he found himself wanting to believe what they said was true. His worries faded. He felt the warm awe and wonder the palace exuded. He hardly noticed the guards pull him to his feet.

A wide grin spread across Jerum's face and showed his three remaining teeth. 'The man in gold chose me?'

'Sure,' the second guard said, half-heartedly swatting at a gnat buzzing by his nose.

'The man in gold chose me,' Jerum repeated in quiet awe, his eyes misted with wonder. He followed the guards down the street and up towards the palace. At last, he would walk beneath the high ceilings and see the carved wooden pillars.

Not long after, a nearby linen merchant who stood idly between trades happened to let her bored gaze fall to the spot where Jerum had been sitting. It seemed to her that something should have been there. She pondered it for a moment but couldn't put her finger on it. Then, a prospective customer neared her booth, inspecting the turquoise linens. She turned to attend to the customer and forgot all about Jerum's empty spot.

Dane paced the throne room. His helmet was off. Although the suit was powerful and its interior comfortable, it got rather stuffy at times. Now his helmet sat on the throne's armrest, allowing fresh air to soothe his fragile, hideous head—a skinned plum set upon a tottering neck. His bald scalp was webbed with blue veins. His face was practically featureless: his nose worn down to a nub and his lips thin and colorless.

Exposed, he had shut the doors and windows so that no sunlight would burn his translucent skin. A table with food had been set out for him—fresh bread, thick cuts of beef, fine cheeses from the south, and bunches of deep purple grapes—more than one man could eat. Of course, he couldn't eat *any* of it.

In the half-dark, he paced the throne room alone. Something was troubling him. He didn't understand why he was so nervous. This should have been easy.

You must do this, he told himself, *to survive.*

There was a knock on the throne room door. Dane strode over to the throne and returned the golden helmet to his head.

'Enter,' he said.

In walked the pair of guards he had sent out into the city. They had brought back a beggar just as he had asked—an old man with long greasy hair and rags that barely covered his emaciated body. The guards left without a word.

The beggar, thinking himself alone in the vast dark room, trembled. With wide eyes, he looked about the walls and ceiling like a child lost in an old museum. Then his eyes fell upon Dane, who was standing by the throne, obscured by shadow. Upon seeing the gold armor, the beggar fell to his knees and pressed his face to the ground.

'My master!' he cried.

Dane took in a deep breath. *This is really happening...*

He took an object from his belt, a device he called a *metovita.* It looked like a metal star that filled the palm of his hand. There were glassy pads on one side and little wires that stuck out from the points. The wires automatically attached themselves to small outlets on one of his gauntlets. Once the metovita was connected, tiny needles on the inside of his suit pricked Dane's skin, ready to inject.

Dane walked slowly to the beggar.

'Stand,' Dane commanded.

The beggar did as he was told. Dane put the metovita against the beggar's chest. He paused. The old beggar looked up at him. Here was a face streaked with grime and deeply creased with age—the face of a human. The eyes were so trusting, and tears of joy flowed from them.

'I've waited so long to come here,' the beggar smiled, showing his three remaining teeth.

Dane pulled his hand back and turned away.

'Guard!' he called.

Immediately, one of the guards from earlier opened the doors.

'Do any of you have a sack or bag on hand?' Dane asked.

The guard didn't have anything of the sort, but his hands unconsciously went to his pants pockets and his eyes stupidly roved the throne room as if there would be a sack just lying around.

'I'm afraid I don't, my master,' the guard said.

'Go find me one,' said Dane, waving the guard off and sending him on his errand.

As Dane waited, the atmosphere in the throne room grew uncomfortable. There stood the old beggar, wringing his filthy hands, not knowing what he should do or say. He stared at Dane with excited expectancy. Dane couldn't endure the awkwardness. He was a man accustomed to the comforts and pleasures of the Dream; in worlds of his imaginings, he had long since banished such feelings.

'Sit there,' he said suddenly, pointing to the table with food. 'Eat.'

The old beggar looked at the table, dumbfounded. His expression said, 'How could this be for me?' Apparently not wanting to disobey an order or disappoint Dane, he gingerly stepped over to the table and sat down. At first, he nibbled at some bread, but it didn't take long for his hunger to overcome his apprehension. Soon he was devouring a thick cut of meat.

As the beggar ate, Dane went over to one of the windows and opened it. He stared out at the city below and the walls of the gorge beyond, his thoughts far from the view.

You're like a god, he told himself. *You're above all this. They're nothing but insects. No one misses an insect.*

At last, the guard returned holding an empty potato sack.

'Good,' Dane stated. 'Put it on his head.' Dane turned to look back out the window so he wouldn't have to endure the beggar's confused expression as the sack covered his face.

'Bring him to me,' Dane commanded.

The guard yanked the beggar away from the table and brought him to stand before Dane.

'Leave us,' said Dane.

The guard nodded and left the throne room, the doors closing behind him with a deep bang as if to emphasize the heavy finality of what Dane was about to do.

Then, with the resolve of a man set on jumping into cold water, Dane turned from the open window and pressed the metovita hard against the beggar's chest. There was no face now to prick his conscience. Just a sack.

Now! he commanded himself.

He activated the metovita and it began to hum and glow red. Dane gasped—energy was flowing into him from the beggar's chest, the tiny pinpricks in his suit feeding his withered body.

The sensation was incredible—it swept over him and sparked like lightning through every fiber of his body and every synapse of his mind. He sensed the spinning of the molecules within him and the spinning of the universe without. The symphony orchestra of life—the pounding percussion of anger, the triumphant brass of joy, the hissing strings of fear, the solemn woodwinds of love and longing—all of it sounded at once and crescendoed into a fortissimo that shook Dane's being.

He was Prometheus stealing the gods' fire. He was the conquistador drinking from the Fountain of Youth. He was Adam biting into the fruit. To take a man's life and his essence and bring it into his own—there was nothing Dane could compare it to, not even in the Dream. What had been his life until that moment? What had been the joys he had sought before? Neither ecstatic drug nor romantic climax could compare. The pleasures of the Dream were but dim reflections of what Dane felt now.

Here was his immortality.

The beggar moaned in agony. He pounded on Dane's chest and tried to push away, but there was no breaking free from that metal grasp. As the life drained from him, he grew weak, the fight in him diminishing. His fists no longer pounded but feebly tapped against the chest plate in gentle, languid movements. Then his knees gave out from under him.

Dane caught him.

'Stand!' he commanded, annoyed by the beggar's weakness. 'You still have some strength yet.'

Whatever reservations Dane had felt before were completely washed away by the flood of pleasure that swept over him. He drained the life from the beggar's chest, greedily taking in every drop.

Soon there was no more moaning from the beggar. No more breath. The metovita stopped humming and glowing and the flood of pleasure subsided. Dane let the lifeless body fall to the floor. He stared at it, feeling like an infant pushed away from a breast run dry.

'Guards!' he called out, and immediately several guards returned to the throne room. 'Bring me another.'

Chapter 17

The pine had been chewed to bits. All that remained of the once towering spike of timber were the wood chips strewn across the forest floor and a splayed trunk half wrenched from the earth, its roots still clinging to the topsoil. Exodus knelt, grasping a handful of soil and letting it run through his fingers.

'A dragon did this.'

'What makes you think that?' Corvala asked.

Her father removed something from the stump and tossed it to her. It was a tooth as long and sharp as a woodsman's knife. Too big to belong to a bear or a manticore. Whatever had left this here was big enough to do to a tree what a dog did to sticks. Corvala felt her heart quicken, and her gaze instinctively searched the woods around her.

'One has moved into Thorn Shroud,' her father mused. 'That would explain why the manticores are moving away from the forest's interior.'

Some of the nearby trees had great scrapes across them—some as wide as wagon beds. Resin had dripped in and scabbed over where the bark had been torn away. The trail of scrape marks went down a hill and disappeared into the forest's depths.

'We're not going that way, are we?' Corvala asked.

'No,' Serapha replied. 'That is our way.'

They moved on from the ruined tree and went farther into the trackless wilderness where the branches blocked out the sun and the columns of trunks created a monotonous maze. All the travelers had to go on was Serapha's guidance and her assurance that she knew the way. It was midmorning, and yet Corvala was already growing weary. She hadn't slept well the night before. There had been a chill in the air, and her bedding had been nothing more than supple branches and piles of dead needles. The earth had sapped Corvala's warmth even as she'd huddled next to her father. But there'd been something else, too—the fear that she would dream again and follow her mother on another trail of madness. Despite her building exhaustion from the sleepless nights before, her mind kept bringing up the ever-blinking worry of sleepwalking and wandering off. The madness—the code Serapha called 'Sky Mantle'—had awoken from its long hibernation. It had shown Corvala what it could do: take her by the mind and throw her body to the beasts. Who knew where the depths of sleep would take her? So, she had skimmed upon its surface, drifting in and out of the darkness of her present mind, opening her eyes each time to find Serapha standing watch, the woman's gaze ever piercing the night beyond.

Corvala must have given into her weariness at some point during the night because she'd been deep in sleep when her father woke her in the morning. He had gathered up wild carrots and edible mushrooms. It wasn't much, but it was something to put in their stomachs. When offered, Serapha declined their food. Corvala hadn't seen her eat or drink anything since they'd first met. She wondered if creatures like Serapha—an 'instrument', or whatever she was—ever needed food, water, or sleep. More items to add to this woman's growing list of oddities.

Now they were deep into the rhythm of their hike, putting the chewed-up tree far behind them. Breakfast had been hours ago, and who knew when—or what— their next meal would be. Probably more scavenged vegetables, raw and gritty. Corvala remembered the food she had packed up in the saddlebags for the journey, ripped away by goblins. What she wouldn't do now for that dried meat and slightly stale bread. The thought of it made Corvala's stomach growl. Her mind drifted to roast pheasant, its grease dripping as it turned over a fire. All she would need was a taste. Just a wing… and a leg… and the breast. Maybe she'd eat the whole thing. And a warm slice of bread with a pad of butter melting into it…

A playful chatter in the treetops interrupted her daydreaming. Corvala looked up to see a troop of nimakas, perhaps a dozen in all, jumping from limb to limb in the nearby trees. They were cat-sized creatures with fiery orange fur and mischief written all over their faces. Their lanky limbs never kept still, and their spidery fingers trembled for something to snatch. In the valley, they were known as the little bandits who broke rabbit snares and raided chicken coops. Now they jabbered away, their squeaks and screeches sounding like a long string of incoherent questions. Corvala just rolled her eyes at them, and Exodus and Serapha paid them no heed. The nimakas, still shrieking, followed the small company, shaking branches and tossing down twigs and pinecones. Some even dared to swing down and rap Corvala on the top of her head. Up and down they went with their little game. In one moment Corvala knocked away a hand trying to pull on her braid and, in the next, she felt droplets on her face—a nimaka peeing onto her path. Corvala sprang away from the stream of urine. Then she felt something pulled off her back. One of the little beasts had snatched her fiddle right out of its sheath.

'Sir William!' she cried. Her hand reached out to take it back, but the thief scurried up into the high branches with its new prize.

'Give it back!' Corvala yelled.

The nimaka screeched and leaped away, springing from tree to tree. Corvala cursed and ran along the forest floor, giving chase. From behind, her father yelled something at her, but she didn't stop to find out what. She was too busy keeping her eye on the fiddle above while making sure not to trip on exposed roots and downed branches in her path. Pushing through a patch of undergrowth, she came to an eroded edge of turf and nearly stumbled down a steep slope. A wide pit lay before her and, at its bottom, a small fetid pond. The nimaka scampered through the trees dwindling at the pit's edge and came to a stop at a high bough well out of Corvala's reach. It began to investigate the fiddle—sniffing at it and working its jaws around the edges. Corvala grit her teeth and clutched at her heart as the creature banged on the wood and twanged a string.

'Stop it!' she cried.

The nimaka became quickly disinterested in its find—not food but just another piece of wood in the forest—and tossed the fiddle aside. Corvala froze and her heart leaped within her chest as she watched the fiddle spin through the air. The weave of pliable branches below slowed its fall and, after several agonizing moments, the fiddle fell with a dull thud. It skidded, rolled, and slid down the sloped sides of the pit before dropping into the pond. Corvala hurried after it, sliding down the scree and loose dirt to the pond's edge. Just as the fiddle's body was filling with water and about to sink, Corvala grabbed it by its neck and fished it out.

She began shaking the water from the body of the instrument, cursing quietly, then stopped—something buzzed. Something else crackled. She looked up to see Serapha at the other side, her arm plunged into the shallows. Bolts of jagged light shot from her hands and illuminated the depths.

'What are you doing?' Corvala shouted.

Serapha pulled her arm out of the water and the greenish pulsing light in the pond ceased. Her hand was glowing just as it had when she had given Corvala a shock.

'I was saving you from being eaten,' Serapha said flatly.

Before Corvala could ask what she meant by that, a slew of small fish, bullfrogs, and painted turtles plopped up to the surface—all dead, their bellies to the sky. Then came a huge shape floating up from under the lily pads and algae—not an arm's length from where the fiddle had fallen into the water. Corvala yelped at the sight of it and stumbled back several steps. Whatever it was, it wasn't moving. Catching her breath and steadying her nerves, she took a step closer, squinting at the beast. The slippery skin that blended in with the water plants, the bulging eyes the size of dinner plates, the mouth large enough to swallow a person... it was a devil frog, a titan of an amphibian larger than an ox. Now it was dead, floating on the surface like a small island.

Her father rushed down the steep ground to the pond's edge where she stood. He gave one look to the dead devil frog and then led Corvala away from the pond.

'I thought you would've learned by now not to run off in these woods,' he said, carefully controlled anger bubbling beneath his flat tone.

'I had to,' Corvala responded, hugging the fiddle to her chest. 'Mother gave it to me.'

To this, Exodus said nothing.

The two of them found Serapha waiting for them on the forest's level ground. Corvala was about to thank Serapha for saving her when she noticed something strange. Serapha, eyes half-closed, was in one of her trances again. This time a harsh humming noise came from her body as though her insides were straining to work. A moment later the noise stopped and Serapha's eyes opened fully.

'Are you all right?' Corvala asked.

'I used most of my remaining energy in the water. I am now at a critical level. I cannot make the distance to the Elijah Tree.'

She didn't appear tired. Indeed, her appearance looked as unbreakably healthy as always, her posture unfatigued. But Corvala didn't think it was her place to question the person who had just saved her life. And hadn't she said something about waking up from hibernation and starting with her energy low?

'Take some rest then,' Corvala said. 'We'll get you some food. But you have to eat this time.'

'I cannot recover with rest and food as you do. I need a power source that produces electricity. Only when I am recharged at this kind of source will I be able to escort you to the Elijah Tree.'

An odd statement. Then again, this woman was altogether odd. She produced lightning from her hands and eyes. It reasoned—in a strange way—that she would live off lightning.

'Where can we get it?' said Exodus.

Corvala gave her father a sideways look. Was he suddenly interested in Serapha's welfare? Perhaps he wanted to make sure she was truly weak before they made themselves free of her.

'According to my internal mapping system,' Serapha replied, 'there is a possible source approximately nine miles from here. If the source has maintained a measure of integrity, then I will be able to use it to recharge.'

'Let's go then,' Exodus said.

Corvala blinked at this. Here was the man who had fought with Serapha, resisting her with every ounce of his strength. Now he wanted to help her. It didn't make sense.

They left the pond and began their detour, Serapha leading the way. Once she was far enough ahead, Corvala came in step beside her father and whispered, 'I thought you wanted out of this. You tried to kill her.'

'I was desperate then.'

'So now you've seen the light?'

'I won't pretend to understand all of this.' Her father shook his head. 'Do you remember our encounter with Morgan Capel a few days before the trial?'

'How could I forget?'

'I wasn't much different than him.'

Corvala elbowed his side. 'Oh, go on! You're not that bad.'

'Think about what he did then.'

'Gave you the spit even after you saved Rhonie.'

'Did I act so differently?' His question was colored with a tinge of guilt. He looked ahead to Serapha. 'And she's saved you twice now.'

He wasn't entirely correct. Serapha had also saved her from the Capel gang in the underground chamber and from the mob that had stormed their house, so the count for rescues was really up to four. Her father had only been conscious for two of them, and Corvala wasn't about to interrupt him with that detail. What she knew only reinforced his point.

'What do you think she is?' Corvala asked. 'A demon?'

Exodus scratched under his chin. 'Don't know. The devil and his demons kill and destroy. This woman heals. I've only seen her kill goblins and that devil frog.'

'So you trust her.'

'No,' he said, his tone becoming grim and his eyes narrowing. Corvala could see there was conflict within him. 'A rancher protects his calves only to slaughter them himself. Who knows what she has planned for you? But... if she speaks true, this might be the best chance at getting you cured.'

For several moments he said nothing more, and Corvala thought he'd leave it at that. Then, under his breath: 'Your mother would want me to try.'

Chapter 18

On the outskirts of Dawn's Landing, a group of women gathered around a well to fill their jars and share the town gossip. Their chatter stopped when one of the children playing nearby let out a frightened cry. Down the road came a man riding a wulgyre. There were no thumping hooves to announce its coming; this creature moved on silent paws. The man was cloaked in gray, wore a metal helmet, and carried a metal staff topped with jade.

'Rook!' one of the women gasped.

She and the others dropped their jars and gathered up their children, pulling them back from the road to cover their little faces with their hands. As the man passed them by, the women kept their eyes to the ground and muttered prayers over the children huddled about their legs.

Vlaren was unmoved by their regard for him. He understood. This backwater town would certainly have its share of stories when it came to Rooks. Vlaren had heard them all. Rooks could stare into your soul and find the gravest of your sins. They made entire villages disappear on account of one guilty person. And, of course, they could stunt a child's growth upon eye contact. It was rubbish—most of it, anyway. Vlaren never disputed the stories since a frightening reputation came in handy at times. No doubt the women would draw circles in the air after he had passed them by.

He rode Lobeka towards town. Before he got through the outskirts, a man wearing a wide-brimmed hat and a sword sheathed at his side came up the road to meet him.

'Hail there, Rook,' he said, raising his hands. 'We were expecting you.'

The message of boundaries was clear. The little powers-that-be didn't want Vlaren riding his beast into the heart of town. A Rook would cause too much of a disturbance. Through the holes of his helmet, Vlaren set his dark eyes upon the man. The man looked away, acting as though something down the road had caught his attention.

'You must be the sheriff,' said Vlaren.

'That I am. Kilagrin's my name.' The introduction was clearly out of habit, for the sheriff flinched when he realized what he had done: given his name—his precious mark of identity—to a Rook. What power had he handed over to this hunter who shifted through the holy and unholy realms?

The superstitions of these people would never cease.

'Kilagrin,' Vlaren said, ruminating on the name and watching the sheriff grit his teeth at the sound of it. 'I'd like to see where the sighting happened.'

'Yes, sir.'

The sheriff, quick to obey, led the way on foot while Vlaren rode behind. The wulgyre kept pace with the sheriff's hurried steps. Kilagrin would often cast a wary look over his shoulder to catch sight of the beast's wolfish-feline eyes or her muzzle, which was nearly at a level with his chest. He led them around the town to what must have been the Judge's house.

'She stood up there,' he said, pointing to the roof. 'Shouting down on us like something out of a storm.'

'Who did?'

'The demon.'

The sheriff let the word hang out there as if it would hold weight with a Rook. Vlaren gave him only a disinterested *hmm*.

Village folk were quick to blame demons for their own mischief. If there was anything of the Ancients present in a crime, which was rare enough, it was normally only an experiment in forbidden knowledge gone wrong. A closet warlock or witch would stumble upon some text explaining how to forge powerful weapons or craft potions that would give them unnatural abilities. They would work on such things and then—*boom!* Their blazing failure would give them away. Such pursuits were demonic, Vlaren supposed, in the sense that they tried to draw out of the dark powers of the Ancients. But did they involve actual demons? In almost all cases, no.

There was an important distinction between *demons* and the *demonic*. It was like the difference between a blacksmith and his metal or a potter and her clay. Demons created the demonic. They were the invisible spirits that floated on the wind and whispered temptations to unwary minds. The Ancients had heeded these whispers and been inspired to build the machines and devices that had brought about their downfall. The artefacts of that bygone age were demonic. Some things, like guns, still carried power. Others were just scrap, merely bearing the unholy taint.

The difference between *demons* and the *demonic* was sentience. Sometimes demons would enter Ancient machines and give them life and movement. The Rooks had a name for this kind of demon: a machubus. They were rare. Vlaren had never seen one, and neither had his master, Rook Eramez. Eramez's master had reportedly had an encounter, but only once, and it had occurred a long time ago. He had been investigating ruins deep underground. There lay the machubus, trapped under rubble. It had entered the form of a beast with metal limbs and greasy black blood and breathed great plumes of smoke. Vlaren doubted that such a thing had come to Dawn's Landing.

Vlaren got down from his wulgyre and looked over the Judge's house. From the outside, he could see none of the usual signs of attempted devilry. No burns from an explosion. No broken glass.

'Did you search the place?'

'No,' replied the sheriff. 'Thought it best to leave that to you. Didn't want my boys spoiling anything you might find interesting.'

By the way the sheriff was hanging back, Vlaren could tell it wasn't the integrity of the investigation that had kept him from going in the house. He was afraid of that place as if it held an infectious evil. Good. At least the scene had been left undisturbed.

'Some members of our community also saw the demon out in the woods…' Kilagrin tried to explain, but he trailed off. Vlaren wasn't paying attention. He turned away from the sheriff and walked up to the porch, opening the front door and going inside. There was nothing spectacular about the place. A table, a pair of chairs, and some shelves with boxes and jars. A typical house out in the sticks. Vlaren ran his fingers over the table. There was a bit of dust, but no powdery residue from unnatural chemicals. Nothing incriminating in the bedrooms either—just some drawers left open in a rush to gather supplies. Returning to the main room, Vlaren saw something had been recently burned in the fireplace—a book by the looks of it. When Vlaren tried to lift it from the grate, it crumbled to ash. To burn something so valuable as a book—disposed evidence, no doubt.

'Did you find anything?' the sheriff called from outside.

Vlaren ignored him. After a preliminary look, there wasn't much to go on. While a burned book was something of interest, it wasn't enough to ascertain whether a demon had been summoned. He could take the investigation deeper—moving the furniture, searching the loft, lifting the floorboards, and scrutinizing every detail of the place. Indeed, the lure of the Hunt made this method appealing. He enjoyed using his keen senses to find clues that evaded the eyes of others. But the Judge and his daughter were already on the run. He didn't have time for that. Instead, he pressed a button on the side of his helmet. With a mechanical whir, jade lenses filled the round eyeholes.

Here was part of what made Rooks feared: their ability and authority to use magic devices. The helmet, along with the staff, was of Ancient making, given life by small power cells. The Rooks were permitted to use these tools because they aided in the Hunt for other Ancient devices. Magic to dispel magic. Hellfire to fight hellfire. People thought a Rook could see into their souls and discover their secrets. The helmet didn't work that way exactly, but it did give him the ability to see things others couldn't.

Through the lenses, everything took on a greenish tint. Vlaren looked around and saw a trail of ghostly white passing through the house. The Rooks called it etheris— residual energy invisible to the naked eye. The etheris trail took a turn about the rooms then went out the front door. Vlaren followed it outside and stepped back from the house to take in what he saw. What had looked like an ordinary home before now wore an otherworldly veneer. There was a great cloud hanging over the house, and from its mass lanced out misty streaks. An explosion of energy frozen in time—the place where the demon had made her show of power.

Vlaren blinked and adjusted his lenses.

'Is everything all right?' the sheriff asked timidly from behind.

Vlaren must have been staring. So much etheris!

'Go to your mayor,' Vlaren commanded. 'Tell him to double the guard and to double their vigilance. If anything else unusual happens, send word to Pillar Dark right away.'

'What did you see?'

'You only need to know my command. Now, do as I say.'

The sheriff shrank back at the Rook's rebuff, biting his tongue and retreating to town.

Vlaren scanned the surrounding meadow. He spotted the trail of etheris leading from the house towards the forest to the west, the infamous Thorn Shroud. It seemed the stories of these backwoods people could be true after all. What else but a demon—a machubus—could have left behind so much etheris? There was only one way to find out. Vlaren jumped on Lobeka's back and rode after the trail of trace energy. The Hunt was on.

Chapter 19

'Are you going to make it?' Corvala asked.

Serapha's insides groaned again, this time more weakly than before. The farther they had traveled, the more she waned. Her pace had slowed and gave way to spells of jerkiness, but she kept going.

'We are close,' was all she said in reply.

She directed them through a thick growth of ponderosa and lodgepole pines. The sky was overcast, and the hollow voice of the wind sighed through the branches. Corvala thought she could spy something ahead: a gray shape cutting across the forest. A perimeter wall. Or what remained of it.

Approaching the wall, Corvala could see it had been built of thick blocks and reinforced with metal beams. It had once stood as a formidable barrier—perhaps fifteen feet high—but now most of its blocks had toppled over and the beams were rusted and exposed. Serapha led them through a wide breach where the wall had completely crumbled. On the other side lay more gutted structures of various sizes. Some had been reduced to little more than their foundations while others had a few walls still standing, albeit cracked and broken. They were fuzzy with moss and scaly with lichen, absorbed into the earthen tones of the forest. Bones of the Ancient World swallowed up long ago by Thorn Shroud.

Knowing that goblins were drawn to ruins such as these, Corvala kept an eye out for any sign of their presence—a camp of small dwellings or contraptions strung through branches. She stuck close to her father's side as Serapha led them deeper into the decayed settlement. She could tell he didn't approve of their coming here. Although his expression was as serious and focused as usual, the slight narrowing of his eyes betrayed feelings of uncertainty. To enter ruins was to go against the law. It had been one thing to rush into the goblin camp to save Corvala's life, but this was something else. Now they were walking into a forbidden land by their own free will. Considering the other crimes that had been pinned to their names, this might have seemed trivial in comparison, but she knew that this was a—

As they turned the corner of a building, her thoughts halted. Out of the building's shadow, something huge reached for her. Crab-like and metal. Her chest seized and she grasped her father's arm.

He put a hand on her shoulder and steadied her.

'It's all right. See, it's dead.'

The metal crab—which would have stood nearly as tall as Corvala—lay sprawled over the low remains of the building's wall, its many eyes empty and lifeless. A large hole had been blown through its carapace. Looking around, Corvala saw that there were other metal beasts, some like the crab, others larger. They lay in rusted heaps between the trees and among the fallen structures. All dead, all nearly fallen to pieces. History told of how demons had possessed forms such as these. Moving within machines, they had filled the world with fire, smoke, and war, bringing the civilization of the Ancients to its end. The foul spirits had long abandoned these metal husks. Still, Corvala made sure to give them a wide berth.

'What happened here?' she asked.

'There was a battle,' Serapha replied, 'during a time when energy was growing scarce. The soldiers stationed here were defending their power source from invaders.'

'For your sake, let's hope the invaders didn't succeed,' Corvala said.

And for my sake as well.

She couldn't help but think what it would mean for her if this place had nothing to offer Serapha. The mission would be left incomplete, and it was only by completing it that Serapha would cure her. Or, at least, those had been the terms before. Maybe Serapha's current weakness would change the deal. If the mission ended, called on account of energy loss, maybe Serapha could use what little remained in her to cure Corvala. Longing rose in Corvala's chest. Her oncoming madness done away with. No more waiting. No more journey crossing the paths of beasts. She would be free—a new person.

But what of Serapha? She would be left spent and lifeless. They would at least give her the honor of burying her among the metal husks. *If that's what it takes to cure me.* Even though Corvala knew it was an evil thing, she couldn't help thinking it.

Serapha didn't appear discouraged by the remnants of battle and continued to move forwards. Corvala and her father followed her through the ruins, stepping over crumbled walls and rusted war machines. Across their path lay a tree that had been chewed to bits—just like the one they'd seen earlier. The smell of resin lingered in the air.

'The dragon,' Exodus said. 'It's been at work.'

Corvala's eyes followed where her father pointed. There was another tree chewed. Then another and another. Dozens—no, hundreds, the forest gradually thinning out. The three travelers came to the edge of the surviving trees and took cover behind the remains of a crumbled wall. Beneath the overcast sky there lay a clearing, desolate and vast, the land blasted and scorched. Blackened stumps spiked from the earth along with beams of twisted metal. A blight of ash within Thorn Shroud.

What drew Corvala's eye stood at the center of the clearing. Like a behemoth coming out of the earth, a structure of slab and metal rose up out of a rocky hill. It was the largest building Corvala had ever seen, even larger than the buildings in Ryperia, its heights rounded and crowned with three columns. Dozens of thick metal tubes reminding Corvala of veins emerged from its sides in all directions and snaked down the hill, disappearing into the ground.

'What is that?' Corvala whispered in unsettled wonder.

'It is a geothermal powerplant,' Serapha replied with a twitch.

Corvala shook her head, not understanding but also not surprised it would have such a name.

Serapha twitched again. 'It is a facility that possibly contains the energy I need.'

Despite its commanding presence, the structure had suffered considerable decay. It was split with cracks and streaked with rust. One of the walls at its base had a wide opening broken through. Something big had dug into the foundation, pushing up mounds of rock and dirt and forming a tunnel that went into the hill. At the mouth of the tunnel lay piles of bones, elk and deer antlers poking from them.

Corvala didn't know much about dragons, but she had heard somewhere that they were drawn to power. Volcanoes, waterfalls, mountain peaks where lightning struck—places where Mother Nature exuded her strength. It reasoned that dragons would be drawn to Ancient power sources as well.

'Looks like the beast has bedded down right next to what we're looking for,' said Exodus, voicing the same conclusion.

Corvala kept her eyes on the dark throat of the tunnel. She imagined that, at any moment, a large shape would emerge and cross the distance to where they hid. Suddenly the clearing didn't seem so wide anymore, and it felt like the tunnel was uncomfortably close. A shiver ran through Corvala's limbs, and she shrank a little lower behind the crumbled wall.

Perhaps there was another power source they could find, one that wasn't guarded by a monster. Or maybe now was the time for Corvala to discuss her cure with Serapha. At least, once they got a safe distance away.

'What are we going to do?' Corvala asked in a hushed tone, hoping they'd move towards a new plan.

Serapha took a different meaning from her question. 'I will go in and charge my core.' With that, she marched out into the desolate clearing.

'Serapha!' Corvala wanted to cry out, but she forced her voice into a sharp whisper. 'Get back here!'

Then her father stepped out from the cover of the crumbled wall. He watched Serapha, his mind deliberating.

'Stay here,' he said to Corvala at length.

'Are you going to get her back?'

'I'm going with her.'

'What?' Corvala cried, barely able to keep her voice down. 'There's a dragon!'

'Stay here,' Exodus repeated. 'We'll be back soon.' And he went off after Serapha.

Corvala was about to shout after him, but she cut herself off. It would be foolish to raise her voice in such a place.

'Fine,' she muttered to herself. 'You walked into your stoning. Why not walk right into the belly of the beast?'

Corvala fidgeted with the hem of her sleeve as she watched them cross the desolation towards the beast's lair.

'Don't worry, Sir William,' she said to her fiddle. 'They'll be all right. Let's hope the dragon isn't even home.'

'The power source will be at the lowest levels of the facility,' Serapha said as they crossed the burnt clearing.

Exodus studied the old structure, looking for a way in. The tunnel beginning at its base was undoubtedly the most direct route to where they wanted to go, but it was too wide and open and would leave them exposed as they made their approach. They needed a more secretive way in. Looking up the hill, Exodus saw a boxy section of the building with rows of broken windows.

'Up there,' he said.

Going over boulders and crags, they climbed the bleak hillside into which the structure was built. Serapha wasn't as quick as before, and the occasional humming from her insides turned intermittently to grinding. Although she said nothing of her state, Exodus suspected she didn't have much time. They came to where rubble piled against the wall and provided them holds by which they could climb up to one of the windows. Most of the glass had been broken and cleared away, and the opening was wide enough for them to pass through. They entered a large room. Metal tables and chairs lay strewn about the ground along with rusty forks and knives and broken plates and mugs. A layer of ash and dust covered everything. Serapha made a beeline towards a metal box affixed to the room's back wall. Above it were stamped the faded words:

CALDERA LIGHT & POWER

UMATILLA GEOTHERMAL ENERGY STATION

EMERGENCY SUPPLY

The box, Exodus saw, contained various small instruments. Serapha took out a tubular ring that looked to be made of translucent glass. She rubbed her finger over the ring and offered it to Exodus.

'Use this to light your way.'

The ring started glowing. Exodus cautiously studied the device. There was no denying the wonder it provoked—how the Ancients could capture light in such a simple vessel—but it was a small taste of what led to their downfall. Forbidden demonic magic. Serapha might as well have been offering him a torch lit by the fires of hell. Exodus gritted his teeth and took the glowing ring. It felt wrong in his hands. Everything about this place felt wrong, as if its shadows and decay could seep into him, tainting his inner being with patches of gray mold.

He had to remind himself—not for the first time that day—why he had come here, why he had dug himself in so deep. He thought again of the night his wife had gone to bed and blown out the candle, and how that had been the last time he'd seen her. He wouldn't let it happen again. Lord forgive him, he'd go through hell to get his daughter cured.

From the room opened a hallway that went deeper into the facility. Serapha stood by its opening, head twitching and eyes blinking rapidly.

'Serapha?' Exodus said.

She stopped, then looked at him. 'My apologies, sir. Right this way, sir.'

Exodus thought her formality odd but said nothing of it. He stepped into the dark hall, the glowing circle lighting his way. Serapha didn't carry a light, and Exodus wondered if she would even need one if she had been on her own. They passed various openings where doors had fallen away, leaving naked hinges to reach out for nothing. Within the shadowy rooms, Exodus could make out long tables with chairs seated before upright glassy panels. Some had large metal boxes sprouting tangles of colored cords that ran across the floors and up the walls. The hall split in different directions, and Serapha had them take a right at one corner and a left at another as if she knew where she was going. They came to a metal door at the end of a hall. More faded words, these stamped upon the door's imposing front.

'I am sorry, sir,' Serapha said, coming to a halt. 'I cannot go any farther. This door says only authorized personnel can enter. We do not have the authorization to go beyond this point.'

Exodus looked the door over.

'That has nothing to do with us. The men who made that rule are long gone.'

Serapha just stood there, staring at the door. Then, after a twitch, she turned and faced him.

'State your name and rank, soldier.' It sounded as though she were issuing a challenge.

Exodus met her gaze, his brow furrowing. 'You know who I am.'

'You do not have authorization to pass.' She held up her hands, barring him from approaching the door.

Exodus snorted. He was half-tempted to let her have her way; to turn around and leave her here to guard this empty, cursed place until she ran dry.

'You're fading fast,' he said. 'But you need to get a hold of yourself. Remember why we're here. Your energy.'

Serapha stared at him for a long while, the silence stretching out in the dark, until her head twitched, and her hands fell to her side.

'Yes. My apologies. Would you like me to reboot? Negative. Cannot reboot at this time. According to my calculations—approximations—evaluation—' She came to an abrupt pause, and then, 'The power cells should be this way.'

She pried the door open, revealing a flight of stairs that wound in rectangular spirals down into the darkness, farther than Exodus's light could reach. Down Serapha and Exodus went, the air growing staler and colder with every level they passed. They were descending deeper into the hill, into parts of the structure unseen from above ground. By the time they reached the bottom of the stairs, Exodus's light illuminated his puffs of breath.

'This is omega level,' Serapha said.

There was a single door of thick metal. Serapha pulled the latch and the rusty hinges creaked in protest, but the door jerked open. A dim light shone through and a wave of heat washed over Exodus. He found himself on a plat-form looking out over a massive chamber. It looked as though the underworld had been hollowed out from raw stone and built up with metal. A labyrinth of tubes went in all directions. Some were small enough that Exodus could have put his hands around them, while others were wide as pillars, coming down from the vaulted ceiling high above and plunging into the earth. Out from where the tubes penetrated the ground ran cracks and fissures that glowed with reddish light from below. It was as if fire burned beneath the surface, and the air above the cracks rippled with heat. Exodus could already feel the sweat forming on his brow.

Many of the tubes fed into the center of the chamber where there stood rows of gigantic cylinders. Each was as wide as a cistern and twice as tall as a house. Their tops and bases were metal, and the middle columns appeared to be ringed with cloudy glass. Blue light pulsed within them. It mixed with the reddish light coming up from the ground, giving the chamber an otherworldly quality. Although the light wasn't bright, Exodus sensed power coming from the cylinders. The air crackled with it, making the hairs on his arms stand on end. This was no doubt the energy source Serapha had been talking about. It gave off a deep hum that wasn't heard so much as felt.

Over the deep tones there came the occasional high-pitched chirp and squeak. Exodus looked up to see tiny forms flittering through the dark. Bats. By the light, Exodus could make out thousands of them roosting up by the ceiling. The occasional pair of wings would drop from the colony and fly to one end of the chamber, where a massive hole had been torn through the wall. Rock and soil had been pushed to the sides of the opening and a steep tunnel had been bored upward towards the surface—through layers of earth and stone and the floors of the structure above. It must have led to the wide entrance they had seen outside at the structure's base. It was a way in and out for the bats.

And for the dragon.

On the far side of the chamber, a great form shifted in the shadows. It lay beyond the glowing cylinders, practically blending into the raw stone of the chamber.

Exodus hid the glowing ring behind his back and crouched down by the wall behind. Focusing on the dragon, Exodus studied its enormity. It was as long as a fortress wall, with ridges and spikes running down its back like battlements. Horns crowned its head, and a whole armory of teeth lined the length of its top jaw—a mouth that could easily swallow a man whole. The dragon lay asleep, its body forming a semicircle around one end of the rows of cylinders. By its head lay a pile of dirt that had been shaped into a bowl. There, Exodus thought he could make out round objects.

Eggs, he realized suddenly. That's why the dragon had come here—to give her young a warm nest. She would protect it fiercely.

'A lifeform guards the energy cells,' Serapha said in a low voice. 'Judging by its size, we would not overcome it in combat. The mission, therefore, is compromised.'

Serapha was right. There would be no fighting a beast that size. An ant didn't battle a lizard; it was eaten. Instinct and common sense gave Exodus pause. He could leave right now and go back the way he had come—go back to the daughter who was waiting for him. The mother dragon would be none the wiser.

But what of his daughter's cure?

'Let's get your energy,' he said at length, wiping the sweat from his brow. 'We'll be careful.'

They took a flight of metal stairs down from the platform and crossed a rickety walkway towards the center of the chamber, treading quietly and carefully. Exodus kept an eye on the sleeping dragon as they slipped between the rows of cylinders. On the far end, the beast lay sleeping, its breath louder now, like the swelling of a storm. Being so near the source of the blue glow, Exodus felt the power more intensely. The pulsating light hummed through his bones and nerves, tingling through his palms and fingertips. Serapha went down the narrow aisle to a cylinder with a steel compartment built into its side. She was about to open its hatch when her hand froze and her head began to twitch again.

'Focus,' Exodus said, taking hold of her shoulder. 'What happens next?'

The twitching stopped and Serapha looked at Exodus. 'I plug into the power cells—cells—cells and charge up.'

'How long will that take?'

'Approximately one hour and forty minutes.'

Exodus looked back along the row of cylinders at the dragon's scaly side, its dead skin sloughing off in ragged swathes just above the belly. The beast lay still. For now.

'Is there a quicker way?'

'My core can be put directly into the power cell interface. That method of charging would take twelve
minutes. But you would have to handle my core since I
will power off without it.'

'I suppose that'll have to do.'

Serapha opened the hatch to the steel compartment to
reveal a nest of wires and knobs set around an aperture.
She flipped a few knobs and the aperture opened, letting
a thin ray of the raw blue light shine through.

'You will need to put my core in there and take it out
when it is done charging,' Serapha said.

Without further instruction, she pressed a finger to
various places on her torso. Her body began to make
strange snapping noises as if pieces of her insides were
coming undone. Then something happened, something
out of a bizarre dream—Serapha's chest split and hissed
open. No bone, no blood; no lungs, no heart. Just an assortment of metal contraptions forming the inside of a
body. Exodus tightened his jaw as a shudder ran through
him. As a Judge, he had seen many things out of the ordinary—but nothing like this. Still, if his job had taught
him anything, it was to remain composed at the sight of
something terrifyingly odd. He couldn't afford to be
mesmerized—especially with a dragon nearby. Now was
a time to accept the odd and focus on the task at hand.

'Here is my core,' Serapha said.

She pointed to the center of her chest where there was
a cylinder—a miniature of the ones looming above them.
It also had a blue glow, albeit weak and faded.

'Do you understand what you are to do? If you do
not, ask your questions now. I will not be able to do anything when my core is taken out of me.'

Amid something so foreign and bizarre, his head was
full of nothing but questions. Where to begin?

'How will I know when—?'

Serapha's head slumped forwards and she collapsed. Exodus caught her mid-fall and tried to put her upright. Her body had gone rigid and wouldn't stand, so he laid her on the ground and shook her shoulders. There was no response. She was out, though her eyes were frozen open.

Exodus stared at the opening in her body. This was it. He clenched and unclenched his fist then reached into her chest. It was warm, but not the soft warmth of a body; it was a metallic warmth, a cooling pan off the stove. He took the core and it came out with a snap. He brought it to the open compartment in the larger cylinder and put it into the ray of blue light. The core was drawn inside and the aperture closed shut. Now all he could do was wait and see if he had done it right. He sat by Serapha and kept an eye on the dragon. He thought of Corvala waiting, sitting outside at the edge of the clearing. Her worry would be growing by the minute. Perhaps she'd be plucking at that fiddle of hers to keep herself calm. Exodus told himself she'd be all right.

The minutes dragged out in the deep hum of energy and the occasional chirp of a bat. There in the cool half-light, surrounded by the shadowy reaches of the chamber, Exodus sank into dark and distant memories. His being underground reminded him of his childhood— another life and another name, back before the Judges had got to him. He'd often hidden from his father, crawling along his belly across the dirt to that low place under his house where the cobwebs tickled his nose. He'd hear the stumbling of his father's boots across the floorboards above. Bottles clinked amid slurred curses. All too often there would come the loud smack of his father's hand against his mother's face, her long sobs to follow.

There were other memories of secret places in the dark, though none as terrible as his childhood refuge. He recalled the last rite of his training. Back then, after years of study and struggle, he'd walked a secret tunnel from

High Court into the Moss Kettle Mountains. He'd been given no light and had groped his way through the long dark. At last, he'd come to the Judge's haven: Cloud Heim, a mountain valley of green. At the valley's center stood an enormous tree—a species of its own, for its leaves were unlike any found on lowland trees. The Judges called the valley sacred because the tree served as a bridge between the heavens and earth, its roots holding the depths of the valley and its branches reaching into the clouds. When Exodus finally emerged from the tunnel into Cloud Heim, he found the council of Judges gathered at the base of the tree, waiting for him. It marked the end of his time as an apprentice. The elders placed their swords on his shoulder and declared him a Judge.

What would they think of him now? Would they condemn him for breaking his oaths?

He looked over at Serapha. An abomination at his feet. She was the one who had dragged them into this. His hand moved unconsciously towards the hilt of his sword. It would be so easy. He could ram the blade into her already-open chest and break what was inside. But no—Corvala needed her. For now.

He stared at the mechanisms inside her torso, spying then something he hadn't before. A metal plate bearing a symbol: a broken pot with fire rising above it. Beneath were etched the words:

GIDEON ROBOTICS ®

Exodus took a sharp intake of breath. His sword—the very blade he had thought to stab her with—bore the same symbol etched into its torcarda. What did this mean?

The aperture hissed and out came Serapha's core. Exodus tore his eyes from the engraved plate within her. *Stay focused.* He retrieved the core, which was no longer dim but emitted a bright glow like the cylinders all around him. Carefully, he placed the warm core back in Serapha's chest, feeling it snap into place. Metal parts began to move and the chest closed, the seams vanishing. Serapha's limbs shuddered with life, and her hands opened and closed. Picking herself off the ground, she stood up in a rigid pose, a soldier standing to attention.

'Rafaela, Seraph class seven,' she announced. 'Reporting for duty, sir!'

Her loud voice echoed through the chamber. Exodus winced and raised his hands, gesturing towards the dragon. Down the row of cylinders, its scaly body shifted in place. Slowly—terribly—the body began to scrape along the ground.

'We need to go,' he hissed.

'I did not power down correctly,' Serapha replied none too quietly. 'Do you wish me to reboot?'

No time for this. He picked up Serapha and threw her over his shoulders as he would a fallen comrade. He rushed down the rows, heading back the way they had come. Serapha didn't appear the least bit bothered by what was going on.

'Rebooting, sir,' she said, speaking into his ear as he ran.

Exodus skidded to a halt at the end of the rows of cylinders and shot a hurried glance at the platform and the metal door they'd come through. It was just across the way. He was about to make a break for it, then froze. He edged back between two cylinders. Eyes like dwindling suns were peering through the darkness into the cool half-light. Exodus could feel the dragon's gaze searching for him. The beast's great neck bent his way and a gigantic leathery snout emerged from around the corner. He could see the forked tongue slithering in and out, tasting the air. Too close. Much, much too close. The tip of the tongue slid across his shoulder.

The dragon snorted, drawing back to full height, and Exodus ran.

Chapter 20

Exodus spun and hurled the glowing ring. It flew over the dragon's snout and skidded across the chamber floor. The great shape of the dragon shifted away, following the light. Exodus sprinted on between the rows of cylinders, Serapha bumping around his shoulders, heavier than he'd expected. The dragon swept ahead, still chasing the light, blocking Exodus's way with a wall of scales. He ground to a halt, breath coming in ragged gasps, and scanned the room. There—a sequence of large metal tubes running along the floor and upwards at a steep angle, leading to the structure above. He followed them down, finding a great split hewn into one of them, and slipped into the cracked opening, bringing Serapha's still form with him. It was cramped and dark, and Exodus had to crouch down to fit.

Just like the crawlspace under his old house.

He felt his way forward in the dark. At first the way was flat and even, but then it ascended steeply. Gritty residue and a sticky substance he preferred not to think about kept Exodus from slipping as he crawled upwards, every inch a struggle, his breath cloying and hot around him. Serapha—Lord, how heavy could one woman be?—

ground along behind him. The way turned to the left as it continued rising, and ahead Exodus saw the faint glow of light. Not the unnatural blue glow of the cylinders—daylight. *Almost there.*

His going was slow and careful work, but eventually he carried Serapha out the tube's broken end. He found himself in the cavernous tunnel the dragon had bored through the building. Its earthen walls led through rooms and halls torn in half, and beams, floors, and ceilings came to abrupt and jagged ends, some jutting dangerously into his path. Dirt and rubble shifted beneath his feet. There was still a steep climb between them and the daylit opening above. Below, the tunnel turned, putting the chamber and dragon out of sight.

'Reboot complete,' Serapha announced in a loud voice. 'Restart required. Do you wish to restart?'

Exodus winced. 'Quiet!' he whispered.

'I am sorry. That command does not compute. Do you wish me to restart?'

Exodus was already on the move, hauling Serapha as quickly as he could up the now-trembling tunnel.

'Do what needs to be done,' he hissed.

'Restarting.'

From below there came a deep and guttural growl. Exodus cast an eye back to see the dragon round the bend. The great chamber shook as her claws ploughed through rock and iron alike, her sunlike eyes fixed on Exodus.

Exodus had stared down many enemies who wanted him dead, but this was no murderous thug or gang of bloodthirsty thieves. This was a force of nature, a beast risen from the underworld. Fear—strange, foreign fear—flooded Exodus's veins. Instinct jolted his legs to flight and he ran up the steep tunnel. He pushed his body up and up, lungs burning as he carried Serapha, but it felt like he was hardly moving, the loose ground shifting beneath his feet. Dread sank a weight in the pit of his stomach. He'd never make it. The opening ahead... too far.

He pushed despair aside and gritted his teeth. Turning to the side of the tunnel, he ducked into the shallow remains of a room, climbing over metal beams and wires. He slammed through a crumbling door, hearing behind him the crashing of walls torn apart. Exodus risked a look back. The dragon's snout and claws burrowed easily through the heaped debris behind, and the image of a lizard digging for insects flashed unbidden in his head. Parts of the building tore away, the platform collapsing behind Exodus as he ran. The dragon pulled back, its throat becoming a deep red like metal hot from the forge. Exodus reached the end of the hall—the way to the left blocked by debris, the right obscured by a collapsed ceiling leading up to the floor above. Already Exodus could feel the coming warmth, could smell the incendiary resin. Up he went, the fallen floor groaning beneath his and Serapha's combined weight. A roar of heat erupted from behind him and a wave of fire consumed the corridor below. Smoke billowed around him as plaster burned. He ran, throat thick with ash, spots dancing in front of his eyes, heart racing—all that mattered was putting distance between himself and the fiery throat behind.

Beneath him came a rumbling of blocks breaking, a groaning of metal bending. A great crack sounded as the entire floor split and crumbled. He staggered, half-fell, and groped for something, anything, to hold on to, his other hand catching Serapha's wrist as she slid free, but it was too late—he fell, Serapha sliding alongside him, downwards, bits of wall and ceiling plunging down alongside him, tables and chairs and metal boxes kicking up dust. All spun in Exodus's view as he slid and scraped into a heap of rubble.

Pain erupted in his legs, but there was no time to pay it any heed. He scrambled out, coughing clouds of dust, clawing and panting as he rose. They were back in the dragon's tunnel—farther up now, but still a hard run to the opening above. Exodus blinked, head swimming. It felt as though the world was about to tip forward again, sending him plunging down the steep slope.

The dragon roared behind. Exodus spun to find it had pulled its head free from the rubble and now reared to a fearsome height, its throat molten with a coming blast. Exodus's fingers clung to the ground beneath him, and he steeled his nerves to face what would come.

Then a high-pitched screeching echoed in the tunnel, interrupting everything. It grated against the ears and shivered the spine. Exodus turned to the source of the noise and saw a lone figure at the mouth of the tunnel high above.

Corvala.

She was sawing vigorously at her fiddle. Backed by pale daylight, she appeared like a stalwart yet diminutive angel playing a fearsome harp of judgment. Exodus's heart sank. There was no way he could reach her in time to drag her to safety—and yet still he ran. He cleared the steep grade, closing the impossible distance, and through his snorting breaths and his heart pounding in his ears he heard something swelling in the depths as if in response to the fiddle's cry. It started faint but quickly grew. At last, Exodus realized what it was he was hearing: thousands of tiny creatures chittering and shrilling in the dark.

Bats. They flew up from the chamber below, first only a few, then dozens, then hundreds. In no time at all, there swarmed a cloud of thousands, filling the tunnel with a rushing wind. The dragon, overwhelmed by the numbers, shook and bit wildly at the air, snarling and puffing fire. It spun about with the swarm. Exodus ran up the slope, only for a force like a moving wall to slam into his back. The dragon's tail. It knocked the wind out of him and sent him careening through the air. His head struck broken blocks, his mind reeling, lost in a world of curling smoke and shrieking bats. He was five again, little legs running through a field towards the woods, his drunken father roaring and raging not far behind. Home burning. Mother perishing in the flames. Smoke and fire reaching for him.

Then a hand took hold of him. A strong hand. Exodus opened his eyes. It was Serapha. She pulled him to his feet and got him running again, up the tunnel to where Corvala stood, eyes wide and frantic. Now all three of them ran across the bleak clearing of burnt stumps and twisted metal. They came to the clearing's edge and dived inside the ruins of a small building. Looking back, Exodus saw the swarm of bats still rushing out the tunnel. Eventually, the dark cloud dispersed into the air. The dragon's head rose briefly, but the beast paused at the mouth of the tunnel. It sniffed the air and stared for a long moment at the empty clearing. Then, after scraping its claws against the ground in a show of ownership, it disappeared back underground.

'I figured it out,' said Corvala after catching her breath.

'Figured what out?' Exodus said.

'How dragons make their fire. They eat trees to get the resin and the resin gives them their spark.' It was her nerves talking, Exodus knew.

'You got that all on your own?'

'I was bored. You took forever.'

'You were supposed to stay put,' Exodus said, but his reprimand was half-hearted.

'It was my turn to save your life.'

'How did you know about the bats?'

'I didn't.'

Corvala then let out a long laugh, one tickled by nerves and relief. Exodus couldn't help but grin. In the moments that followed near-death, it was sometimes good to laugh.

It wasn't long until they were on the move again, and Serapha had them back on course to the Elijah Tree. She looked well, acting and speaking as she had before. Still, something left Exodus unsettled. He had seen things— seen her inner workings—and it had ripped away her human façade. If she wasn't human then what was she? From what he had been taught, animated machines had demons inside. A machubus! But now those teachings seemed incomplete. She had healed him and had saved Corvala on more than one occasion. Now she had saved him from burning ruin. Would a demon do any of these things?

No. Serapha was... something else.

Then there was the odd, stilted way she'd talked down in the facility. He'd grasped hints of what she was, or of what she'd once been before this mission, before her time locked away in the secret vault. It sounded like she had served with soldiers. Now, with the Ancients gone, she had been repurposed. Exodus could relate. He, too, had a former life, one better forgotten.

And now, at least, he knew her full name. *Seraph Rafaela.*

The people would call her a demon, but Exodus could no longer see that. According to the scriptures, demons were fallen angels, brought down from heaven by the Red Dragon, the devil. And yet there were other forces at work in the world besides demons. The unfallen angels, those who fought *against* the devil. It was said that angels were the ones who had come down from heaven to give the first Judges their swords, which bore the mark of broken pottery and fire. The same symbol etched above Serapha's core.

Seraph Rafaela.

Maybe she was a seraph after all. An angel.

Chapter 21

Dane lounged on his throne, his mind and nerves drifting through a pleasant stupor—a tingly, sugary mist. An orphan lay dead at his feet, the life drained from the body. There'd been a newness to the little girl, a freshness missing in the older men and women Dane had consumed. The exhilaration of taking her life had been that much greater. To have the child's tender youth become his—what blissful delight. His was life eternal, and the city was rid of one begging waif. Everyone benefited.

As he sat there in the fading haze of his pleasure, the door to the throne room opened. In walked a guard to fulfill the evening routine. He threw a blanket over the girl and gathered her up in his arms. She was as limp as a sack of flour and perhaps just as small. Dane paid no heed. He stared at the ceiling. Under his helmet, his eyes were half-open, his mouth half-smiling. The guard moved gingerly so as not to disturb Dane and closed the throne room door quietly behind him when he left. After a while—Dane couldn't tell how long—the pleasure left him. His limbs began feeling stiff, and his mouth stuck with dryness. After a drink of cool water from a silver goblet, he looked out the window to the city below. It was quiet that night, the streets subtly lit with torches. The mountains that marked the gorge walls were invisible in their own vast shadows. Above their peaks, the sky shouted with stars, the wide band of the Milky Way extending from east to west.

Dane thought it was funny. He had spent centuries in orbit and yet never looked out at the stars. Such was his life shut in his pod, deep in the Dream. He stared up but found no wonder there. No mystery, no awe. Nothing could impress him now that he had tasted the entirety of a person's lifespan in the concentrated dose of a few minutes. Everything else—even the vastness of the universe—was drab in comparison. There had been a time in his life when he had looked to the stars in wonder. He had lived on Earth then. That was long ago, before Olympus. Before the Divide and the Treaty.

Dane looked out into the night. On earth, he had once seen skylines of cities glittering with electricity. Now he saw a settlement of wood and stone lit by primitive torches. Long ago, he had seen humanity at the height of its power, the keenness of its collective mind. Now he saw what the people of Earth had become. They ran around in animal skins, poking at one another with spears. How far they had sunk, deep into a dark age of superstition. Yet they had brought this upon themselves. They deserved what was coming to them. All of it. What he was doing—it wasn't wrong. It was their doing. Yes, *their* doing.

Then an image of a twitching hand came to mind: a child's hand trembling in weak protest. The image came uninvited, the way conscience-pricking thoughts do. The orphan's face had been covered, but Dane had seen the child's hand. So small and fragile. While he had taken life from the body, he had seen the hand reach out for some kind of salvation. Perhaps an instinctual reach for a mother who wasn't there. Who knew? The hand had fallen lifeless to the floor shortly after.

I killed it.

Dane looked at the floor where the little girl had been and immediately back outside. Heat spread around his neck. He'd never felt anything like this in the Dream. He'd almost forgotten what guilt was like. He began pacing, his metal boots clanking on the stone floor. But no matter how fervently he paced, no matter how many circles he walked, he couldn't escape the hot grip of guilt on his neck. He couldn't shake the thoughts. He still saw the hand reaching for him.

He felt like a drone locked into its pattern—back and forth, back and forth. He had to get out of there. So, after snatching up the cloth from the dining table, he snuck out the window and climbed down to the garden below. There was a tall wrought iron fence separating the palace gardens from the rest of the city. Dane went to an inconspicuous corner and bent the rods to make an opening. Before he left, he took off his suit and hid it in a rose bush. No unnecessary attention for the golden man this evening. A crowd of mindless worshippers was the last thing he needed. He did keep the mechanical supports for his arms and legs and a small metal band around his head to protect him from the signal of the patheograph. Without it, he'd be forced to worship his own image—a mirror-into-mirror infinity of folding into himself. Eternal madness. Dane shuddered at the thought.

Armor stripped off, only his jumpsuit remained. He tied the table cloth over his head as a makeshift cloak and passed through the opening he had bent, heading out into the city. There was no sun to burn his translucent skin, yet still he drew himself deep into his cloth cloak. He kept to the shadows, unsure of where he was going, hoping only to get away from the scene of his deed. As he walked, he thought hard, searching for what could rid him of this hot, prickly guilt. He tried to justify his act with logic. He was a superior breed of human, a god, and these people—if they could be called that—were far lesser beings. He took what he needed to survive. Is a lion condemned for killing a zebra, a hawk for eating a mouse? No. They merely follow the natural order of things. And so was Dane.

It was solid logic, a watertight defense. And yet it was absolute rubbish. It did nothing to mollify his feelings. It was like an itch he couldn't get rid of no matter how much he scratched. Life in the Dream, where all unpleasant emotions were pushed aside, had left him with the inability to cope with this reality. Logic couldn't remove it, and yet it was the only thing he could use. Round and round his mind went, getting nowhere.

Then, like so many guilty men before him, he wandered into a church for reasons he couldn't comprehend. He wasn't even sure how he'd arrived there. Perhaps it was the church's size that had drawn him. The palace and the church were the largest structures of the city, situated like diametric poles to one another; perhaps as the palace repelled him, the church had pulled him in like a magnet to the desperate. Or perhaps what had drawn him was the warm yet unobtrusive candlelight that shone from the building's open doors. While the upper levels of his mind had waded through a fog of useless thought, the lower levels had been guiding his feet. Had those parts been so primordial, taking him to light like a moth to a porch lamp?

For whatever reason, he now found himself standing by the back pews of the sanctuary. The center aisle led to the altar, where a multitude of candles stood, a choir singing a quiet hymn of light. Behind them stood a towering cross, shaped from the stone of nearby mountains. Kneeling before it was a priest clad in rough cloth, deep in his evening prayers.

Dane had never been a religious man. It wasn't that he opposed religion; thoughts of God had just never come to his mind. On Earth, he had been too busy with his projects and studies. In the Dream, he had everything taken care of. Religion had always been something far away, an island he would hear about from time to time that he never thought of visiting. There was no empirical evidence of God to interest him, no voice calling. Yet here he was in a church. Cold logic could not temper the heat of his guilt. If anything, the pressure was building like steam within him. He needed release. Perhaps this was why he had come here. He sat down in the back pew, uncertain how these visits worked. Not knowing what to say, he cleared his throat loudly. The priest stirred and rose from his prayers. As he came down the aisle, Dane watched him. The man even *looked* like a priest—he had a cherubic face, and Dane imagined him fluttering down from the ceiling of the Sistine Chapel. Dane pulled himself deeper into his cloak so that his hideous face was obscured in shadow.

'How can I help you?' the priest asked in a light voice.

'I have come to… confess.' The word came out with some uncertainty. A confession was something a criminal gave to the authorities. While he couldn't bear to see himself as a criminal, Dane couldn't deny it—he wanted to confess, to open the valves and release it all. Not to God, necessarily, but to somebody.

'You wish to confess your sins to God in heaven,' said the priest, nodding sagely. He leaned in closer to Dane and spoke softly: 'Or do you wish to pray to the golden man who now sits on the throne?'

Dane should have been enthused by how well his patheograph was working—how it had infiltrated even the religion of these people. Instead, to his surprise, he was appalled. That he was seen as a deity, a source of hope and comfort, a being people prayed to—it was revolting! He had been handed an idol with gold on the outside and death on the inside. And that idol was him.

In his darkest hour, the priest, with all sincerity, had offered him something poisonous, and only Dane knew it. He was trying to escape from himself, not pray to himself.

'Don't speak to me of that man!' Dane growled. He pushed by the priest and stormed out the church.

Where he was going he didn't know, but he moved with fierce purpose. He had to get away—away from this place he had infected. He passed through the city gate, then down the river and up a path into the mountains. His mechanical supports hissed and whirred as they carried him along. Once he was far enough from civilization, he stopped. He had come to a ledge overlooking the gorge. Torches flickered in the city below. Above, the Milky Way spanned the sky in a vast arch. Within its band, two bright stars looked down on him like a pair of eyes. The eyes of the universe—of God. They appeared compassionate.

Dane dropped his cloak in the presence of those stars. Except for the thin layer of his jumpsuit over his skin, he was exposed. No golden armor. Just him and the heavens above.

'If you're really there then strike me down,' he challenged. 'I'm no good for this world.'

He spread his arms open wide and waited. A minute passed. Then another. The stars remained still, and no punishment came.

'That's what I thought,' Dane scoffed. 'You're as much a fraud as I am. At least I exist. You're nothing but empty darkness.'

Returning to the city, he went to the palace gardens and took the pieces of his suit from under the rosebush. Once his armor was on, he used its strength to climb up to the throne room's window. He had failed to find comfort. There was only one thing left to do.

'Guard!' he called.

The guard on evening watch obediently stepped inside.

'Bring me someone old—better yet, someone from the prisons. The worst of the criminals.'

The guard bowed and exited.

Dane fidgeted, anxious for the coming pleasure. Taking the life of a bad man should tide him over. Not another orphan—that had been cruel. These people may be insects, but it was better to give the young a chance. Tomorrow he would quit his habit and find something different to sustain him. For now, he would allow himself one last pleasure.

Chapter 22

Serapha stalked ahead through an old patch of forest. True, all of Thorn Shroud was old. This section, however, seemed older than the rest. The trees grew taller, their trunks thicker, their boughs shaggy with moss. Rotten logs rose like small hills, the hollows underneath providing safe havens for pill bugs and emerald salamanders. Ferns spiraled from the forest floor as green sprigs from a forgotten time, surviving patiently on whatever rays of dim sunlight fell through the roof of branches and tendrils of mist. Judging by the damp mystery of plants and soil, they were entering the very heart of Thorn Shroud. The Elijah Tree was close. Corvala could feel it.

'I wonder if it will hurt,' she thought aloud.

Serapha assured her that the connection with the tree wouldn't be painful. It would be similar to when Serapha had read her mind—a strange sensation followed by a brief headache.

'No,' Corvala said. 'I mean, will the intruder feel anything?'

Serapha had explained that when the Sky Mantle code activated the Elijah Tree's defense system, the tree would release something called *nanotech*—tiny devices imperceptible to the human eye. The devices would come off the tree like a cloud of pollen and converge upon the intruding Olympian.

'It is highly probable they will feel it,' Serapha said after a slight pause.

'Why kill them? Are they guilty of a crime?'

'I do not know who the intruder is or what they are doing. Neither can I make moral judgments on what is good or bad. But I can discern what is and what is not allowed. The people of Olympus are not permitted to come to Earth because they have great power. They know this. They signed the Earth and Sky Treaty and agreed to keep it. They could harm the people of Earth, who do not have the same level of technology. The Elijah Trees were put in place to defend the people of Earth if ever that Treaty was broken.'

Corvala thought of the handful of warlords who were said to have embraced the demonic. She'd heard the stories: fierce and exiled warriors who roamed the wild deserts of the south, outside the bounds of civilization. They had unearthed weapons of the Ancients, scrap creaking with rust, and were ever a bane to the spearmen guarding the southern borders of the Norwestor Dominion and its neighboring kingdoms. Yet Serapha spoke of an intrusive power from the heavens, something that sounded more threatening even than these desert raiders.

'What are the chances?' Corvala said, shaking her head. 'This intruder could have flown over someplace else. I wouldn't have seen it. There'd be no dream to lead me to you and we wouldn't be out here in these woods.'

'The organization I served left as little to chance as possible. It implanted codes into many people, all of whom were designated to be the encoded watchers. Sentries, they were called. Their ability and responsibility would be passed down through the generations. Many Elijah Trees were planted for them to find.'

'So, you're saying there are more people... like me? How many?'

'I do not know. Family trees may have increased the original number. Some codes might have deteriorated over time, and some bloodlines may have ended completely.'

'But there are others,' Corvala mused.

Even if there were just a few, there were other people out there like her and her mother. All of them had something in common—a guardianship. Corvala suddenly felt big and small all at once. She was part of something much larger than herself, and yet she was a mere piece of it. She was a Sentry. Such a thought made her dizzy with confusion and relief. What her mother, grandmother, and ancestors had passed down to her—she was going to fulfill it. Not only did Corvala feel a new connection with her mother, but she also felt a new appreciation for her father. Just as he acted as Judge and brought justice to the world, so would she. Maybe not with a sword as he did, but in a different way—a more powerful way.

And someone would die. The sobering thought dampened her revelation.

They entered a mossy glade where round boulders rose from the earth like prehistoric eggs. At the center grew a tree standing high above the others. She knew what it was even before Serapha spoke its name.

'The Elijah Tree.'

The entire glade fell under the cover of its outstretched branches. Corvala studied the swollen roots. Thin veins of silver ran through its bark and, above, its leaves were seven-pointed stars with flecks of deep blue. It was a broadleaf unlike any Corvala had seen before—not an oak, maple, or ash, nor any species she could recognize. She felt so small next to its immense trunk and under its overarching boughs.

Something was off. Many of the branches were dead and bare, robbing the tree of its majesty. Then she saw it, the source of the condition: a great swathe torn from the trunk, claw marks framing it.

'The dragon got here first,' Exodus said. 'Many months ago, by the looks of it.'

It made sense: the largest beast of the forest was bound to seek out the largest tree. The mark of its claws and teeth no doubt let the other beasts know that this was a dragon's territory.

Although the tree stood firm, the wound was deep. Fungus would have entered the timber, its corruption spreading to the inner core. The tree was dying.

'Touch it,' Serapha commanded. 'You must try to make a connection.'

Corvala placed her hand on the trunk. She thought she could feel the sudden pulse of something deep within, a flicker of a reaction, but it was so faint—maybe she was imagining it. Then there was nothing but the feel of the rough bark under her palm. She walked around the tree and tested various areas around the base of the trunk.

'Nothing's happening,' she said.

'That does not compute. The Elijah Tree must function for the mission to be complete.'

'What now?'

'You must try again.' Serapha reached out and placed her hand on the trunk to demonstrate the action. Then she pulled her hand back. 'You put your hand against it,' she said again and repeated the motion, this time harder, the blow landing with a heavy thud.

'You put your hand against it.'

Thud!

'You put your hand against it.'

Thud!

'You put your hand against it.'

Crack!

Serapha's hand burst through the bark and struck a rotten hollow where fluids had collected. Water poured from the break and flowed like lifeblood down the tree. The acrid stench hinted at rot and strange chemicals. Serapha stared for a long moment at the hole she had made.

'I can see this Elijah Tree no longer functions,' she said at length, regaining her stalwart composure. 'The damage is too great.'

Corvala watched as the liquid pouring from the tree pooled near her feet, forming a greasy puddle with an iridescent surface. All of the enthusiasm that had come a moment ago withered quickly away. She had been a fool to think anything good could come of the ability that ran through her bloodline. It was the curse of madness. Nothing more.

'So, what now?' she asked. 'Can I be cured?'

'No. We are not yet done. We must find another Elijah Tree.'

Corvala looked up from the puddle and stared at Serapha in disbelief. A woodpecker knocked on a hollow bough above.

'Another?'

'For security purposes, I was given the location of this one but not the others. There is the possibility of finding another if we do an investigative search.'

'That would take forever! Think of what it took to get to this one.' Corvala shook her head. 'Why can't we just say it's over and you cure me now?'

'As long as there is an intruder on this world, I must have your code remain intact as a possible resource.'

Corvala's heart sank. 'So, you won't help me.'

'Only when the mission is complete will I dismantle the code,' Serapha replied.

Corvala stood there, dumbfounded. It was her failed audition with Solomon Swain all over again, only a thousand times worse. She had lost her chance of leaving the valley with the Windborne, and now she had lost her chance to cure her coming madness. It was supposed to be right there, within arm's reach—but it had crumbled with the rotten timber. It would be better to have never known of the cure in the first place.

'Wait a minute,' her father said. He was standing in the glade, his arms crossed and his eyes studying the enormous tree. By his grim expression, Corvala could tell weighty thoughts and decisions were stirring in his head—more than he would let on.

'I've seen a tree like this before.'

'Another Elijah Tree?' Corvala asked weakly.

'Perhaps. The Judges hold an old secret: Cloud Heim, a valley in the Moss Kettle Mountains, where a sacred tree grows.' He looked down from the upper branches to Corvala. In his eyes, she could see the stern resolve she knew so well. 'We may have a second chance at this.'

Chapter 23

The goblin camp had become the picking ground for crows and magpies, and the stench of carrion hung heavy in the air. Squat bodies, bloated from the day's heat, lay strewn about in various contortions of death. Arms and legs twisted. Toothy mouths hung slack, tongues lolled out in the dirt. Some of the warty faces still possessed the ghost of fear and agony from their final moments. Others already had their eyes pecked out. It was a gruesome scene that jarred against the gentle clinking of metal pieces strung through the trees.

Vlaren paced about the camp, the tip of his metal staff tapping the ground. Lobeka had found the remains of a horse and was cracking open the bones to get to the marrow inside. She rejected the goblin meat and rightfully so. They were tainted creatures with rotten flesh. Vlaren looked over the deep gashes on their bodies. This was the Judge's work. Over twenty goblins cut down. Vlaren had known stalwart warriors overwhelmed by fewer. This Judge he hunted was dangerous. This was no surprise: Judges weren't recruited solely for their moral fiber. They had to have the muscle and grit to dole out justice with a sword. This Judge would be especially fierce given that his daughter was with him. *Don't get between a beast and its young*, the adage advised.

There was also the woman with them—the one the sheriff had called a demon. The etheris she left behind suggested his claim was true. Vlaren had been taught that demons inhabiting mechanical forms—machubi—had metal limbs and joints, tubes filled with oily substances. This demon took on the aspect of a human. The scriptures told of how demons possessed people, like the man at the tombs. *I am Legion for we are many*. Occasionally a person claiming to have a demon inside them would come to Pillar Dark looking for healing, but they never had the aura of etheris about them. This woman Vlaren hunted… she was a different case. A machubus with the aspect of a human? Whatever she was, she was also dangerous—after all, not all of these goblins had been slain by a sword. Others showed signs of blunt trauma, and many more had broken limbs and necks. She and the Judge would not be captured easily.

Vlaren welcomed the challenge. So far, tracking had been easy, the path laid out by a clear trail of etheris. It wasn't as strong as it had been at the Judge's house, and it would eventually fade away altogether. For now, though, there was still enough for him to follow. Never before had Vlaren seen a trail remain so obvious for so long. It felt like cheating. In most cases he'd have no etheris to go by and would have to rely on the standard spoors— footprints in the mud, for instance, or scrapes against a tree.

To most, the language of the Hunted was an utter mystery. To Vlaren it was an open book. Sometimes— perhaps most times—there would be pages missing. That made the story all the more alluring. He'd have to fill in the blanks and use what he knew of his quarry to determine what they would do next. It was an irresistible game. If his quarry was particularly kind, they would give him a challenge by covering up their tracks and putting down false trails for him to follow. There was the fond memory of the witch who tried to lose him through a blizzard, and the dealer of forbidden books who had worked out of a labyrinthine swamp. On those kinds of Hunts, his senses would come fully alive and a thrill would come upon him in a great rush.

Although following an obvious trail of etheris was dull, the details Vlaren had collected piqued his interest. There was more to the story than what he had been told. It was interesting that the small company had moved on from here. If they had been any witch or warlock on the run, they would have hunkered down in this camp. It was an ideal spot for those enthralled with the demonic—a patch of Ancient ruins hidden deep in the woods with a wide assortment of Ancient knickknacks hanging from the trees. It had everything his typical quarry would have been looking for in a hideout—and yet the woman, the Judge, and his daughter had moved on. It seemed they were looking for something other than a refuge. Not running *from* something; going *towards* something.

According to the report from Dawn's Landing, the Judge's daughter had summoned a demon to enact vengeance on those who stoned her father. From his reading of the tracks, Vlaren saw that the girl had broken away from the woman, making her way down a creek that led to her capture by the goblins. It was a curious thing that she would summon the demon only to run from it later on. Vlaren hadn't read any signs of a fight or struggle on the way here. The old stories warned of how the demons made seductive offers that turned bitter in the end. Perhaps the girl wanted out of her situation and therefore fled. After the battle with the goblins, it looked like the Judge and the woman had a tussle. Then—according to the tracks—the three of them continued on their way together peacefully. The relationship the Judge and his daughter had with the woman was turning out to be something unusual indeed.

Vlaren could understand why the girl had summoned the demon. People were capable of doing desperate things to save those they loved. However, learning the motives of his quarry and determining whether they were guilty or innocent wasn't his concern. Let the Judges work for justice and righteousness. Rooks cared only for the Hunt.

Two Claw Pass through the Moss Kettle Mountains was a major thoroughfare for trade. Farmers would go north to sell their crops in Ryperia, and going the opposite way, merchants would come off the river to sell their wares south of the mountains. Normally there would be a fair number of wagons and pack animals traveling, but Rook Eramez encountered no one on the mountain road. Only wind through the trees. He brought his wulgyre mount to a stop at a vista overlooking the Landsong Gorge. Down below snaked the Colmane River, and on its southern bank sat Ryperia. The old Rook perched upon his saddle with rigid posture, leaning forward and staring long at the city. Above its center, there glowed a powerful light—a radiance like a star settled atop the palace. Not blinding but calm. Not burning with fire but pulsating with energy, faint halos rippling through the air. Eramez studied the glow, reaching beneath his helmet to stroke the white tuft of his beard. A strange magic was at work here.

His wulgyre pawed at the ground and nipped at the air, yet there were no biting flies around to elicit such behavior. Eramez patted the creature on the neck.

'Peace, peace.'

He pressed the button on the side of his helmet, dropping the jade lenses into place. Given the power of the light, it was hardly a surprise to find his vision blotted out by cloudy white, and yet he gasped at the overwhelming abundance of etheris before him. On past Hunts, he had encountered faint wisps of the stuff, like a man of the desert who had only found trickles of water; now he had been plunged into an ocean.

'By the wreck,' he whispered.

His hand unconsciously drew a circle in the air, but even as he did, a hint of a grin tugged at the corners of his mouth. He couldn't help but think of the glory a discovery of this magnitude would bestow upon him. All of Pillar Dark would want to learn of what he had found, and the throne would certainly want to know, earning him an audience with the Archon himself. Eramez closed his eyes and took a breath. All in good time. Now for discipline. If the power—no doubt demonic—could fill the gorge with etheris and block the city from sight, then it was something he couldn't contend with on his own. He would need to send for reinforcements. Eramez thought of sharing glory with others and plucked a hair from his chin.

Since his lenses prevented him from seeing anything clearly, he pressed the button on the side of the helmet so they would retract. They didn't move. He tried again and again, but the mechanism was stuck. Such was the trouble with these Ancient devices. Frequent glitches meant constant maintenance. He took the helmet off so he could see again. At that moment, the wulgyre bucked and he dropped the helmet so that it bounced across the road, into the weeds.

'Wicked beast,' he grunted and flicked the wulgyre's ear.

He dismounted to retrieve the helmet, and as he did, he felt something odd. His attention was drawn to the light over the city. Somehow, he could feel it now—could feel it pressing against his senses. A part of him knew he should put his helmet on, block out whatever powers were reaching for him, and ride away from that place. Yet there was something alluring about the light that kept him looking.

'Lord, protect the windows to my soul,' Eramez muttered, an old prayer to ward off evil.

He kept on staring at the light, and the more he stared, the more he felt a presence behind it. He could picture it vaguely—out of the radiance, a golden figure. It beckoned him. There came a voice, not so much heard as thought. A voice of promise and power. A whisper that somehow filled the gorge and his mind.

Come to me.

Eramez remembered the testing he had throughout his training. When he was an apprentice, his master would pretend to misplace an Ancient device, leaving it behind in a tucked-away space where no one would see it. It would be a small and unassuming object—a bit of shine no one would miss. Although Eramez always knew it was a test, he struggled with the desire to take what tempted him. Even now he pondered what was locked away deep within the secret parts of his mind—a fascination with the Ancient ways and desire for their power. That was why he had become a Rook. Not necessarily to destroy Ancient technology but to be near it without punishment. All the amazing things he had encountered crossed his mind. Messages sent across the world in an instant. Moving pictures. The wonder of flight. The writings and artefacts that pointed to these things were mere shadows of that fallen age. Now the golden presence enticed him to take the deep knowledge he always longed to possess. And behold the power of that presence! To fill the gorge with etheris! It promised the fullness of Ancient knowledge.

Come to me. I will teach you what I know.

Eramez stared long at the city. Discipline—he needed discipline.

My knowledge is the most beautiful of disciplines.

Eramez stepped forward. He tried to lead his wulgyre, but it pulled away and ran back up the pass they had traveled, disappearing around a bend. No matter. Something inside his head was changing his thoughts, but he didn't care. Indeed, he welcomed it. All the secret desires he had kept locked up for so long could now go free.

Behold the glory offered to you.

He would see this wonder for himself. He picked up his helmet and staff and began walking towards the city. Perhaps the golden presence would find them to be a pleasing gift. Maybe he would reward Eramez with knowledge.

Chapter 24

They left the dark cover of Thorn Shroud without any ceremony or looking back. Corvala, Exodus, and Serapha descended the Gloaming Hills, clearing the forest's western edge to where the trees thinned and gradually gave way to wide fields and scrubland. They were heading west towards the Landsong Gorge and High Court within. From there, they would take the Judge's secret path to Cloud Heim, where her father had described a massive tree that might be another Elijah Tree.

Corvala didn't care two licks. She knew she should have been grateful for even the possibility of a cure—the possibility there was something to help her when all the healers and even the Ancients' texts on medicine had been unable to provide answers. Here was a whisper of hope. She had no desire to listen to it now. She had passed through Thorn Shroud and the lairs of beasts to get to one Elijah Tree. And for what? To be told her cure was possibly—*maybe, might be*—in a mountain valley several days away… on foot. Heaven forgive her for not jumping for joy.

When the raindrop fell on her cheek, she was hardly surprised. It was only fitting that the weather matched her mood. The thunderheads were still a way off, rolling in from the west. A few scattered drops continued to fall, forerunners of the heavy rains to come. In the fields of grass and scrub, they spotted a growth of trees set in a depression between two hills. It wasn't much, but it was better than standing out in the open. They arrived under the cover of branches just in time, the hard rains coming fast behind them. Corvala was about to huddle against the base of an oak when her father called to her.

'Over here,' he said.

In the crux between the two hills was a shadowy space beneath a rock ledge. It was the mouth of a small cave, so concealed by underbrush that she probably wouldn't have seen it if her father hadn't pointed it out. It was chilly inside but dry. When Corvala's eyes adjusted to the dark, she could see the cave was roomier than she had guessed, the ceiling tall enough for them to stand comfortably. At the back of the cave was an assortment of shapes, much too square or rectangular to be natural stone. Peering through the dim light, she could see they were crates and chests stacked on top of one another.

'A thieves' den,' Exodus said, wiping away a thick layer of dust from one of the crates. 'Been left alone for some time. We shouldn't be bothered while waiting out the storm.'

Outside the cave, the rain fell hard and didn't show any signs of stopping. Serapha stood watch by the entrance, peering out into the storm. Exodus took advantage of their wait by settling down against the chamber wall and shutting his eyes. Although Corvala knew she should do likewise, she couldn't help wondering if there was any food stored here. A jar of dried meat or wizened fruit, perhaps. Probably not. No one would want to attract bears or other animals with that stuff. Corvala's hunger for something other than roots and mushrooms made her search anyway. Maybe she would find a crate of wine bottles. That would wash away the taste of dirt in her mouth, and it would certainly help her mood.

Wrenching the lid off a chest, she found silver utensils within. Another chest held copper bracelets. Rummaging in the boxes, Corvala found a wide collection of goods: metalwork, swathes of fine linen, fur pelts, jars of paint—the kinds of things carried by traveling merchants. But no food. As she searched, she came upon some long wooden boxes with an image stamped upon them: a flower in flames.

'The Bright Kin,' Corvala whispered, rubbing her hand almost reverently over the image.

Every performance troupe had their mark, and Corvala knew them all. For the Windborne, it was an eagle rising out of a cloud. The Bright Kin was a performance troupe from the coast who occasionally wandered east to the Elkhorn Valley. They were run by the famed Madame Mercury, a woman who held herself with the refined manner of a lady but had the fierceness of a wild cat. The flower in flames captured the essence of her elegance and burning passion.

Corvala gingerly opened the boxes. Inside she found all the costumes needed for a proper show. There were clothes of indigo, ochre, and scarlet for jugglers and musicians. The bear hide cloak for the Man o' Beasts, the tamer of wolves, eagles, and manticores. The black and green cloth and the fearsome-grinned mask for the Demon. And the robes of the Clumsy Priest. The sight of all these costumes was enough to bring a blush of warm cheer to her cheeks amid her sour mood.

Her grin fell when she thought of how these costumes had come to this cave. The Bright Kin had been robbed. Corvala pictured their caravan out on some lonely stretch of road, thieves armed with spears and knives surrounding them. There would be Madame Mercury, putting herself between her troupe and their attackers, a blade threatening her midsection. Despite the menace, she would uphold her ladylike dignity while she cussed out the highwaymen looting her wagons. Although Corvala wasn't part of a troupe yet and had never performed for an audience before, she counted herself among those who called themselves performers. She looked over the stolen boxes of costumes and felt a shade of the Bright Kin's loss. Her hand unconsciously went to Sir William in a protective grasp. The theft was no small thing. It took time for a troupe to build up its wardrobe, and the dyed fabrics alone would have cost a small fortune. None of this belonged here. Not in the filthy hands of thieves.

She thought of ways to get back at the men who stole this hoard. An idea came to mind.

'When we get to High Court,' she mused aloud, 'there'll be people on the lookout for us. We'll need disguises so we won't be recognized.'

Exodus didn't stir at her voice. Still resting, he half-opened his eyes and looked over at the boxes of costumes.

'No,' he said and returned to his rest.

'Why not?'

'It's stealing.'

'It's not stealing if we take it from thieves.' Corvala ran a hand over the bright cloth in the boxes. 'We can pose as performers.'

'No,' Exodus repeated.

'Then how are we going to get into High Court unnoticed?'

'Not dressed like clowns.'

'Look at you,' Corvala said, throwing a hand in her father's direction. 'Look at all of us. We look like fugitives.'

Their passage through Thorn Shroud had left their shirts and pants dirty and torn. They would fit in with beggars—or prisoners. They couldn't expect to enter High Court without suspicion and scorn dressed as they were. And Seentha's gray clothes of slick cloth displayed a style from a different time that would certainly draw attention.

Serapha, still looking out at the rain, added her opinion. 'A disguise would improve our probability of not being identified.'

'Thank you,' Corvala said, resting her case.

Before her father could add further objection, she began sorting through the clothes, searching for something they could use. Among the bright and garish, she veered more towards cloth of subdued colors, something that wouldn't draw too much attention to itself. She also looked for clothes that would fit them, so it wouldn't appear as though they had hastily raided a drying line.

After much deliberating, she took for herself a sleeveless tunic and pants, both colored cedar-green and with golden ivy designs embroidered at the seams. For Serapha, she picked out an indigo mandarin shirt and pants with flames worked into the short collar. Both outfits were gaudy in comparison to the everyday clothing of common people, but she had found the plainest. For Exodus, it was more difficult to choose. The robe and cowl of the Clumsy Priest would have been good for their purposes, allowing him to blend in with the priests who went to High Court. But the robe was much too small. So was the bear hide cloak and vest of the Man o' Beasts, which was a shame since her father fit the serious nature of the part. Corvala ended up choosing an alligator skin vest with a fox tail collar and a wide-brimmed hat with a long pheasant tail feather stuck in it. When Corvala handed him the outfit, he gave her a long stern look. He eventually took it, grumbling something about showiness. The first thing he did was pluck the decorative feather from the hat.

Going to a private nook in the cave, Corvala changed into her tunic and pants. It felt good to wear new clothes. And not just any clothes—the cloth cut for a performer. She looked down at herself and ran her hands over the soft fabric. Oh, what she wouldn't do for a mirror to see herself now! She closed her eyes and pictured herself dressed as she was, walking out onto a stage, Sir William in hand, an entire town gathered to listen to her play. She could almost feel the expectant eyes upon her, hear the first passionate note she would draw across the strings.

'The rain has stopped,' Serapha said, breaking Corvala from her fantasy.

It was time to move on to High Court and show the world her new disguise. The thought made her grin. It was the part she was born to play.

Chapter 25

The road meandered alongside the wide Colmane River, the Rainier Kingdom on the far shore. Corvala had never been to the kingdom of the north, and it didn't look like she'd be able to visit it on this trip. She, her father, and Serapha followed the river's patient push west through fields and scrubland. Up ahead sat a small village on the riverbank.

'Remember, we're not drawing attention to ourselves,' Exodus said. Although he looked ahead as he spoke, Corvala knew his words were directed at her. 'Say little if nothing at all. A shut mouth will make up for these clown suits.'

'They're not that bad,' Corvala retorted, looking down at her shirt. 'They have a little more flash than most, but nothing that's going to give us away. Serapha's not complaining.'

'I was not made to understand the appropriateness or popularity of one type of clothing over another. I want only to succeed in my mission. If what I am wearing helps me to achieve this, then so be it.'

'See,' Corvala said, turning to her father. 'Even Serapha agrees with me.'

Exodus said nothing. Corvala could tell he wasn't excited about leaving the wilds and reuniting with civilization dressed as he was. Especially with that wide-brimmed hat. He had never liked hats. In his opinion, they were a vanity that sat on the highest part of the body, and anyone who needed to wear them must be trying to make up for something they lacked. If he could throw his hat in the river, he would. But he understood that the brim concealed his eyes, and that meant anonymity. So, he allowed the hat to stay.

As they approached the village, Corvala felt her stomach rumble.

'We should make a stop for food and supplies,' she said. She patted the empty knapsack on her father's back—another item they had taken from the thieves' den. Each of them carried one now.

'I don't like that idea,' Exodus said. 'We need to keep our heads low. Better if we didn't do business. No dealings. Just pass through unnoticed.'

Corvala's stomach rumbled again in protest. If she had to swallow another dusty root...

'How will we eat?'

'We'll make do,' Exodus said. 'Besides, we don't have any money to buy food.'

Corvala reached into her knapsack and pulled out a heavy bag that jingled with coins. 'This should do.'

Exodus looked at her with severe eyes. 'Where did you get that?'

'It's a gift from our former hosts.'

Exodus grunted in disapproval. 'We already took more than we should have.'

Corvala hefted the coin bag from one hand to another. 'We'll put it to good use.'

'Regardless, it's dark times when you live off dishonest gain.'

'We're already in dark times. And besides, the money is better in our hands than in the hands of thieves.'

'So you may think,' Exodus replied.

The village of Red Jack was nothing more than a few dozen shacks raised on stilts. It stood near the river's edge where the water was slow and held harbor slips where barges were tied up. When Corvala, Exodus, and Serapha entered the village from the main road, they received a few looks from the old fellows sitting on their porches. None of them gave the small company too much scrutiny. At the center of the village stood the inn, which had a trading post and tavern. Corvala, Exodus, and Serapha climbed its wooden steps and entered through the creaking door. They came to the dim and dingy common room that smelled of pipe smoke and fish. Bargemen, along with a few women and barefoot children, were gathered inside for their drinks and evening meals. They were a rough-looking bunch, all grimy and many scarred. They huddled around small greasy tables and coddled their mugs, and Corvala could hear Rainier and Washona accents mixed into their conversations. At the other end of the room, a band was setting up with a guitar, banjo, goat-skin drums, and double bass.

'Let's make this quick,' Exodus muttered.

Corvala rang a bell on the front counter. A large woman came from the storage rooms in the back. Thick-armed, calloused hands, and square jaw, she looked every bit as rough as the men coming off the river. The only vestiges of femininity about her were her tightly wound braids that ended with little bows.

'What can I get you?' she said. She had the drawl of river folk: long and lazy, like the flow of the Colmane.

'We'd like to stock up on food for the road,' Corvala said.

'We've got bread, dried fish, and pickled eggs.'

After Corvala let her know how much they wanted of each item, the woman went into the back rooms to fill their order.

'Excuse me, miss,' said a gruff voice.

Corvala turned, confronted by a stocky redheaded man with an eyepatch.

'I take it you're a fiddler.' He nodded to Sir William sheathed at her back.

'Yes,' Corvala said, taking a half step back.

The man leaned in expectantly, close enough that Corvala could see a louse in his whiskers and smell the beer on his breath.

'Know how to play 'With Luck Like Yours' and 'South of the Good Life'?'

Corvala nodded apprehensively. *What's this all about?*

He listed off more songs, and of course she knew them all—any fiddler of Stag Ridge who had an ounce of talent could saw those tunes.

'Good,' the man snorted with a satisfied smile. 'I'm on guitar with the band. Hutch, our regular on fiddle, is out. Nasty jab from a catfish spine. Won't be playing for a while. But now that you're here, you could fill in for him. In exchange, I'll see to it that Marge gets you and your friends a meal on the house. Plus an honest cut from the tip jar.'

Corvala, biting her lip, turned to her father. With his elbows propped on the counter, he gave her a sideways glance that said, 'You walked yourself into this.' Dressing up like performers had been her idea, so now she had to play her part.

'Sure,' Corvala replied, turning back to the guitar player. 'I'll help you out.'

'Good.' He gave Corvala's hand a hardy shake. 'Name's Russell.'

Corvala was about to say her real name before she stopped herself. Bargemen and river folk lived on the routes where rumors flowed, and the people of Red Jack had undoubtedly heard the strange news from Dawn's Landing. They might even know the fugitives' names.

'Call me Juliet,' Corvala said, using a name she had once read in an obscure play.

'Come with me, Juliet. I'll introduce you to the boys.'

As the tavern filled with river folk coming in to get their dinner, the band opened with 'Don't Need No Saddle,' and Corvala played right along. There were appearances she had to keep up. Even so, she couldn't help feeling nervous on stage, even if it was a small stage. This was her first time playing for an audience like this. Forty, maybe fifty people, gathered in a dingy tavern. It wasn't how she had pictured her first show, but it was a show nonetheless. She relaxed a little when she realized most of the men in the tavern weren't listening. They were murmuring amongst themselves and chowing down on fried fish and boiled potatoes, the music thrumming out the mood. Corvala saw her father and Serapha seated at a table in the back. Marge, the large woman from behind the counter, put plates heaping with food in front of them. Corvala's stomach growled at the sight of a decent meal, but she forced herself to focus on the music. She even started to have some fun, letting the upbeat songs put a tap in her step. Russell would often glance over at her with an appraising look and nod with approval.

When the band neared the close of the first set, Russell turned to Corvala and said, 'How about we shake this crowd up some. Know 'The Devil Went Down to Georgia'?'

Corvala nodded. It was an old song dating back to the time of the Ancients. It told the story of a young man named Johnny who competes with the Devil in a fiddle-playing match. As the story went, the contest took place in the mythical land of Georgia. Stories and songs like these, as far as forbidden knowledge was concerned, fell into that gray area between what was and wasn't allowed. Russell didn't look concerned. Little villages like Red Jack didn't have much to worry about when it came to the Rooks and the powers-that-be policing their music.

The drummer snapped out the beat, and Corvala's strings sounded with quick mischief. The people in the tavern perked up, stopping in their conversations and looking up from their plates and mugs. They recognized the song immediately. It wasn't every day Russell risked an Ancient song. It seemed he wanted to show off the new talent that had come in off the road. It had been a long time since Corvala played 'The Devil Went Down to Georgia,' so her memory was only half a step ahead of the music. Fortunately for her, it was a relatively easy song despite its rapid tempo. If anything, its quickness helped her cover a few mistakes. Her fingers flew across the strings. Russell rambled off the lyrics, and in no time at all the whole tavern was singing along and stomping their feet in time with the music. Even Marge, Corvala could see, tapped her knuckles against the counter. Just as the band enlivened the room, Corvala felt the crowd's vigor tingling in her limbs. The thrill of the stage pulsed in every nerve. The crowd gave her energy, and she poured every ounce of it right back into her music. Maybe it was only a dingy tavern, but here she found a shred of glory. When the band punched out the final notes, the room erupted with applause.

'Let's give a hand to tonight's fiddler, Juliet!' Russell announced. 'She's coming to us all the way from—'

He leaned in close to Corvala and whispered, 'Where're you from, kid?'

'Hard Scrabble,' Corvala answered hastily.

Then Russell, turning back to the crowd: 'All the way from Hard Scrabble. Let's give her a proper Colmane welcome.'

The applause swelled up again. Corvala bowed to hide her blushing face, reminding herself she was playing the part of a performer who was accustomed to applause. When she rose, Russell clapped a hand on her shoulder.

'They love you. How about you lead the next one? Your pick.'

He pushed her to the front of the stage, and the room grew quiet in expectation, all eyes on her. Under the sudden pressure, her mind went blank. All the songs she knew vanished.

All except one.

No—she couldn't do that one! She racked her brain for others, but the music wouldn't come. Her breathing grew quick and shallow, and her ears and cheeks tingled wildly from nerves. The quiet in the room drew out uncomfortably. Russell leaned in and asked, 'You got this?'

'Yes,' she said, nodding much too vigorously. 'I got this.'

She took a deep breath and drew the bow across the string in a long note. The sound came unhurried and solemn. As she played, she could hear her mother singing the familiar lullaby—words only Corvala could hear.

When peace like a river, attendeth my way,
When sorrows like sea billows roll
Whatever my lot, thou hast taught me to say
It is well,
  it is well,
    with my soul.

The music drew her in, apprehension melting away. It was just her and her fiddle, her mind becoming a still pond. She felt almost weightless as the music flowed through her fingers. Here there was no mission, no beasts, and for a blessed minute all was well.

When Corvala drew out the final note, the impression of it hung in the air. In that liminal moment between sound and silence, with strings still humming noiselessly beneath her fingers, Corvala returned to herself, rising out of the music that had once been there, eyes blinking as if waking from a dream. For many moments the room was still. Then a man at a front table started clapping. More joined in, and pretty soon everyone was on their feet, swelling the room with cheers and applause. Corvala looked to the back to see her father smiling, a look of pride on his face. Her heart swelled. His smile meant more to her than all the praise of the crowd.

Then she caught sight of someone else. Someone who hadn't been there a moment before. There in the middle of the tavern, white gown untouched by the grime of the place.

Her mother.

Corvala froze. The crowd was suddenly muted, as if a heavy invisible blanket had fallen over everything. Corvala's mother spoke in a clear voice.

'If you can keep your head when all about you are losing theirs…'

Corvala blinked. Her mother was gone, and the room's volume came roaring back. The air suddenly became unbearably stuffy, constricting around her throat. As her mind reeled from the vision, she excused herself and nearly tripped off stage.

'Hey, Juliet!" Russell called. 'Where're you going?'

She gave no answer but pushed through the crowded room towards the exit, enduring the quizzical stares and slapping away a few pawing hands. Only when she stumbled out the door and onto the tavern's porch did her lungs open up and take in the cool evening air. Still, she hurried down the road towards the village's edge, not sure what she was doing. There was no running from her visions. Instead, she slipped beneath a raised house and leaned against one of its stilts, giving herself time to breathe. Not a minute later, Exodus and Serapha found her.

'What happened?' her father asked.

'I got stage fright,' she muttered.

Exodus caught her by the shoulders and forced her to face him.

'You might've blown our cover. Now tell me the truth. What's going on?'

Corvala met her father's eyes but didn't know how to respond. The truth was too shameful, and she felt her mouth clamp shut. Fortunately, a voice from the road pulled away her father's penetrating stare.

'Hey!' called out a young man coming towards them. Corvala recognized him as one of the faces she had seen in the tavern.

'Excuse me,' he said, approaching tentatively. 'I work crew on the *Salamander*. My captain sent me to ask you something.'

'What is it?' Exodus said.

'Cap wondered if you'd want passage downriver. We're going west on the Colmane if that's where you're headed.'

Exodus eyed the young bargeman with suspicion and asked, 'How much?'

'Nothing at all. Cap's only asking that she'd play for us a little along the way. Long floats down the Mane can get mighty boring. A little music would do us some good.'

Exodus paused to consider the offer. Corvala could guess what he was thinking—passing through a village of pirates was one thing; being stuck with them on a barge was another. He would be worried about his daughter, not knowing what the bargemen would try to pull while they slept. And being stuck with a crew in close quarters meant lots of questions.

'I'm afraid we can't,' he said at last.

'You can't?' the young man asked, scrunching his brow.

'We appreciate the offer, but we'll walk.'

'Walk? The gorge? That's so far. And robberies are on the rise. Besides, it'll be dark soon.'

Corvala thought of thieves lying in wait at the roadside and remembered the den they had encountered.

'Maybe we should take the barge,' she said, looking at her father.

She could tell he was weighing the options in his head. Neither the road nor the barge sounded good to him.

'What do you think?' he asked, directing his question to Serapha.

'Taking a boat is more efficient than walking.'

'Fine,' he grumbled. 'We'll take the barge.'

Chapter 26

Vlaren remembered all his Hunts as a Rook. But some Hunts were more memorable than others. There was a time early on in his career when he had to track down a dealer of illicit goods—demonic chemicals the Ancients had once cooked up, potions and powders that gave one visions of heaven and hell and all the pleasures and nightmares in between. This dealer went by the alias Obsidian Fox. He was particularly crafty, never showing his face to anyone and seeming to cover long distances as if by magic. When Vlaren tracked him, he would follow trails that led nowhere. At these dead ends, there would always be the mark of a fox, something like an etching on a tree or a painted mark on an alley wall. Vlaren knew they had been left especially for him. Just as he lived for the Hunt, it seemed the Obsidian Fox did as well—not as the pursuer but the pursued.

The tracking on his current Hunt possessed challenges of its own. Riding through Thorn Shroud, he had followed the trail of etheris left behind by the machubus woman. When he had left the forest and rode out into the open hills, dark thunderheads rolled in and overcame him. With lightning crashing all around, he and Lobeka had found scant shelter in the hollow of a hill. He wrapped his helmet in his cloak, but the damage had already been done. The lenses were fragile, designed to pick up faint hints of trace energy in the air, not powerful blasts of lightning. Such exposure damaged them, much like looking into the sun damages the eye. After the storm had let up, Vlaren tested out the helmet. Instead of seeing a trail of etheris, he saw ghosts of lightning bolts burned into the lenses. The damage wasn't permanent. The lenses only needed a few chemical baths to become as good as new. To get that repair, however, he'd have to go back to Pillar Dark. Since there wasn't time for that, he'd have to continue without the aid of lenses.

Having ridden a fair distance to find cover from the storm, he'd left the fugitives' trail. Even if he could find the point where he had left off, the heavy rains had undoubtedly washed away any sign of their passing. He had dealt with worse and welcomed the challenge. No more etheris trail. Now he had to use his wits. From what he knew, the fugitives had taken a winding course through Thorn Shroud. But it hadn't been aimless. They'd directed their path towards certain peculiar stops along the way—the ruins with the dragon's den and the massive tree at the heart of the forest. Now their trail had gone west out into the open hills. They would either go south towards the Aery province or veer north towards the Landsong Gorge. It had to be the latter. That's where Eramez had gone, and something told Vlaren that his current Hunt was connected to his old master's investigation. It was just a hunch, but sometimes when the ground wouldn't reveal any spoor, a hunch was all the tracker had.

Vlaren had found the Obsidian Fox on a hunch. After a long Hunt, he had followed the Fox's trail to a wide river out in the wilderness—It was the fugitive's old ruse: find water. Water meant no trail and no scent left behind for the hounds. So Vlaren had to decide whether his quarry was the type to go upstream or downstream, whether he'd get out on the near bank or the far bank. As Vlaren debated which way to go, he remembered his quarry wasn't a simple prisoner on the run. This was the Obsidian Fox, one who showed a love of wit and cunning, a love for the Hunt. Then Vlaren knew. He simply waded across the river to the other side. And there, hidden behind a stand of cedars near the bank, was the Obsidian Fox. He sat comfortably on the soft grass as if he had been enjoying a picnic, a small teapot and teacup at his side. He took off his fox mask, and Vlaren saw that he wasn't a he at all. *She* was a lithe old woman with a grandmotherly face.

'Good work,' she said with a raise of her cup. 'I was wondering when you were going to find me.' She coughed into a handkerchief, leaving a stain of blood. Then she took a drink. 'What a fun game it has been.'

The poison seized her heart, and she died with a contented smile on her face. Vlaren gave her a burial by that river, for she had been a worthy opponent.

That had been years ago. Now, after a half day's ride through the open hills, he found himself at another river, the Colmane. The road went along its bank and took him into the village of Red Jack. He gave the old fellows on the porch quite a stir, their eyes growing as wide as saucers. When he dismounted from the wulgyre, he sensed many eyes watching him from half-opened doors and shutters. Since the main road ran through the village, the people had probably seen their share of Rooks pass through. But it was enough of a rare occurrence to leave them unsettled. Vlaren preferred it that way. People who feared you were easier to work with.

Lobeka nudged Vlaren's arm, so he took a pair of dead rabbits from the saddlebags and threw them to her. She snapped up each one in a single bite. Vlaren gave two sharp whistles, and she sat on her haunches, her limbs at the ready while her eyes roved the village. Leaving his mount to watch the road, Vlaren took up his staff and entered the most prominent structure in the village: the inn. He took inventory of the room on the lower floor. Being close to the middle of the day, the place was quiet and mostly empty. There was just a single table occupied by some locals having their lunch. A large woman behind the trading post counter sat picking at her nails with a knife. Vlaren pounded his staff against the floorboards to get everyone's attention. When the men at the table saw him, they started in their seats. Vlaren kept still for a moment, letting his presence sink in. Let all the myths, rumors and nonsense they had heard do its work. Let them feel that trepidation down their spine.

'Who's in charge here?' Vlaren asked.

The men at the table immediately pointed at the woman behind the counter. 'She is,' one of them replied.

Unlike the men, the woman retained her composure, planting her fists on the counter and bracing her wide shoulders for this encounter with a Rook.

'You the owner?' Vlaren asked.

'No, I'm the Archon's mistress.'

Vlaren stepped over to the counter, ignoring the quip. 'You must keep an eye on things.'

'Depends what you're looking for.'

'A large bearded man, a dark-skinned woman, and a girl. They might have passed through here not long ago.'

'There were three folks like that last evening. What of it?'

'Do you know where they went?'

'Don't keep much track of such things like that. But I think I heard they took a barge out from the docks early this morning.'

Vlaren could tell the woman was cutting to the chase. The faster she got him out of there, the better.

'Which way were they headed? Upriver or down?'

'That I don't know. A few barges left this morning, some going downriver, some going up. I don't know which of them your people took.'

Vlaren read the woman. She wasn't lying. She had no reason to. There was no affinity between her and the trio he was hunting.

Vlaren turned to the men at the table. 'Do you know which way they went?'

The men looked at the floor or their meals, too afraid to address a Rook.

'How about you?' Vlaren asked, singling one of them out, a gangly man with long greasy hair. 'You look like you might know.'

He looked up with stricken eyes, probably thinking the Rook was reading his mind, studying a history of petty crimes. Whatever frightening myth he had skittering around in his head, it made him talk.

'I think they left on the *Salamander*. I'm not sure. They might have gone on the *Reed Queen*. That one pulled out of here this morning, too. Did you catch which one they went on, Gitty?' He tapped the man sitting next to him.

Gitty didn't dare look up from his plate of fried fish as he shook his head. 'I didn't see nothing of them after they left here last night.'

Vlaren could tell these men weren't liars, just ignorant. He preferred confronting liars. Liars would give up their secrets once broken, and he had broken plenty. Recognizing empty pursuit, he turned away without a word and left the men to their meals, but he suspected they wouldn't have much of a stomach for food after his visit. He could practically hear their sighs of relief as he went out the door.

His investigation at the docks proved just as fruitless. Some of the dock workers had seen the trio, but no one was certain which barge they had taken or which direction they were headed. Opinions conflicted and stories didn't match up. It didn't matter. Vlaren had been right about their coming this way. He knew they would go downstream through the Landsong Gorge as it cut its way through the Moss Kettle Mountains. The gorge was over eighty miles long, and there were many places within it they could go. He thought about where the trail had led him so far—the goblin camp, the dragon den, and the enormous tree. There was something piecing these places together, some clue pointing to where they were headed. Then an idea came to him, a secret known by very few. It was just a hunch. But sometimes a hunch was all he needed on the Hunt.

Chapter 27

The cool of night had settled on the Colmane River. The barge *Salamander* was beached on a gravelly island. It was a good spot to stop for the night since it provided safety from any bands of thieves that might be roaming the Colmane's shores. The *Salamander*'s crew had made camp under the island's few trees. A fire crackled in the center of camp, and the crew sat around it contentedly, their bellies full of the trout they had roasted over the flames. Corvala played her fiddle for the evening's entertainment.

The captain and owner of the *Salamander*, Captain Jarrett, sat with his wife Petunia on comfortable wooden chairs as they listened to Corvala. Jarrett was a short, stout man with fierce eyes, thick swarthy limbs, and cheeks bristling with mutton chops. Petunia was plump as well as cheery and hale with a ruddy complexion. When Corvala saw the couple together, she thought of a silly song she might write one day—'The Badger and the Pumpkin.' While Captain Jarett appeared indifferent to Corvala's playing, Petunia sat listening with a rosy-cheeked smile and clapped her hands in time with the music.

From what Corvala had seen while floating down the river, Jarrett growled orders and grumbled about staying on schedule. His other barge, the *Lily Pad*, hadn't returned from Ryperia, and he was anxious to see for himself what had happened. He suspected the barge's crew had turned mutinous and taken the vessel for themselves, which was another reason he had come this way— to find this crew. But the men murmured about how there were hardly any barges coming from the opposite direction. The only ones being pulled upriver along the towpaths had launched from closer ports. None had launched from Ryperia or its surrounding villages. All that they heard were foreboding tales that sounded too outrageous to be true—stories about a golden man.

Jarrett had dismissed the news—'Just a bunch of superstitious nonsense spread by the bargemen'—but Corvala couldn't help but wonder if this was the intruder come down from the heavens. From what she remembered of the shooting star—or the flying vessel, rather— it had flown towards the Landsong and the regions northwest. The details added up. All the more reason to get to where they were going—and quickly.

The men were spooked. But Jarret was paying them prime coin, so they kept their mouths shut when he was around. Who knew why the captain had brought his wife along? She worked counter to his grain of desired efficiency. As the crew had been busy at the oars, Petunia had casually strolled about the deck, watering the potted flowers she kept in precarious places. She'd often stop the crew members at random moments and give them unasked-for advice. 'Rudy, you should be married, a strong, handsome young man like you.' Then moments later—'Don't slouch, Kugen. It's bad posture.' From what Corvala saw, Petunia was the one who was really in charge of the whole operation. The crew may have answered to the captain; the captain, however, answered to his wife. All Petunia had to say was, 'Now, now Mr.

Jarrett,' and he would do as told. Corvala figured that it hadn't been the captain's idea to bring performers onboard but his wife's, the woman making the request of her husband while they had been dining at Red Jack's inn. Just as Petunia had potted flowers to beautify the barge, she'd have music to beautify the voyage.

Even after a long day at the oars, spirits were high that night, and the special presence of good music was an excuse to break open a keg of beer—much to Jarrett's chagrin. But Petunia patted his arm and said, 'Let the boys live a little.' Frothy mugs were passed around, and after a while, the crew was laughing easily along with the music.

Corvala had started that evening with some jigs and reels that had them all chuckling and clapping. Now, with the moon up and the hour late, she was playing softer, slower strathspeys, hoping it would help the crew nod off to sleep. She did this more for herself than for them. The crew had pushed mugs of beer on her between songs. She wasn't much of a drinker, so she just took sips. Even so, after a couple of hours of playing and drinking, the booze began to take its toll. Her hands felt farther off, and she was making slipups in her music. With drowsy eyes, she played one last ballad about a drunk who falls asleep on his horse and wakes up in a town full of beautiful women. She concluded with a bow, but the crew wanted more.

'Give us another!'

'Yes! Play some more.'

Corvala didn't have another one in her, not with the beer dulling her senses, so she gave Petunia a beseeching look. Woman to woman, the captain's wife would understand.

'Quiet, boys,' Petunia called from her seat. 'Give the poor dear a rest.' She turned a forced smile on Corvala. 'You can stop if you'd like. Or you can play more. Whatever you wish.'

'I think I'll call it a night,' Corvala yawned.

Petunia's smile waned. She managed to say, 'Thank you, Juliet. It was absolutely lovely.'

Corvala—or Juliet as she was known to the crew— gave one last bow and went to sit down with her father.

'How about you, Hamlet?' one of the crew members called out. 'Got anything for us?'

The camp turned its attention to where Exodus sat. Upon being called to perform, he kept a calm composure, but Corvala thought she could see a shade of dread. Put among a pack of criminals and violent men, he'd comfortably bring all things to order. But have him play pretend at being a traveling performer, and he was out of his element.

'What's your act?' someone asked.

'I do… magic… tricks,' Exodus replied.

'Magic!' Petunia cried, clapping her hands together excitedly. 'How lovely! Give us a show.'

'I'm afraid most of my equipment has been taken,' Exodus said, forcing himself into his role. He shook his head dolefully. 'Thieves these days.'

Corvala was impressed. It wasn't a great lie, but it was more than she expected of her father.

'Surely you can give us one trick,' Petunia begged.

The crew bellowed their agreement and looked expectantly at Exodus. Corvala felt a nervous tingle run down her back, her hands gripping Sir William tightly. Exodus kept calm and assessed the crew. To Corvala's surprise, he nodded in compliance with their request.

'I can do one trick,' he stated. 'I need to borrow a coin.'

One of the crew members quickly produced a kwet and handed it to Exodus. Exodus held the coin up for all to see, then clasped his fist around it. When he opened his hand, the kwet was gone. There were murmurs of amazement. The most astonished witness was Corvala, her mouth fallen open in disbelief. It was nothing but a simple parlor trick, but to Corvala—whose wits were numbed by booze—it was an impressive work of magic. One done by her father, of all people.

Exodus pointed to Captain Jarrett and said, 'Check your vest pocket.'

The captain looked put out at being given a command, but after a nudge from his wife, he did as he was told. He reached into his vest pocket, and to his surprise, there was the copper kwet. The stern Captain Jarrett was suddenly caught up in a bit of wonder.

'Would you look at that?' he said, with an amused smile that showed off a few of his gold teeth.

The crew called for more tricks. Exodus had to turn them down, since he didn't have any more up his sleeve. Still, the crew insisted. It didn't matter that all of his supplies were 'stolen.' He was a performer, wasn't he? He could pull something out of his hat.

Corvala grew nervous again, but then Serapha spoke up.

'I may be able to entertain you,' she said, calling attention to herself. 'I can throw things in the air and catch them.'

For a moment, those gathered around the fire were at a loss for words, unsure of what she was driving at.

'You mean you can juggle?' someone asked.

'Yes,' she replied. 'I can juggle.'

'Oh, I would love to see that,' Petunia cried out gleefully. 'Go on, Hippolyta, show us some juggling.'

Serapha—Hippolyta to the crew—gathered a pile of fist-sized stones from around her feet and kept three in her hand. She started juggling, and after a while, she kicked up one of the stones from the pile and began juggling four. She flicked in another so it was five. Another and it was six, then seven, then eight. She kept adding and adding until a dozen stones were spinning in the air. Some seated around the fire gasped in amazement, watching her hands move with speed and smooth precision. If her act hadn't been astounding enough, she split her juggling loop in two so that each hand juggled six stones on its own. She concluded by throwing all of them in the air at once and catching them on her outstretched arms. At first, the crew sat in silent awe of what they had seen. Then they exploded in cheers and applause. Corvala found herself clapping as well. She knew Serapha to be agile and quick, but she had never seen a spectacle like this before. Then again, what could Corvala expect? Serapha wasn't anything natural.

'Given what I have witnessed of your behavior, it is highly improbable that you will allow me to conclude now. Therefore, I will juggle more for you. I have heard that people are impressed when knives are juggled because knives are sharp and therefore dangerous. In the likelihood of impressing you, I will juggle knives. Do any of you have knives I can juggle?'

The crew looked at one another, jaws slack and befuddled by what she had said.

'I have one,' a crewman said at length, offering her the clam knife from his belt.

The men then produced blades of all kinds—hunting knives, filet knives, daggers. Serapha collected them all and began juggling.

Corvala watched, amazed by the hidden talents her company possessed. More pressing than the entertainment before her, however, was a question tickling the front of her mind. She leaned in close to her father and gave him a nudge with her elbow.

'I didn't know you could do magic,' she whispered.

'It's not magic. Just a trick.'

'But how did you get the coin in the captain's vest pocket?'

'I didn't. The coin was already there.'

Corvala gave him a quizzical look.

'I could see a sag in the pocket,' Exodus explained. 'No doubt from the weight of a kwet. Captain probably forgot it was there.'

'So, you just hid the coin you had and made a lucky guess about another.'

'A calculated guess,' Exodus corrected.

Corvala grinned at the clever trick. 'How did you make the coin disappear? That one I can't figure.'

'Let's just call it sleight of hand,' Exodus replied, and he gave her one of his rare smiles. Corvala thought he would leave it at that since he turned his gaze towards Serapha's juggling act and took a long draught from his mug. But he continued, 'I wasn't always a Judge, Corvala. I had a… former life.'

'What do you mean?'

'I used to be a pickpocket.'

'A *pickpocket*?' she gasped. Such an impossible idea shook her out of her drowsiness. 'You're kidding.'

'It's true,' he said. 'Tonight, I relied on old skills—the skills of a thief. They're rusty now. But I still have them, it seems. Quick hands to make a coin disappear. Eyes to notice the coin in the captain's pocket. Don't like those assets. Even so, they came in handy tonight.'

Corvala rarely heard her father talk about his past so openly. Maybe it was the beer loosening his tongue. Whatever it was, Corvala welcomed it heartily even as it shook her up. Her father, a former criminal? It couldn't be so.

Exodus paused, looking into his mug as though it held secrets only he could see. Then he set his jaw in resolve and continued his story.

'After I was orphaned as a child, life was rough. Ended up in the port city of Sockeye. Stealing to eat. Stealing to impress other street kids. Back then, I thought it was the best I could get. An older boy named Dirk took me under his wing. Wanted to make something of me, I suppose. Every day we picked and stole. Every day he taught me the trade. Then a job went south, and Dirk ended up killing a woman. That's when a Judge got involved.

'Judge Abraham. He found Dirk and killed him. Found me, too. Showed me mercy, though, because I was young. Only about eleven or twelve. He gave me a choice: turn my life around with a Judge's training or die right then and there.'

Corvala shook her head in tipsy bewilderment. 'Why are you telling me all this?' she breathed.

For a moment Exodus paused. 'Because now's a good time.' Then after a few more moments, he spoke again, his eyes locked on the fire. 'I know you wonder why I did it—why I allowed the Capels to stone me. Why I would give them the chance to take me away from you. No vague notion of good drove me. I saw myself in them, what I could've become. Maybe I was being merciful. But I did it for myself.'

Corvala looked long at her father and felt like she should've said something. Her mind felt slow and her tongue thick. Besides, whatever she told him would've been cut off by the burst of wild cheers and applause from around the campfire. Serapha had given her grand finale—catching all the knives and then flinging them in rapid succession, each one sticking to a different tree about the island. It was a masterful—and terrifying—display of marksmanship.

After the applause, Captain Jarrett gave the word for everybody to get to bed. It was late, and he wanted to get an early start in the morning. With a few groans and pro-tests, mixed with plenty of yawns, the crew retired to their bedrolls and hammocks. Even Petunia couldn't ar-gue with her husband's order. Her head was drooping, and her eyes were heavy, so she shuffled off to her quar-ters aboard the beached *Salamander*.

As Corvala lay on her bedroll by the fire, she thought of how the three of them had pulled off that evening's performance. Each of them had played their part and played it well. There would be no doubt in the crew's mind that this trio was a troupe of traveling performers—even if that was a lie. The thought made Corvala grin. Besides their successful ruse, she thought mostly of what her father had told her. He had been a pickpocket; she still couldn't get over that. Perhaps she never would. She wanted to sit with that thought, ruminate on it. But her drowsiness eventually took over. As the campfire died, she dozed off, dreaming of flying knives and disappearing coins.

Chapter 28

The Colmane River flowed along the base of the Moss Kettle Mountains, carving out the Landsong Gorge. The gorge was wide, a breadth of three miles in some places, and extended nearly eighty miles before it reached the western coast. Down the gorge's slopes and cliff faces, there flowed waterfalls and streams that fed into the Colmane, making the rocks and earth mossy with life. The *Salamander* floated down the river and through the gorge where a fertile basin hummed with green. Even the villages on the river banks seemed to have sprung up from the soil, their floodwater stilts standing like tree trunks and their clay shingled roofs hosting gardens of ferns.

The *Salamander* made a stop at the little port town of Echo Bend where their passengers disembarked.

'Goodbye, Juliet!' said Petunia, vigorously shaking Corvala's hand. 'Goodbye, Hippolyta! Goodbye, Hamlet! Your work is lovely, absolutely lovely!'

Captain Jarrett delivered a curt farewell. He seemed distracted, as if he was itching to find out what happened to his lost barge, the *Lily Pad*. The strange lack of boat traffic coming from the west end of the gorge had made him even more anxious. After a simple wave and a nod, he ordered his crew to cast off. No time for lollygagging, not while there was daylight burning. So, the *Salamander* continued downstream, as Corvala, Serapha, and Exodus entered Echo Bend.

The little town sat at the foot of the stairs leading to High Court. It was a hive of activity for all the people going up and down the mountainside, pilgrims from the eastern and western roads, coming and going from the boats at the docks. Like any town, there were inns for the weary and stores where travelers could buy supplies. What made Echo Bend unique was its many booths where self-proclaimed lawyers hung out their shingles.

'Get your forms stamped and notarized here,' they shouted. 'Don't climb the two-thousand steps only to learn you're missing papers. Talk to me. I'll get you what you need.'

This bustling economy—a rich mixture of sizzling street food and hasty legal advice—thrived on the town's proximity to High Court. It was all noise and busyness, a stark contrast to the quiet wilderness the three travelers had recently left. With the buildings crowded so tightly against the foot of the steep mountainside, Corvala wondered how the whole town didn't go tumbling into the river. She tried to mimic her father's plain and inconspicuous demeanor, but she couldn't help feeling like a fugitive while she walked among the crowds, thinking that someone might turn to her at any moment and say, 'Hey! Ain't you that girl who ran from Dawn's Landing?' She reminded herself their disguises would put up a sufficient front. Their performer outfits may have been a novelty in the backwards village of Red Jack, but not here in Echo Bend. There were people wearing clothes of all different fashions—farmers in rough spun cloth and wealthy merchants in fur-hemmed tunics. There were even brightly garbed performers panhandling at every other street corner. Corvala was just another face in the crowd.

'Don't worry,' she whispered to Sir William. 'No one's looking for us here. What fugitive would run towards the law?'

After walking a few blocks into town, she was relieved to find most people were too focused on their own business to give her any attention. Corvala overheard a middle-aged woman at a lawyer's booth, her eyes wild and her voice shaking.

'...Haven't seen her in over a week. She went to Ryperia to visit her aunt. She was supposed to be back by...'

Her plea was swept away in the passing crowds as Corvala moved on. More supplications took its place from other desperate petitioners. Words like 'missing' and 'gone' punctuated the air. Something was wrong. The bargemen had spoken of towns and villages being emptied and people following a strange golden man. Captain Jarrett had dismissed the rumors as foolish stories. Corvala began to wonder if he was wrong. What if there really was a golden man? And what if he was the intruder from the heavens?

Echo Bend's main road led to a tall archway at the edge of town. Beyond the archway, steep stairs climbed out of the gorge and ascended the mountainside. Corvala joined those who gaped at what lay ahead. She craned her neck back to see where the stairs ended, but they disappeared into the contours of the cliff face. High Court was hidden up there, somewhere near the peaks and clouds. This wasn't Corvala's first time coming to High Court, having visited with her father when she was little. Why he had brought her along on that trip, she couldn't recall. What she did remember was that he carried her the whole way up. Now she would climb the stairs herself.

Or perhaps not.

'Look over there,' she said, nudging her father. 'They can carry us up.'

Parked near the archway were a few dozen palanquins with their carriers resting beside them. Although the palanquin carriers weren't large burly men, they looked built for the task of carrying people up the mountain. They were incredibly lean, and their legs and shoulders appeared to possess a wiry strength. Their signs read: *twelve tocs per person*. Corvala thought the price a little much but believed they could afford it. There was enough in the bag of coins she had filched from the thieves' den.

'I do not need the assistance,' Serapha replied. 'I do not fatigue as you do.'

Exodus didn't even bother to look over at the palanquins but just shook his head. 'We don't need the attention.'

Corvala considered the mountain gloomily. 'It's so far up,' she whined.

'You've walked across Thorn Shroud,' Exodus said. 'You can walk up some stairs.'

'Come on. We can afford it.'

'That's a waste.'

'The money we have—it's not from savings. It sort of fell into our lap.'

'We stole it.'

Corvala rolled her eyes. 'My point is, it came to us as an extra, so we can use it on something extra. Don't we deserve an easy break?'

'Save the money. You may need it for something important.'

'So now you want to keep it? That's interesting because you were the one who was against us taking it. Why don't we get rid of it now? Hand it to those nice men over there so they can give us a ride up the mountain.'

Exodus turned on her, his expression darker and more severe than the occasion merited. Corvala shrank back a little. Something was troubling him, and she could tell it didn't have to do with palanquins and money.

'Would you spend what you have on laziness?' he said, concern in his voice. 'How will you care for yourself when I'm—?' He cut himself off.

'When you're what?' Corvala asked with a slight tremble.

Scratching his chin, Exodus turned from her and looked up the mountain. 'Nothing,' he said. 'Let's get going.'

There were five High Courts found throughout the Norwestor Dominion—one in the north, south, east, and west, and one in the capital city of Belcastan. High Court North stood at the top of the stairs climbing up from Echo Bend. It was not uncommon for those who made the climb to think or ask aloud, 'Why is this place so out of the way? Why couldn't it have been built down where we could get to it easily?' The answer to those questions was threefold, the first having to do with keeping unimportant business away. The builders and planners of High Court North figured that if a case was important enough, people would make the climb so they could be heard. Those with trivial matters would take one look at the stairs and think, 'Maybe I don't need to air out my grievances after all.' The second reason for the High Court's location had to do with the relationship between the Order of Judges and the Norwestor Dominion. Since the two were separate entities that served and policed one another, the place where the two met had to be neutral, hence a convergence on the mountain heights where no people dwelled. The third reason for High Court's location had to do with authority. When people made the climb up the stairs, they were being told subtly yet firmly that the law stood over their land.

Corvala didn't care much for these reasons as she made the ascent. The stairs were wide enough to accommodate the foot traffic; they were steep as well. Besides the occasional switchback, they went straight up the mountainside, each step rising above mid-shin. Corvala's calves were soon burning with exertion. Her eyes stayed mostly on her feet so she wouldn't trip and stumble. When she looked back, she expected to see they had come a long way. But Echo Bend was in plain sight below, and High Court remained hidden somewhere above. As she climbed, Corvala and those around her would occasionally have to step aside to make way for the rich or infirm taking a palanquin up the mountain. Towards the beginning of her climb, Corvala watched them pass with longing. The farther up she went, the more her longing became jealousy and her jealousy a loathing that those who are exhausted feel towards those afforded rest and comfort. Despite this, she knew she couldn't have ridden up that way and maintained a low profile. Even though she would never admit it to her father, she knew he had been right. The palanquins brought too much attention— and negative attention at that.

Eventually, Corvala found her rhythm, and her soreness dulled as her body accepted the hike up the stairs. Although it had only been a little over a week since she had left Dawn's Landing, the journey had made her body and will stronger. Many other pilgrims making the climb had to pause often to catch their breath. Corvala found herself passing them as she kept up with her father and Serapha. She certainly wasn't springing up the stairs like the palanquin carriers, but she felt a new endurance within her. Despite this growing strength, she was relieved in knowing they wouldn't be taking these stairs down. They had a different route.

It was midday when they made it to the top of the stairs. Before them stood a concave wall in the mountainside, a cliff face that made Corvala feel quite small. At the base of the cliffs lay the grounds of High Court. There was a square with a small stream running through its middle. Forming the perimeter of the square were three massive structures built against the cliff face, each one appearing to have been carved out of the mountain. To the right was the Judiciary Wing where trials took place. In the center was the Fountain Wing, a quiet refuge where priests and pilgrims prayed and meditated. To the left was the Library Wing where thousands and thousands of books on law and medicine, history and theology were shelved. The whole of the area stood like a beacon of civilization, holding a commanding view of the gorge below. Corvala, holding her sides and catching her breath, looked back where they had come and saw wisps of cloud and flocks of white birds below. Farther down flowed the Colmane, a thin glittering band at the bottom of the gorge.

Turning from the view, she spied the tail end of a quiet exchange between Serapha and her father. He was somewhat obscured by the foot traffic, but Corvala could see the grim expression on his face. Then, spotting her, he called, 'Come. We'd better be going.'

Corvala followed him to the colonnade of the Judiciary Wing where they found privacy behind a pillar.

'The door to the secret path is in the lower level of the Library Wing,' he said. 'But the key to open the door—I'll need to go to the Judiciary Wing to get it.'

'People in there will have certainly heard of the fugitives of Dawn's Landing,' Corvala said, looking apprehensively at the large doorway looming ahead. 'The authorities know to look for three. So how about we break up that number.'

Exodus nodded. 'I'll need you to come with me to help me get into the inner halls. Serapha, you wait for her in the Fountain Wing.'

'What about the Judges?' Corvala asked. 'They'll recognize you.'

'Don't you worry about that,' he said, lowering the brim of his hat to cover his eyes. 'Once you're done helping me, find Serapha and go to the Library Wing. The librarians are watchful and don't allow loitering, so be quick.' He cast one more disapproving look at Corvala's and Serapha's outfits. 'And try not to draw attention to yourselves. Go directly to the lower level, all the way to the far wall at the end. Seventh bookcase on the left. Got it?'

With the plan set, Exodus motioned for them to go. Corvala took a deep breath as she followed him through the massive doors and into the halls of justice.

Chapter 29

Doing as Exodus instructed, Serapha went to the Fountain Wing. Passing through its main archway, she came to a large courtyard where a spring bubbled at the center, the source of the stream that ran through High Court's square. Around the pool grew a garden where a few priests picked herbs or sat in meditation. Serapha was about to enter the courtyard and wait on one of the stone benches when a voice called out.

'Tut tut tut. Don't forget to take off your shoes. This is sacred ground.'

Serapha looked to the corner of the courtyard to see a tiny old man sitting on a stool. He was bald, and thick cataracts clouded his eyes. His empty gaze vaguely turned in Serapha's direction. Before him lay a wide assortment of shoes placed in neat rows.

'Bring your shoes to me,' he said. 'I'll keep an eye on them.' He laughed at the joke, one he must have told a million times before. 'Don't worry, you can trust me. Wonder how I do it? It's the smell. I know who belongs to what shoe by using my nose. Keeps people honest. Never got it wrong in my forty years of shoe-keeping.'

Serapha paused.

PROCESSING...

She couldn't take off her boots. If she did, she'd reveal not a human foot but a mechanical one. Deciding it was better to alter Exodus's plan than to get caught, she turned to leave. The blind shoe-keeper called to her.

'Don't go, miss. I didn't scare you off, did I? You don't have to worry. Your secret's safe with me.'

Serapha stared at the little old man.

PROCESSING...

'What secret could you know?' she said in a low voice. 'I have told you nothing.'

'You don't need to say anything. I can sense plenty— and smell it. You're not like the rest of us. There's something different about you, something angelic.'

Serapha took a step back from him.

DOES NOT COMPUTE.

'There I go again, scaring you off,' he said, shaking his head. He tapped a fist on his bald pate. 'Old thought box ain't what it used to be. Come back, come back. That's a dear. I'll pick my words wisely. Not here to scare you. Just have to know what you've come here for.'

'I'm here to wait for my companions,' Serapha replied.

The shoe-keeper grinned, a knowing glint in his empty eyes. 'Of course you are. But I have a feeling you're here for something far bigger. Beings like you don't deal in the trivial matters of the courts. No, you're here for something far more important. I wonder, are you here to solve our problem?'

'I am not aware of the problem to which you are referring?'

At this, the shoe-keeper dropped his jovial tone for a grave one. 'The problem in Ryperia. Something terrible is happening. The city's a vortex, drawing people in and dragging them down into darkness. Only rumors and whispers get out. The public doesn't really know what's going on. I do. What little they say, I catch. Been collecting it and piecing it together.

'From what I've gathered, a man with strange magic has set himself up as a god over the city. He's taking human sacrifices, accusing people of crimes they didn't commit and then having his way with them. It's like something out of the Holy Book. Worse than Ahab and Jezebel. The Judges and priests don't know what to do about it. They're too blind.

'Now I've got a feeling you were sent by God to deal with this problem. Sensed it the moment you stepped in here. The question is, my angel dear, what are you going to do about it?'

The main hall where Corvala and Exodus walked stretched the entire length of the Judiciary Wing. They passed through small crowds and slanted columns of sunlight that shone down from large windows high above. People wandered in and out of archways leading to courtrooms and smaller halls, some of them robed lawyers with heavy books tucked under their arms. Along the wall were people on stone benches, regular folk brought before the law or those who came to have their cases heard—all sitting in the eternal wait demanded by bureaucracy. Corvala and Exodus made their way down the hall and passed a pair of Judges, both of them in their leather uniforms and each with a sword sheathed at his side.

'Know them?' Corvala whispered out the side of her mouth.

'Yes,' Exodus muttered, his head down so the brim of his hat covered most of his face.

'They didn't see us.'

'Of course. They don't expect us here. Sometimes the closer you are, the thicker your disguise.'

Corvala cocked her head. 'Pick that up from your time on the streets?'

As soon as the words left her mouth, she regretted them—their meaning dragging up what must be a painful memory. But her father just shrugged it off.

'I suppose I did.'

The two of them walked on and came to the end of the hall where there were fewer people. In this secluded space stood a door set back in a deep recess in the wall. Etched into the capstone above the door was the symbol of the Judges: a broken pot with fire coming from it. Beneath it stood a bored-looking guard. Exodus drew Corvala to the side, away from the guard's line of sight.

'I'm going in there,' Exodus said, nodding to the door.

'That's where you'll find the key?'

Her father nodded, not really paying attention, his gaze focused on the door.

'I'll need you to get the guard away from there.'

Corvala frowned. 'How do you expect me to do that?'

'Ask him where the permit office is. Pretend you're a naïve girl from the sticks and this big place confuses you.'

'Is that what you think of me?' Corvala asked, giving his side a jab with her elbow.

But her playful smirk vanished when she saw his brow knit with worry—a subtle expression only she would notice. She blinked, and it was gone. Perhaps she had just imagined it.

'You'll do just fine,' Exodus said, squeezing his daughter's hand, his visage firm with confidence. 'If your act can win over a barge crew, then this should be nothing.'

Corvala walked up to the guard by the door. He was young, perhaps her age. He had the dark leather garb of a Judge but didn't yet have his shoulder buckle bearing the Judge's symbol, which meant he was still a tin-blade, an apprentice to a Judge. This menial task of guarding a door was probably part of paying his dues.

'Excuse me,' Corvala said, using the best vacuous bearing she could manage. 'Do you know where I can find the permit office?'

'Just down that way,' said the tin-blade. 'Fourth hall on the right, third counter in.'

'Hmm… over there?' she said, pointing to the wrong place.

'No,' the tin-blade grunted in annoyance. 'Over there.' And he pointed where she ought to go.

'I'm not sure. There are lots of doors and offices here. I don't want to get lost… Could you show me?'

He rolled his eyes. 'Come on.'

Corvala followed him as he led her to the permit office. She cast a furtive glance back and saw her father slip through the unguarded door. Part of her wondered what he'd do if he encountered any Judges in there, but she pushed the worry aside so she could do her part and keep up the act.

Once she was taken down the corridor and to the permit office counter, Corvala sighed in feigned relief. 'Oh, here it is!'

The tin-blade gave her a curt nod and left to return to his duties. Once he was out of sight, Corvala slipped out of line and headed towards the exit in search of Serapha.

The Library Wing looked very similar to the Judiciary Wing: a long hall stretching back from the main entrance. The front half yawned with sunlight streaming down from tall windows. The back half sank into dimness as it extended into the mountain. Running down the entire length were rows and rows of bookcases and various levels connected by stairways. Worked into the stone pillars that held up the vaulted ceiling were statues of scholarly figures. Their stone faces looked down with cold stares, their expressions demanding reverence. There was no talking in these halls, and visitors shuffled quietly from shelf to shelf or sat reading in private nooks.

Upon entering, Corvala and Serapha passed the front desk. The librarian seated there was a pale woman who appeared more at home among the dark archives than the light of day. She looked up from her ledger and eyed the two visitors, her expression conveying strict guardianship of this hall of knowledge. The colorful clothing on Corvala and Serapha's backs may have blended in with the crowds down in Echo Bend, but here in the library, they looked nothing like the scholars who stuck to browns and grays.

'Can I help you?' the librarian asked, voice openly colored with suspicion.

'We're just looking, thank you,' Corvala said.

This earned them a scowl from the librarian, and she went back to her ledger, muttering something about how this was a place for scholarship, not tourism.

Serapha walked past the rows of bookcases while Corvala pretended to be browsing. On the western side of the hall, they found a stairway that descended into shadow. Across the entry to the stairs hung a rope with a sign that read: NO PUBLIC ACCESS GRANTED. After Corvala glanced over her shoulder to make sure no one was looking, she and Serapha slipped under the rope.

The lower level was all dark except for the glow Serapha produced from her hand. As Corvala's eyes adjusted, she could make out more rows of bookcases. The books were bound in wrinkled and cracked leather, their spines bearing fading titles and intricate patterns of silver and gold. Bay leaves stuck out of the fragile pages to keep the bugs away, and there were open jars of salt on the shelves to help keep the air dry. The books here didn't look too different from the books on the upper levels except each volume here had a thin chain that kept it leashed to its place. This must be where the library held its collection of rare and valuable items yet to be copied by the scribes. No wonder casual visitors weren't permitted.

Corvala and Serapha moved carefully through the dark. They followed Exodus's instructions and went to the far wall at the end of the room, coming to the seventh bookcase to the left. Corvala knocked on its wooden back. The boards were thick, but she could hear a hollow emptiness behind them. She started moving books aside, looking for where there might be a hidden keyhole. Serapha reached her fingers around to the back and pulled, the bookcase swinging open like a door. Within lay the opening of a tunnel, the beginning of the secret path Exodus had told them about. The tunnel ran through the raw stone of the mountain, and its length disappeared into darkness. Corvala peered inside, cool stale air brushing against her face.

'That's strange,' she said. 'It's already unlocked.'

'There is no key for this door,' said Serapha.

'What do you mean, no key?'

'Your father was being false with you when he spoke to you about a key. He said you could not know until you and I arrived here.'

Corvala blanched at this. 'Fah… lied…'

'He said it was for your benefit.'

'No!' Corvala said, shaking her head. 'That's not true.'

She turned to the bookcase and resumed her search for a keyhole or any device that might have kept the wood latched to the wall. She convinced herself that Serapha's strength must have broken the lock—that's why the door had opened. She started taking books out one at a time. But as her search came up with nothing and as her desperation grew, she tore books away by the armful. Rare bindings crashed to the floor, their fragile pages crumpling. Only when all the shelves were emptied did she give up her search. There was no keyhole. And if there was no keyhole, then there was no key.

The darkness around her suddenly became more profound, and she shivered with cold.

'Why would he lie to me?' she muttered.

'He said it was the only way you would go willingly. You had to think there was a plan.'

Corvala remembered the private word shared between her father and Serapha when they had arrived at High Court.

'Tell me he's coming for us.' Corvala's voice was shaking now, hope and anger battling underneath. 'Tell me he's coming.'

'He said he wishes for us to go on without him. He said he is staying behind to clear your name.'

The words landed on Corvala's ears, but she refused to receive them. She stood there, stunned, her throat suddenly feeling thick.

'No,' she whispered. Then she shook her head and spoke louder. 'He wouldn't.'

'That is what he told me,' Serapha replied. 'He has elected to stay. Therefore, we must continue the mission without him.'

'No. He'll come for us. Watch! Any moment now, he'll walk down those stairs.'

Corvala looked to the other end of the room where a lonely patch of light shone down the stairs from the level above. She watched and waited. Serapha was putting the tossed aside books back in the bookcase, apparently attempting to hide evidence of their coming here. When she finished, she reached out to take Corvala's hand.

'We need to take the path.'

Corvala pulled away. 'No!' she screamed, upsetting the dusty silence. 'We have to wait for him!'

Then she heard something—steps coming down the stairway.

'Fah!'

'What?' replied a sharp voice from above. 'Who's down there?' It sounded like the librarian, her shadow preceding her as she came.

Corvala's heart sank.

'We need to go,' Serapha said, grabbing Corvala's hand. Corvala didn't resist. She stared down the length of the room, not understanding—not wanting to understand. Serapha ushered her into the tunnel and shut the bookcase door behind them. Now there was only darkness ahead.

Chapter 30

Judge Abraham walked one of High Court's many courtyards—a secluded offshoot of the Judiciary Wing. The walls here were bushy with ivy, and some chickens scratched and pecked at the hard-packed earth. A single pear tree grew up from the center of the yard. Although the courtyard wasn't as impressive as the garden in the Fountain Wing, it was quiet enough and gave Abraham a place where he could be alone to think. He strolled about, casting feed to the chickens. He could have been in his inner chamber writing his book, but it was too nice a day to be inside.

He walked slowly, a mere echo of his former strength. His shoulders, once broad and powerful, were slumped with age. His hair, previously swept back in a lion's mane, was sparse and wispy. Most of his life he had been out in the world, hunting down bad people and bringing about justice. Those days were gone. He had been granted retirement nearly six years ago. No more violence from his hand; no more facing trial by a community. Now he remained in High Court, his sword hung up above his bed where it collected dust. It was for the best, he supposed. Out in the world, he was a throwback, old and weak. In High Court, he was esteemed.

There were no ranks among the Judges, no special titles. They were an Order outside civilian law and therefore bound to no formal hierarchy. Nonetheless, Abraham was seen as an unofficial leader in the Order. He was their elder, one who had survived many battles. He possessed wisdom by experience; therefore, younger Judges sought him out for counsel. Not only how to win with a sword but also how to use a sword wisely and justly.

Given his safety and status in High Court, this was where he chose to reside. Here he could work on his book, his last gift to the world, sharing his adventures so the generations to follow could learn from his successes and failures. As far as most were concerned, he couldn't have asked for a better way to spend his final days. He was comfortable and should have been happy. But something bothered Abraham. Something was coming for him. He sensed its approach the way a beast of the field senses rain coming from beyond the horizon. It wasn't death he felt. Abraham had long accepted the coming of that old visitor. No, this was something else, a choice that would be set before him by God. One final test to see if he was truly a man of justice. He knew it was coming, and it darkened the back of his mind like a thunderhead.

As he fed the chickens in the courtyard, Abraham inadvertently looked up at the sky. The sun was out, and puffy white clouds sailed gently across the blue. This couldn't be a day of reckoning. It was too nice. Indeed, he felt he could sit back and enjoy it for a moment or two. Tossing the last of the feed, he took a seat on a stone bench beneath the pear tree and leaned back against the trunk, closing his eyes. Just as he was about to drift into an old man's nap, he felt a presence nearby.

'I had a feeling you would come,' Abraham said, blinking his eyes open and back to wakefulness. 'I didn't know when, but I knew you would get here somehow.'

He looked to the bench across from him. There sat a broad-shouldered man, bearded, with a face carved by time and tribulation. Abraham smiled gravely at the sight of him.

'Exodus, my boy. Have you come to test me?'

'You know why I'm here.'

Abraham nodded. He had heard of what happened in Dawn's Landing. Everyone who held a post of significance in High Court knew. A girl had summoned infernal powers to raise her father back from the dead and then attack the men who had tried to take his life. It was a crime against heaven and humankind.

'It's your daughter.'

'I've come to clear her name.'

'She consorted with a demon.'

'To save my life. A child will do what she can to save her father.'

Abraham kept his eyes on Exodus but noticed that three other Judges had entered the courtyard and took positions along the walls, like wolves gathering to their alpha. They had certainly learned of Exodus's association with a demonic crime and now regarded him with keen wariness, their hands resting on their sword hilts. Abraham felt the heavy tension of their presence, and though he was sitting, his body suddenly grew weary. He smacked his lips, his mouth dry. Inclining his head towards one of the newcomers, he said, 'Fetch me a cup of water. Would you like one, Exodus?'

Exodus shook his head. One of the Judges by the walls left to fulfill Abraham's request.

'She's just a child,' Exodus said. 'You can show her mercy. Just as you showed me mercy once.'

Abraham nodded and smiled faintly. He remembered well that moment from so many years ago. He could still picture the greasy alleyway in Sockeye. There crouched a creature with its back against the wall, snarling like a cornered stray. Its skin was covered in soot and filth, and it had a feral look in its eyes. Abraham knew the type—those who lived by theft and violence alone, who thought only of taking what they could from the world. Abraham could have killed this creature, and no one would have blamed him. One less wretch in the city's underbelly. But Abraham noticed there was more to this creature. Even though it could have tried to run, it stayed beside a dying companion. Armed with only a piece of broken glass that bled its hand, it prepared to stand its ground against a seasoned Judge. It was that glimmer of something better, something not yet extinguished by the hardships of the streets, that stayed Abraham's hand.

'I took you and formed you into something new,' he said. 'I taught you how to be a boy, then how to be a man. Not just any man, but a Judge.'

Abraham looked at Exodus the way a sculptor looks at his masterpiece.

'The day I found you... I saved your life.'

'You can save another,' Exodus responded. 'You have the authority. Use it to declare my daughter innocent.'

More Judges had entered the courtyard. There were nearly a dozen of them now. If Abraham declared Exodus's daughter innocent, those present would alert the rest of the Order. When the Norwestor Dominion learned the Order had pardoned her, it would have little choice but to pardon her as well. No official or sheriff would go against their verdict, not when the Judges could enforce their will with impunity. Therefore, the Dominion would call off the Rooks, and Exodus's daughter would no longer be a fugitive of the law. Abraham could see it done.

Here it was—the test. The choice that God was laying before Abraham. Would he honor the wishes of the man he had created? Or would he honor the law he had given his life to serve? The wrinkles on his weathered face deepened as he pondered what verdict he'd announce. When the Judge he'd sent out returned with a cup of water, he accepted it without a word. He cooled his thirst, and looked up to the sky. The clouds drifted by, casting their shadows over the courtyard. Exodus and the others waited quietly, hardly moving from their positions. They knew not to disturb Abraham while he was deep in thought.

To be a Judge meant wrestling with justice and mercy, determining what was right and wrong. Once a verdict was reached, it meant having the iron will to carry it through. But now Abraham felt tired, the burden of his role weighing heavily upon his shoulders. Exodus—the little boy he had saved and raised—sat before him in judgment. He felt like his namesake, who had taken his son up to a mountaintop as a sacrifice. Now it was he who held the knife above the altar. He knew what he had to do. Even now God could call to him and stay his hand once more.

My God, he prayed, *I only wish to do what is right.*

When at last he looked down from the sky, it took every ounce of his will to fix his eyes on Exodus.

'I cannot declare your daughter innocent.'

Exodus received the verdict with a stone face, the stich in his brow tightening.

'You won't show mercy?' he asked. There was no surprise in his voice, only shades of sorrow.

'The law is the law,' Abraham replied. 'We didn't write it. We can't change it. All we can do is uphold it.'

'Then let me atone for her crime. If someone needs to pay for what she's done, let it be me, not her.'

Abraham paused to consider this. Of course, Exodus wouldn't give up so easily. The test, it seemed, wasn't over. Another proposition to press against Abraham's resolve.

'You ask me to give you her guilt as if you're the one who could take it,' he said at length. 'If you were innocent, then perhaps I would grant it to you. But you have your own crime to pay for.'

'And what crime is that?'

'Being your daughter's accomplice. She has consorted with a demon, and you have let her run free.'

'Should a father not protect his daughter?'

Abraham rubbed a finger around the rim of his cup and then took a long drink.

'Should a Judge not uphold the law?' he said with a heavy sigh. He had made his decision. Now he had to see it all the way through. 'You have no right to give your daughter special treatment. None of us have that right. When it comes to protecting our own or upholding the law, we choose the law. Even when it comes to those we raised as our own.'

'This is your declaration.'

'My son, I may have been a father to you. But I was a Judge first.'

With that Exodus rose. The others closed in, their swords drawn. Exodus hardly flinched as he kept his eyes locked on Abraham.

'Do you truly believe I would draw my blade against you?'

Abraham studied the man he had just condemned. He had seen countless executions but had no desire to see this one. He could tell the others to do the deed away from here, up at one of the peaks. Maybe that made him a coward, not wanting to be there when the sword fell. He could give the word and have Exodus handed over to the Rooks. There was a chance they'd imprison him rather than kill him. But Abraham knew Exodus would see it as betrayal. Abraham's head sank to his chest, and he placed a withered hand against the pear tree, leaning against the trunk. *So tired.*

A wind blew through the courtyard, and in that moment, another option came to mind. Maybe there was a way to appease both justice and mercy. He could only hope.

'Exodus needs to pay for the crime, and there are payments other than death...'

Abraham shared with the others the plan forming in his head. They could take his suggestion or not. As Judges, they were free to do as they pleased. But he knew they would follow his word.

They took Exodus away and left him alone under the pear tree. He finished his water and looked up to the sky.

My God... have I passed your test? Have I lived up to your justice?

Chapter 31

Dane remembered a time in his life when he had simpler tastes. Through the fog of ages, he could still think back to the flavors of fruit. He remembered when he was just a youth, when there was nothing better than biting into a ripe peach on a hot afternoon and letting the juice run down his chin. Inversely, there was nothing worse than a bad peach. Its golden skin promised something good, but its flesh would be nothing more than dry, grainy pulp. That lie made it worse than mediocre.

Centuries from those youthful afternoons, Dane sat displeased on his throne. He had found something dreadfully similar to a bad peach.

There on the floor before him lay a dead bull. It had been a magnificent beast, fat and healthy, the pride of a wealthy rancher. Its coat was sleek black, and its horns spread out farther than a man's arm span. Such an impressive animal should have brought Dane immense pleasure when he took life from its body. But it didn't. Although the bull brought with it a large quantity of life, the sensation that he experienced was faint. It lacked the waves of rich emotion that came with draining humans. No heights of electric joy nor depths of gloomy sorrow.

Just dry boredom from life in a pasture. The bull's fat and healthy appearance had promised something more, but it didn't deliver. That made it worse than mediocre. Dane looked at the dead bull in sour disappointment.

That's the last beast I'll try, he swore to himself.

As he had managed both his hunger for life and relief from guilt, Dane went back and forth between sapping people and sapping animals. After taking the lives of a few prisoners, his guilt would grow, and he'd try to find relief by draining chickens, dogs, and pigs. None of them satisfied him, so he would ultimately return to satiating his hunger on humanity. He thought the bull would be different because of its magnificence. But it was just like the other animals. Just another bad peach.

He hungered for people, and he found himself needing them more and more. There used to be a time when he drained just one or two a day. Now he was draining half a dozen—sometimes up to ten if his mood called for it. The more life he took, the more guilt he felt. And the more guilt he felt, the more life he took. A vicious cycle. He needed the pleasure to numb the pins pricking his conscience. Indeed, he didn't feel the pleasure as strongly as he had before. Now he was taking life more for the escape than for the ecstasy.

Along with his craving, there were other concerns to worry about. There had been that peculiar man who came to him. The guards called him a Rook. What had his name been? Eramac... Eramez? It didn't matter. All that Dane cared about was the equipment he had laid down as an offering. There was an energy vision helmet and EMP blaster worked into a staff. After the End War and the Treaty, these were the tools used by the natreo zealots to purge the Earth of technology. Dane thought such tools might have perished with time. He had believed he would be impervious to any weapons that were now on Earth, it appeared the tech had lived on in a strange organization following some semblance of the zealot creed. One blast from the staff and his suit would be rendered useless and he'd be trapped inside. Shivering at the terrifying thought, he swallowed the rising lump in his throat.

He had taken his invincibility for granted, but now a crack, however thin it might be, broke down his assurance. There was something out there that could beat him.

He'd been lucky this time. By happenstance, the man the guards called a Rook had taken off his helmet and lost its protection from the patheograph. Dane couldn't count on luck next time. Therefore, he had set up sensors throughout the city to alert him of any kind of tech drawing near, and he had put the word out for the guards to kill any Rook on sight.

What about other threats to his established order? What about Olympus? Dane shook his head. Impossible. As he sat on the throne, the Founders would be dreaming in their pods, as they always had. They never looked into what was happening on Earth. Even so, there was something inside Dane—perhaps the guilt he was trying to bury—that gave him the sense that he'd be found out. *No*, he assured himself. All the Founders thought he was dead. All but Silas. What if, in some future meeting, he let something slip? What would happen then? Dane's throat tightened, and he swallowed.

'Guard!' he called.

He would save his concerns for another time. There had been enough worrying that day, and it was beginning to take a toll on his nerves.

Obeying the summons, a guard came into the throne room and kneeled before the dais. He, like the other guards, now had eyes clouded with white—an unforeseen effect of the patheograph's increasing power.

'Get rid of this thing,' Dane said, waving a dismissive hand at the bull. 'And bring me another prisoner.'

The guard got up but remained standing, nervously clasping his hands.

'Forgive me,' he said, 'but we gave you the last set of prisoners yesterday. There aren't anymore.'

Dane sat unmoving, the momentum of his habit unable to conceive of anything other than unending supply. There had been so many people in those cells. How had he cleaned them out so quickly?

'They can't all be gone,' he said with dark displeasure.

'They are, sir,' the guard replied in a small voice. 'Prison's empty.'

Dane sat with that word. *Empty*. His stomach began to growl, and his mouth felt dry. Even more discomforting was the hunger in his mind that shivered his spine and made his fingers twitch. He longed for life, the richness of humanity absorbed into his body. There was none to be had. *Empty*. He had come to the bottom of the barrel.

Dane stared at the guard. Moments passed in uncomfortable silence. He could see the guard trembling. For reasons Dane couldn't understand, he began to hate the man before him. The feeling welled up within him like bubbling tar.

'It's your fault,' Dane hissed.

'Excuse me?' the guard said, his lip quivering.

'It's your fault the prison is empty.'

'I—I don't know what you mean. I only did what I was told.'

'You fed me and fed me!' Dane took off his helmet, revealing his hideous head—a face crossed with blue veins under translucent skin. 'Look at me! I'm a monster! Inside and out!'

Now the guard was trembling so much his knees shook. 'I didn't mean nothing like that. I just did as I was told.'

'You could've stopped this! You could've refused my request! Now because of you and all the others like you, I have this hunger that can never be satisfied.'

'I can get you more cattle.'

'No!' Dane roared.

He sprang up from the throne, his cell gun out on his right arm. The guard cowered, but Dane fired into the dead bull, again and again, blasting through the sleek hide and into the flesh and bone. When he stopped, smoke rose from the sizzling carcass, and the air was filled with the smell of charred beef.

'I'm tired of beasts,' he said, in a voice quiet yet terrible. He turned the cell gun on the guard. 'All of this… it's your fault.'

The guard collapsed to his knees, blubbering. 'Please don't! I'll make it right. I'll get you people.'

At this, the snarl in Dane's colorless lips subsided, and he paused in consideration of this proposal. The cell gun retracted back into his suit.

'You would do this?'

'Yes!' the guard nodded in desperation.

'You would round up people and put them in the prison?'

'Yes!'

'You would make sure the cells are never empty again?'

'Yes! I promise!'

'You would sacrifice others to save your own skin.'

The guard's mouth opened, but he said nothing. His expression sank into despair as he must have realized he had walked into a trap.

Dane stepped down from the dais and came face to face with the guard. 'Then you and I aren't too different,' he said softly. 'You're a monster just like me, complicit with my sin.'

Dane put the helmet back on his head. Then, in a quick thrust, he pressed the metovita against the guard's chest. He grinned to himself. It seemed his supply of lives hadn't ended after all. Even though the prison was empty, he would find bad men to satiate his hunger. They might be wearing the guise of good and decent folk, but he would find them nonetheless. They would be his peach.

Chapter 32

Corvala fell to the tunnel floor, tearing the rips in her pant legs even wider and scraping her knees, which were already raw from the countless falls before. She winced at the burn in her legs but was growing accustomed to the pain. Here in the darkness where it seemed that every twist and turn had a roughly hewn edge to trip her, the going had been slow and full of stumbles. Serapha, holding tightly to her hand, helped her up and continued to lead the way. Somehow, she was able to walk perfectly fine without groping in the dark—just another one of her strange abilities. Corvala shuffled behind her, the tunnel meandering this way and that. Sometimes they'd squeeze through tight spaces, while at other times they'd pass through chambers where the sound of dripping water echoed in the distance. While in a narrow passage and rounding another bend, Corvala's toe caught on a stone lip and she nearly fell again. She placed a steadying hand against the wall and laughed at herself—a joyless sound, its echoes resembling sobs.

How could I not see it coming? she chided herself. *Why didn't I see his plan? He laid it right in front of me: go to the door without* him. *How could I be so stupid?*

With nothing to see and Serapha allowing her silence, all she had were her thoughts, her mind running through the same string of agonizing questions again and again. *Why did I argue with him about that stupid palanquin? Where is he now? Why didn't I get to say goodbye?*

Turn after turn, thought after thought, time stretched out in the darkness. They had been underground for so long, Corvala had no idea whether it would be day or night in the world above. Hours or a hundred years could have passed since they had started down the tunnel. It didn't matter. They could stay in the dark forever for all she cared.

But eventually, the pitch-black lightened into gray, and Corvala could start to make out the tunnel's roughly hewn surfaces. A sliver of light shone above and the ceiling opened into a crevice. The tunnel gradually became a path at the bottom of a narrow ravine. Blinking in the new light, Corvala looked up to the high escarpments pressing in on both sides. She felt like an insect crawling along the bottom of a crack in the ground. They followed the path until it suddenly ended at a rocky ledge with nothing beyond it but fog. A cold wind blew, brushing against Corvala and raising gooseflesh on her naked arms. She hugged herself for warmth as she peered out beyond the ledge. As if to open a curtain before her, the wind pushed the fog back, revealing a wide ravine. Between the steep mountain slopes lay a verdant landscape velvety with grass and speckled with highland flowers. Feathery banks of cloud rolled down the mountains and drifted overhead, and through their openings shone golden shafts of sunlight that shifted in amorphous shapes along the ravine floor. At the center of the ravine stood a great tree, similar to the one they had seen in the heart of Thorn Shroud. Its trunk rose to a colossal height and its branches spread out in a vast canopy mingling with the clouds.

'An Elijah Tree,' Corvala whispered.

From what her father had told her, Corvala knew that tin-blades came here to swear their vows and become full-fledged Judges. Just like her father had done so many years ago.

If only he could be there now...

Below the ledge, there was a short drop. Serapha jumped first and slid gracefully down the slope of loose scree. Corvala jumped next, but when she landed on the ragged earth, one of her feet slipped out from under her. She pitched to the right to keep her fiddle from being crushed. Falling headfirst, she landed on her side, her palms and leg burning as she scraped her way down the scree, stones tumbling down alongside her. She slid to a stop at the bottom, the taste of blood in her mouth, and remained still. Beyond the physical pain she felt in her body, something within her burst open and released the full force of nothingness upon her. Sobs wracked her body, her breath catching in her throat, and for several minutes she wept facedown into the dirt and gravel.

He's gone. He's gone.

She cried until she had no more tears to shed. Then, with shaking arms, she lifted herself to her knees. Her eyes felt puffy and bleary, and she regarded Serapha with a hard stare.

'You could've saved him,' she croaked. 'You could've found him and fought your way out. But you didn't. You left him...'

Serapha stood there, regarding her with the same flat expression as always. 'We have a mission to complete. It is urgent.'

She put out a hand to help Corvala up, but Corvala didn't take it.

'People are dying,' Serapha said.

Corvala looked up from the ground and wiped her eyes. 'What?'

'I have learned more about the intruder who came down from the space station,' Serapha explained. 'There is a strong possibility that he has set himself up as a deity and is demanding human sacrifice. People are dying, and you can save them.'

'What people?'

'The people of the city called Ryperia.'

Corvala remembered the ominous rumors that had come down the river, remembered the people in Echo Bend desperate to find their missing loved ones.

'I can save them?' she said, her mind digesting the thought.

'Yes,' Serapha replied. 'I believe I have made this point clear on several occasions. You will make contact with the Elijah Tree, and the code within you will activate its defense system, which in turn will locate and subdue the intruder.'

Corvala sat there, dull and vacant-eyed. To have the power of life and death dropped on her amid grief... it was disorienting. Her world had crumbled, and now she was being asked to save someone else's. With a touch, she could see it done. But she couldn't care less about the people of Ryperia. Maybe it was heartless, but it was true. They were a nameless, faceless crowd who lived far from her and meant nothing to her. At that moment she cared only for her father.

What about him? Of all the people in the world to save, why couldn't it be him?

She pondered the ease of falling deeper into despair. But thinking of her father made her remember the morning of his trial and what he had faced for the sake of others—even those who didn't deserve it.

He would want her to save the people of Ryperia.

Corvala wiped her face and looked at the Elijah Tree standing in the center of the ravine. With one touch, she could fulfill her job.

'You are in pain,' Serapha said. 'You do not need to recover. All you need to do is touch that tree.'

Corvala faced the cold wind, her expression heavy with dulled sadness. Without a word she rose from the ground, squared her shoulders, and headed towards the center of the ravine.

The Elijah Tree stood as a massive pillar of timber—not as tall as the mountains around it, but it was higher than many of the cliffs and crags. Unlike the one in the heart of Thorn Shroud, this tree was healthy, its branches full and green. Corvala could see why the Judges revered this place—why they saw it as a connection between heaven and earth. She saw it as something else: a merging of nature and Ancient craft. It represented both her burden and her cure. Because of this tree, her father was—

Focus, she told herself. *You're almost done.*

Corvala climbed over the ground rippling with outstretched roots and came up to the vast trunk with silvery veins running through the bark. If everything worked as it was supposed to, she'd activate the defense system and release a cloud of spore-like devices into the air. The cloud would find this man in Ryperia and subdue him. Probably kill him. Corvala flinched at the thought, but she knew there was no going back now.

With a trembling hand, she reached out for the trunk. First her finger tips touched the bark, then her palm. The sensation pulsed through her immediately—like getting dunked into cold water, her senses waking completely. She felt electricity pass through her and enter the heart of the trunk, but there were no painful jolts or flashing sparks. Rather she found the feeling strangely welcoming. A connection was forming between her and the tree, one that seemed natural. Her bloodline bonding with this six-hundred-year-old organism. A long-awaited meeting now realized.

Corvala sensed the tree stirring from an age of slumber. As it woke, it felt as though she were being lifted and spread out, her arms extending into the clouds and her feet digging deep into the ravine. She knew her body remained on the ground, even as her mind went elsewhere, absorbed into the waking consciousness of the tree. Her eyes opened, and she saw both ends of the ravine, the ground below and the sky above, and the surrounding mountains—all of it at once. With the tree coming into full wakefulness, Corvala's view broadened and the tree plunged her into the depths of time.

Chapter 33

Serapha could see the connection had been established.
Corvala's eyes were closed, and her muscles were rigid.
From where her hand pressed against the tree, the silvery
veins in the bark lit up. A pulsating light surrounded the
trunk, lighting the branches and the roots. All Serapha
could do was wait. The mission would soon be complete.

But there, in the periphery of her vision, a dark shape
moved on one of the mountain ridges—there for a moment then gone. Too short a time for Serapha to identify
what it was. For caution, she took a defensive stance at
Corvala's side. The girl was vulnerable, and the connection had to be completed. There was no pausing the
process, no pulling Corvala away. To do that could damage not only Corvala's mind but also the Elijah Tree.

Serapha's sharp eyes searched through the mist.

SCANNING

There was no sign of the thing she had seen. Just
clouds and wind.

Corvala's perception expanded into an empty space. Unlike the dark nothingness she had felt while walking the tunnel, this place wasn't defined by what it lacked but by what it could be. An empty canvas awaiting the artist's brush; an empty page to be given words. She was in the middle of this vast emptiness and yet somehow felt herself standing on a firm foundation. She looked out at the blank darkness as one waiting for stars to come out. There appeared a point of light, and it expanded into something like a window, giving her the view of a place—a city. It was unlike any city she had ever seen before, filled with towers of glass and metal. They were so tall, Corvala wondered how humans could build such structures. Another window appeared next to the first. This one also showed a city, the view looking up from the streets. From down here, the towers appeared even more imposing. But there were things even higher than these. Far above the distant spires there flew great metal birds, tails of cloud following after them. Another window opened beside the first two. This one looked at black roads crisscrossing in all directions. On the roads there were wagons—at least that's what Corvala thought they were. Like wagons, they moved on wheels. But these things didn't have horses or oxen pulling them. They moved on their own and at great speeds. There were millions of them. They hummed and roared, masses of these strange vehicles barreling down the roads.

More windows appeared, first dozens, then hundreds, then thousands. All showing Corvala a world utterly foreign and fascinating. The world of the Ancients. Not seen through crude drawings but as if she were there. Her mind took it all in. It was as if she were seeing through a multitude of eyes, each pair bearing the capacity to focus on a single window. Somehow, she wasn't confused. The Elijah Tree, it seemed, enabled her to bear the mental load. Still, she felt like a child lost in a festival crowd, surrounded by color and sound that was at once frightening and mesmerizing.

This strange world buzzed with movement and noise. There were people, more than Corvala could count. Crowds of people walking on the street, people ascending and descending the towers, people seated in the speeding wagons. Corvala watched tensely, waiting for them to crash into one another at any moment. But the collisions rarely came. In this chaos, there appeared to be a rhythm that kept things in relative order.

Corvala marveled at these people, for they had powerful magic. In buildings, they could summon forth clean water from strange metal fountains and bring light into dark rooms by just a wave of the hand. Indeed, there were lights everywhere. Even at night, the cities shimmered with luminous colors. People carried light with them wherever they went, constantly staring at flat rectangular devices with glowing surfaces.

'Beautiful, isn't it?'

The voice came from beside Corvala. She looked to see a woman standing there, staring at all the windows before them. She had short auburn hair and the tattoo of a tree on her neck. Corvala recognized her. She was the woman from her dreams—the woman who had pointed her to the underground chamber in Thorn Shroud.

'Not all of it, perhaps,' the woman continued. 'But it had a beauty of its own kind.' She turned and looked to where Corvala stood. 'I believe introductions are in order—at least from my end. I'm Felicity Ferrer. I'm your ancestor.'

'Hello,' Corvala replied hesitantly. 'I'm—'

She was cut off. It appeared the woman wasn't really listening but only speaking, as if a speech had been made long ago and somehow preserved.

'This is the first recording of its kind,' Felicity said. 'We're working with cognitive memory files placed within organic plant matter. It's pretty new tech. Kind of a big deal. But you won't care about that. You're probably wondering why you're seeing and hearing me. If the Elijah Tree is working correctly, then you're seeing the state of the world as it once was.'

Corvala saw the images move more quickly as the sun rose and fell in rapid succession. Years passed, and the cities changed. They spread out across the lands, and their towers rose even taller than before. The people also became stranger. The devices they once carried were now placed inside their bodies. In one scene, Corvala watched in horror as people in green suits and matching masks over their mouths and nose stood over a prone man on a table. With peculiar instruments, they opened up his skull and placed a device that looked like a metal spider inside his brain. When he was sewn up, blinking lights protruded from his temples. The line between humanity and machines blurred as people grew more and more dependent on their devices. They no longer went outdoors but crawled inside egg-like capsules and lay within them for days and even weeks at a time like animals in hibernation. The world outside grew oddly quiet as everyone stayed holed up in their machines, dreaming.

Then the Earth burst with a terrible noise. Metal beasts tromped over the land and screamed through the sky, blasting fire and searing light. Weapons, like great metal spears, launched from ships in the ocean and flew with tails of roaring flame. When the spears struck the cities, they erupted into all-consuming storms of fire and smoke, blasting the enormous towers into rubble and ash, their clouds rising like red trees and mushrooms. From the destruction, hills were levelled and mountains rose. Tidal waves crashed upon the shores, and islands sank. Millions upon millions died. Consumed in fire. Blasted apart by tearing metal and burning light. Crushed under rubble. Drowned in floods. Children cried out and were silenced. Hands reached out and found no salvation.

Corvala saw it all. She watched in horror. She told herself it was only a vision, that nothing could hurt her. But what the windows revealed seemed so real, and the sheer amount of death staggered her. She tried to shrink back and close her eyes, but there was no hiding from this. Her enhanced vision of countless sets of eyes couldn't blink the terrors away. Her mind was fixed on the images, and everywhere she turned there was destruction. The metal beasts tore each other to pieces until there was nothing left to fight. Only when the world lay in ash and ruins did the silence resume.

'The war killed nearly everyone,' Felicity said. 'An estimated fifteen percent of the population survived. Rural folks mostly because they weren't in the cities that got nuked. Humanity limped on.'

Many of the windows before Corvala faded. Those that remained divided into two groups. On the left, she saw windows showing bands of men armed with weapons. These weapons weren't like the clubs and spears carried by the guards in Dawn's Landing. These fired metal and searing bolts of red light. The roving bands scoured the ruins of once-great cities, searching for any machines or devices worth saving or repairing. Sometimes these bands would encounter one another and fight bloody battles over discovered supplies and treasures.

Small communities untouched by the war tried their best to keep their electric power and hold onto what form of the old life they could. They lived in fear of the roving bands of violent men. Sometimes they could ward off their attackers; sometimes they were overrun and destroyed. But with energy running low and resources scarce, their communities gradually crumbled. Many couldn't handle seeing what the world had become, so they retreated to their cocoons to dream and used what little energy remained to escape reality.

The grouping of windows on Corvala's right showed people renouncing what Felicity had called *tech*. They fled the cities and went out to the forests and fields to make new settlements. They learned how to work with their hands—to cut timber and build with wood, to collect reeds and weave baskets, to hammer metal on the forge. They used horses to plough fields and used ropes and pulleys to erect houses and barns. They hunted deer and wild pigs with wooden bows and arrows. For Corvala, these practices were nothing new. They were all part of the way of life in the Elkhorn Valley and the entire Dominion. But she could sense the newness these practices held for these people. They were carving out lives for themselves apart from the ruins of the old world.

'I'll save you the boring history lecture,' Felicity continued, 'and just tell you we didn't all get along. There were conflicts about how we should govern ourselves. The biggest issue, however, was technology. Even after the war, there were still some places where tech remained intact. The question was, 'What should we do with all this stuff that blew our world to kingdom come?' Most people wanted to leave it in the past. I, for one, am among them. Others, however, couldn't picture a world without their gadgets. They have their reasons, but now is the time for a clean start. Not a time for going back into mindless bondage behind a screen. Anyway, humanity had its great divide. Those who wanted tech, and those who wanted to abolish it. The two sides of the debate were irreconcilable, so we split.'

The woman rubbed her temples as if the mere thought of the conflict made her head hurt.

'The technas went into orbit, claiming the space station Olympus for themselves. Given it was off-world and didn't pose a threat to any nation, it remained untouched by the war.'

All the windows before Corvala blinked out except for one. It showed what looked to be a white cylindrical tower coming to a needle-like point. Then great clouds of fire and smoke exploded from underneath the tower. Corvala realized it wasn't a tower at all but some kind of flying machine, for it lifted off the ground and pierced the sky like a great spear. It went above the clouds and into the starry darkness, heading towards something floating above the world. At first, it appeared small, nothing more than a little ring. As the flying machine drew nearer, Corvala could see the ring growing. It grew and grew, filling most of Corvala's viewing space, and yet there was more of it left unseen behind its rounded edges. This must be what Felicity called Olympus. The flying machine, upon its approach, looked like nothing more than a piece of chalk next to the massive ring. Corvala felt herself shrinking in the presence of its immensity. Olympus was like a great wheel looking down on the world and floating among the stars—a flying city with towers spiking out in all directions and vast wings of silver rectangles spread out to reflect the glare of sunlight.

'All the technas are gone,' Felicity continued, 'floating above us in Olympus. Still, the natreos, as you can imagine, don't trust the technas—so the technas were made to sign a treaty before they went into orbit. The wordage is boring. Basically, it says: Keep off Earth. No tech allowed.

'But there's a problem. The Treaty won't be enough. If the technas want to come down in the future, what's to stop them? A document they signed? Highly unlikely. They still have tech. They still have weapons. They'll be able to do whatever they please. Especially now since the zealots are bringing about the Purge.'

One set of windows blinked out as another set appeared. This set of windows showed groups of figures, the ones Felicity called zealots. They all wore uniform pants and jackets of mottled grays and blacks, clothing that helped them blend into the rock and steel of destroyed buildings. They wore helmets with green lenses and carried weapons with green cylinders attached to handles. Like the roving bands from before, these zealots scoured the small communities and city ruins in search of any machines and devices that might still be in working order. But instead of collecting these things for future use, they fired green blasts of light from their weapons, leaving tech smoking and sparking.

Felicity sighed.

'The natreo zealots mean well. They want to free us from the devices that put us into mental slavery—the devices that ultimately led to utter destruction. But by purging the land of every gadget and contraption, we're leaving ourselves vulnerable. We can't let that happen. That's where the Sky Mantle project comes in. We're not quite natreos, and we're definitely not technas. We're our own faction.

'My team and I have been preparing for the time when someone from Olympus decides to come down to Earth. A likely event. We've created a defensive network that will keep future natreos safe. It involves tech, but given the current hatred people down here have for all things with blinking lights, we have to work in unconventional means. Bunkers in caves where we placed Seraph units. Codes hidden in DNA, like the one in me that I pass down to you. And, of course, this tree you've encountered—a supercomputer built from organic matter and made to run off photosynthesis. Beautiful, isn't it?'

More windows appeared in front of Corvala, each one showing various people working on the Sky Mantle project. Some were digging out bunkers, and others went out to hidden places to plant saplings bearing seven-pointed leaves and bark veined with silver.

'I know,' Felicity said. 'It's all very complicated and convoluted. But we have to make do with the conditions we're given. Working in the shadows isn't always user friendly. We wear animal skins during the day and lab coats at night. When it gets tough, I tell myself I'm a secret agent. It helps me get by.' Felicity held a smile, then let it fall. 'If the zealots were to find out about the Sky

Mantle project, they'd burn it down. And my team and I would probably be put to death. Some have already died.'

Felicity paused a moment, a short wave of grief passing over her face.

'If you're watching this,' she went on, 'it means what we've feared has come to pass: someone has indeed come down from Olympus. I guess that they're up to no good. We'll take care of that. More accurately, *you* will take care of that. While you've been watching this message, the code within you has been establishing a connection with the Elijah Tree, a trillion pieces of information finding where they need to go. But it works fast. You'll be done in no time.

'Sit tight. You're about to save the world.'

Felicity faded from Corvala's vision, and Corvala found herself alone in the dark emptiness again. Perhaps not alone. She could sense the presence of the tree working in the background of her mind. Connections were finishing up. Then—*click!*—it was all in place. Everything seemed to be in order.

She felt the Elijah Tree proceed in a new kind of work. It reached into her mind, a strange sensation of many little fingers groping about her head. The tree found what it was looking for and pulled it out to fill the dark space. Corvala saw it was the memory of her father's trial. She was there again in the main square of Dawn's Landing. Fortunately, the tree skipped the painful parts and focused on the 'shooting star' that tore through the sky.

'Shuttle identified,' said a strange metallic voice. 'Trajectory calculated.'

Corvala had revisited this image when Serapha made a connection with her mind. But the tree did more than study what Corvala had seen. It lifted Corvala into the air and had her follow the shuttle as it went. She was flying, hurtling through the sky, the shuttle in front of her. It came in low over a gorge and river that looked familiar, and then it landed in the flinty hills that lay beyond.

'Landing site acquired,' said the metallic voice. 'Contact with Earth: highly probable. Presence of intruder on Earth: highly probable. Permission to proceed. Initiating defense.'

Suddenly, Corvala's frame shook when something struck the tree, and a jolt of agony knifed into her mind. She sensed her body at the base of the trunk—her spine arched back as the pain ripped a raw scream out of her throat. It felt like iron spikes were piercing the base of her skull and driving into her teeth, nerves split by honed points. Under her screams she managed to hear the metallic voice:

'Error. Error. System failure. System fail—'

Chapter 34

Vlaren crouched low in the saddle, holding tightly to the leather straps and feeling his stomach rise into his throat. He rode Lobeka down the steep mountainside at breakneck speed, the wulgyre bounding from the crags in one free fall after another before sliding smoothly into the scree and dashing towards the center of the ravine. The thrill of the Hunt coursed through Vlaren's veins as he closed in on his quarry. He squinted from the wind rushing through the eyeholes of his helmet but locked his gaze on the target ahead—the massive tree pulsing with light. At its base stood two figures, tiny next to the overshadowing trunk. The Judge was nowhere in sight, but Vlaren could see the girl and the woman. Out from where the girl stood, the tree's light radiated in concentric circles that flowed over the trunk and branches. A beautiful spectacle—albeit demonic. The light's pulse quickened by the second. Whatever devilry they were brewing, it appeared ready to release its terrible power at any moment.

The woman spotted Vlaren's approach immediately and launched herself at him with inhuman speed, her stride appearing to match the wulgyre's. *Machubus.* As the two charged one another, Vlaren thrust out his staff like a lance and took aim. A blast of green light fired from the jade tip and screamed through the air, veering towards the woman as it sought her out. Before it could make a hit, she sprang from its path, leaving the green projectile to fizzle out on the ground. She tore up grass as she skidded to a halt, appearing to appraise Vlaren's weapon before ducking for cover behind a rock outcropping.

That's right, machubus. You know what this is.

With the threat of her charge momentarily stayed, Vlaren fired at the more pressing target. Another ball of green screamed through the air, streaking over the ravine and striking the trunk of the massive tree. The veins at the point of impact sizzled then burst in an explosion of splintered wood and burning bark, leaving a smoldering gash near the base of the trunk. The girl threw her head back and released an agonized scream as she fell to the ground. At the sound of her distress, the woman broke from cover and sprinted back for the girl. Vlaren kept his aim on the tree and relentlessly fired, each shot blasting away huge chunks of wood, rending the gash wider. The tree started to tilt, groaning under its colossal weight. Then the ravine echoed with a resounding crack as the trunk split. The tree collapsed from its majestic height, its branches tearing through the clouds as if to bring the sky down. It crashed into the ravine wall, and there it remained, leaning precariously against the mountain.

As the woman ran to the base of the tree and scooped up the girl's limp form, Vlaren rode hard on her heels. At the bottom of the ravine, there was nowhere for her to go. But then, as Vlaren aimed and fired at the moving target, she made an unexpected move: she vaulted over the splintered trunk and started sprinting up the steep angle of the leaning tree. Vlaren's shot trailed her for a moment but veered off and dove into the tree, seeking the larger power source—like lightning seeking the taller object. *Got to get a closer shot.* Riding hard, Vlaren pressed his mount to follow. Lobeka leaped from the ravine floor then ran up the trunk in pursuit, her claws digging into the bark to keep hold. As they climbed higher up the tree, Vlaren clung to the saddle, the strap biting into his hand as gravity pulled at his back. The tree groaned beneath his mount. Wood popped, split, and belched acrid chemicals that caught fire from the sparking lights. Vlaren drove a knee hard into Lobeka's side, having her swerve just as a gout of flame erupted from a split in their path. He spotted the woman running ahead, her pace unflagging. She nimbly dodged the flames spitting from the quaking tree—*by the wreck! How did she move so fast carrying the girl?*—and made it all the way up to the lowest boughs where the fire engulfed leaves and branches.

Where are you going? Vlaren scanned ahead to where the upper boughs had taken hold on the crags. *There!*—a cliff with a flat edge leading to a smooth slope, a way of escape into the mountains. Not if he cut her off. Vlaren followed her into the fire's red breath. All around him the air crackled with falling embers and branches crumbling to cinders. Smoke and fumes raked at his throat and shook him with a bout of coughing. The tree creaked ominously as limbs burned away, sounding as though its hold on the ravine wall was steadily weakening. Lobeka panted and frothed as she ran through the flames, her flanks sleek with sweat. Not far ahead, the woman sprang from one branch to another. Vlaren blinked away the stinging smoke as he pointed his staff and took aim. He fired, the green blast striking the branch ahead of her. It sparked and burst into flames, breaking just as she set foot on it. She fell, clutching the girl with one arm and catching a tree limb with another. She hung suspended over a long drop to the ravine below. At last, an unmoving target. Vlaren closed the distance and aimed his staff.

A series of cracks thundered in the ravine, many limbs and boughs breaking at once and losing their hold on the crags. The tree fell. In an instant, Vlaren felt as though the world had dropped beneath him. He clung to the straps to keep from being lifted off his seat as the tree made a scraping fall against the cliffs. The woman, still holding the girl, was lifted into the air as the tree rolled. The force propelled her upwards, and she swung from the branches and onto the safety of the cliff ledge above. Vlaren dropped as she quickly rose out of sight. He whipped Lobeka around, kicking her sides and spurring her into a mad dash down the falling trunk. When they cleared the branches, the wulgyre made a desperate leap from the burning ruin. Just behind them, the tree came roaring down and slammed to the ground with a terrible crash—as though the fiery heavens of the end times had collided with the Earth. The ravine shook with an explosion of fiery wood. A hot blast swept through the ravine and thrust Vlaren and his mount toward the quickly approaching ground. Something struck Vlaren in the back, toppling him from the saddle. He hit the earth at a violent roll while rocks and dirt clods pummeled him on all sides.

Once he stopped, he was on his back, looking at the sky. Gasping for breath, he felt the firmness of the ground beneath him even as his vision spun with smoke and floating sparks. Several minutes passed before he could raise his head. He pulled his helmet off and rubbed his temples, his skull and spine throbbing. His wrist, judging by the swollen and already purple skin, was either broken or severely sprained.

I've had worse, he thought groggily.

When his vision stopped spinning, he tried lifting himself from the ground. As he propped himself on his elbow, he sensed something wrong, something *in* him. He looked down and saw that out from his side stuck a piece of splintered wood. It was only a few fingers wide and no longer than his forearm, running through his lower back and out the front.

Maybe I haven't *had worse...*

Hopefully the wood had missed his liver. He'd have to leave it in. If he took it out, the wound would bleed freely, and he could die. A wound like this was beyond his skill to heal. He needed aid—and soon.

Lobeka padded over to him and started licking a cut on one of her forelimbs.

'We got beat, old girl,' Vlaren said. 'At least we did some damage.'

He grabbed one of the wulgyre's saddle straps and carefully pulled himself to his feet, wincing. Even the most minor movements tugged the wound at his side. The tree was still alight, though much of the trunk had burned down to smoldering embers. If it had been a normal tree, the blasts from his staff would have done nothing. Although the blasts were frightening as they screamed through the air, they were harmless when they met with wholly organic matter. This tree, however, had the demonic taint within it, and whatever magic it had possessed was now burning. The catalogers of Pillar Dark would chastise him if he didn't return with a piece of it to study. But he didn't have time to wait around for the flames to die down so he could take samples. If the catalogers wanted one, they could have the wood from his side.

It was hard to tell how much time he had. If his bowels had been pierced, he would go septic in a matter of hours. A slow and painful way to go. If he was lucky, the wood had only pierced the muscle. Vlaren thought for a moment. The closest place he could go for help was High Court where priests would tend to him. Most of them knew the basics of medicine, and their shelves would be well-stocked with healing herbs. The Judges wouldn't be too happy about having a Rook in High Court. What did it matter? He could weather their disdain if it meant survival.

Vlaren climbed onto Lobeka, favoring his left side as he did so. The ride around the mountain ridge would take a couple of hours. He might have to take it even slower if a quick pace and jostling ride proved too painful. As he turned his wulgyre in the direction they had come, he looked up to the cliffs where the woman and the girl had made their escape.

The Hunt may be delayed for now. But it was never over.

Serapha ran at a relentless sprint over the mountain ridges, her mind mapping out the most efficient route of escape. She carried Corvala, who was unconscious and likely wouldn't wake up if left untreated. The girl's mind had been deep within the programming of the Elijah Tree, the connection infinitely complex and fragile. In many ways, her nerves and synapses had become an extension of the tree, and the only healthy way to leave such a connection was by a methodical yet gentle unravelling. The process could only be done by the programming itself, if all had gone to procedure. But when the tree had been destroyed, Corvala's nerves and synapses had been ripped away. Now the girl lay limp with sporadic moments of violent convulsions. Before Serapha could assess the damage, she had to get as far from the hunter as she possibly could. She knew the man's gear—the helmet and modified EMP emitter—and knew that one blast from his staff would destroy all her circuitry.

The loss of the Elijah Tree left her processing what she would do next. Since she didn't have access to the location of where others grew, finding another wasn't a viable option. Not with the urgent circumstances in the city called Ryperia. That, however, presented another objective. Serapha had a lead on where she could find the intruder from Olympus. Based on what she had heard from bargemen on the river and the blind man at High Court, the intruder was posing as a deity over the city.

DETERMINE ACTION

PROCESSING...

SEEK OUT INTRUDER

Her decision was made in an instant, for she wouldn't allow herself to go without a purpose. Not while her system still ran and her structure was in tune. The most reasonable course of action was to travel to Ryperia and confront the intruder herself.

Trees on the mountainside flew by as she descended into the Landsong Gorge. In the early evening hours, she came down to the river and found a small raft tied to a rickety dock. Unhindered by human ethics on stealing, she untied the raft and pushed out to the middle of the Colmane where the current carried the raft downstream. Laying Corvala on the deck, she placed her hands on the sides of the girl's head and assessed the damage.

PROCESSING...

Sensing Corvala's brain, Serapha pulled up an image of what looked like millions of gossamer threads intertwined with one another. In most places, the web was healthy, lively sparks running up and down it. But in other places, the strands looked torn, sparks fizzling at frayed ends. Damage to the synapses.

INITIATE REPAIRS

Serapha produced the metal spur from her wrist and inserted it into Corvala's neck. The spur injected a fluid containing countless nanobots designed to heal human tissue. Serapha sent the microscopic robots to work, signaling them where to go and instructing them to repair the frayed ends. It was similar to the work she had done for the girl's father. He had suffered trauma from several blows to the head, so Serapha had had to address contusions in specific areas. Corvala's damage, however, was subtler, albeit more widespread. There were millions of tiny tears throughout the cerebrum. Both the father's and the girl's cases required the nanobots to put together what was broken and re-establish connections between the synapses.

Serapha had healed many people with head wounds. Indeed, she had healed almost every kind of wound that existed. Before she had been re-purposed by the Sky Mantle project and hidden in the bunker, she had been military property and assigned to a company of soldiers. At times she had fought alongside them but mostly provided healing when they were wounded. While some of her human counterparts in medic units broke down at the sight of blood and gore or wept when they lost patients, Serapha came to the hospital table with no emotion—a doctor's instrument. Yet she knew there was more to people than the sum of their biological parts. They had thoughts and feelings that complicated things. Pain, fear, and panic could affect the outcome of surgery, could put a patient into a state of shock. To increase the chances of survival, she would say everything would be fine when it wouldn't be; she would hold a patient's hand while they were in pain. These practices didn't fit into her default logic, but it wasn't her place to question how humans functioned. She was programmed to serve them and heal their bodies, not fix their idiosyncrasies.

Serapha took her hands from Corvala's head.

REPAIRS COMPLETE

The girl would need to rest. The code within her was still intact, a possible tool in the unforeseen future. But the only Elijah Trees known to Serapha had been destroyed, and therefore Corvala couldn't contribute to the mission now.

Serapha would have to find a secure place to leave her before she went to Ryperia.

Sometime in the early morning, approximately an hour before sunrise, Serapha spotted a stone structure on the water's edge. Half of the structure stood on the bank while the other half went out into the river. It appeared abandoned. Cattails grew all around its walls, and a big willow pushed up against its base. Serapha used a pole to punt through the arched doorway and brought the raft to rest in the muddy shallows within the structure.

SCANNING

The inside was one large room with tall windows along its side. The windows were empty except for the jagged bits of glass that remained at their edges. At the far end of the room was a round stained-glass window up near the ceiling. Part of the window was broken, but enough of it was intact to show parts of a cross formed out of gold-colored glass. Serapha deduced that this had once been a place where humans had worshipped. Now pigeons nested on the window ledge at the base of the cross. The ceiling had collapsed in some places, and most of the beams were rotten, but this half-flooded church would suffice as a shelter.

Serapha brought Corvala to a corner of the room farthest from the water's edge and laid her on a soft bed of moss growing over the floor. Here the walls would hide her from anyone passing outside, and the remains of the roof would keep her mostly dry if it should rain. The girl would survive.

Serapha wrote a message on the muddy bank, one for Corvala to find when she woke. Once Serapha finished, she got on the raft and pushed her way out the door, out into the river where the current carried her downstream.

DESTINATION: RYPERIA

Chapter 35

The village was quiet. Doors and shutters lazily swung in the breeze. Chickens scratched and pecked in the roads, but there were no people to be seen or heard. It was morning, and a fog had rolled into the Landsong Gorge, making the abandoned riverside village all the more eerie. Atop a horse, Exodus rode through the village and surveyed its emptiness. A few weather-battered garments still hung on a clothesline. In a fenced yard, the body of a dog lay tied up to a stake. Dead from starvation. It was as if the people had simply walked away from here. So it had been with the other villages Exodus had passed through on his ride from High Court. This had something to do with the intruder Serapha had mentioned—Exodus was certain of it. It was no coincidence he was finding emptied huts soon after he had been dragged into Serapha's mission. Somehow this intruder had made thousands of people vanish from their homes.

Now if I could just figure out how...

After running from the law, Exodus was now working for the law. Funny how fate worked out. Under Abraham's suggestion, the Judges had issued him a horse and sent him out to investigate the mysterious silence from

Ryperia and the abandonment of the surrounding areas. If he could, he was to find Malachi, the Judge stationed in Ryperia, to whom messages had been sent but none returned. Going out on this investigation, Exodus openly wore a Judge's jerkin and shoulder belt with the bronze buckle, although he was technically still a criminal in the eyes of the Order. There were no guards to watch him, but Abraham had him on a short leash. The old Judge knew Exodus wouldn't run from this job—not while his daughter's innocence was on the line.

For Exodus, this journey was his path of penance. If he found out what was going on in Ryperia, his name would be cleared. It was a small cost. But then again, his crime had been small in comparison to his daughter's. In the eyes of Rooks and the other Judges, she had summoned up a demon. The gravest of heresies. Exodus was merely an accomplice. To atone for *her* crime in addition to his, he'd need to do more than simple reconnaissance. He'd have to 'face dangers proportional to her crime'—Abraham's words. Maybe then her name would be cleared as well. That was Abraham's promise. Exodus could sense that the old Judge didn't have much hope in it. He had sent Exodus out with the same voice and expression he used when sending a man to the chopping block.

Riding through the abandoned village covered in fog, Exodus couldn't help but wonder if he was getting in over his head—if he was riding into the dangers Abraham had in mind. He kept his horse at a walk, watching his surroundings and listening, careful not to ride into a trap. An abandoned village would be the ideal place for an ambush. Lots of empty houses where marauders could hide. At first, he heard nothing more than the soft clucking of chickens. Then there came the sound of voices. Exodus stopped his horse and listened. He put his hand on his hilt, ready to draw. Out of the fog walked two women coming up from the river. Exodus's sword hand fell at ease. Judging from the women's kerchiefs and plain clothing, they were of humble means. One looked young, an awkward thing, all knees and elbows. The other was older, thin as a broom, frizzy hair peppered with gray. They each carried a bucket of water in one hand and a heavy stick in the other. The two chatted quietly with one another and kept their eyes on the ground as they carried their loads. Exodus could hear their singsong drawl, the accent of those who lived on the other side of the Moss Kettle Mountains. It wasn't until they were a few paces away that the older one looked up from her trudging and noticed Exodus in front of them. She gasped and dropped her bucket, immediately shielding the younger woman and holding the heavy stick out like a club. The younger woman whimpered and also held up her improvised weapon, but it was clear by her trembling hands she didn't know what to do with it.

'Stay back,' the older woman warned even though Exodus hadn't made any move toward them.

'Peace,' Exodus said, raising his hands to show he meant no harm. 'I was passing through here and heard you coming.'

'Then you just keep moving along now,' she said. 'We don't want no trouble.'

'I will. But first please tell me what happened here. Where is everybody?'

The older woman looked him over and stared at his bronze buckle with the symbol of broken pottery and fire.

'You a Judge?'

Although his circumstances made the answer complicated, he gave a simple nod.

'You don't have any business here?' asked the older woman, pointing tentatively at his sword.

'My business lies elsewhere.'

At this, the older woman lowered her club and motioned for the young woman to do the same.

'It's all right,' she said, patting her on the arm. 'He's here to protect defenseless folk like us.' Then she turned an expectant glance at Exodus, one that said, 'And you *will* protect us, right?'

'I'm out to help,' Exodus said. 'Which is why I want to know what happened here.'

The older woman shrugged. 'You want to know why this place is empty? We'd like to know the same. We're not from here. Passing through like you.' She picked up her empty bucket from the ground. 'We were just fetching water. Going to boil our breakfast.'

'You're camped here?'

'Kind of,' the older woman replied. 'I always think of camping as bedding down on the earth. We're using a house.' She immediately grimaced and ducked under Exodus's gaze. 'We're no squatters, mind you,' she added nervously, shaking her head in earnest. 'Just two women on the road. And staying in a house gives us more protection than sleeping outdoors, if you follow. We only stayed there for the night, and we'll be moving on after breakfast. We'll even tidy the place up a bit before we go. Not that we made much of a mess in the first place.'

Exodus waved his hand to show he wasn't concerned with any of that. 'What brings you here?'

'That's a story, sir. But it's not fitting to stand out here and chat. Not while there's breakfast to be had. Lena still has her water. I was going to boil mush in one pot and eggs in another. Looks like it's just mush this go around.' She tapped her club against her empty bucket. 'Why not come and join us? Mush ain't the tastiest to be sure, but it fills the belly. And a full belly's what's needed on the road.'

Before Exodus could answer, the older woman took his horse by the reins and began leading it down one of the village's side roads.

'Name's Eudora, by the way. This is my daughter-in-law, Lena.'

The younger woman shyly looked up at Exodus with doe eyes and then quickly looked back down to the ground.

'Can't start a day's travel without a good breakfast,' said Eudora as she walked them down a dirt path through the village. 'We'll get you fed in no time. Luckily, I brought extra oats.'

Eudora's quick shift from defensive to welcoming didn't escape Exodus's notice—using hospitality in hopes of winning an armed escort through this foreboding land. There was a certain amount of urgency in Exodus's assignment in Ryperia, but he wanted to know what brought these two women here. Perhaps their story would shed some light on the emptiness around them. Besides, he didn't mind an excuse for having breakfast. He hadn't eaten much since leaving High Court the day before.

Eudora took him to the house where the two women had stayed the night. It looked like any of the other log cabins in the village, their two mules tied to the fence. Inside, the stove already had a fire going.

'We didn't take nothing from here,' Eudora said, bracing for an accusation Exodus never put forward. 'Except for a bit of firewood.' She poured water from Lena's bucket into the kettle on the stove.

'You asked why we're here,' Eudora went on. 'It's a long story. I'll give you the short of it. We come from a little farm just to the south of the gorge. We're looking for my son, Lena's husband. We haven't seen him in over a week. He went to the city to sell some of our crop. We had a good harvest of corn last year and thought we'd sell the surplus for extra money. He left home with a loaded wagon and that's the last we saw of him.

'It's normally two days to town from our place and two days back. When that time passed, I wasn't too worried to begin with. Stuff happens on the road. Your horse eats something what makes it sick. A wheel breaks. Bad luck. But then more days went by than you could blame bad luck for. Lena and I started to get worried. And I was thinking, 'Good Lord! He was taken by thieves!' But then I start hearing stories about people who went Ryperia way and never came back. Lena's cousin went there, and no one's heard from him. There's my uncle's boy and sister's brother-in-law. Same thing.

'We don't know what's going on, Judge. I want to find my boy. I want my Victor. I'm just a widow, and Lena's just a girl. Victor's all we have. We had to go out and get him back.'

'You haven't seen him, have you?' Lena asked, speaking up for the first time, her voice timid yet hopeful. 'He's got hair that sticks up in places like straw. And he has a birthmark on his right cheek that looks like an oak leaf.'

Exodus shook his head. 'Haven't seen anyone on the road.'

Lena looked down at her hands folded in her lap. Then she started to cry softly. Eudora went and embraced her.

Exodus couldn't help but feel pity for the young woman. She reminded him of Corvala. Same dark hair, not much older. He sighed heavily. Where was *his* girl? Was she safe in Serapha's care?

'I'm going to Ryperia,' Exodus said, his words meant to assure himself just as much as they were meant to ease the women. 'And I'm going to get to the bottom of this.'

'Since that's where we're going, why don't we go with you?' Eudora asked. It wasn't really a question. By the intensity in her brown eyes, Exodus could tell it was her plan.

'If I told you no, my guess is it wouldn't do any good.'

'No, it wouldn't. We're going to Ryperia with or without your help.'

Exodus didn't need the two of them as a burden. And yet he couldn't let them go by themselves into this strange unknown with nothing but clubs for protection. He let out a heavy sigh.

'It's not a good idea,' he answered. 'You can't get in the way.'

'We won't,' Eudora assured.

The kettle came to a boil, and Eudora added the oats to make her mush.

'Lena, go get some mugs and spoons from our packs. You don't mind eating mush from a mug, do you?'

Once Lena had left the house, Eudora turned to Exodus and spoke in a low voice.

'I know it's forward, asking to come along. But happening upon a Judge going our way—that's a stroke of luck you can't pass up. We're going to need all the help we can get. I reckon there's something supernatural going on here. I think it might be—' She looked to the door to make sure Lena was gone '—might be ghosts haunting the gorge. Couldn't sleep a wink last night. Kept hearing a voice whenever I nodded off. Something coming from far away. Kept calling me, urging me to come. Never had a thing like that happen in all my life. Didn't tell Lena. She gets real frightened by that kind of stuff. But Lord above! Ain't that strange? Think it has something to do with my boy?'

'Perhaps.'

Exodus said nothing more. There was no way she would understand what he believed was going on—how an intruder from the heavens was behind these disappearing people. Even Exodus himself didn't understand it. He supposed he'd find out soon enough.

After a quick breakfast, the women packed up and took to their mules. Exodus led the way on his horse. Lena kept quiet while Eudora tried talking to him about her son and the farm where they lived—about how great a farmer he was. Exodus paid little attention. He was more concerned about what could be lurking in the fog. He kept a watch on the curling vapor and kept his ears listening for what might come. Everything on the road was still.

Their way went along the bottom of the gorge and followed the bends in the river. Eudora was talking about something or other—bragging about a huge squash her son had grown—when they came to a stream that fed into the Colmane. Over the stream, there was a wide stone bridge. Exodus knew this bridge and knew that Ryperia wasn't far. If it weren't for the fog, they'd be able to see the eastern gate of the city.

'We're close,' he said in a low voice, a cue for Eudora to keep quiet.

Before they crossed the bridge, Lena stopped and pointed up ahead. 'Look!' she cried. 'The sun.'

Up ahead shone a bright golden light through the fog. For people who had been hemmed in by gray, the sun would have been a welcome sight. But something was off. It was late morning, but the sun sat low in the west as if it were late afternoon. No, it wasn't the sun. This light seemed too close, coming from the heights of Ryperia, perhaps. The more Exodus stared at it, the stranger it seemed. There was something there... something taking shape. It was as though the light held a presence. A golden being.

It beckoned him to come.

Exodus pulled his gaze away. He saw Eudora blinking and waving a hand in front of her face as if she were batting away invisible gnats. Even the horse and mules appeared bothered, snorting and stamping their hooves.

'I hear it again,' Eudora said. 'That voice from my dreams. Do you hear it?'

Exodus bent his head forward and listened. He heard nothing. Instead, there was a faint feeling in the back of his mind—a thought forming that had yet to take shape. Maybe someone was calling him, but he couldn't yet make out their words. Whatever it was, it felt wrong.

'That's where everyone's gone,' he said at length. 'The light. It draws them in.'

'What are we going to do then?'

'We can't go any closer,' he said at length. 'Not yet.' This was his one chance to clear his daughter's name. Not a time for hasty decisions.

'What are you thinking we do then? Go back?'

'I'm not sure yet.'

'My boy's in that city,' Eudora said, batting at the invisible gnats. Her head turned quickly in the direction of Ryperia as though she had heard something. 'I'm going in there to get him.'

She prodded her mule to continue onward, but Exodus prodded his horse forward to block her way.

'The light bewitches you,' he said. 'It's a trap. I'm not going to have us walk into it.'

'I'm not abandoning my boy,' Eudora shot back. 'You're a Judge. You're supposed to help us.'

'I'm not sure I can.' It pained Exodus to admit this even though he knew it was true. The power of that light—it was something beyond him. Something beyond the reach of his sword. It might have shone as a bright light, but Exodus sensed dark magic was at work. 'We might have to alert the Rooks.'

'That'll take too long! My son's a stone's throw away, and you want to turn back.'

'Listen. We need to—' Exodus cut himself off.

Lena had moved away from them and was slowly urging her mule over the bridge. Her body sat languidly in the saddle, and she held up a limp arm towards the light, reaching for it.

'Corvala!' Exodus shook his head. 'Lena!' The young woman kept going as if she hadn't heard him.

Exodus turned his mount and rode over to her, taking the mule by the reins and making it stop in the middle of the bridge.

'Lena!'

The young woman didn't acknowledge him but gazed at the light. She had a glazed expression of awe and wonder, and her eyes were beginning to cloud over with a faint white film.

'He's calling to me,' Lena whispered. 'Can you hear him?'

'Lena,' Exodus said, shaking her shoulder. 'Resist. It's a spell.'

'He's calling.'

Exodus shook her harder. Lena blinked her eyes as if waking from a dream. The white film faded away as she looked at him.

'Please don't hurt me,' she whimpered, cowering.

Before Exodus could say anything to calm her, there came the clipping of hooves galloping across the bridge. Eudora sped away, disappearing into the fog and riding straight for Ryperia.

'Eudora!' cried Exodus, but she was gone. Biting off a curse, he turned to Lena. 'Stay here! Don't follow me.'

'What's happening?' Lena asked.

'I'm finding out. Get back,' he commanded, pointing to the other side of the bridge, 'and don't cross over.'

Exodus spurred his horse and went after Eudora. As he drove his mount down the road, the light above the city grew ever brighter. Exodus didn't look at it, but somehow he could feel it. The overpowering presence. In his mind, he could picture it vaguely—a golden man.

Then there came a voice, not so much heard as thought. A voice of promise and power—a whisper that somehow filled the gorge through which he rode, a voice that filled his mind.

Come to me.

It felt like someone was at the door to his thoughts, pushing to get in. Exodus braced himself, pushing back. He held the reins tighter and bent all his concentration on the road. Still, he felt the voice, its call growing stronger and stronger the closer he came to the city. He'd have to work quickly. Get Eudora and get back to the other side of the bridge, beyond the reach of the bewitching light. The horse cut through the fog, running at a full gallop. It nearly ran into the mule when the braying creature appeared out of the wisps, no Eudora in the saddle. The mule snorted as if tormented by a swarm of biting flies and galloped right past Exodus, back the way he had come.

Exodus rode on until he heard voices. These were more substantive than the voice in his head. Pulling back on the reins, Exodus slowed his mount and proceeded at a careful tread. Like the mule, his horse was also distressed, snorting and whinnying. Even the beasts could feel the wrongness of the light. Out of the fog, Exodus could see the vague shape of the city gate and a dozen gray figures standing before it. The guards of Ryperia, at least four of them armed with spears. Between Exodus and the guards stood a single figure: Eudora. Her dress was torn, and her arms were scraped, signs she had been thrown by the mule.

'Where's my son?' she shouted, brandishing her club. Her voice wasn't directed at the men with spears but at the light shining above the city. 'Bring him to me!'

A pair of guards left the gate and began approaching her. Exodus could see their cudgels in hand.

Exodus rode forward and shouted, 'Stop!'

The guards, who must have noticed him materializing out of the fog, turned their attention to him.

'Who are you?' one of them called.

'I'm Judge Exodus Keen. I've come to retrieve the woman.'

'She's in the realm of our god. She cannot leave.'

Exodus narrowed his eyes as he studied them. Their god?

Come to me, rang the voice in Exodus's mind. *She waits for you.*

'Corvala!' Exodus gasped but then shook his head.

'You serve Governor Grimshaw,' Exodus shouted, putting his focus on the guards, his words strained. 'You serve the Dominion. You will acknowledge my authority. Now let me retrieve the woman.'

'Grimshaw is no more,' another guard shouted. 'There is only Dane. He is the one we serve.'

Exodus nodded in grim understanding. This was the madness, the dark magic in the air. The intruder from the heavens had set himself up as a god, and Dane was his name. Exodus could feel his presence, could feel it shining from the light.

Come to me, the voice echoed in his mind. *She waits for you. Come to me, and you will see her again.*

Despite the guards' defiance, they made no move to seize Eudora. Perhaps they feared the challenge of a mounted warrior even though the spearmen would make short work of his horse. Or maybe the reputation of Judges gave them pause. For whatever reason, the guards remained by the walls, appearing to wait for his next move. Eudora continued limping towards the gate. Exodus judged the distance, figuring out whether or not he could make a break for Eudora and get her into the saddle before the spearmen skewered his mount.

There is no need to fight, said the voice in Exodus's mind. *Come to me.*

He gritted his teeth and shuddered, as if he could shake off the voice. Then he heard the clip of hooves coming from behind. Looking back, he saw Lena riding towards him at a trot.

'No!' Exodus shouted. 'Go back! Get back to the bridge.'

'He's calling,' she said, her eyes once again glazed over with white film.

'Get away from here!'

The young woman still approached, coming up beside him. He could grab her mule by the reins and get her out now, leaving Eudora behind. Or he could try to save both of them, first riding to Eudora and risking the spears. As Eudora limped ever closer to the guards, his mind raced through possible outcomes. But it was impossible to think clearly, the incessant voice pushing its way in.

Come to me. She is waiting for you.

'No... she's not!' Exodus seethed.

Then came a loud moan from the road. 'Victor!' Eudora cried. 'My son! Tell me where he is.'

Exodus fought to keep focused. He blinked hard and gritted his teeth in determination.

'Stay here,' he said, turning to Lena. 'I'm going to get—'

Pain exploded in the back of his head. He struggled to hold onto consciousness as he felt his body fall from the saddle and land on the road. Bits of color and darkness swirled around the edge of his vision as he saw Lena come to stand over him. Her club was heavy, but a swing from that frail arm shouldn't have brought him down, not when he had weathered far worse in past battles. In those fights, however, he had never had his mind strained and weakened by powerful spells.

'He's calling to us,' Lena said, pointing to the golden light. 'We must obey. We must go to him.'

The fierce hue pressed in, and with it came the presence.

Come to me—this time not an alluring voice but a forceful command.

What remained of Exodus's will fell to the sheer force that crashed upon him. The door to his mind broke asunder, and the golden light consumed him—the power of the tide pulling him into the depths of the sea. Once within the golden man's grasp, he found it strange that the light was no more, and perhaps it had never been there at all, only shining as a façade. For now, there gaped before him the empty nothingness of the abyss, and it was the god's to fill.

Chapter 36

From the cover of pines and ferns, Serapha scouted out the Landsong Gorge below. The Colmane River ran along the bottom of the gorge, and on the other side of the river stood the city of Ryperia. From the hilltop where she perched, Serapha had a clear view of the walls and buildings below. Above the city's largest structure— what looked to be a palace—shone a powerful light. From it came something unseen, something detected by Serapha's sensors.

ANALYZING

There was a signal, a frequency. Her internal decryption program determined the data contained in the signal.

RADIO: NEGATIVE

TELEVISION: NEGATIVE

WIRELESS: NEGATIVE

This was a new kind of signal. One that resonated with the electrical impulses found in the human brain— the same impulses she had repaired in Corvala and Exodus. Judging by her analysis, she determined the light shone from a transmitter that altered human cognition.

PROCESSING...

EVIDENCE OF TECHNOLOGICALLY ADVANCED PRESENCE

DETERMINE ACTION

PROCESSING...

COURSE OF ACTION:

    1. FIND POINT OF ENTRY

    2. DESTROY MIND-ALTERING DEVICE

    3. NEUTRALIZE INTRUDER

The walls were too tall for her to jump, and the gates were heavily guarded. It wasn't guards that concerned her but the Olympian himself. If he had created a device to control the minds of humans, then logically he had other inventions—weapons that could make him a powerful enemy, maybe even more powerful than Serapha. Taking him by surprise, however, would give her an advantage. To keep that advantage, she'd have to find a secret entry point.

ACCESS MEMORY FILES: MAPPING

According to her memory, there had once been an urban area here in this wide section of the gorge—back before the End War. There had been factories and industrial plants where Ryperia now stood. At this part of the river, the Chinook Dam had been this region's source of hydroelectric power. According to Serapha's mapping system, it should have been right in front of Ryperia, under the large bridge that spanned the Colmane and led up to the city's northern entrance. From what Serapha could read from the terrain, centuries of flooding had raised the riverbed and water levels and would have left the dam submerged.

SCANNING

The upstream side of the bridge was significantly shallower than downstream. Something lay beneath the bridge had piled up the rocks and mud to the upstream side.

PROBABLE PRESENCE OF CHINOOK DAM

POSSIBLE POINT OF ENTRY

Approximately one hour after sundown, she left her cover among the pines and ferns and went down the mountainside to the northern bank. Keeping low, she crept to the middle of the bridge and slipped over the side. Unlike the upstream side of the bridge, the river was deep, and her dive took her over a dozen meters down to the bottom. She clung to a boulder on the riverbed so the strong current wouldn't drag her downstream. With her advanced night vision, she looked to the bridge supports above and the foundation on which they stood: a sheer wall of concrete.

CONFIRMED VISUAL ON CHINOOK DAM

After all these centuries it still held up, a testament to its exceptional engineering. Serapha's hands found holds on half-buried stones in the riverbed and her feet pushed through the gravel as she crawled against the recirculating current near the dam. At its base, she came to the outlets where the dam's water discharge would have flowed. All of them were buried with rocks, but one of them less so. There was just enough of an opening for Serapha to slide through.

POINT OF ENTRY ACQUIRED

ACTIVATE BUOYANCY COMPENSATION DEVICE

Small air canisters inflated a pair of rubber pouches inside her body, giving her a measure of flotation. She swam up the water discharge of the dam and into the large cylinder where the turbine had once turned. Clearing out the petrified sticks and debris clogged inside, she swam between two of the turbine's blades, up to where the generators were housed. From there stretched out a sunken hallway lined with tubes and pipes. Unlike the river's swift flow, the water here was still as glass. Besides the snail trails that meandered over the thick layer of silt on the floor, it appeared as if nothing had touched this hallway in centuries. Serapha swam down its length, disturbing the age-long stillness with a rhythmic stroke that kicked up swirls of silt from the floor and pipes. The hallway led to other sunken tunnels—some formed from concrete walls, others carved out of raw stone. By Serapha's estimation, the water table here must have been honeycombed with flooded cavities and passageways throughout the underground ruins. After swimming into several dead ends, she discovered a vast underwater cavern. Part of it had caved in, but great steel beams held up what remained of the vaulted ceiling. Throughout the cavern loomed massive shapes—giant machines, arranged in long rows. A factory frozen in a moment of industrial progress. Down the assembly line ran a chain of construction robots in various stages of incompleteness—all covered in a slimy film and encrusted by tiny mussels.

MODEL 407 MAMMOTH EXCAVATORS

Each one was a beast of treads and hydraulics and bore a pair of huge steel claws for digging and lifting rocks. Some were merely metal frames at the beginning of production. Others were nearly finished, needing only a few rivets and a final line to be welded. At the sides of the conveyor belts were large robotic arms that had once done the assembling. Now they bowed in eternal rest from their labor. What had once been a place of rhythmic clanking and sparks had become the silent domain of eyeless albino fish.

LOCATION: THE LEE-VAUGHN PRODUCTION CENTER OF CONSTRUCTION EQUIPMENT

Serapha swam through the submerged ruins of the factory and came to a stairwell on the far side of the cavern. Inflating her rubber pouches to their fullest, she made a quick ascent up the stairwell and broke the water's surface. Once above the water table, she climbed a rusty flight of stairs on foot to the entrance of another underground chamber. Like the cavern below, there were parts that were caved in. But where it was whole, cement columns rose from the floor and held up rusted metal beams crisscrossing the ceiling. In the center of the chamber stood over two dozen robotic excavators, all completed and appearing ready to be shipped out for construction work that would never come.

Within these industrial ruins of the bygone age, Serapha observed that a more recent—more primitive—

element had been introduced. Crude chains wrapped around the excavators' limbs and were staked to the cement floor with large metal spikes. The back wall held words painted in red, now somewhat faded:

I SAW AN ANGEL

COME DOWN FROM HEAVEN,

AND HE LAID HOLD ON THE DEVIL

AND BOUND HIM A THOUSAND YEARS.

Under the painted words, there was what looked to have been a large doorway framed with cement and rebar. It was now, however, walled over with roughly hewn stone blocks.

PROBABLE EXIT

Serapha looked around at the various Model 407 Mammoths.

SCANNING

She walked down the center of the chamber, the hulking machines towering over her on either side. One of them would provide the means of making an exit—one not too corroded or broken down by time. As she searched the machines, she evaluated their current circumstances. Here they had sat through the centuries, rusting and without purpose. Mighty though their claws and limbs may have appeared, they were nothing more than heavy scrap among the ruin, unable to fulfill their purpose. Serapha knew there would come a day when she would have too many parts worn and broken to be worth fixing—and it was very unlikely that she could be fixed at all in this new primitive world. Her eventual fate was to be thrown to the scrap heap just like any other machine. It was not a fate to lament; it was simply the way the world worked. For now, however, she was whole and with a purpose—one she planned to accomplish soon.

As she scanned, she sensed a spark of energy in some of the excavators. They may have looked dead, but there was still a hint of life in them. According to Serapha's sensors, some were hibernating, much like she had done in her underground vault. Unlike her, they had massive power cells designed for months of intense work without recharging. In their restive state, however, their cells could last for centuries. Some of the hibernating machines still had some energy left. Not enough to organize an assault on the intruder from Olympus—even if she managed to find a way to bring the excavators above ground. There should be just enough power for what she needed.

Going down the rows, opening up their hatches and looking inside, she found that most of the machines didn't work. Their wires were corroded or chewed through by rats. There was one, however, that appeared to be in working order. Serapha unlatched a compartment on its side and revealed a computer interface with buttons and a small screen.

PROGRAMMING OVERRIDE

Being far more advanced than these robots built to lift and smash, she soon accessed the activation codes and had the internal systems humming. Gears turned, and the engine shuddered and then roared to life. Serapha gave a command, and the machine's caterpillar treads clanked into motion. The chains trying to hold it in place strained then snapped. When the robot reached the blocked off doorway, it thrust out a claw arm, and the blunt steel edge smashed through the walled off doorway.

'Go to sleep,' Serapha commanded.

The robot immediately retracted its arm and returned to hibernation.

Serapha passed through the newly made opening and entered a cavern that appeared to be a cistern. At the far end stood arches and pillars built to hold up the ceiling. High above, there was a shaft leading up to a grate, the moon shining through and water dripping down. The grate was over a dozen meters above, too high for her to reach. But on the opposite side of the cistern was a conduit. She squeezed inside and snaked her way against a slippery layer of algae and slime, crawling to a shaft that fed down into the conduit. There was another grate above, one Serapha could reach when she stood. She paused and listened. Silence.

NO THREAT DETECTED

She opened the grate, climbed out of the conduit, and entered what looked to be a storage room full of crates covered in grime. The room had a heavy wooden door, and when Serapha pushed against it, she found it was locked on the other side. One solid shove with her shoulder, and it swung open, the latch wrenched from its place.

She found herself at the end of an aisle lined with metal bars: cells to the right and left, dozens of people packed inside. One child whimpered weakly in his mother's lap, but it was the only sound in the whole jail. The prisoners sat silently on the ground and tilted their attention to Serapha, their expressions vacant and eyes clouded. They showed little interest in her sudden appearance and bowed their heads, returning their gazes to the floor.

ANALYZING

NO THREAT DETECTED

The far end of the jail held another door. Unlike the one she had just broken through, this one was reinforced with iron. Behind it came the murmur of muted voices. Guards most likely.

DETERMINE ACTION

PROCESSING...

She spied a high window in one of the cells—too high for a human to reach but not for her. Grabbing two of the cell's bars, she pulled in opposite directions. The pistons in her arms extended, and the bars groaned as they bent into an opening. She slipped into the cell, deftly placing her feet on the few spaces of floor unoccupied by prisoners. Their slumped forms hardly budged as she passed, and none made a move for the exit she had created.

PROCESSING...

INCONGRUENT HUMAN BEHAVIOR

EFFECTS OF MIND-ALTERING DEVICE

As she walked around the prisoners, she noticed a bearded man with broad shoulders hunched over in the corner. He was larger than the others, and his clouded eyes stared at nothing, his expression—which had once been full of stern resolve—was now hollow, as if the lights within him had grown dim.

EXODUS

PROCESSING...

PROCESSING...

PROCESSING...

'Exodus,' she said. 'What are you doing here?'

He looked at her, his eyes squinting in faint recognition.

'Serapha,' he murmured. 'Where's Corvala?'

'She is safe. Why are you here?'

'I was brought here. It's...hard to remember.'

'I will get you out of here.'

She jumped up to the high window and, with feet braced against the wall, bent the bars just as she had before. Slipping through the window, she crawled out onto open ground. The cells, it appeared, had been dug out below street level. She turned back and reached a hand down to Exodus, but he didn't move. He looked up, eyes clouded.

'Come,' Serapha called.

'I can't,' he replied.

CURRENT BEHAVIOR: ABNORMAL...DOCILE

'You can reach me,' she said. 'I will pull you out.'

'I can't,' he repeated. 'It's against... his law.'

'Whose law?'

'The golden man's.' Exodus sighed and turned his eyes to the ground.

Serapha didn't have time for this.

DETERMINE ACTION

PROCESSING...

He wasn't crucial to her mission, and in his current state of mind, he would only be a burden if she brought him along. She determined it would be better to get him *after* she destroyed the device, when he was no longer under the effects of its signal.

'I will return for you' she said, then left the jail and entered the streets of Ryperia.

This section of the city appeared quiet with no patrolling guards in sight. She scaled a drainpipe and came to the top of a building where she could see the bright glow shining from the heights of the palace.

DISTANCE TO TARGET: APPROXIMATELY 230 METERS

She bounded from rooftop to rooftop, moving quickly and quietly, disturbing nothing except a few roosting pigeons. Nearing the palace, she sprinted along the peak of a roof and leaped from the edge, flying above a street and over the iron fence that surrounded the palace grounds. She landed in a garden of hedgerows and fruit trees. From the cover of a hedge, she scanned the grounds. A pair of guards patrolling along the fence passed a couple meters from where she hid. Once they had their backs to her, she slinked from her cover and dashed from shadow to shadow through the garden, heading towards the palace.

The palace rose to a height of three stories, and ivy grew up its basalt walls in thick knots. Finding holds in the ivy, she scaled the walls and reached the roof. Here, above the palace's southern wing, the slate roof slanted to a peak, but the eaves were flat and formed a lip wide enough for Serapha to traverse. She stole along the edge and came to the center of the palace where the dome and spire rose up before her. Metal rungs were bolted to the blocks forming the dome, and Serapha ascended them two at a time. Reaching the top, she came to stand at the base of the spire where the mind-altering device shone.

Her vision cut through the light, and she saw that the thing itself was unassuming—a sphere that could fit in her hand—and it was attached to the spire with nothing more than a few pieces of fusing wire. But Serapha could sense the great power that radiated from it, manipulating the cerebral functions of a hundred thousand people. An egregious breach in the Earth and Sky Treaty. Here she would fulfill her purpose. She reached out for the sphere, her hand poised to crush it.

The air cracked with a bang and a blast struck her arm. Thrown back, she tumbled down the dome roof to the stone ledge below. Before she could get up, a dense weight slammed her to the stone surface and pinned her there. She lay prone with a gauntleted hand pressing down on her head, another clamped to her leg. Looking through the vice-like grip of metal fingers, she saw a figure crouching over her, glinting in the sphere's glow.

A man in golden armor.

Chapter 37

'Who are you?' Dane demanded.

The woman in his grip didn't answer. His gaze fell to where her arm had been. All that remained were wires and metal rods jutting out of her shoulder, the broken ends still smoldering red from his cell gun blast.

Not a woman… an android.

Dane's body stiffened. *Impossible. Not in this primitive world.*

'Who sent you? Silas?'

The android's remaining hand shot out and grabbed his arm. Sparks flew, and an electric shock jolted through Dane's suit, functions flickering out. His armor suddenly became slack, and Dane's frail body collapsed under the dead weight. Through his visor lenses, he saw the android roll on top of him, looking down with impassive eyes. To be beneath someone—something—it caught him off guard. Terrifying surprise tightened his chest, and his heart fluttered against the thin bones of his ribcage. Dane watched in wide-eyed fear as the fist came down and struck him between the eyes.

The helmet clanged, muted by the padding against his ears. The android struck again and again, pummeling the faceplate with inhuman speed—*bang! bang! bang! bang!*— coming within mere millimeters of Dane's eyes. He blinked at each blow, watching the world go strobe as the beating rained down. Before his hot, panicked breaths fogged up his visor, he watched as the android's jackhammer blows wore away its synthetic skin from the knuckles, revealing the metal joints beneath.

Still, his armor held. Despite what he felt, he knew his suit could withstand an entire army's fury without incurring a dent. But—*gah!*—what a headache that fist was pounding into his skull—*bang! bang! bang!* If he had any teeth, they would've rattled out of his jaws by now. With the incessant clanging reverberating in his ears, he barely registered when the suit hummed to life and recovered its functions. Dane felt power coursing around him once more. He shook off his astonishment and snatched up his wits. *Enough of this!*

He blindly thrust out his arm, his palm slamming into something, and the android's weight lifted off of him. It gave him a chance to push himself up to his side. His defogging system cleared the visor lenses just in time for him to see the android launch itself at him again. It railed series of blows at the neck joint as if it were trying to take off his helmet. Dane growled and swept out with a kick, knocking the android from its feet. He pushed himself forward and swung down with his fist, The android rolled away just before the crushing blow cracked the stone.

The android pressed the attack, but once on his feet, Dane blocked and met it blow for blow. During his six hundred years in the Dream, he had relived almost every battle scenario possible. He had fought in the mud of trenches and on the heights of ramparts, from atop charging warhorses and in the thick of clashing infantries. The centuries of experience had honed his mind to a keen edge, and he studied the android just as he had a thousand other foes he'd faced in the Dream. The android was quicker, but Dane had cunning to perceive its moves. It deftly hit Dane's armor in various places, seeking out a weakness. A low kick to the knee tested the joint, but Dane's leg held firm. Using the force of the kick to leap back, the android avoided Dane's swing. He feinted right then jabbed with his left. The android adjusted its dodge too late, and the fist clipped its shoulder, knocking it off balance. Dane moved in and thrust his fist upward. The android's head snapped back—half its neck split, sparking wires breaking free. The android lifted into the air and off the palace roof.

Dane looked over the roof's edge, surprised to see the android picking itself up from where it had crashed on a stone path, its head cricked hard to one side. It sprang to its feet and ran for the iron fence that encircled the gardens and the palace grounds. Defeated, it appeared to be trying to escape. Dane fired his cell guns down on the fleeing android, aiming for the legs. He didn't want it completely destroyed. Not yet. He had questions— questions that only intact memory files could answer. Shots from his cell guns rained down on the garden, tearing up shrubs and blasting holes in the lawn. The android dodged the blasts even as it vaulted over the fence. Dane jumped from the roof, his suit absorbing the impact of the three-story fall. He launched into the chase, his suit giving him inhuman speed as he tore across the garden and broke through the palace fence, out into the quiet streets of the sleeping city. Now the rapid clanking of his boots broke the quiet as he sped past darkened buildings. The android ran only a block ahead, then ducked down an opening between buildings. Agile, it turned on a dime and kept speed, outmaneuvering Dane's bulkier form. Just a fleeting shadow disappearing around the next corner. But on the straights, Dane closed the distance bit by bit, his legs pumping like pistons. The chase drove him down a market street. The android leaped over wagons and slid around the stalls. Dane ploughed through the obstacles, crushing and splintering as he went, speed unhindered. The android took a right down a side street. When Dane rounded the corner, he caught a glimpse of it throwing aside a grate in the street and dropping down a hole.

Dane halted at the hole's edge, nothing but darkness below. A trap perhaps, although unlikely. There was only one way to find out, and he had questions that needed answering. He dropped into the darkness, falling the distance of several stories before his feet landed on the stone ground. Night vision revealed an underground cavern glistening with stalagmites and stalactites. No sign of the android. No sign of a trap. Dane trod carefully down to the lowest level of the cavern to where a narrow portion of it had been walled off with masoned stone. There was a break in the wall, probably where the android had gone. As Dane passed through the opening, he looked up to see a great metal beast looming over him, claws raised. Dane leaped back, ready to fire his cell guns, but then noticed the monster didn't move. He stared a moment at the half-rusted thing, recognition entering his mind. Not a monster—a robotic excavator, the kind he had once seen working construction sites so long ago. Looking around the room, he saw that more excavators lined up in rows beside cement columns. At the far end stood a doorway girded by metal. Although some of the chamber was caved in, he could see it for what it was: not another cavern but a warehouse. Ruins from the world he once knew, hidden here deep underground.

Dane took a few steps inward, sensors scanning the chamber for any sign of the android. Part of his mind was intrigued by the oddity of this place—so incongruent with the world above. Then he snapped to focus when he spotted a figure move between excavators, darting away from him. Suddenly, a rumble echoed through the chamber. Dane spun towards the nearest machine, the one that had startled him. Its engine roared, and it started to move. Dane snapped his arms forward out of instinct, his cell guns firing. The excavator—indifferent to the blasts that scored its armor-like exterior and punched into its motor—stretched out its hydraulic arms. Even as it belched smoke and fire from the damage, one of its massive claws tore a cement column from its base. As pieces of the column crashed to the floor, the rusty girders it had supported groaned ominously and a violent tremor shook the chamber. Dane stopped firing and looked up. Just as the excavator demolished another column, the ceiling broke open with a scream of metal and a massive slab of raw stone fell through and crushed the machine's front end. The chamber quaked, and the ceiling cracked and crumbled. Dane paused a moment, cell guns raised as he scanned for the android. Then he leaped back just before a car-sized chunk of rock crashed into where he had been. More stone fell around him, and he ran back to the break in the block wall. As the room caved in around him and as more machines were crushed, he cast a glance over his shoulder. Through the dust and falling rubble, he saw the android slip through the doorway on the other side of the warehouse chamber and out of sight.

The patheograph still glowed upon the palace spire, still spread emotions that demanded worship. The android hadn't touched it. Dane's cell gun had made certain of that. But something had changed in the patheograph. It pulsed at a steady rhythm as always, except now, every twenty beats or so, the light would flicker with a shade of blue—a small error in the system.

Dane looked out into the city and gorge beyond the walls. Torchlight in the distance marked the positions of roving patrols, the guards he had sent to search the city and the surrounding areas for a one-armed woman. They wouldn't find the android, of course. It would be long gone by now. But he had to make the men do something. Perhaps their searching would keep the android from coming back. It was a Seraph class if Dane's memory served right—once an elite servant of the military. How it had survived the Purge and six hundred years of a primitive Earth was beyond him. It couldn't have been holed up down there with the robotic excavators. Not without a power source. And it was in too good a shape to be from the rust and ruin down there. Something else was at play. Perhaps Silas had sent an android down from Olympus to check on him. Dane couldn't be certain. If only he had got hold of the android's memory...

More cracks formed in his perceived sense of invincibility. First the man with the EMP blaster, the one the guards called a Rook. Now an android. He wasn't the only being in this primitive world with the power of tech.

The patheograph flickered blue again. It was so faint, a casual observer wouldn't have noticed. But Dane did. A new emotion had made its way into the device's broadcasting cycle: doubt. Dane had seen it on some of the guards' faces when he had ordered them to search for the one-armed woman. Something was wrong, and they could sense it. Someone had defied the golden man and had got away with it. Doubt colored the men's eyes—doubt in their god. It was there for a moment, then it was gone, fear and awe taking its place. But the doubt had been there, and now it tainted the patheograph—however small that taint may be. Perfection with a small stain wasn't perfection at all.

Dane's mind grew dark and the heat of frustration rose to his cheeks. He could try to fix the device, but that would mean turning it off. If he did, all the emotions it had gathered would dissipate, and the people would be unloosed from its hold. He'd have to start over, proving to the people once again that he was a god and gather their feelings. Even so, he couldn't guarantee the worship would come back. He'd have to let the device keep running. Perhaps he'd show some great feat of strength to invigorate and multiply the wonder and fear the people felt for him. Something to overpower the flicker of doubt.

As much as the imperfection in his device bothered him, there were other pressing matters. He had to make sure the android, and more machines like it, couldn't get to him or the patheograph. After the Rook had come, Dane had placed sensors around the city—simple sensors modified to detect electrical devices at work. The android had used the underground passage to bypass the ones he had placed along the walls. If it hadn't been for the sensors on the palace, he wouldn't have been alerted and the android would've reached the patheograph unhindered. It was too close. Security had to be strengthened, but he couldn't just stand here on the roof, guarding his invention. That was no life for a god. Something needed to be done. He pressed his palm to his helmet as if it could relieve him of his splitting headache. Plans could come later. Right now, he'd get relief the best way he knew how.

When he descended from the roof to the throne room, there was a pair of guards awaiting him. They stood silently, knowing better than to ask questions when their god climbed in through the window. Between the guards stood a dozen prisoners, all with bags over their heads. The guards had come to know their god's appetites. He would need to sap a hefty share of life to ease the frustration caused by this night's failure. Dane appraised the stock, looking at which one to take first. There was one figure who stood out from the rest. His brawny form appeared chiseled from stone, and he stood nearly a head taller than the others. He wore a uniform of sorts.

'What's this?' Dane asked mildly curious, tapping the buckle on the man's shoulder strap. It bore the image of a broken pot with fire coming out of it.

'It marks him as a Judge, sir,' replied one of the guards.

'A Judge?' The man certainly didn't look like a judge, not by Dane's estimation. This wasn't a wizened old man hidden within black robes; here was a mountain of a man.

'What do your Judges do? Oversee trials?'

'They protect the people,' said the guard.

'Ah... protect.'

The judge was a fine specimen. Taking a life full of such strength would be a rich experience indeed.

But the presence of strength only reminded Dane of his newly acquired weakness. The flicker of doubt running through the city. The heat of frustration flared through him again. With a growl, he pressed the metovita against the Judge's chest, longing to drown the emotion.

Then an idea came to him. *Protection.*

The idea grew. He could see the blocks of a plan rapidly coming together to form a wall and then from a wall to a stronghold in his mind. Protection. Perhaps the solution to his recent problem stood right there in front of him.

Chapter 38

Corvala's mind rose out of darkness, out of the abyss into which she'd fallen. Up from the oceanic trenches of the earth and into the world of the living, she floated into the gray realm of not-quite-awake and not-quite-asleep, gathering what faculties she could along the way. First came feeling, most notably the dull throbbing in her head—lingering effects of a disaster she couldn't yet remember. Her sense of hearing followed, the sound of running water trickling into her burgeoning consciousness. A flowing river perhaps. She could feel the soft, damp bank beneath her—could feel her body settled onto the moss and loam. After a long while of floating beneath the surface of wakefulness, her eyes blinked open. There was a roof above punched with holes and littered with bird nests in the rafters. She looked up at the sunlight streaming through, time stretching out languidly as she built up the will to rise. Eventually, she sat up and found herself inside an abandoned building, all the windows empty except for the half-broken stained-glass window above. She guessed this place had once been a chapel, but now half of it was flooded, the river flowing outside the door. She didn't remember how she got to this strange place. What she could remember were the countless images of a strange world. A dream? The images blurred together, and none of them gave her any hint of how she had come here.

Wading into the water that flooded the chapel, Corvala went out the door and into the shallows of the river to wash her face and take a long drink. Steep green slopes formed the banks on either side of the river, and she could see she was in Landsong Gorge once again, the southern edge of the Rainier Kingdom on the opposite shore. After a minute or two of watching ospreys catch fish from the river, she went back inside the chapel where she found something written on the sand.

I HAVE GONE TO RYPERIA TO CONFRONT THE INTRUDER. I MAY RETURN.

—SERAPHA

Upon reading the words, events started to clear. She had made contact with the Elijah Tree. It had shown her millions of wonderful and horrible things. Not a dream exactly, but a vision that had been given to her. The tree had been working on something—the mission. It was about to complete the mission when something went wrong. The vision had been cut off; the tree stopped in its work. The last thing Corvala could remember was the nerve-splitting agony that had torn through her mind and body. She had plummeted into utter darkness. She couldn't remember what happened after that. Serapha had brought her here. Why she had done that remained a mystery. Corvala rubbed her temples, trying to clear the dull throbbing in her head. There was no way of telling how long she had been unconscious or how long Serapha had been gone. Since the Elijah Tree had failed, the woman had gone to face the intruder herself. With nowhere else to go, the only thing Corvala could think to do was stay there and wait. Perhaps Serapha would return.

Corvala didn't remember falling back to sleep, but she woke from her bed of moss with a start. It was still daytime, the light through the holes in the roof slanting differently than before. Hours had passed while she had been sleeping. She wondered what had woken her, but then she heard it—the sound of something wading through the shallows. She told herself it was Serapha returning. Even so, she was too frightened to call out. Corvala waited and listened. The sound of stirred up water was coming closer. She looked around for a rock or a heavy stick. Finding neither, she pressed her back to the wall, her breathing growing quicker.

What came through the flooded doorway looked as if it were from the land of the dead: a woman with her arm torn away and her head nearly wrenched from her neck. Corvala opened her mouth to scream, but no sound came out. Her throat seized, and it felt as though the blood drained from her body. But staring at the creature's face... she realized it was one she knew.

'Serapha?' she trembled.

Metal protruded from her open shoulder, and there were thin bits of metal coming out of the split neck. No blood though, and Corvala remembered the knife Morgan Capel had stabbed into Serapha's back. Then it dawned on her, the moment's terror replaced by realization. Serapha was a...

'Machine!' Corvala whispered.

Strangely enough, she wasn't surprised. With all that Serapha could do, it made sense. The Elijah Tree had shown her what the old world had been like; Serapha was a remnant of that world of metal and blinking lights. Despite the realization, the damage to Serapha's human façade disturbed her.

'What happened?' she asked, forcing herself to look away from the torn flesh on Serapha's face and neck.

'I encountered the intruder from—from—from Olympus.'

Corvala went out to her and took her by the remaining hand. 'Are you hurt?'

'I cannot feel pain,' Serapha replied, letting Corvala lead her to dry ground. Her steps were jerky, as if her legs were having a hard time working together. 'I am—am—am not in optimal condition, but I am still functional.'

It was hard to believe Serapha could be beaten. The woman—or machine, rather—had thrashed goblins and the Capel brothers as if they were nothing. Whoever had beaten her this badly must be powerful indeed.

With a voice that stuttered and cracked, Serapha managed to tell her what had happened: how she had infiltrated Ryperia and fought a man in a mechanical suit. The intruder from Olympus—the man in gold from the bargemen's stories. He was bewitching the entire city with a device that controlled people's minds. Corvala listened, stroking a finger up and down one of her fiddle's strings. Before her contact with the Elijah Tree, she would've found Serapha's report hard to believe, but she had seen the power the Ancients possessed and the destruction they were capable of wreaking upon the world. A terror of the past had returned.

As Serapha finished her report, she said, 'You must address this problem.' In her flat tone, it sounded like a mundane detail tacked onto the end of a story.

Corvala stopped stroking the string and scrunched her brow.

'Come again?'

'The mission remains incomplete. You must finish it.'

Corvala stared at Serapha, baffled, then leaned back and barked a laugh.

'Something in your head must've got knocked loose.' Her gaze returned to Serapha's damaged body, and her laughter died. 'No offense,' she muttered at length. 'But you're joking, right?'

'I am incapable of taking offense to anything. Also, my few attempts at humor have been mostly unsuccessful.'

Corvala blinked. 'We tried the trees, and it didn't work. What do you want me to do—walk on over to Ryperia and politely ask the golden man to stop?'

'No. There is another possible solution.' Serapha's head twitched. 'When you—you—you were connected with the Elijah Tree, a man riding on a predatory animal destroyed the tree using a staff that fired a corrosive EMP blast.'

Corvala cocked her head in confusion, but the mention of a beast and staff teased out an image in her mind.

'A Rook!' she gasped in realization. She unconsciously let her gaze drift to the door as if the Rook would appear there at any moment. She shivered. 'How is *that* helpful?'

'If he can destroy the—the—the Elijah Tree, then he is capable of subduing the intruder in Ryperia and destroying the mind-altering device. You must go to him and warn him what the intruder is doing. If—if—if I approach him, he will most likely destroy me.' Another twitch of her head. 'But you are made of organic matter. His—his staff will not harm you. You can deliver the warning.'

'Find the guy who's hunting us... Do you know what would happen to me?' Corvala shook her head and looked to the mud at her feet. 'No thank you. I've done enough for this mission already.'

'I cannot dismantle the code until the mission is complete,' Serapha reminded her.

'What good is the cure if I spend the rest of my life in a Rook dungeon?'

Several moments of silence passed before Serapha spoke up again.

'I saw your father in Ryperia.'

Corvala looked up from the mud, shocked.

'What…?'

'He was in the jail,' Serapha continued.

Corvala suddenly felt off balance and put a hand against the wall to steady herself.

'How did he… Is he all right?' she asked, her breathing becoming shallow.

"I do not know how he came to be there,' Serapha replied. 'His mind has been altered by the intruder's device. I attempted to free him from the jail, but he refused my help.'

'What will happen to him?'

'I do not know.'

Even though the day was warm, Corvala felt a chill sweep over her like a ragged shadow. The rawness of grief returned as a splitting ache in her chest. Her back slid down the chapel wall until she was sitting on the ground, her hands gripping at the loam. The tears were rolling down her cheeks even before she realized she was crying. First, she had nearly lost her father to death by stoning. When he had come back to life, she had lost him to the Judges of High Court. Now he was in the clutches of the golden man. What more could she lose?

She looked up to the ceiling. Through one of the gaping holes, she could see sunlight piercing the clouds.

How could you be so cruel, God? First you take my mother. Now my fah. Am I next? If so, just reach down and squash me now. The wait is agony. Do you know what it's like to have the heart ache I have? Do you even have a heart? Do you even care?

Corvala dug her fingers deeper into the loam.

Please…help me.

She stared for a long while at the sky, then turned her gaze to the muddy ground. It was foolish to think the answer to her problems would come falling from the heavens. She saw Serapha's shadow fall over her feet.

'If you want to save your father, you must contact the one you call the Rook.'

'No…'

Corvala doubted any Rook would listen to a girl who had summoned a 'demon.' They'd lock her up. Then she and her father would both be in cells.

A wind blew through the gorge, creaking the roof and rippling across the river. Corvala hugged her knees to her chest and became still; an idea was drifting into her mind.

The answer... falling from the heavens...

'I saw where it went,' she said with sniff and rubbed her eyes. 'The falling star—the shuttle. The Elijah Tree showed me.' She looked out the doorway, out to the river and the opposite shore. 'Maybe there are answers.'

'Answers to what questions?'

'To who the golden man is and how he can be beaten.'

'I do not know if the shuttle can show us any of those things.'

Corvala slowly got up from the muddy ground and brushed herself off. She had come this far; she could go a little farther. For her father's sake.

'We have to try.'

Within the darkness she felt, there was the faintest flicker of light. It wasn't hope. Not yet. But it was something. And something was all she needed right now.

Chapter 39

Vlaren winced as he rose from the bed, and his hand went instinctively to his bandaged side. The priests had removed the sharp piece of wood, stitched up the wound, and given him herbs to fight infection. They wanted him to stay for a couple of days so they could observe him and make sure the wound didn't fester. But Vlaren had to leave. He had spent too much time there already.

His bare feet met the cool stone floor. He was in a narrow, austere room with a cross hanging over the bed. There was a small desk in the corner holding his cloak and helmet. His crossbow and staff leaned against the wall in the opposite corner. The sunlight of late morning was streaming through the room's small window, and by Vlaren's guess, it was only an hour or so until noon. He muttered a curse. The priests must have given him something to help him sleep. He had wanted to leave before daybreak, for the Hunt was still on. His quarry's lead was growing by the minute, but fortune had not completely abandoned him.

During his brief stay here in High Court, he'd heard the priests talk about the strange silence coming from Ryperia and the surrounding villages—whispers of a golden man and his alluring power. A mystery to be sure, even though some of the fragments were coming together. Rook Eramez had gone to Ryperia, and it couldn't have been mere coincidence that the Hunt had taken Vlaren closer and closer to the city. That's where he'd find his quarry.

His sprained wrist throbbed with a dull pain and made gathering his things slow work. Eventually, he was dressed and had all his gear ready—except his boots. He walked barefoot to the main courtyard of the Fountain Wing. Priests tended to the garden in the open space and walked the gravel paths around the bubbling fountain, murmuring their morning prayers. Vlaren found the shoe-keeper seated beside the archway that served as a threshold between the large courtyard and the rest of High Court. That's where he found Lobeka also. Vlaren was surprised to see that she hadn't gone off by herself but had come to lie beside the shoe-keeper. He didn't seem to mind. Other priests cast the wulgyre a wary eye and gave her a wide berth. But here sat the bent old man, stroking her behind the ears. She perked up when Vlaren approached.

'I need my boots.'

The old man inclined his head in Vlaren's direction, his eyes cloudy with cataracts looking into nothing.

'The Rook has awoken,' he said with a smile. 'I was just enjoying the company of your pet here. Sweet girl. We could use her around here to chase away the ground squirrels. They like to eat our garlic.' He continued to scratch the wulgyre's head. 'Now what was it you needed from me?'

'My boots.'

'Of course! What else would it be?'

Vlaren waited a few moments, but the old man made no move to get his boots. He just sat on his bench appearing to be lost in thought.

With the Hunt itching at his back, Vlaren reached for his boots himself. As he did so, a cane rapped him on the knuckles.

'Let an old man do his job,' the shoe-keeper said.

With rickety movements, he rose from his bench and walked the tidy rows of shoes and boots, sniffing occasionally. Eventually, he came to Vlaren's boots.

'It would be better if you stayed and mended up. Don't want to fall apart at the seams.'

'I'll survive,' Vlaren replied.

'Sounds like you're in a hurry.'

'I am.'

The shoe-keeper nodded. 'Ah yes…you Rooks and your Hunt.'

He picked up the boots but didn't hand them to Vlaren right away.

'Can I tell you something?' The question hung in the air for a moment, but he didn't wait for Vlaren to answer. 'I used to be like you,' he said. 'I used to wear the helmet and carry the staff. That was another life many, many years ago. Then I was blinded and saw the light. I learned what I was missing.' He leaned in close to Vlaren as if to share with him a secret. 'I sought after the demonic and missed the angelic. I tracked down the footprints of my quarry even as I missed the fingerprints left behind by God's hand at work.' He shook his head, his expression somber. Somehow, he came to appear even more aged than before. 'When you look for evil, that's all you end up seeing. Don't make the same mistake I made. Don't let the Hunt take your soul.'

Vlaren accepted his boots and left the Fountain Wing. Mounting the wulgyre, he winced as pain tugged at his side. He took the reins in his good hand and began to ride down the steep steps to Echo Bend. Pilgrims on the stairs parted before him, some cowering. He paid them little heed. He was focused on the Hunt. Part of his mind considered the shoe tender's words. They unsettled him more than he cared to admit.

Worries for another time. For now, the Hunt was calling.

Chapter 40

To the north of the Colmane River and the Landsong Gorge, the land grew ridged with flinty hills. The Rainier Kingdom claimed to rule this region, but none of its roads ran through it, and the presence of Rainier troops was rare. The hills bore a harshness to fend off the hand of civilization. Not that there was much that civilization would want to take. It was a craggy wilderness patched with scrub and colored a barren gray. Even though the maps marked this land as the southern reaches of the Rainier Kingdom, everyone knew who its true rulers were. The trolls. And any human who entered their domain was either desperate or crazy.

Desperation had driven Corvala to leave the Norwestor Dominion and enter that land—although she wondered if there hadn't been a little madness as well. This wasn't the first time she had entered a dangerous place for her father's sake. Hadn't she walked into Thorn Shroud in search for healing ingredients? She and Serapha had crossed the river at a ford and now walked among the flinty hills, deep into troll territory.

This is madness... this is madness...

This is for fah...

Corvala had never seen a troll, but she had heard of their savagery. Stories from the north had come down to the Elkhorn Valley and told of how trolls ate people and wore their victim's bones. Corvala shivered at the thought of her ribs strung around some beast's thick neck.

She and Serapha stole quietly through the low areas between the hills, hoping to go unnoticed. Corvala led the way. The Elijah Tree had shown her the flight of the shuttle and where it had most likely landed. Although the hilly terrain forced her to make deviations from a direct route, she could somehow picture the shuttle's location in her mind. They were getting close; she could sense it.

Something else lay ahead. She could smell it on the breeze—the stench of rotting meat. The closer they came to their destination, the more pungent it grew. Not far off, crows and magpies circled in the air. The ominous sign sent a prickle down Corvala's nerves. With a cautious step, she turned a bend in a small valley and saw the source of the stench. Dead trolls littered the ground. They had tough gray skins and bodies built like huge apes. When they had stood, they must had been twice as tall as a man. Now they lay bloated in the sun, over thirty bodies. The stench putrefied the air, and clouds of flies gorged themselves on burst innards. The taste of bile rose within Corvala, and she fought to keep down her last meal. Serapha investigated one of the bodies, a wide hole blown through its back. Looking around, Corvala noticed the other trolls had holes in them as well. A massacre.

'Did the intruder do this?' Corvala asked.

'That is most likely the case,' Serapha answered.

Corvala shuddered. She didn't know what was more disturbing: being surrounded by all this death or knowing there was a powerful being who had caused it.

She and Serapha gingerly stepped around the splayed limbs and hulking forms. As they rounded the base of a hill, they came into view of the shuttle. It sat in an open area between the hills, a short distance from the carnage. It appeared just as Corvala had seen it in her vision. Sleek pieces of metal formed into a triangle like a spearhead. But the vision hadn't given her a sense of its size. It was massive, and Corvala guessed it would have filled most of the town square back in Dawn's Landing. Serapha walked directly underneath it while Corvala held back, unwilling to trust the three insect-like legs upon which the shuttle sat.

'What are you doing?' she called.

'I will a—a—attempt to open the loading ramp.' She opened a hatch on the shuttle's underbelly, revealing a mess of wires and knobs. 'This is a Hermes 870 shuttle. It is designed to—to—to be opened with a key code. Since we do not possess the key code, I will need to override the locking system. Since I am not in optimal shape, this process may take longer than it usually would.'

Her one hand began fiddling with the knobs and wires. Corvala watched for a minute or two but then started to pace anxiously around the shuttle. She didn't know what she expected to find inside. She had hoped it would reveal the answer to their problem—reveal a weakness in the Olympian intruder perhaps. But now that she had seen the dozens of dead trolls, her hope in finding something useful began to falter. She could only think of the intruder's terrible might.

She paced around the shuttle and scanned the grim landscape, keeping an eye out for anything that might come roaming in their direction. One of the crows pecking at the dead made a loud croak and flapped its black wings. It flew across the valley and passed in front of something built into a hillside. A stone doorway. Tucked back into a hollow, it was easy to miss. Curious, Corvala crossed over to the opening. The door of stone had been moved away and lay on the ground. It couldn't have led to a troll cave; no troll would have fit through. The smell of filth came from within, but it wasn't nearly as bad as the stench of rotting meat that hung heavy over the small valley. Corvala took a step inside. After her eyes adjusted to the dark, she saw a large stone box—a sarcophagus. She had entered a tomb.

On any other occasion, she might have been unnerved in such a place. But considering all the death that lay just outside, remains hidden within a sarcophagus seemed mild. Rather than eeriness, Corvala was struck by how strange it was to find a human tomb here in the middle of the troll lands.

On the sarcophagus lid was a metal emblem shaped like a tree. Tucked under the edge of the emblem was what looked like a small piece of paper. Corvala picked it up. It was glossy to her touch and had an image on one side. Like the images Corvala had seen in the Elijah Tree, this one was a perfect representation of reality—a moment frozen in time. Two people, arms around each other's shoulders. Corvala froze. She didn't know who the man was, but she recognized the woman. Short auburn hair and a tattoo of a tree on her neck. The woman Corvala had seen in the Elijah Tree and her dream.

Her ancestor.

She looked over the sarcophagus. There were words engraved on the lid.

HERE LIES FELICITY FERRER
BELOVED DAUGHTER & FIERCE FRIEND

'Felicity,' Corvala breathed.

She ran her hand gently over the lid, feeling the history of what lay beneath, the span of centuries only inches away.

Her hand grazed the metal tree emblem. To her surprise, a light flickered within the emblem, and a cool blue glow filled the room. Corvala leaped back in fright. Over the sarcophagus hovered Felicity Ferrer.

Corvala caught her breath and stared at the ghost. Part of her was too shocked to move, let alone run away. But another part of her didn't want to run. Not from this woman who was mysterious and familiar all at once. A woman from her bloodline. She held Corvala with piercing eyes.

'Many people ask me why I have chosen to stay on Earth,' the ghost said. 'The answer's simple: this is home. Here I have the ground beneath my feet, sunlight to keep me warm, and fresh air to breathe. Yes, living here is hard. But it's real. And it's worth fighting for.' She rubbed her eyes, appearing exhausted. 'If you're listening to this, it means I'm gone. And I guess I just have one more thing to say...

...Dad, I'm sorry. I could never join you on Olympus. I know you think I'm throwing my life away. I'm not, though. As I said before, being trapped in a pod is no life at all. You've bent over backward to give me a future without death. But that's not for me. *This* is for me.' She pointed to the ground. 'This is my home. And I have a lot of work to do.' She wiped her eye, denying a tear to fall. 'We've fought bitterly over this... but that doesn't mean I've stopped loving you...I love you more than the distance between us.' She let out a heavy sigh. 'I wish we could hike Shenandoah again. One last time.'

She pressed her face into her palms, and for several moments she was quiet. Then she reached forward, and her image blinked out. Words took her place.

END OF HOLOGRAM

The light went out, and the tomb became as dim as before.

Corvala took a long breath. She looked down at the small piece of paper in her hand, studying the picture of the man. His features were sharp, and his receding hair was grayed at the sides. He was smiling, and there were creases at the corners of his kind, intelligent eyes.

'He must be your father,' Corvala whispered.

She stared at the image of those two people—two ancestors of hers.

Then a loud noise shook her from her thoughts. Something like a trumpet blared, filling the hills with a repetitive clamor. Corvala rushed out of the tomb. When she had last seen the shuttle, it sat ominously still. Now its underbelly was a riot of flashing red lights. The sound was so ear-splitting, Corvala clamped her hands over her ears. The shuttle rattled, and mechanical joints protested, the sound of creaking metal joining the din. The back end opened like a drawbridge and met the ground with a loud clang. Not long after, the blaring stopped, and the valley grew quiet once more.

'What was that all about?' Corvala said, coming to stand by Serapha near the opening in the shuttle.

'I was unable to override the locking system due to my—my—my system not running optimally. Therefore, I activated the sh—sh—shuttle's emergency exit protocol, which has fewer restrictions to bypass.'

Corvala shook her head. 'Let's hope we're the only ones who heard that.'

The two of them walked up the ramp into the shuttle. They entered a long metal tube with two rows of seats, one on each side, facing each other. The vison had shown Corvala the vehicles and vessels of the Ancient world. Some were built for luxury while others were more utilitarian. The shuttle appeared to fall into the latter. It was spartan, the seats rigid and straight-backed, and the tube was mostly raw metal, an occasional mixture of plain letters and numbers painted in black on the sides. At the front end of the shuttle, there was a separate compartment with a pair of seats set before a window. Countless knobs and buttons filled up the panels. Corvala didn't dare touch any of them. Who knew what kinds of Ancient magic they could release?

'Is this where we'll find answers?'

'I am not certain what you expect to find. But if this shuttle has—has—has any information on the intruder, we will find it in its main computer.'

Serapha sat down in one of the front seats and opened a panel revealing more parts. She reached inside, pressed her hand on a black sphere hooked up with wires, and went into one of her trances again, her body growing rigid and her eyes rolling back in her head. Corvala imagined she was studying the device the same way she had once studied Corvala's mind. Hopefully she'd find out more about the intruder and learn of a weakness.

As Serapha did her work, Corvala wandered the shuttle. She opened a few compartments in the walls of the tube and found more assortments of knobs and buttons or boxes with strange-looking tools. She didn't know what these things could do, let alone if they could help with their problem. Could any of these things help them defeat a false god? Could any of them help save her father from prison? Serapha would know, but she was busy at the front. One thing at a time. Despite how alien the shuttle was, she kept looking around as though she knew what she was looking for. It was better than sitting by idly.

Even though the Elijah Tree had shown her visions of the Ancient flying machines, it felt strange to be inside one and to hear the light clank of its metal beneath her feet. What was stranger still, however, was where this shuttle had landed: right next to the tomb of her ancestor. Corvala didn't know what to think of the coincidence. It was too odd… too unreal. It could have been the madness in her—the code—doing its mischievous work. The tomb and the ghost—they could have been a hallucination. The product of her wanting so desperately to find something here. If she were to go back into the valley, maybe the tomb would be gone. Maybe it would just be a shallow cave in the hillside. It couldn't have been real; it was too great a coincidence.

But then she put her hand in her pocket. The small piece of glossy paper was indeed there. She took it out and looked at the picture. Felicity and her father, both smiling back at her. Corvala came to the back end of the shuttle to the ramp and looked out in the direction of the tomb.

What does all of this mean? she thought to herself.

She stared out over the valley of the slain, lost in her thoughts. Then something moved in her view. A few hulking shapes crested the hilltops. They were hard to distinguish from the boulders, gray and massive as they were. On long, thick arms and squat legs, they lumbered across the ridge.

'Trolls!' Corvala gasped.

The noise from the shuttle must have drawn them.

There were three of them. They stopped at the hilltop to survey what lay below then descended into the valley.

Corvala backpedaled from the ramp and ran to the front of the shuttle.

'Trolls!' she cried, shaking Serapha. 'They've found us!'

Serapha snapped out of her trance. In a flash, she sprang down the main tube to the back of the shuttle. Corvala followed. The trolls had entered the lowland between the hills. Two were sniffing at the dead while the third cautiously approached the shuttle. It moved over the ground on knuckles and squat legs, its beady eyes surveying the craft. Then its gaze came to where Corvala and Serapha stood at the top of the shuttle ramp. With a loud grunt, it alerted the others.

Corvala stepped back, instincts telling her to run; but, trapped in the shuttle, there was nowhere to go. Serapha flipped open one of the shuttle's compartments and pressed the large red button within. The ramp began to rise. At the deep humming of its mechanisms, the trolls became spurred into motion, charging forward. Their tusked jaws opened in predatory hunger, their desire for human flesh appearing to overpower their wariness of the shuttle. They barreled forward, their leathery fists pounding the earth. Corvala shrank back, urging the ramp to rise faster. The troll in the lead reached for the closing gap just as the ramp banged shut. Not a moment later, the back of the shuttle resounded with a thunderous clang. The floor shook, and Corvala nearly lost her feet. Serapha took her by the hand and led her sprinting to the front of the shuttle, the sound of pounding coming from behind.

Serapha placed her in one of the front seats and strapped her in. Corvala clutched Sir William. The trolls still pounded from the outside, and Corvala felt like she was on the inside of a metal drum. Serapha belted herself to the other front seat and began pressing buttons and turning knobs. Lights flickered on, and the shuttle hummed to life. A deep roaring came from below. Then the pounding and shaking stopped altogether.

Corvala felt the shuttle moving. Outside the window, the hills fell away as they rose higher and higher.

'We're… flying!'

'It is how we get away from the hostile creatures,' Serapha replied.

Corvala stared dumbfounded out the window: flight, the great marvel of the Ancient world. She sometimes dreamed of flying while she slept, and the dreams always swelled with absolute freedom—her skimming the clouds, high above the worries of the world below. But now that she was flying in real life, she dug her fingers into the armrests and felt her breathing quicken. Such a massive metal thing couldn't possibly hold itself up in the air for long. She closed her eyes tight. Any moment the shuttle would stop climbing and plummet to the hills. Corvala waited for it to happen, but when at last she opened her eyes, she saw the shuttle keep rising higher and higher into the sky.

'Where are we going?' Corvala cried out over the dull roar.

'The shuttle has its course set on autopilot. I cannot control where it is going, but I will attempt to override its navigational system. I may not—'

The shuttle suddenly roared louder, drowning out Serapha's voice. An invisible force slammed into Corvala, pressing her into her seat. It shoved her throat into her belly and eyes deep into her skull. She screamed, her terror mixing with the clamor all around. The shuttle rattled violently, sounding as though it would shake loose and fall to pieces. They tore through the clouds and into the blue beyond. And the sky grew dark, and the compartment around her grew dark…

…and the shadow spread…

…and she could feel herself sinking into it…

When Corvala came to, everything was quiet. She didn't remember the shuttle stopping its roaring and rattling, but now it hummed quietly. She felt dizzy, and her insides were gurgling with nausea.

'How long was I out?' Corvala groaned, staring at the window. It was dark outside with the stars spread before them.

'I was not checking on—on—on your consciousness,' Serapha replied, her hand on some knobs and buttons. 'You could not have been unconscious for more than four minutes.'

'That can't be.' Corvala shook her head in disbelief. 'It was day when we started. Now it's night.'

'We are no longer in the atmosphere,' Serapha said. 'We are in what you call 'the heavens.''

Corvala put a hand to her chest. 'Something doesn't feel right.' Her body was too light—as though it could fly away, as if her spirit would lift from her. Then Sir William floated in front of her. She stared at the fiddle and barked out a mirthless laugh. This was it; this was her madness taking over.

'What's happening?' she asked, poking Sir William and making her fiddle spin slowly in the air.

'We are experiencing weightlessness. This is what—what—what happens when you are high above the Earth.'

'How high are we...' Corvala's question drifted off, for out the window a great sphere came into view, so massive that they could only see a part of it curving before them. It swirled with colors—blue, green, white, and brown—like a giant marble.

'By the wreck!' Corvala breathed. 'Is that...'

'Yes. It is the world.'

Corvala stared. It had been one thing for the Elijah Tree to show her the heights and depths of things she could have never imagined, but that had been like a dream. This, however, was the unbelievable rising up before her open eyes.

Up ahead, she spotted an object suspended over the Earth. At first it was small—a speck of light mixed in with the stars—but as the shuttle carried them over the globe, it grew larger and larger. It was a great wheel spiked with towers, just as Corvala had seen in her vision at the Elijah Tree.

'I cannot override the navigation system,' Serapha said. 'The shuttle is taking us to Olympus.'

Chapter 41

The mountain stood impossibly tall, and below it, the orchestra spread out impossibly vast. The string section alone would've covered all of Russia, and the percussion section would've filled India. Along with the manmade instruments, there were elements of nature and wild beasts. Elephants and whales, cicadas and songbirds, thunderheads and sea waves. The winds from the four cardinal directions. All of them awaited Silas's command. The man himself stood atop the mountain and looked down at the creation that had taken the span of many lifetimes to perfect. By the power of the Dream, he could see all the members of his immense orchestra. The instruments, beasts, and elements were silent before him, ready for their conductor to begin. Silas held his baton aloft, ready to unleash the orchestra's power and fill the universe with his music.

Before he could start, however, a beeping sounded in his ears and words appeared in the air in front of him.

YOU HAVE 1 NEW MESSAGE

Silas groaned. As much as he hated being interrupted during his conducting, he knew he couldn't ignore this. Messages rarely came to him while in the Dream, but when they did, they were usually important. He nodded to accept it, and new words appeared before him—just a single line of text.

SHUTTLE BR-578 HAS ARRIVED.

It took a moment for the words to register. A shuttle coming here? But why? Then it dawned on him. The shuttle's arrival could only mean one thing: Dane had returned. The mountain and orchestra immediately disappeared as he plunged into cold dread.

Silas disconnected from the Dream. An unpleasant feeling as always: the sensation of having his entire being sucked through a straw and spat out on the other side. A hatch opened above him, and he emerged from his pod like a blinking newborn. Even though his surroundings were dimly lit, his eyes needed to get accustomed to being used again. His frail naked body was deposited on a platform where robotic arms came to care for him. One to help him to his feet and attach the mechanical supports along his spine and spindly arms and legs. Another robotic arm to drape a white gown over his body. Once he was dressed and able to stand and move, the robotic arms retreated and the pod pulled back from the platform and returned to its place. The platform where Silas stood extended out into the middle of a massive cylinder. The home tower held thousands of pods arranged in concentric circles and suspended by metal beams and mechanical lifts. Layers were stacked on top of one another, filling the interior of the cylinder. There were other home towers like this one all around Olympus, and all of them together held the millions of residents who hibernated and dwelled within the Dream. For a place so densely populated, it was dead silent and still. As far as

Silas knew, he was the only one awake. He would need to take care of his current problem quickly and secretly. Cold sweat started to bead on his brow. Not a minute out of the pod and his body was already responding to the anxiety.

As fast as his mechanical supports would allow, Silas hurried from his home tower through a set of sliding doors and came to another platform beside a monorail. A small, ovular train awaited him on the track.

'Take me to shuttle bay E-7,' he said as he took a seat in one of the cars.

The train left the platform and sped down a tube. After a few minutes, it arrived at his stop. Silas got off and walked the hallway towards the shuttle bay. It was quiet and empty. No one else, it seemed, had been alerted to the shuttle's arrival. A small relief.

The double doors to the shuttle bay lay ahead. Silas's glassy fingers nervously tapped against his thighs. What was Dane doing here? He was supposed to be in exile—*secret* exile—not coming up here for who-knows-what. What if the other Founders got the message about the shuttle's arrival? No, no, that couldn't be. Silas was the only one who had access to that kind of information. Wasn't he? His hands clenched into pathetic fists as he regretted having shown his old friend mercy. He should have cast the man into space, preventing any of this from happening.

Just outside the shuttle bay, the decontamination chamber hummed. When the doors slid open, out came not one but two figures. To Silas's shock, neither one of them was Dane. One was a girl who looked almost as bewildered as he did, and the other was a half-destroyed android, one of its arms torn away and its head askew, neck broken. Their tattered clothes stood in stark contrast to the sterile white of the walls, and they smelled like the harsh decontaminant that had been misted on them.

'Who are you?' Silas asked, his hand moving to the white band on his opposite wrist.

The girl—who had her head swiveling in all directions and her eyes wide with astonishment—turned to notice him for the first time. Her expression of wonder fell away as she held back a gasp of surprise and distaste. Was he really that hideous? Silas shrugged his robes a little higher, hoping to hide more of his body in its folds.

'Answer my question,' he demanded. 'Who are you? What are you doing here?'

The girl collected herself before she spoke. 'We came here by mistake. We just want to get back down to where we came from.'

'Where's Dane?' Silas asked, looking towards the de-contamination chamber to see if anyone remained inside or if anyone was still in the shuttle bay beyond. 'Did he come with you?'

The girl shook her head.

'How did you get the shuttle then?'

'We found it.'

At this Silas wrinkled the nub of his nose. The answer of a thief if he had ever heard one! Before he could question them further, the android spoke up.

'Dane—is that the name of the intruder, the one who has broken the Earth and Sky Treaty?'

The android's gaze, the way it didn't blink and the way its head kinked hard to the right, unsettled Silas. More alarming, however, was the accusation behind the question. Silas froze even as an uncomfortable warmth ran across his skin. His dark secret brought into the light. Even though he didn't feel himself move, he must have nodded since the android continued as though he had answered its question.

'Since we are here, we will report his crimes to the authorities.'

'Crimes?' Silas asked, emphasizing the plural, his voice darkened with apprehension. What else had Dane done besides trespass onto the planet?

The android told him what it had seen. Dane's mech suit, his mind-altering device, the prisoners he held, and—worst of all—the rumors of human sacrifice. As Silas listened, his body grew more and more stiff, as though his flesh were petrifying where he stood. The strangers had no proof for these accusations, but what did it matter? Dane's release from his death sentence and his escape to Earth had been found out. The arrival of the girl and the android with the shuttle was proof enough for that.

Only when the android finished its tale did Silas release a breath and break from his stiff position. Trembling now, he looked back at the platform and wondered what would happen if the other Founders rounded the corner in that moment and learned what was going on. They would be outraged that he'd gone back on their order and would name Silas complicit in Dane's crime. Then he'd be the one cast into space. It suddenly became difficult to breathe. Silas bent over and clutched at his chest. The scratchy heat on his neck grew more intense as it crept up the back of his skull. What was this feeling he had hidden from for so long? Guilt?

'Take the shuttle,' he panted quietly. 'I'll give you the clearance, but you must go. Now!'

'What about the intruder?' said the girl. 'Are you going to do something to stop him?'

Silas ignored her question. 'Go!'

If he turned away from them, then he could pretend they weren't there. They had never come at all. He could go back to his pod and forget this whole thing ever happened. He felt like a child crouched over and covering his eyes, but he didn't care. So many unwelcome emotions were threatening to pull him apart at the seams, and he didn't know what else to do. He just needed a moment to pretend the world around him had vanished.

A hand took him by the shoulder. Not a crushing grip, but firm. He turned to see the android standing over him. Why hadn't it left yet with the girl?

'The authorities must be made aware of his crimes,' it said.
Silas pulled away, and the android released him.

'Don't touch me!' he snarled. 'Security! Security!'

He frantically pressed a button on his bracelet. From around the corner at the end of the hallway came five black and white security droids hovering through the air. They surrounded the girl and the android and trained their tasers on them, thin ribbons of electricity leaping between the prongs. One of the droids searched the two, running its metal insect-like limbs over their bodies and into pockets. The girl cried out when the droid pulled a fiddle from a sheath at her back. She reached out to grab it away but then withdrew when the other droids blared menacingly and jabbed their tasers in close.

Silas studied the android and the girl. What to do with them? In his desire to get rid of them quickly, perhaps he had been too hasty in offering them clearance on a shuttle. He had made the mistake with Dane and look at what that had got him. He wouldn't make it again. If they wouldn't go willingly, then Olympus's security would show them the door. That would rid him of his problem.

'Take them to the airlock for ejection.'

No big loss. He assured himself this was true, because if it wasn't, the guilt would be crushing. The android was little more than scrap, and the girl would have a quick end to her already short and miserable life.

The security droids clamped onto their wrists and started dragging them away. Silas could hear the girl struggling but refused to look at her.

'No!' she cried out. 'You have to help us!'

The droid that had searched them remained with Silas, offering its findings for his inspection. He looked the objects over, if only to distract himself from the girl's cries. The droid had found two things on her. There was the fiddle with the face of a man carved on the top scroll—a strange object to bring into space—but it was the other item that drew his attention. His eyes grew wide, transfixed. A photo, one he knew well. There were blotches along one edge where the decontaminant had made the ink run, but the image was mostly intact. A picture of him and his daughter hiking the mountains at sunrise.

'Wait!' he shouted. The security droids stopped pulling the pair down the hall. The girl, straining against the metal claws that held her hands behind her back, twisted around so she could see him.

'Where did you get this?' He held up the photo.

'I found it,' the girl said.

'Like you *found* the shuttle? Tell me *where* you found it!'

'In a tomb.'

Silas nodded solemnly, running a finger over the photo's edge. 'Then Dane did as I asked.' He tried to remember where the photo had been taken, the name of the mountain range escaping him. Too many centuries between then and now. In an age when everything had gone to digital, printing photos was an almost archaic thing to do. But when Silas had left Earth for the last time and headed up into orbit, he had wanted at least one thing he could hold. When Dane left, Silas decided it was time to let go and give it back.

He looked at the girl, his lips pinching in a scowl. 'This wasn't yours to take!' he cried, waving the picture in the air. 'You stole from my daughter's tomb!'

The girl just stared at him. 'Daughter?' she said at length. 'Felicity was your daughter?'

This took Silas off guard. He hadn't heard that name spoken in a long time, not even by his own lips.

'How do you know her name?'

The girl cocked her head. 'How can you be her fah? She was alive hundreds of years ago.'

Silas felt his scowl deepen. 'You intrude on my home and question who I am. Watch yourself. I'm the one asking questions. Now tell me, how do you know her name, and why do you have her photo?'

'I have a… connection with her.' Then realization lit up her face. 'Which means I also have a connection with you… if what you say is true.' She started staring at him, studying him, as if her eyes could peel back the flesh and years that covered his face.

'Stop it,' he snapped. 'What are you doing?'

'Those eyes,' she said in genuine wonder. 'By the wreck! You could be him—the man from the picture!'

'I know who I am. And I have no connection with Earth anymore. Especially not with some girl who steals a shuttle and comes up here uninvited.' He had had enough of this nonsense. It was time for the security droids to take them on their way, but before he could give the word, the girl spoke up.

'Wait! I know I must be nothing to you. But what of your daughter? You must care for what she stood for— her work. She served to protect the world, and now it's in danger.'

'What do you know of my daughter's work?'

'It's a long story.'

'Make it quick. My patience is running out.'

The girl looked at the android and took a deep breath before she spoke. She told Silas about what Felicity had done after the signing of the Treaty. How this girl could know such things was beyond him. Not even he knew the nature of his daughter's work since she had been so secretive about it. The story could be just a ruse, but he found himself letting down his guard and listening intently. Maybe he longed to learn something new about his daughter. Apparently, she had developed a code that was passed down her bloodline, and the girl had inherited it. Seeing Dane's shuttle fly over her home had triggered the code, which then led her to where the shuttle had landed. Silas could tell the girl wasn't sharing everything with him. When she mentioned something about a tree, the android spoke up and said, 'We will not talk about that.' Despite the details left out, Silas got the idea that his daughter's project had to do with Earth's defense against intruders. Intruders like Dane.

'And that's why we need your help,' the girl said. 'We need to continue what your daughter started.'

The girl's plea hung in the air, waiting for Silas to reply. He looked at the photo. Two figures from another time, both happy with full, genuine smiles and arms clasped around each other's shoulders. In the background, the sun was rising over the mountains. Shenandoah—that was the name of the range. Daughter of the Stars.

'She loved you to the very end,' said the girl, desperation growing in her voice and tears starting to form in the corners of her eyes. 'Please, I need to help my fah.'

He should have sent them to an airlock and been done with them. But then the girl had brought his daughter into it.

'Release them,' he said with a wave of his hand.

The security droids did as they were told. Once the clamps were off the pair, the girl rubbed her wrists and sighed in relief even as she warily watched Silas to see what he would do next. He stood there, evaluating the situation. A thought came to him, and he immediately doubted the wisdom in it, but it was the only thing he could think of that would assuage the guilt that continued to twist his innards tighter and tighter. Something could be done, but Silas wasn't going to be the one to do it. If Dane had caused the problem, then Dane could fix it—indirectly at least. That was the best Silas could offer.

'Come with me,' he said.

He led them to the monorail platform where they boarded the train, and the ovular cars took them through the tubes of the space station. The ride was short, but the awkward silence in the close confines made it seem unbearably long. He told himself that despite the discomfort, this needed to be done. Even now he could feel his guilt lessening somewhat. Soon this would all be over and he'd be back in the Dream getting lost in his music. The train took them to another platform. After they got off, Silas led the girl and the android down a hall to a nondescript door. He swiped his bracelet over a panel, and the door opened.

'This is Dane's workshop,' he said. 'Take what you need, but you must be off Olympus in one hour. After that, security will not allow your presence.' He raised a hand to indicate the five droids that hovered beside him and that would remain outside the door while the girl and the android gathered what they needed. 'When you finish, take a shuttle and go. I'll make sure you have clearance.'

With that, he turned from the girl and the android and walked away.

'Wait!' the girl called to him. 'What are we supposed to do here?'

He turned back to face them. This was the best he could do. At least, that's what he told himself.

'I'll leave that for you to figure out.'

He walked the hall, leaving the girl and the android behind and coming to the platform where the monorail train awaited him. He entered the ovular car and let out a sigh of relief as the mechanical supports lowered him into his seat. Perhaps he should report this encounter to Empyrean. No, another time… when he was ready. He had done enough for today. The train sped down the tunnel, taking him back to his home tower and pod. He stared blankly out the window and clutched tightly to the photo of him and his daughter.

Unlike the sterile white halls outside, the workshop was a clutter of metal. Devices and machine parts hung from the ceilings and walls. There were tools of various sizes and shapes and large metal capsules stamped with symbols depicting fire. Tables and standing boards held the drawings depicting plans and designs.

'Can any of this help us?' Corvala asked.

Serapha walked over to one of the room's tables. Above it was what looked to be half a dozen metal arms of various sizes and shapes, all of them jointed like insect limbs.

'This is where I—I—I can get repaired.'

Corvala nodded. 'Let's start with that.'

Serapha pressed a few buttons on a pedestal then lay down on the table. A line of red light shone from above and passed over her body. Then the metal arms began to work, each one focused on its task. So many deft and precise movements. Pieces of metal connected to Serapha's empty shoulder and began building a new arm bit by bit.

As Serapha was being repaired, Corvala wandered around the workshop. There had to be something useful in here.

'What's this?' Corvala said, standing by a mannequin displaying a tightly fitted suit of black. She ran her finger along the suit's sleeve. The material felt smooth like something between silk and snake skin.

Serapha looked up from the table where she lay. 'It appears to be a cloaking suit.' Her voice was beginning to sound better, not crackling like it had before. 'It bends the light around the wearer, making them nearly invisible to the human eye.'

It seemed that Dane had once thought of roaming Earth in secret. The plan must've changed, however, and he decided to go the opposite route—to draw attention to himself in radiant armor and make himself a god.

When the metal arms finished their work on Serapha, she got up from the table, and Corvala could see she was whole once more. Her head was back on straight, and the split in the neck was gone. Her new arm looked different. Rather than being covered in flesh-like material, this one was covered in bands of metal, like tightly fitted armor. The repairs had been surprisingly quick, only a dozen minutes or so.

But their time in the workshop was running out.

Serapha inspected the capsules marked with symbols of fire. 'We need to formulate a plan.'

'And fast,' Corvala said. She looked at the mannequin with the cloaking suit. 'I think I have an idea. At least the beginning of one.' She clapped her hands together. 'Let's get to work.'

Chapter 42

Pedren stood at his post above the northern gate of Ryperia. Hodge stood watch nearby, leaning on his spear. Both of the guards looked out at the bridge that crossed the Colmane and the docks where the barges were tied up. Very little moved in front of the city. Some days a bewildered traveler or two would come down the road, drawn by the light over the palace. Yet even that was becoming less of an occurrence. No more barges floated down this region of the gorge anymore, and the roads were empty. Pedren and Hodge kept diligent watch anyway.

Before the golden man's arrival, they would have probably had a seat and started a game of cards, maybe sneak a few sips of whiskey if they knew the captain would be away. But now that Dane ruled the city, all the guards wanted to do was please their god. Drinking and gambling while on the job was unthinkable. Duty first. Besides, Pedren didn't have any money anymore to spend on cards or whiskey. He hadn't been paid since the golden man arrived. Still, he showed up for his duty. His coffer in the barracks was growing empty, but that didn't bother him. Neither did the white film that appeared over everyone's eyes. He supposed his eyes looked the same. He didn't even care that the last he had seen of his father and uncle was when his fellow guards had seized them for no reason. The light above the palace soothed Pedren, spoke to him. He was just happy to serve the god who had graciously come to live in his city and protect the people with his might.

Yet in the last two days, something had changed. There was a rumor among the guards that a woman had dared fight the god. Perhaps the golden man wasn't as mighty as everyone had originally thought. A whisper flitting through the city shadows; not something spoken in public. Pedren had heard it from another guard the night before while they had been walking a secluded alley. Even before being told, however, Pedren knew something was off. It was as though he felt it in the air. Even so, it was such a small doubt, like a single gnat come to buzz a circle around his head. He'd swat the idea away, and it would be gone for a time. The god having a weakness—impossible! The golden man was the pinnacle of strength. He had slain an army of trolls. Nothing could stop him. So Pedren ultimately rested on that assurance.

The flags above the gate snapped wildly from a powerful gust of wind. A gale blew through the gorge, whipping up dust from the road below.

'The storm's come,' said Hodge. 'Could feel it coming all this morning, what with my fingers popping so much.' The grizzled old guard was always talking about his aching joints.

For an hour, dark clouds rolled in over the gorge and Ryperia. People on the streets were heading home for cover, and Pedren braced himself for foul weather. It was miserable being out on the wall during a storm, exposed to so much wind and rain, but he would stand and endure it if it meant fulfilling his duty to his god.

A deep rumble came from the clouds. At first, Pedren thought it must have been thunder. But the rumbling didn't stop. It grew louder and louder. Pedren stood beside Hodge, and the two studied the clouds with a wary eye. The noise kept coming. It couldn't have been the weather; this was unnatural. Then something tore through the clouds—a massive spearhead trailed by smoke and fire, metal and terror roaring down on the city. The market and streets in the distance burst into a panic, people crying out and fleeing in all directions. Pedren stared at the falling thing with dread. Two opposing forces wrenched at his mind. Part of him wanted to abandon the wall and run for his life. Another, the part that was sworn to serve the golden man at all costs, demanded he remain at his post. The latter won out. Even so, his sense of duty couldn't keep him from cowering behind the ramparts.

The beast from the sky flew in low over the city and, to Pedren's horror, came to land in front of the gate where he stood. He had to clamp his hands over his ears at the wind-tearing roar. Fire blew from its underbelly, and three metal legs emerged to meet the ground. By the time the noise died down, more guards had responded and came to stand on ramparts above the northern gate. They were nervous, holding tightly to their clubs and spears. The captain arrived only moments after. The red feather in his helmet fluttered in the wind like a frightened bird. Though he tried to keep his composure, his voice trembled as he spoke.

'Steady, men. Steady.'

On the metal beast, a door opened. Out came a woman—if she could be called a woman. She looked like a creature born from the coming storm. She radiated with power, and her eyes shone with lightning, her voice boomed with thunder.

'Tell Dane I have arrived,' she announced. 'Tell him I bring a challenge. He is to appear before me. Alone.'

The captain stood awestruck.

'Do as I say,' the woman commanded.

The captain nodded in fearful compliance and turned to Pedren. 'You heard her. Go to the palace and deliver the message.'

Pedren rushed from the wall top and down the stairs. But as he passed the gate, he thought he saw something come in through the opening—a shimmer in the air that almost looked like a transparent form of a person. It was there for a moment then gone. It must have been a trick of the wind combined with the fear that was already stirring inside him.

Pedren shook his head clear and moved on. He ran with all speed towards the palace, although he did so with trepidation. He had bad news to deliver to his god.

'Too close,' Corvala murmured to herself.

The guard had looked right at her when she had slipped into the city, and he'd noticed something was off. She had escaped his gaze by running from the gate and ducking into the cover of an alley.

Serapha had warned her the cloaking suit would make her hard to see but not completely invisible. If someone stared long enough or got close enough, they'd be able to see the cloaking field folding the background around her, and they might be able to make out her shape, especially if she moved. Corvala looked down at her arms and saw only blurred patches of air. It felt strange not being able to see herself clearly, as if she were a ghost moving around without a body. She pressed a button on her wrist, and the cloaking suit turned off, making her body visible again. No need to use it now since she had got through the gate. Serapha had told her it would be best to conserve its energy when she could. Corvala pulled back the suit's hood and threw on a rough-spun poncho with ragged edges. She also wore a metal headband, which didn't quite fit with her disguise as one of the city's poor. But Serapha explained how important it was for her to wear it, as it protected her from the mind-altering device. Corvala had seen what the device had done to the guard, how it made his eyes glaze over with white film. Not wanting a similar fate, she made sure her headband was on tight.

She peeked out from the other end of the alley. People ran in all directions, some retreating to their homes and others trying to get as far from the shuttle as they could. In the distance, a bright light shone from the palace heights—the device bewitching the entire city. Corvala studied it with a grim expression.

'All right,' she whispered. 'Let's go bust that thing.'

Dane stood outside the doors of the palace and looked over the city below where the shuttle's arrival had put the people into an uproar. Dane recognized the shuttle, a Hermes model—the same kind he had flown down from Olympus. It confirmed the fears that had been nagging at him ever since his encounter with the android. Somehow the Founders must have learned about his escape to Earth, and now they were coming to make him pay for his crime. Yet why would Silas—the only Founder who knew what had become of Dane—open his mouth when it would get him in trouble? Something else must have been at play here, something Dane couldn't put his finger on. But what did it matter? There was no time to solve mysteries. The enemy was already at his gate.

For a moment, he didn't feel like a warrior in a suit of armor but a fraud in a ridiculous costume. He felt exposed, forgetting the strength of his suit and thinking only of the soft flesh and the frail bones that squirmed within their metal casings. The jig was up. Olympus had come to peel back the gold and show everyone who Dane really was. Nothing but a lump of meat to be dumped from a can.

Get a hold of yourself.

His sense of survival kicked in. Now was not the time for self-pity or cowering in fear. Who was he? Weak—no! Frail—no! He was strong. True, he had Dreamed, and his body had softened like the other Founders, but unlike them, he had forced himself to leave his pod at times and continued to work with his hands. From countless hours in his workshop, he had produced inventions while the others slept and slept. If they had come down for a confrontation, then they would do so with standard skeletal suits holding up their brittle forms. He had his suit of armor built for battle. The question was, could he bring himself to hurt or even kill his fellow Olympians? His eyes narrowed in grim certainty. If they had been willing to cast him into space, then he would have no problem putting them in the ground.

A crowd was beginning to gather around the palace, pressing against the iron fence and reaching through the bars. They cried out to Dane, terrified. Of course they were. They had never seen a shuttle before, and these primitive people feared what they didn't understand. Dane looked up at the pathograph radiating from the palace's highest spire. Before, its flicker had been occasional and slight—the doubt of a few guards creating a minor taint. Now, however, the light sputtered chaotically with new emotions. A terror of metal and fire had fallen from the sky, and the pathograph was picking up the people's fear of the shuttle and broadcasting it back to them, even as it demanded worship of Dane. Two emotions jockeying for dominance, like two radio stations clashing different songs on the same frequency. If Dane didn't do something about it, the problem would only get worse. The people would doubt his power and their awe for him would diminish.

Harsh yells came from just outside the palace grounds. Guards fought back the crowd as they opened the gate and let in another guard, one shaken and out of breath. He ran up the steps and kneeled before Dane.

'Speak,' Dane commanded.

'I have a message, my god. A woman came out of that… thing. She wants you to come and face her.'

'Did she have dark skin and short hair?'

The guard nodded.

Dane smacked his gums. So, the Founders hadn't come down themselves. He shouldn't have been surprised they would send an android to do their dirty work for them. Since he had beat the other to scrap, they must've sent another one to face him like before. Were their strategies that lacking in imagination? Then again, what could he expect from minds confined solely to the Dream? Dane cast a glance at the palace spire. Although he was a little hesitant leaving the patheograph while a threat was present, he wasn't going to leave it completely unguarded. Special measures had been put in place establishing the patheograph's security.

Dane left through the iron gate, the crowds parting for him as he went, looking at him with awe and wonder as he passed. But there was fear and doubt in their eyes as well. He would fix that. Olympus would learn that its feeble reach wouldn't be able to pluck the city from his grasp. The people would see the android torn to pieces, and their worship of him would fill the patheograph once more. All of this would be resolved in one fight. Two birds killed with one stone.

Ryperia was proving to be a labyrinth. The streets twisted every which way except the way Corvala thought correct. To make matters worse, she had nothing to guide her since her view of the palace was blocked by the tall stone buildings that hemmed her in. The wind howled down the street, rattling the doors and shutters. After the gust passed, Corvala heard another sound—the approach of many feet. Around the bend appeared a hushed crowd. At its head strode a man clad from head to toe in golden armor.

Dane.

Even from a distance, Corvala could see he was an imposing figure. His armor radiated strength and seemed to glow with its own light. All the eyes of the crowd were on him, the people watching with hushed reverence and expectation. Corvala knew that under the armor was a body as frail and pitiful as Silas's. Still, she couldn't help but feel a sense of awe at Dane's portrayed magnificence. That was the power she was fighting against—the man who had imprisoned her father. The man who took lives. Upon seeing her enemy, Corvala supposed the bitter taste of anger would rise in her throat. But it didn't. There was no human face on which to latch such feelings. No evil grin she could hate. No eyes full of darkness she could judge. Just an emotionless metal mask. A force of destructive power. If Corvala felt anything it was a heart-quickening fear.

She shrank into a small side street to avoid Dane's gaze and to get out of the way of the coming crowd. If Dane had left the palace, it meant he had accepted Serapha's challenge—a distraction to buy Corvala some time to get to the palace. If she could ever *find* the place. She took a few turns down narrow ways and came to a wider street. With the buildings opening up, she caught sight of the palace in the distance, the pulsing glow coming from the spire. She was about to continue on her way but then stopped when she noticed the building before her: a big block of a structure set apart from the others. Formidable stone walls with heavy wooden doors at the front and iron bars over narrow windows. Ryperia's jail.

Corvala's breath caught in her throat. That was where Serapha had seen her father. He could still be in there.

The plan was for her to go straight to the palace while Dane was away. Her father's wits had been addled, and he wouldn't leave the city until the mind-altering device was destroyed. Or at least that was what Serapha had told her. Exodus hadn't responded to Serapha's urging to leave his cell. But Serapha was a cold machine. Maybe he would respond to his daughter. Corvala looked at the mind-altering device shining from the spire and then turned back to the jail.

It would only take a moment. Just a quick look to see if he was all right.

A group of guards stood by the jail door, two of them armed with spears while the others carried truncheons. They weren't lazing about as Corvala would've expected. They kept a vigilant watch, some of them looking about nervously. Ducking back into the cover of the side street, Corvala took off the ragged poncho and turned on the cloaking suit. A patch of blurry air concealed her once more, as she blended into the street and buildings around her. She went down the side of the jail until she came to a grate at the bottom of the wall, a window to the jail's lower level. Serapha had told her Exodus was in one of the underground cells. Corvala had to get down on the ground to look through the bars. There were around twenty figures huddled on the floor below. None of them looked like her father, but it was hard to tell in the dim light.

'Fah!' she called in hushed tones. 'Exodus! Are you in there?'

No one answered or even bothered to look up at the window. They kept quiet, their heads down.

Corvala was about to move down the jail wall to check the next window when a pair of guards turned the corner and came her way. She crouched down against the wall and kept still, hoping to go unnoticed as they passed her by. Her hand reached for a little mechanism tucked in a holster at her side, what Serapha called an *electric pulse gun*, the closest thing to a weapon they had found in Dane's workshop. It had a limited amount of power, most of which would be needed to destroy the mind-altering device. Hopefully, if she was careful—and lucky—she wouldn't have to use it now.

'...and maybe it's his wife,' one of the guards said.

'Don't be thick,' the other replied.

'Me, thick! Don't you know your mythology? Gods had wives. You know... goddesses.'

'She came to fight him.'

'So? My wife and I fight all the time, and we still manage under the same roof. Maybe this will all blow over. And by tomorrow they'll get to making little god babies.'

'You *are* thick.'

The guards were only a few paces away from Corvala. She tried to keep still, but her shoulders kept trembling. Her finger went to the trigger of the electric pulse gun.

One of the guards stopped suddenly. 'What's that?'

For a moment Corvala thought they had noticed the blurring effect of her cloaking suit. But they weren't looking at her; they were looking towards a darkened side street. In the shadows stood a figure cloaked in dark gray and wearing a metal helmet.

'A Rook!' one of the guards yelled.

He went to raise a horn to his lips and then he let out a cry of pain. A bolt took him in the hand, and he dropped the horn. Before the other guard could react, a flurry of gray fell upon him. A metal staff swung in a blur. *Crack! Crack!* Before Corvala could fully realize what had happened, the two guards lay on the street. The Rook stood over their unconscious forms.

And he was looking in Corvala's direction.

She froze in terror, perfectly still. Even so, she swore he was looking right at her. The jade lenses were concealed within the helmet, and she could feel his eyes upon her. His dark piercing eyes. She could feel her heart pound and blood course through her veins. In a dreadful moment, she understood why it was said a Rook could look into a person's soul.

Shouts sounded down the street, and a company of guards came around from the front of the jail.

'Over there!' one of them cried. 'A Rook!'

The Rook spun away and disappeared down the side street from where he had come, the company of guards attempting to chase him. After they passed Corvala by, she got up and hurried away.

Too close. Much, much too close. Now, keep to the plan.

She took the wide street and continued on her way towards the palace.

The crowds followed Dane to the city walls and stopped at the northern gate. It was as if they had been halted by some unspoken rule—an understanding that the matters to take place outside the city were for gods only. They watched from beneath the arches of the gate or went to stand atop the walls with the guards. Here were the brave followers of the golden man, come to see him face his challenger.

Dane put the city behind him and strode down the road until he came within a dozen paces of the android. The shuttle that had brought it down loomed not far behind. The android had pitched its challenge outside the city—less risk to the people. An intentional move, no doubt. Seraph class androids aided in combat and tended to the wounded; it was against their programming to allow innocent civilians to be harmed. He had counted on that and had made arrangements accordingly.

Studying the android, he noticed it was the same one that had attacked him before. Its neck had been repaired, and the arm he had blown off had been replaced with an all metal one.

So, it looks like our fight will go into round two.

Not in the cover of night this time, but with the eyes of the city watching. This was the way of the old mythologies, a challenger come to usurp an old god—the stronger to take the place of the weaker. For the ancient Greeks, Ouranos fell to his son Kronos. And Kronos fell to his son Zeus. Dane, however, would break this pattern, for he was the stronger. The people would bear witness to the power of their god as he destroyed this inferior machine. And their worship of him would increase a hundred-fold.

They watched in hushed anticipation, their silence settling over the walls. Only the wind and distant thunder could be heard. Dane and the android watched each other, waiting. Moments drew out, the distance between the two combatants straining to the point of cracking. Elements waiting to be released.

Then Dane launched forward, his cell guns unleashing a hail of fire.

Serapha sprang from right to left as she bolted toward Dane. Hot blasts of light streaked past her only inches away, threatening to shred her to pieces. Yet she still ran toward the danger. She yanked a small canister from her belt and hurled it at Dane. It hit the ground at his feet and exploded in a cloud—their battleground consumed by bluish, powdery smoke. Red flashes lit up the inside of the cloud as Dane's guns continued to fire. Serapha ghosted through the smoke and towards her target, running wide of the blasts. The wind howled and tore her smokescreen to a ragged veil. Through the tendrils of vapor, Serapha saw Dane turn and lock onto her—but a moment too late. She dove under his arm, slamming a hand against his chest. Electricity shot from her palm, knocking him to the ground.

TARGET TEMPORARILY IMMOBILIZED

He would be down for only a moment, and it would take several minutes for Serapha to build up another charge. From a small pouch on her belt, Serapha took out two bundles of fusing wire and crammed them into Dane's cell gun. The wires immediately fused themselves to the metal inside of the barrels. Serapha was about to fuse a third bundle to the suit's elbow joint, but then a gauntleted fist struck her in the chest and sent her rolling across the stony ground. She looked up to see Dane rise to his feet, his power returned. His arms shot forward to unleash another hail of fire, but Serapha watched—as if in slow motion—his gun barrels swell and glow red. In a flash, they exploded, bits of shrapnel hissing through the air. Dane stumbled back, looking at his smoking bracers where the guns had been. All that remained were splayed, blackened pieces of metal. With a loud grunt, he ejected the ruined weapons from his armor and closed in on Serapha. She got up like a cat rising from a crouch, letting him bring the fight to her.

The first blow aimed for her head. The destructive power of his fist swept through empty air as she made a deft backstep. With his guns down, she could keep her distance, and she was in no hurry to engage in this fight. She dodged the next blow and the next. When a pocket opened, she would land a few punches of her own, but evasion was her strategy. No attempts to break off

Dane's armor. No attempts to bring him down. Not yet anyway.

Dodge and evade. Dodge and evade. Keep Dane fighting. Buy Corvala time.

The clouds above Ryperia grew more ominous by the minute, and lightning cracked behind the peaks of the Moss Kettle Mountains. The sky was ready to burst with rain; Corvala could feel it coming. She tried to shrug it off, knowing more important matters were at hand. Peeking out from an alleyway, she looked across a wide street to a structure of pillars and fine cut stone. The governor's palace. Along with being located at the highest part of the city, it also stood atop a steep incline, the surrounding gardens terraced and a wide stair leading up to the front entrance. The Elijah Tree had shown Corvala far larger and taller structures built by the Ancients, but she hadn't been tasked with scaling their heights. Her eyes crawled up the three-story-tall walls of the palace, up to the domed roof at the palace's center. On the dome's spire, the mind-altering device shone bright against the darkened sky. Corvala had to cock her head back to look at it and caught herself staring, mouth hung open. She shook her head. One thing at a time. Worry about getting in first, then the climb.

The palace had been built in the name of grandeur rather than fortification, its only protective boundary being a tall wrought iron fence. A group of four guards stood by the gate, the only way she could see in. Even with her cloaking suit, there would be no way to sneak past four pairs of eyes without being noticed. She thought back to when she had sneaked backstage at the Windborne show to get an audition with Solomon Swain. If only her present task could be as simple as passing through a curtain.

But even then, the only reason her entry had been possible was that something had distracted the Windborne's security. That gave her an idea.

Looking over the palace grounds, she spotted a guard patrolling along the fence. She left the cover of the alley and cut across the wide street. Being out in the open, she felt exposed, thinking that at any moment the guards at the gate would spot her—that she was just pretending to be unseen and they would catch her in her silly game. But even though they were only a dozen paces away, they kept looking ahead and not at her. Shaking, she reminded herself, *I'm invisible—I'm invisible!*

The patrolling guard walked just on the other side of the fence and appeared completely unaware of the obscured figure nearby. Corvala took out the electric pulse gun and pointed it at him. She put her finger on the trigger just as Serapha had shown her and slowly squeezed. The small device buzzed in her hand like an angry cicada, its vibrations running up her arm. She was about to yelp and drop the gun, but then it released its power and shot off a ball of sparks through the fence. The sparks hit the guard in the back, and he cried out and fell to the ground. For a moment, Corvala stared in heart-stopping horror, wondering at the power she had unleashed and afraid she had killed the man. He laid in the grass twitching and his eyes blinking in bewilderment. Corvala let out a strained sigh of relief at seeing him alive.

The cry set off a commotion at the gate, and three of the four guards left their post to see what had happened. Corvala, running along the other side of the fence, went past them unnoticed. She came up to the gate, and—with a slightly better understanding of how to aim and a diminishing feeling of guilt—she shocked the remaining guard posted there. With a yelp, he convulsed and fell to the ground. Before the others could respond, Corvala opened the gate and slipped inside.

The gardens provided abundant cover with overgrown shrubs. Corvala took the paths over the terraces and around the grounds to the back of the palace. Serapha had told her of a wall trellis there she could climb. When Corvala saw the trellis covered in ivy, however, she immediately had her doubts. Too high and too rickety, and it only went up to the second story. Serapha must have leaped to holds and footings beyond Corvala's reach. There had to be another way—a safer way—to get to the roof high above.

Walking along the outside of the palace, she came upon the coal chute. The chute had been used recently, as evidenced by the bits of coal scattered on the ground, which was odd since there was no reason to heat the palace in these warm summer days. As Corvala opened the lid, the rusty hinges protested with a loud creak. Corvala stopped and looked around, but it seemed no guards had heard. She continued to lift the lid, revealing an iron grate over the opening. The fasteners were nearly rusted through, and one of the bars had fallen off. With some prying and pulling, Corvala was able to bend the weakened metal and make an opening just wide enough for her to squeeze through. It was a tight fit, and the rough rusty metal scratched against her, but she pushed onward. Over halfway in, she felt something tugging against her side—a piece of metal snagged on the hem of her suit. She couldn't back up to undo the snag. Too much of her weight was going forward down the chute, and she was slipping. The fabric tore free, and she slid down into the darkness below.

The chute dropped her on a pile of coal. Coughing from the coal dust, she picked herself up from the floor. She was in a dark room with a low ceiling and rough walls. The large furnace sat in the center, its pipes running up to the floors above. It filled the room with heat, and Corvala could already feel herself beginning to sweat. The room smelled heavily of smoke. Beneath that was something else, a smell Corvala had encountered in the valley of the slaughtered trolls. The stench of death.

By the red light glowing from the furnace grate, she saw the room contained some large bins. As her eyes adjusted to the dim light, she could see the bins were filled with ash. And bones. Human bones. Over a dozen skulls protruded from the ash, empty sockets looking at her. Despite the room's heat, a chill ran through her. She backpedaled from the bins only to run into a wheelbarrow in the corner, a burlap sheet thrown over it. The bulge in the sheet told of a form underneath, and out from under the sheet's edge dangled a hand, the flesh greenish and dead.

Corvala bolted for the door and tumbled into a corridor. Shutting the door behind her, she leaned against it to still her shaking nerves. So the rumors were true. The golden man—Dane—was taking human sacrifices. A horrid thought crossed her mind—why her father was in prison. For who would a tyrant sacrifice but his prisoners? Her father could be next... or he had already been laid before Dane's horrific altar.

No, she couldn't think that. He was still alive; he had to be. She gritted her teeth, willing herself to believe it.

The sound of footsteps came from the stairs leading to the basement corridor. A plump servant woman was coming down carrying a bucket loaded with kitchen scraps, presumably going to the furnace room to have the rubbish burned. Corvala pressed herself against the wall, hoping to blend into the corridor's shadows, but the servant stopped and stared right at her. The woman's plump cheeks went pale as a sheet, her eyes grown wide with horror as if she had just seen a ghost. It was then Corvala noticed the problem with her suit. Her arms were flickering in and out of visibility. To this woman, she *was* a ghost. A phantom from the palace's pit of death. The servant fainted.

Corvala spotted the tear in the cloaking suit, running along her left side. The whole suit fuzzed and flickered for a minute or two. And then its cloaking ability went out altogether. No matter how many times she pressed the button on her wrist, the suit wouldn't work. She stood there in the bowels of her enemy's palace with no-where to hide. Panic threatened to take hold, but balling her hands into fists, she fought to keep her calm. Panic hadn't helped her in Thorn Shroud, and it wouldn't help her here. She'd think of something. She had to. Other-wise it'd be her bones that wound up in the ash heap.

Dane threw power into the punch—enough to knock that head clean off its shoulders—but the android side-stepped the blow, the fist flying barely an inch past its cheek. He growled in frustration. He knew the android was baiting him to fight while keeping just out of reach. It had danced away from every attack while he stomped over the rocky ground like an oaf. Knowing it couldn't match his strength, the android had turned this into a battle of attrition, waiting to tire him out. His breathing was heavy, and he blinked a bead of sweat from his eye. Even with his mechanical supports doing the work, his frail body was beginning to fatigue from all the move-ment. He cast a glance at the city wall where the people stood. All watched in silence and rapt attention, waiting to see which power from the heavens would come out on top. Many gazed at him in wide-eyed wonder and wor-ship, but there were those with arms crossed, regarding him with a glint of suspicion. In the distance, Dane could see the light of the patheograph flickering wildly because of their doubt. He snarled and threw another punch, stra-tegic calculation giving way to the anger that trembled through him. The blow went wide, his balance tipping, and the android easily leaped aside with a kick to his shoulder, toppling him to the ground.

A gale howled through the gorge followed by the echo of thunder. Dane, on hands and knees, heard the rain begin to fall and clink against his armor. Let the android think it had this fight; let it think he was tiring. He had cunning to match its speed. He launched himself off the ground and at his foe, his arms a sudden flurry of punches. The android dodged fist after fist. But then he held one back—a feint. The android spun away only to find itself round into Dane's grasp. His gauntleted hand caught it by the wrist, armored fingers digging into the synthetic flesh. With a swipe of his other hand, he grabbed the android by the ankle and lifted it to the lightning cracked sky. The crowd on the wall roared with a savage cheer, a cry for violence. Dane pulled and could hear the android's metal joints groan as he was about to tear it in two.

But then it slammed its free hand against his head, a surge of electricity jolting through his suit. The power went out, and Dane fell in a heap. The cheering died. Lying on his side, he could see the people on the wall standing silently in the rain, looking down on him from the walls with blank stares. Hot shame burned in his cheeks. Everyone had seen him fall like a withered flower cut down by a breeze. He impotently watched as the android ran away. His shame turned to white hot anger. His suit—as if powered by the rage that blazed in the pit of his belly and boiled in his throat—hummed to life once more. This was his city—*his!*—and he wasn't about to lose it through humiliation.

Once all systems were back online, he clawed over the ground until he was on his feet again and charged after the android. It ran to the shuttle and up the ramp, apparently thinking it could make a fool out of him and fly away. Dane snorted in dark pleasure; all the android had done was trap itself onboard. Nowhere to dance away from his punches now. He crossed the distance in a matter of strides, and his boots clanked up the ramp. Down the length of the cargo compartment, he saw the android in the cockpit, working the controls. The cargo bay door closed behind him, and thrusters on the underside of the fuselage began to roar, lifting the shuttle into the air. Dane charged down the compartment to the cockpit. As he made a lunge for the android, it launched itself forward, breaking glass in a streamline dive through the cockpit window.

Dane watched the river and the ground below steadily shrink beneath him. Only then did cold dread sink in as he made a terrible realization: he had run right into a trap.

Serapha dove into the river and activated her buoyancy device to float her to the surface. Above, the shuttle was still rising. She pulled a detonator from her belt, flipped open its cap, and pressed the button. The front end of the shuttle immediately exploded in a fireball, and the engines in the underbelly burst into flame. The whole vessel spun in mad circles before it careened to one side and plummeted from the sky. Like a blazing meteor, it smashed into the bridge. Metal screaming, stones breaking. The crash split the bridge support in two and sent it crumbling into the river. The wreckage—what remained above the water—settled precariously on the stone ruin, its insides engulfed in high roaring flames. Serapha swam to the part of the bridge that remained firm and climbed out of the river. Coming in close to the wreckage, she scanned what remained of the fuselage. There was no sign of Dane; just scrap and remnants of the shuttle's frame within the raging fire. The threat had been eliminated.

Putting the wreckage behind her, she turned to face the city. The mind-altering device's light shone through the rain. She had given Corvala plenty of time. The girl should've disabled it by now—unless something went wrong.

Serapha was about to sprint towards the city when a shape leaped from the smoke and fire, faster than she could respond. It hit her square in the back. A well-aimed blow that shook through her frame and snapped her chest plates open. Her energy cell sprang free and flew from her body, bouncing along the bridge. She fell to the stones, becoming still. With what residual power remained in her system, she saw a pair of golden boots step over her and run towards the city.

Then her power went out.

Chapter 43

The wide gallery of the palace was eerily quiet, its walls displaying a variety of animal heads. Mostly deer and elk with a few bears and manticores. Corvala hoped this room would lead her closer to a stairway. She started walking the gallery's length, her footsteps creaking on the polished floorboards. The mounted head of a troll looked down on her as she passed, its marble eyes watching her, spotting her as an intruder. On edge, she practically jumped when she heard the sound of approaching footsteps. Three guards appeared at the opposite end of the gallery. She looked to the floor and scooted to the side for them to pass. She wore the guise of a servant, her smock and off-gray apron courtesy of the serving woman who had fainted in the lower level. Although her outfit was much too baggy, she played her part the best she could. Keep her eyes down, stay timid, hold a bucket to look like she was in the middle of chores. She had fooled a whole tavern into believing she was a traveling musician; she could fool these three into thinking she was just another servant.

Then again, what was she thinking? They'd see through her disguise. They'd catch her with rough hands and bring her to Dane. Any moment now. Corvala kept her eyes on the floor, struggling to keep herself from wincing, waiting for the terrible thing to happen. But it didn't. The guards kept moving, giving her hardly any notice. Just another domestic. A few moments after they passed, Corvala started breathing again.

Coming to the end of the gallery, she found an opening to a stairway. She took the flights up to the third floor where there stretched a hall lined with doors. She waited at the top of the stairs and listened. When she was certain there were no guards around, she went from door to door, peeking inside. Almost all of them led to unoccupied spare bedrooms. Near the middle of the hall, she came to a nondescript door that practically blended into the wood paneling. It opened to a large closet with mops, brooms, and other cleaning materials. And at the back was an iron ladder bolted to the wall, leading to a hatch in the ceiling. Corvala's eyes lit up. She climbed the ladder, and sure enough, the opened hatch took her to the roof.

Rain splashed upon her face as she crawled outside. Here above the palace's eastern wing, the roof was sloped slightly so the rainwater flowed to the gutters at the edge. Corvala crept gingerly across the roof's slippery surface to the base of the dome. On the spire high above, the light shone through the sheets of rain. Corvala looked around and found metal rungs going up the steep curve of the dome. She was on the first rung when a hand grabbed her by the ankle and pulled her down. She shrieked, thinking a guard had taken hold of her. It was far worse. She lay on her back and looked up, blinking in the rain. The figure who stood over her was cloaked in gray and wore a helmet. The Rook pinned her down with the end of his staff and studied her.

'You,' he said in an even voice. 'The girl from the demonic tree… is this your magic as well?' He pointed to the light.

Corvala paused, too frightened and perplexed to say anything.

'Speak,' he said, driving the staff harder into her chest.

'No,' she gasped, the word pressed out of her. 'I'm trying to stop it.'

'I have no time for lies.'

'My fah,' Corvala pled. 'Please... I need to save him.' All she could do was meet the Rook's gaze and hope he found earnestness in her expression. But there was no connection with those cold, shadowed eyes.

'The bewitched of the city,' he said. 'How do you free them?'

'That's what I'm trying to do.'

In the midst of her fear, Corvala remembered the pulse gun in her smock pocket. She reached for it, but the Rook stepped on her hand, his boot squeezing her fingers against the stone. Pain flared up her arm.

'Please,' she cried, desperate tears mixing with the rain on her cheeks. Her goal was only a stone's throw away. She had come too far to be stopped now—lying under a Rook's boot and staff.

'Please,' she whimpered.

Then, out of the corner of her eye, a figure appeared from the torrents of rain. A flash of gold accompanied by clanking metal.

Dane.

But not as she had seen him before. He looked as though a mountain had fallen on top of him, the glory of his armor gone. The metal was scored and dented, and pieces had been torn away. Still, he barreled forward, if only by a fraction of his former power. The Rook turned to face him, raising his staff. Dane knocked the staff away, sending it clattering to the ground.

Sudden lucidity stung Corvala like the cold rain. No time to gawk. She had to move. While Dane and the Rook faced off—neither focused on her—she rose to her feet and scrambled up the rungs. There was the sound of a struggle behind her. Her foot slipped on the wet metal, but she caught herself and forced herself upward, rung after rung.

Vlaren stood his ground. With the steep rise of the dome to his right and the precipitous ledges on either side of the roof, there was no room for escape. The stormy sky seemed to hem him in on all sides and force him to face his opponent. The golden man's boot crunched against the stone as he moved in to engage. Despite the ruin of his armor, it sparked and fizzled with demonic power. Surely the etheris radiating from it would have been blinding had Vlaren the lenses to see it. Here was the mystery revealed, what the Hunt had led him to. A wonder of the Ancient world never before seen and an apex prize for a Rook. But Vlaren knew this power was beyond him. The armor showed no weakness, and Vlaren was without his staff, not daring to turn from his foe to search for it.

He winced as he ducked a blow, his stitched-up wounds pulling at his sides. He barely dodged another strike that would have broken his ribs to gravel. As he leaped back, he happened to see a deep chink in the armor, just beneath the left armpit. The golden man's stance left no clear shot. Still, Vlaren reached for his crossbow and fired, the bolt aimed directly between the golden man's eyes. The golden man instinctively lifted his arms to block the bolt, exposing the chink. In one fluid motion, Vlaren dropped his crossbow, drew his knife, and lunged forward, the thrill of the Hunt rushing through his nerves as never before. Finally, a prize worthy of his skill—within the reach of his blade. If only the sprain in his wrist hadn't jolted pain up his arm and slowed his thrust by a fraction...

The golden man swung his fist down on Vlaren's shoulder. Bone shattered, and Vlaren cried out in agony. Knocked to the ground, his head hit the stone and the world plummeted into deeper darkness.

As Corvala climbed, something began to materialize through the obscuring rain. A group of figures on the top of the dome. At first, she thought they were guards, but there were no uniforms. Just a dozen men and women tightly packed together, standing at the base of the spire. They made no move towards her but just stood there, watching her. All of them were drenched and appeared oddly undisturbed by the rain. It looked as though they had been standing there for hours—maybe days even. Their faces were creased with weariness but their expressions stalwart in obedience. Cautious, Corvala left the final rung and came to the top of the dome where she could stand. The people were only a couple of paces away. When she drew near and took out the electric pulse gun, they raised knives. Not at her but to their throats. They didn't say anything but just stared at her with their ghostly white eyes. Corvala met their empty stares, the pulse gun gripped in a hesitant hand.

One figure stood a head taller than the others. A man with a beard and broad shoulders.

'Fah!' Corvala gasped. Her breath caught in her throat. Hope and relief swelled within her chest even as she cringed at the knife at his throat.

A flash of recognition lit his eyes as he looked at her. A spark of resistance to what held his mind. Then it was gone. Only empty paleness remained.

'I wouldn't try anything if I were you.' said a voice behind her.

Corvala turned around to see Dane climbing the rungs. His movement was sluggish, and occasional sparks sizzled from the exposed mechanisms of his armor. Serapha must have caused the damage. Yet it wasn't enough. Somehow, he had bested her and bested the Rook. Below, at the base of the rungs, lay a crumpled figure beneath a gray cloak, his staff laying out of reach. Now Dane's gaze locked onto her. Although he wasn't the power he once was, she suddenly felt very small standing in his presence. The image of the manticore at Apostle's Grove came unbidden to her mind, how its fearsome yellow eyes had locked onto her, its jaws thirsty for blood. Once again, her heart thumped the rhythm known by all small, defenseless prey. Now the beast was gold, the clanking metal of his approach keeping time with the rhythm. Corvala wondered how the beating of her terrified heart that pounded in her ears wasn't echoing throughout the entire gorge. She took an involuntary step back, closer to the people ready to kill themselves, her father among them. He wouldn't save her this time.

Death before her. Death behind. She couldn't win.

The patheograph wasn't flickering as violently as before. The people had seen Dane survive an explosion and a fall, had seen him strike down the android. The fear and wonder they felt toward him—the worship for him as an immortal and almighty god—had returned to the patheograph's circulation. Even so, it still flickered slightly as a hint of doubt remained. That wouldn't do.

The crowds had followed him from the walls. Now they pressed against the iron fence around the palace, and more stragglers were coming, adding to their numbers. The eyes of the city were on the palace heights. On him...

...and on the girl.

She was the source of doubt that tampered with the patheograph. She stood higher than he did, stood in defiance of him. And the people saw it. Even if her defiance bore no true threat, it was something none of them would dare to do on their own, so it stirred up the curiosity of the masses, gave them that hint of doubt.

Dane would make quick work of her. She was trembling at the sight of him. Soon all of this mess would be resolved, and when it was, he'd find reprieve by enjoying an extra portion of his special indulgence.

'They have strict orders,' Dane said, ascending the last rung and rising to his feet. 'If anyone tries to tamper with my invention, then they'll cut their throats. Do you want their blood on your hands?'

The girl said nothing, just kept trembling. This negotiating would have been easier with the android. They were programmed to heal and protect the innocent. That's why Dane had put the prisoners here. No civilian casualties permitted—an android law. Dane hadn't counted on a human trying to destroy the patheograph. Its power should have protected itself, keeping people docile. It was then Dane noticed that beneath the girl's disheveled handkerchief was a metal headband, similar to those he had designed. It was a wonder how one of *these* people had got a hold of something like that. Could she have been from Olympus? It didn't matter. Dane was more concerned with the pulse gun in her hand. One shot from that could overload the patheograph and destroy it.

Yet despite her weapon, he had the power in this situation.

'Give me the gun. Or I'll give them the order myself.'

The girl looked back and forth between Dane and the prisoners. Then she tossed the gun to Dane so that it landed at his feet. He crushed it with a stomp of his boot. As he moved in toward her, she backed away. But still, she stood, a wavering defiance to his power. He could kill her now. It would be so easy. A swift snap of her neck.

He remembered the crowds below, watching how this would play out. They had seen him defeat the android, a being come down from the heavens. It could defy him because it was more his match—its speed against his strength. This girl, however, was a shivering wretch, no different than the people below. Her insolence might raise questions. If she could defy the golden man, why couldn't they? A potential taint on the patheograph's signal that wouldn't be easily erased.

But if she brought about her own destruction…

Dane grinned to himself. The girl yelped when he tore her headband away and broke it in two. She was his now, taken by the power of the patheograph.

Obedience. That was what the people needed to see, what they owed their god. Willful obedience.

He took a knife from one of the prisoners and tossed it to her feet.

'Take it,' he ordered, 'and face the people.'

The girl did as she was told, picking up the knife and turning to face the crowds below. Now all the city could see her clearly.

'Tell them,' he said in a low voice, 'that you were wrong, and that you must pay for your disobedience.'

'I was wrong—'

'Louder!' Dane ordered.

'I was wrong,' the girl shouted so the people could hear her. 'I must pay for my disobedience.'

'Good. Now cut your throat.'

The wind whipped at Corvala's hair. She looked down at the street in front of the palace where thousands had gathered. All of them looking at her. She noticed something. Of all the people gathered there, her eyes were drawn to a single figure in the middle of the crowd. A woman in white.

Her mother.

Somehow, the vision of her mother was clear, even as all the people around her grew fuzzy in Corvala's view. She could hear her mother's voice over the storm, as clearly as a voice next to her.

'If you can keep your head when all about you are losing theirs…'

Her mother left the old poem hanging in the air. Now Corvala understood why, clarity rushing in. Dane was right about her. She was wrong. She'd been wrong this whole time.

She laughed and drew the knife across her throat.

Chapter 44

Dane watched as the girl's body went limp, like a marionette cut from its strings, tumbling down the dome to the flatter roof below.

In the Dream, Dane had relived the exploits of the great conquerors, bringing entire civilizations to their knees. Today's victory was much smaller in comparison. But it was real. Not a reconstruction of history as it played out in his mind. No security of multiple lives as in the games. This had been a true fight. He had defended his title as god over this city, and it had cost him. He ran a finger over his breastplate where a sizable piece had been torn away. He'd have to run an extensive diagnostic to get the full extent of the damage. Undoubtedly there would be parts in the suit just barely holding together and fluids leaking from tubes and valves. The suit still supported him and served as his strength, but it wouldn't last. Heavy repairs were needed before it broke down entirely.

Along with his armor, there were other concerns to think about. If this attempted coup had shown him anything, it was that his defenses weren't as strong as he originally thought. He would need to rethink how he protected himself and his domain, preparing for more serious future threats. Olympus could send others. And there were those men with helmets and cloaks to think about—the Rooks.

The worries gnawed at his mind, more than he could bear since his mind was so consumed by its thirst for pleasure. He felt like he was going to be sick, his stomach in knots. The city defenses and the suit repairs would have to wait. He'd had a difficult day, and it was time to rest on his throne and have the feast of lives that was his due.

At least the patheograph was back to—

Looking up to the light on the spire, he saw something was off. Now that he had set everything aright, the patheograph was supposed to be pulsing at a healthy rhythm again. But it was still flickering. Something was wrong. The crowds were still gathered around the palace, watching the rooftops with expectation, as if something had been left unfinished. Dane looked down to see what they were looking at.

The girl.

She was standing at the base of the dome and near the edge of the roof. Dane froze and stared in disbelief, eyes wide. She was *standing*! How could that be? He had watched her die.

In his utter shock, he barely noticed her holding the Rook's staff, taking aim. There was a flash from the tip, a glowing green streak screaming through the air. It looked as though the shot would go wide by a foot or two, but then it veered towards Dane, seeking out the power in his suit. It struck him full in the chest, not knocking him back but being absorbed into his armor. Popping heat rippled all around him as mechanisms sizzled and circuits fried. It felt like stinging bees swarming the inside of his suit. He yelped and tried to leap back in pain, but the suit didn't respond. It froze up, locked in a forward lean—his weight tipping headlong little by little. He fell headfirst, down the dome like an empty can clanking against the stone block. Tumbling towards the front of the palace—where there was no flat ledge to catch him—his body rolled off the guttered edge of the roof.

Down... down...

He crashed on the stairway below. Though the armor took the brunt of the impact, the force shook his bones and rattled his skull, the stone steps cracking beneath him. He lay on his back, the rainy sky spinning above him. He tried to get up but couldn't move. The suit remained unresponsive. His scrawny limbs pushed and pressed within their casings, but the shriveled muscles couldn't budge the heavy armor. It felt like he was encased in cement, and no matter how much he tried to wriggle and writhe, he couldn't *move*! His breathing grew shallow, and a cold sweat broke out over his body as the terrible truth dawned on him. This wasn't like the minor outage from the android's shock. No quick reboot of the system; the system had been destroyed. His armor was now a powerless husk—a prison fitted to his body. He felt hot with panic, shrill terror rising up and bursting from his throat, the scream trapped in his helmet.

Through the lenses of his visor, he could see people gathering around, looking down on him. There was no reverence for him in their eyes. Only confusion. It felt like the armor was closing tighter around him—all those people pressing in on him, looking *down* on him as if he were some piece of garbage on the ground. He squeezed his eyes shut to escape their stares. Soon the people would figure out it was all a sham. He was no god. They would remember the lives he had demanded for sacrifice, and they would demand their primitive justice, the rage of an entire city falling upon him. They would try to rip him from his armor to punish his flesh, but damaged as his suit was, no tool they possessed could break him free. The metal was too strong.

It would be a mercy to be torn apart by a mob's fury. A quick death. But that wouldn't be his fate, for he had built his prison too well. His frail body would find its own way to expire, and already he could feel his throat getting dry. The irony weighed on him like the thick, impenetrable alloy all around his body. He who had known the thrill of drinking in the lives of others would have a death drawn out by thirst. In the meantime, he felt an itch on his nose, one he could never scratch. But what itched him even more was the maddening thought at the forefront of his mind: how had he been beaten? The girl had been in his power, controlled by the patheograph. How had she defied him and survived? He lay on the cracked stones, powerless and broken, mind raging, never to know. How had she done it? *How?*

Corvala looked over the edge of the roof and down at where Dane lay, assured he wouldn't be getting up again. She stretched her neck from side to side, her body aching from her tumble down the dome, but she had needed to look convincing, playing dead and letting her limp body take the hits. She had played the part well. Already her arms and legs were showing the signs of blows, and she was sure there'd be bruising all over. It didn't matter now. Corvala rubbed her hand over her throat, her flesh whole and unwounded. She hadn't drawn the sharp edge of the knife but had used the flat, harmless side. Yes, she'd played her part well indeed.

Stepping back from the edge, she turned and noticed the place where the Rook had fallen was now empty. He was nowhere in sight. Cautiously, Corvala carried his staff and limped towards the rungs on the dome. The storm above was rolling away, the rain subsiding. She could hardly believe what had happened. She had defeated

Dane—even after he had destroyed her protective head-band. She should have fallen under the control of his mind-altering device, should have obeyed him and cut her throat. But for some reason, neither of those things had happened. Instead, her wits had been unaffected, and at the last second, she had found a way to trick him. The best she could figure was that the Sky Mantle code blocked out the power of his mind-altering device. One madness keeping another madness from getting in. Whatever the code was doing, it was allowing her to keep her head when everyone else was losing theirs.

Now she would save the others. Save her father.

As she made the slow climb up the rungs, pain flared through her aching limbs, but she didn't care. She could only think of what lay at the top. She would blast the mind-altering device with the Rook's staff, and then—with the spell broken—her father would blink as if waking from a dream. Corvala would rush to him, and he would embrace her.

Rung over rung, she reached for the top. The song that had so haunted her steps drifted into her mind, and for the first time, she understood the meaning of the words.

> *It is well,*
> *it is well,*
> *with my soul.*

Epilogue

Two weeks later...

Corvala drew out the final note across her fiddle. She opened her eyes, only now realizing she'd had them closed while playing. In the chair before her sat Solomon Swain, master of the Windborne. He studied Corvala with an even stare, twisting the end of his tremendous moustache. The two of them were in a middle of a large tent where crates were stacked in the corner and costumes hung from racks. Outside, performers and stagehands moved about, cleaning up after their recently finished show. Corvala had been fortunate to catch the troupe master before he retired for the night, and she counted herself especially fortunate he had granted her this audition.

He asked her to play the song again. After she finished it a second time, he didn't say anything for a while, stroking his chin in thought. Corvala didn't shrink back from his evaluating gaze. There was a time when she would have looked down and fidgeted with her fingers. But there was no nervousness in her now. After breaking a spell over a city, what was a simple audition?

'You're a long way from home,' Solomon said at last. 'I've been in this business longer than you've been alive, and I can spot the runaways from a mile off.'

'I'm not running from anything,' Corvala replied.

'Just come for a second try, eh?'

'Something like that.'

'A long hike. And to know it might be all for nothing if I send you back.'

'You won't,' Corvala stated, surprised by the sudden confidence.

Solomon barked a laugh. 'You've got some salt in you!' He rubbed a hand over his bald head then let out a sigh. 'If I turned away every performer running from something, my troupe would be a third of what it is and not worth half the price of admission. I suppose it wouldn't hurt to have another character with a question-able past.'

'Listen, I haven't done—' Corvala cut herself off. Her heart skipped a beat. 'Are you saying... I'm in?'

'If I said no, you'd only come bother me again farther down the road.'

The joyful disbelief tingled across Corvala's nerves, and she had to hold her tongue to fight back a giddy squeal.

Solomon got up from his chair and made to leave. Then he stopped and turned to her. 'How'd you find it?' he asked.

'Find what?'

'Your song.'

Corvala thought for a moment. Then the answer became plain to her. 'It was handed down to me.'

Solomon nodded in understanding and then strolled out the tent.

Corvala found her father at the center of camp. He was helping tear down the bleachers in the main tent and loading the boards onto wagons. He no longer wore his Judge's jerkin and shoulder belt but a simple shirt and a buckskin vest similar in style to the other men of the work crew. When he saw Corvala, he came over to her and took her off to the side where there wasn't so much noise. He normally didn't like to break off from work like this, especially when others were carrying heavy loads. But he knew Corvala had important news.

'I got in,' she said with a wide smile. An incredible thing to declare, that she was now a part of the Windborne.

'Of course you did,' her father said matter-of-factly.

Corvala wouldn't enter the Windborne alone. Exodus had met with the troupe's manager of labor and supplies earlier that evening and had got a position in setup and tear down. The manager must have picked up on his fighter's strength because he said Exodus could also work security during the shows. Corvala knew her father wouldn't mind the simple work with the troupe as he had grown accustomed to helping the people with their chores in the Elkhorn Valley. Corvala would take on the performer's life. For her father, however, his time with the Windborne was only temporary. Something to last him until their names were cleared.

Exodus had sent a message to Abraham of how he and Corvala had completed their atoning task in Ryperia. The old Judge would approve, but it would take some time for his word to get out and for the Dominion to officially declare Exodus and Corvala innocent. The Rooks wouldn't be easily placated. Until they were, Corvala and Exodus would wear the guises of Juliet and Hamlet of the Windborne.

'You should get to sleep,' Exodus said. 'Early day tomorrow. I'll be by when I'm finished up here.' His calloused hand gently cupped her chin. 'I'm proud of you.'

High praise coming from her father. Corvala blushed.

She left him to his work and walked through the camp. It was a place of colorful tents and exotic beasts, music and spicy scents. It was her home now—a home that traveled the face of the Earth. Tomorrow, the Windborne would take the road south toward Belcastan, the capital of the Dominion. The caravan would be on the road right after breakfast.

At the far edge of camp, Corvala arrived at where her tent was pitched. Serapha was inside, sitting cross-legged at the back. She wore plain clothes of brown and gray, the too-long sleeves concealing her metal arm.

Corvala remembered when they had found Serapha outside Ryperia. A lifeless body near the burning wreckage on the broken bridge. Exodus had found the glowing power cell nearby and had placed it inside Serapha's chest. She had come back to life, and now she was as sound as ever.

'What was the outcome of your audition?' she asked.

'I made it,' Corvala replied, smiling to herself as she readied for bed. She was tired, but she wondered if her excitement would let her get to sleep. She lay down on her bedding and closed her eyes.

Then Serapha spoke up. 'I will be leaving tonight.'

Corvala rolled over to face her. 'Where are you going?'

'I must find a new purpose.'

'What...?' The strange statement caught Corvala off guard. She sat up and shook off her drowsiness. 'What are you talking about?'

'Now that you have been accepted into this community, you no longer need my protection. I have served my purpose. Therefore, I must find a new one.'

Corvala sat there in the dark, not knowing what to say. A part of her had known this moment would come, but she didn't think it would come so suddenly. Something within her began to ache. A touch of coming loss.

'Before I go,' Serapha said, 'I will fulfill my part of the bargain by dismantling the Sky Mantle code within you.'

The cure. A chance Corvala should have jumped for—to finally be rid of the coming madness. It had been the very reason she had followed Serapha into Thorn Shroud and begun the arduous journey. Yet now with the cure held out to her freely, she hesitated.

For as long as she could remember, she had regarded the thing within her—the Sky Mantle code—as a curse. It had killed her ancestors and had left her shunned by her people. Yet it had also saved her in Ryperia and made her a Sentry for humankind. It wasn't entirely a thing of destruction and had proved to be much more complex than she had originally thought. Such was the inheritance from her mother. Perhaps all gifts from parents were part blessing, part curse.

With solemnity, Corvala nodded, allowing Serapha to proceed. It wasn't as painful as she thought it would be. Just strange. Even as her body remained whole, she felt as though many delicate fingers were taking apart the tiny pieces of herself and gently putting them back together. After nearly an hour of pricking sensations and waves of warmth, Serapha removed her hands from the side of Corvala's head.

'I will go now,' she said, rising from where she had been kneeling.

Corvala came outside and bid her farewell. Serapha gave her a nod and then walked away from camp, disappearing into the night.

As Corvala watched her go, her hand unconsciously touched the side of her head. It didn't feel like anything had changed. Deep down, however, she knew she had lost something—even as she had gained her dreams that day.

She stared out into the darkness, the unknown ahead.

'Don't worry, Sir William,' she said, stroking her fiddle. 'God cuts our path.'

THE END

Acknowledgments

When people think of a book-in-the-making, the image that often comes to mind is of the author at work: an introvert hunched over his or her desk, shut off from the rest of the world and completely absorbed in the story on the screen. While this is a big part of a book coming into existence, the image is incomplete. When it comes to publishing a book (and publishing it well), an author can't function as an island. It takes a team of good people—as it did with this book. I'd like to thank them all.

My thanks to Chris Arnold, Helen Blakeman, and the team at Heroic Books. You believed in the story and gave me a chance, doing most of the heavy lifting to see it produced. Heroic was a fun ride while it lasted. Fred Johnson, my editor, turned up the volume on my action scenes and masterfully made the story all that it could be. Nat MacKenzie did a wonderful job on the cover, capturing the essence of the story into an image.

This story has also been produced as an audiobook, and this project was made possible with the help of the backers on my Kickstarter campaign. All my backers are generous, but some of them went above and beyond by being *extra* generous. My thanks to Tanda Fitzsimmons, Brett McKenzie, and the Puleos. Tiffany Morgan Baker, the audiobook narrator, did a wonderful job bringing the story to life with her voice.

I also have to mention my writer's group in La Grande: Sean Crow, Will Bowman, Alex McHaddad, and Heather Rekow. You took the early drafts of this story—pieces of my soul on the page—and you utterly crushed them into millions of jagged pieces. And for that I thank you.

To my students at NCA who bugged me to get mentioned in my book—here you go. You've been mentioned. Happy now?

I thank my wife, Jessenia. Without your support, I wouldn't be able to live out my dream putting stories to the page. Thank you for your sacrifices and putting up with my wandering writer's mind.

And of course, I thank God for giving me my imagination and giving me the opportunity to tell this story.

Photo credit: Bethany Bracht

Jason Link is a high school English teacher by day and an author by night. He lives with his family in Nicaragua.

You can learn more about him and his work at **epicjason.com**.